GRIMMSBANE

BOOK ONE OF STEELEYE

NICHOLAS APPLEYARD

TWC
THE WRITING
COLLECTIVE

Interior design by Joseph Sale.

Cover art by J. Mathias. Cover design by Joseph Sale.

To Donna, who has been finger-tapping for 30 years of holidays as I just "finish this page". I hope you give it a go, and the next two books won't take so long, honest!

To Ella Narissie, who I'm hoping will catch the writing bug, and fill the world with wonder.

To those amazing Facebook groups who are 24/7 there with tips and help and critique, whether you want it or not!

To my late brother, Richard, he would have gotten a kick out of it; I miss you, mate.

To Eve Vesela, our family's number one cheer captain and photoshopper!

I would like to thank Lisa Cowan, beta reader extraordinaire, and J. Mathias, for his incredible art.

And of course to my luckiest find over the last couple of years, an editor that understands you can write a book and still be very dense! Thank you Joseph!

FOREWORD

I'll start by saying this Foreword is the hardest thing I've ever had to write.

I first met Nicholas Appleyard in 2021. We were introduced by a mutual friend, the fabulous author Tia Wojciechowski. I had done editing work with Tia, and she was beta-reading Nicholas's novel. Nicholas needed someone to give his manuscript a proper developmental edit; and Tia also said she thought I would love reading Nicholas's work.

She was totally right.

When Nick first sent me his manuscript, he was extremely apologetic. He seemed concerned about whether or not the story would have any relevance for today's audience, and confessed that he'd had a love affair with the pulpy sword and sorcery novels of the '70s and '80s—and magazines such as *Heavy Metal* —that he'd never quite let go of.

I let him know that he'd found the right editor.

But it wasn't just a shared love of those classic fantasy tales that endeared me to Nick and his work. What struck me immediately was the ferocious passion of his writing. When I first took

Nick on as a client, one of the only things I knew about him—from his own lips—was that he was "getting on in years". I'll admit that I succumbed to the human tendency to stereotype, and had a series of expectations, all of which Nick completely dashed. His writing was not only passionate and rousing, as any good fantasy epic should be, but hair-raisingly supernatural, romantic, blackly comic, and deeply psychological. At times it was a struggle to edit his manuscript because I simply wanted to read on and discover what happened next. I should also note here that Nick was a complete joy to work with. We shared much banter about the state of affairs in the world and foibles and oddities of fantasy literary. When Nick found out I was also a writer, he immediately purchased one of my books and committed to reading and reviewing it. That was the kind of generous person he was. There was no need for him to do this, the payments for editing were more than adequate, but he believed in reciprocity, goodwill, and mutual support. On top of all of this, Nick gave me lots of advice on fatherhood.

By the time I crossed the halfway point of the book, I knew that *Grimmsbane,* the tentative working title for the novel, was a special, special book. And Nicholas Appleyard was a special writer. The great poet and critic Andrew Benson Brown once said that, "The qualities of meaning, truth, and beauty have an ever-lasting essence, and the poet who wields them is able to dress timeworn subject matter in new clothes—to garb us in the raiment of a living antiquity." In other words, not only was *Grimmsbane* a wonderful homage to the sword and sorcery epics of old, but a complete revivification of the genre. If those epic, pulpy paperbacks were to make a comeback, Nicholas Appleyard was setting the example of how to do it. Not only this, but *Grimmsbane* possessed the qualities of "meaning, truth, and beauty" which are so rarely found in contemporary fiction but which elevate a work to the level of the sublime.

In early 2022, Nick told me he had cancer. He had been suffering from quite a few health issues, such as panic attacks and palpitations, and began to suspect there was an underlying problem. The tumours were clustered around nerve centres, and hence not only incredibly stubborn and difficult to remove, but also treatment would cause visual and vocal impairment.

Nick had been working on his novel for more than 45 years. Life kept getting in the way. I had been gently encouraging him towards self-publishing the book; I was confident it was going to blow people away. Though Nick was initially still hesitant (anyone would be releasing their first book), as is often the way of these things the diagnosis clarified priorities and lit a fire. Nick decided that waiting for a publisher or agent to pick the book up, given his health, was a bad move. We agreed that the time to strike was now. So he asked me to help him get the book ready. When Nicholas asked me how much it would cost to do all the formatting, cover-design, etc I told him to leave it. I was going to help him get the book out; I considered it a mission from God.

Nick underwent intense gamma- and chemotherapy, along with several surgeries. I know it's an oft repeated cliché, but Nicholas really was a fighter. Not only that, he retained his brilliant sense of humour despite the harrowing physical ordeal he was going through. I continued to work on all the bits I could that didn't require his input, and when he was well enough, he would check in with me. At the end of one of these check ins he signed off with the following quip, "Any day that ends in me picking up a 'do not resuscitate' card from the doctors has got to have been a doozy." Not only did Nick retain his humour in the face of his body falling apart, but he retained his faith. One morning he told me that because his dizziness had subsided, he would be able to properly pray again—and this filled him with joy. Nick compared himself to a Templar, a holy man dedicated to the good fight, and indeed he was, for not only was he fighting cancer but he was a real veteran—no wonder the war scenes in *Grimmsbane* were so frighteningly vivid.

By November, it seemed like Nick was on the mend. The tumours were receding. He still had problems with vision, balance, and growths in his brain, but we thought the worst was over. We made frantic progress to try and get the book ready. We were so incredibly close. By December, all we needed to do was write a description for the book and to sort out the technical side of uploading the book into KDP and choosing keywords. I was certain that by January 2023, the book would be out, and Nick would have realised his lifelong dream of 45 years.

But on Christmas Day, I received a message that Nicholas had passed away. He died on Christmas Eve.

To say I was shocked and devastated is an understatement. Nick had long ago stopped being my client and become my friend. I can't pretend I knew him well, or that we were drinking buddies, though I would have liked to have been were circumstances different. But one thing I did know about him—and that we shared—was a faith. I can't help but think that God took Nick on that auspicious day to spare him from further suffering. That doesn't make it any easier. The ways of the Lord are unknowable and mysterious. He comes like a thief in the night.

Nick knew this well, for one of the key themes of *Grimmsbane* is death: how we cope with the death of loved ones, how we live with ourselves when we feel responsible for those deaths, the everlasting scars of taking another life, and how we meet Death when he finally comes for us. Indeed, the book opens with a fearsome clan of Northmen attempting to scale a dreadful mountain peak known simply as The Death because of the lives it's claimed. Throughout the novel there is a cunning juxtaposition: the villains of the story are forever trying to cheat death or else master it, but the heroes fearlessly meet it.

Therefore, in a tragic way, there could be no more fitting

legacy to Nicholas Appleyard—his life *and* death—than the book you now hold in your hands. Indeed, Nick admitted to me that he had inserted himself into the tale—as even the great poet Homer is said to have done—in the form of the cheeky, roguish bard Artfur:

> "Artfur had practiced his lute, singing songs of heroes or long-lost kingdoms. Though getting on in years, his voice remained strong and clear, and his company eased the rigours of travel."

Though Artfur describes himself as a mere "spectator" in the "game of heroes", he proves far more courageous and capable than he first appears, helping the main character, Steeleye, on his more daring ventures. In one particularly moving scene, Artfur reflects upon Helgen, his niece whom he has adopted due to the death of her mother:

> "How wrong can an old fool be?" he asked. "She has become as a daughter to me, and she will rise far above any station that I had hoped for myself; she has real talent, she does!"

I cannot help but wonder if this was Nick's subtle way of passing the torch on to his real daughter, Narissie, whom the book is also dedicated to, and who also has a talent for creative writing.

Needless to say, after speaking with Donna Appleyard, Nick's wife, we agreed that Nick would want the book to finally come out, with the proceeds going to his daughter. One of the only things I knew about Donna was that, in Nick's words, "She has the patience of a saint" and indeed I found that to be the case as I bombarded her with endless irritating but important technical questions which she always answered with consideration and kindness. I'd like to take a moment to thank Donna and Narissie for helping get this book over the finish-line. My heart goes out to you both, along with my deepest condolences. I hope I did right by Nick.

They say that fiction mirrors reality, but the opposite is really true: reality mirrors fiction. All things begin in the invisible world of archetypal forms Plato described, where truth, meaning, and beauty originate. Our world is a shadow of this greater world. And when we start living our life in accordance to the true world, not our false one, when we listen to the promptings of the Divine, we begin to discover our destiny. That is why so many works of fiction: poems, plays, novels, even films—prove eerily prescient.

Though I will remain forever saddened by Nicholas Appleyard's untimely death, I hope that his book does prove prescient, and that the torch is passed—either to his daughter or someone else who knew and loved him—and that the epic story of Steeleye and the Grimm lives on.

In his author bio, Nick wrote, "*Grimmsbane* is his first book, but hopefully not his last." I think, given Nick's jet-black sense of humour, he would appreciate the tragi-comedy of leaving this in. But in truth, *Grimmsbane* will not be Nicholas Appleyard's final book. This is an inspiring work, a work that sets the imagination on fire like the great tales of old, and I have no doubt that his world, his mythology, his rich characters, and his compelling narrative will catalyst the birth of new storytellers all around the globe.

Nick, you finally did it. Your book is in print. You made it. I'm so proud of you. You smashed it. I love you and miss you, man.

—Joseph Sale, January 2023

PART ONE

CHAPTER I
GATHERING SHADOW

R annulf leaned forwards into the howling wind, his eyes narrowed against the stinging snow and hail. He stood upon a treacherous pathway winding around the side of the forbidding mountain known in the Northlands simply as The Death. The pathway was only seven or eight feet wide, littered with fallen debris and snow, snaking for several miles from the lowlands in the East, over the shoulder of The Death, and then into the Northern valleys and beyond. Rannulf struggled several more steps, thankful for the winter gear he wore: heavy woollen garments, fur-lined boiled leather armour that held much of the wind's bite at bay, a huge fur cloak and hood pulled snug, and a thick woollen scarf wound tight about his face, leaving only his squinting eyes to be pelted by the hail.

Ahead, he could just make out several hunched figures struggling much the same as he. Einar, his sword brother. Also Wolfrumm, his younger brother by blood. Along with a dozen others that he had carefully detached from his father's party. Young warriors, fierce and headstrong, tired of peace, tired of the drudgery of his father's reign.

Resting a moment, Rannulf turned to look back along the pathway, a particularly harsh gust of wind pushing him against the mountain, rattling his teeth in his skull. He was glad it had pushed him that way; the other way was death, nothing but freezing air and the mountain falling away steeply, to be lost in the maelstrom that beat about its heights.

Behind him, almost invisible in the blizzard, was the rest of his party, another ten men: old, past their prime and their best, just like his father, whom he could just make out at the head of the struggling line.

For the briefest moment, he doubted his present course, and then, as if something deep within him recognised a weakness, dark thoughts of hatred and fury welled inside him, coursing through his veins like bile. The familiar voice, the one that had been invading his dreams for so long, and of late even his waking moments, came to him loud and insistent. It had at first been a shadow, then a slithering, malevolent presence. Now it was as if he shared his very being with this dark entity. Nay, the entity was most dominant, with the old Rannulf cast into a dark corner where he could only watch in horror at the terrible things he was made to do.

Behind the scarf, his lips pulled back into a snarl at the sight of his father: the great warrior, the noble leader, the bringer of peace to the warring clansmen of the North. Aelrik the Bearslayer, Aelrik the Wise, Aelrik the Just. Rannulf tore his scarf free and spat through his red beard into the snow. His face was contorted, twisted and livid. Had anyone who knew Rannulf seen him then, they would have been hard pressed to recognise the once proud and dutiful son. That which possessed him had momentarily come too far into the world of man. As the young warrior stood upon the ledge, glaring back at the straggling line of clansmen, a different visage emerged from within the heavy cowl, something dark and terrible, something beyond the ken of any on that storm-blasted mountainside.

No sooner did it become apparent, than it was gone. Once more, the face was that of Rannulf. But still, there was a look of craftiness about him that his father would not have believed possible.

Rannulf scanned the wall of the mountain, his gloved hands passing over the ice and rock in a frantic fashion. Satisfied what he sought wasn't here, he continued along the ledge, his hand trailing against The Death.

It was just as he turned a particularly sharp bend on the ledge, where it was little more than four foot wide and the footing more treacherous than ever, that his questing fingers found what they sought. Glancing back and forth, Rannulf assured himself that he was unseen. Not only did the contours of the mountain hide him, but also the snow had thickened, and the wind, if anything, was more violent, swirling flakes forming an almost impenetrable curtain.

Here, high upon The Death, a huge rune-engraved iron ring could be seen protruding from an aperture in the mountain. The great ring was threaded through the final link of a mighty chain which disappeared inside the mountain. Just as Rannulf had dreamed, just as the persuasive voice within had told him it would be. Beyond this ring and chain, there was an ancient mechanism, built eons ago in the age of the Horde, built by their greatest mages and strongest backs. So utterly defeated was the will of Rannulf that he grasped the iron ring with both hands without pause or hesitation. The iron was heavy, the runes were hot to the touch even through gloves, but Rannulf bent to his task with a feral grin. He heaved upon the ring. Like his father, he was huge of stature and sturdy of body. His hands were strong and held the iron like a vice. He heaved again until his arms shook with the effort and his fingers ached, but slowly more of the great chain links came into view.

Overwhelmed with the presence of the dark entity, Rannulf roared loudly in triumph as the chain came free faster and faster. There came from above a great cracking sound, as if the sky itself had split asunder. Deep within the mountain, wheels turned, cogs groaned, and ancient weights and counterweights shifted and moved. The mountain shook and vibrated. Letting the chain fall to the ledge, Rannulf made his way back along the path until he could see his back trail. The mountain still groaned and rumbled, louder and louder, as if a creature of rock and stone within the peak convulsed and twisted. Rannulf set his eyes upon his father's party in the distance.

Between Rannulf and his father, high above the ledge, an enormous slab of black stone groaned and tipped. It seemed to balance precariously for a moment, and then to the horror of the beaten and withdrawn Rannulf, and the glee and triumph of the creature that now stalked the world in his guise, the great stone fell. It plummeted down the mountainside with a sound like thunder. The Death shook underfoot. The ledge convulsed and writhed as the great stone crashed into its surface. Huge plumes of snow and black mountain rock burst into the air, more and yet more boulders and snow avalanching down the mountainside, obliterating the ledge, scraping it away as if it had never been.

It was quite some time later, with Rannulf still crouched upon the ledge staring back to where the rest of the Northerners had been, when his sword brother Einar came and placed a hand upon his shoulder. "Thank the Morriggu and her crows you are still here Rannulf! When I heard the mountain giving way, I thought we had lost you."

"No, the mountain gave way further back, though I fear for my father and the rest of the Clansmen!" Rannulf's voice cracked as he shouted over the sound of the storm. He and Einar both stared back along the trail. For long moments they saw nothing but the snow and the shattered ledge, and then from the maelstrom emerged the figure of a man, and then another and yet another, until all the remaining Clansmen had gathered close to where the ledge had been obliterated.

"It is your father!" exclaimed Einar, clearly elated to see the remaining members of the party safe and well. "But the trail is gone, and they cannot climb over The Death, certainly not in the teeth of this storm." Einar gripped Rannulf's arm in his concern. "What are they to do? They are a full day's hard march back to the Spring Gathering camp, and the storm will have taken its toll of them the same as it has us; they will be hard pressed to make it."

More warriors came back along the ledge, led by young Wolfrumm, each stunned by the news that was swiftly passed among them. The younger son of Aelrik pushed to the front of the gathering and stared dumbstruck into the snow. His father and his comrades were only a hundred paces away, but it may as well have been a thousand leagues for all the help that could be offered.

Rannulf turned from his party and beat his hand upon the mountain side in a show of grief, hanging his head low in apparent defeat and misery. Dimly, over the roar of the wind, he could hear the men shouting and yelling at one another as they tried in vain to come up with a method of rescue for their Clan chief and the other stranded warriors. He waited, listening to his brother volunteer to scale back along the mountain, and in turn be told it was madness by the others. He heard them squabble like maids as they argued on one course of action or another, but Rannulf knew it was hopeless. The mighty Aelrik and his loyal but ageing retinue were stranded.

Making sure that he wasn't seen by his men, Rannulf stole a glance back into the storm. His father stood tall and unbowed. Even at this distance and in such poor visibility, the power of the man was apparent. Had he been alone, Rannulf was sure that the old warrior would have made the attempt to climb The Death, and he was also sure that he would have succeeded. But not all the stranded men were as vital as his father, and Rannulf knew the chief would never abandon a comrade.

It was all coming to pass just as the whispering voice within his skull had predicted. It was time for the Clans of the North to follow a different path, a younger more vibrant leader. One not afraid of leading men to battle, one who would bring loot and slaves aplenty back to the halls of the Northern warriors. For too long, the world's greatest fighting men had stayed confined in their frozen realm. A new power was rising in the world, one that would sweep away the old ways, or so the voice had said. It was time for men like Rannulf to align with the new order, time for blood and swords, time for the strong to rule.

The entity within Rannulf found himself shaking with passion as he remembered the promises that were whispered, as he saw again the visions of conquest and victory that had been granted to him. It was at this moment that the very last vestiges of Rannulf, son of Aelrik, brother to Wolfrumm, were swamped and erased for all time. The darkness swelled within the body of the warrior. All thoughts of compassion and concern for his fellow men were snuffed out like the flame of a candle. This new Rannulf raised his voice like a whip over the arguments of his fellows. "There is nothing we can do to help them," he shouted, "and if we stay here much longer, then the chances of making it back to our halls ourselves becomes less and less."

His gaze fixed each of the waiting and despondent warriors; his confidence and leadership were sorely needed. "All is not lost for them," he said. "A little over a quarter mile back along the path there is the entrance to the caves that lead through The Death. With luck, my father and the rest will be back and roasting a deer in the Hall before even we return." He saw some of the men nodding with relief. Just like that, he had eased their guilt at deserting comrades on the mountain. Gradually, each of the warriors turned away from the older Clansmen, looking to Rannulf for guidance. This was easier than he had expected. Euphoria filled him as he turned his back upon the distant figure of Aelrik, a grin spreading beneath his beard.

"But the caves lead to Ash Ul M'on!"

Wolfrumm, loyal little Wolfrumm, whom, Rannulf suddenly decided, was not long for this world of men. "The caves are much easier than the trail, 'tis true," Wolfrumm went on. "But then there is the City of the Dead, Ash Ul M'on to pass through. None would dare such a thing! Why else do we always suffer the mountainside? It is because only horror resides in Ash Ul M'on." Wolfrumm took hold of his brother's arm and looked beseechingly at him. "Please reconsider, Brother. There must be something we can do?"

Rannulf gripped his brother by the shoulder. "If there were any other way, I would take it, Wolfrumm. Do you think I would desert father here if there was no other choice?" He motioned the rest of the men to get a move on, and then bent his head close to that of his brother. "You and I shall lead a rescue party to the City of the Dead ourselves. If there is no sign of father when we return. We shall storm the Pit itself to get him back home safe. Trust me, little brother."

Wolfrumm tortured himself longer still, though he knew his brother was right. He turned his face towards his father, who raised his arm in salute and walked back along the trail. He was soon gone from sight, as if he had never been. Wolfrumm had seen eighteen winters, had twice been in battle, had slain men and been sick to his stomach after. He had felt his bowels loosen as he waited in his first shield wall with the din and clash of raging war all about him, but never had he felt so stricken as he did now. He carried axe and sword, yet was totally helpless to give any aid to his own father. He thought again of the crumbling towers of Ash Ul M'on, the jagged and forbidding walls, the dark alleyways forever locked beneath the ice of centuries, and shuddered, though not from the cold.

Ash Ul M'on had once been a thriving city, a capital of trade and commerce, the seat of High Kings, with colourful pennants fluttering from its walls. It had ruled over the North for over a hundred years, until it had succumbed to the shadows. Avarice and greed had stalked the halls, treachery and violence soon followed. Then came the Horde, those evil and shambling creatures that knew no reasoning or brotherhood.

The Grimm Horde had swept over half the world, following the whim of the dread witch Aihaab. The High Seat of kings had become the City of the Dead. And even now, none would enter its grim streets; tales of grisly deeds, strange shapes seen along the walls from the distance, kept children and grown men alike awake at night and jumping at shadows.

Wolfrumm shuddered again as he stared at where his father had stood but a moment ago. His gloved fingers sought out the sword hilt at his waist. With a curse, he spun to his brother. "We must make haste then Rannulf. It looks like father has the same idea as you, and we have a long way to go if we are to be of any use to him."

Rannulf watched the younger warrior hurry along the ledge, and allowed himself a smile. They could have wings upon their heels and it would do the old wind bag little good. His fate was sealed.

Aelrik the Bearslayer would perish with his toothless cronies on the ice plateau outside Ash Ul M'on. His legend would be crushed, his body broken, and his bones scattered for the crows. The bearded warrior who had once been Rannulf, now more than he seemed yet far less than he had been, laughed into the raging storm. Elation filled him, and he gave praise to the shadows that had shown him the way, and had given him the opportunity to strike the first blow in the new war. Aelrik was doomed, and Rannulf would soon be a general of the New Horde, and lead it into battle for the Empress, the new power in the world of man.

* * *

AELRIK BEARSLAYER WAS A HUGE MAN. He stood almost seven feet tall, with shoulders well over a yard across. His hair was long and braided, still showing signs of the red that had been so bright in his youth, though now layered with silver. His face was fierce, with its bristling beard and stern eyes as grey as a stormy sky. The wind caught his cloak and it stood behind him as a banner, revealing bright polished silver scalemail. A broad girdle about his middle held a great sword and a dagger, their scabbards affixed by chain links.

He was a man of many legends. His name was truly given, as in his prime he had done battle with a great white bear that had been killing the Clansmen's cattle. With spear, shield, and axe, Aelrik had faced the beast, and after the fight of his life had emerged victorious, if battered and bloody. That had been the closest Aelrik had ever come to defeat. He had fought in countless battles, leading his fighting men South to help the realms of men over twenty years past, when those lands had been beset by armies of evil. A Mage had arisen, taking the mantle of Master of the Horde, and Aelrik and many other Kings had gone to defy him.

Hewla had sent him thither. The Crone had told him all the realms of humankind must stand shoulder to shoulder against the darkness, that powerful wizards and witches of great evil were once more stalking the lowlands. Along with their magics, they brought a savage beast, a brutal creature bred for war. These were the Grimm. The tales went that centuries ago, the Grimm had been human in another realm, but they had given themselves over to darkness. Vile sorcerers and demonic forces had enticed them, had corrupted them, twisted them in soul and body, tortured their spirit until only savagery remained. Savagery and hunger, for the Grimm were cursed with a lust for the flesh of humankind.

Aelrik and the southern Kings had fought the Grimm and their terrible master. For a year, the clash of steel rang loud across the land. The Grimm had been driven back to their shadowy haunts, their master slain. So horrible was the war, that it seemed even the Grimm had had their fill of blood, for nothing more was heard of them or their like.

It all seemed so long ago....

Yet now Hewla the Crone believed the darkness had returned. Aelrik had listened to her wise words, for she had a gift well beyond his ken. She had told him that she believed that there were, amongst the young men of the Clan, those that had succumbed to the shadow. She had warned him of a revolt that was brewing amongst the younger warriors. And so he had watched. And he had waited. And sure enough, he began to see with his own eyes that there were subtle changes afoot. There was a slyness, a shiftiness amongst the warriors. Quarrels were now more commonplace. It was as if they took offence at the slightest thing. Young men he had known from their birth seemed to be changing.

There were none of those youngsters among his followers here upon the Death. His fierce eyes noted his companions, each a stalwart of many campaigns and skirmishes. Each had stood, sword drawn in battle line, many times. Aelrik was proud to call each friend.

"That's buggered it then," said Rothgar, a grizzled veteran with only one eye, a leather patch covered the grisly empty cavity of the other. He, along with all the others, was looking to where the path had been sliced away.

Aelrik's second on this journey, Fredach squinted through the swirling snow, and then with a shrug, he called above the wind to his chief. "There is only one course of action left to us."

Aelrik leaned into his lieutenant, and nodded, "It's not a course of action that I particularly relish."

Rothgar was close enough to hear the exchange and looked at the two men. "What course of action?"

The others had now gathered close to hear what was going on. Aelrik cursed inwardly, but he knew there was no option for them, so better to get on with it. "A little way back along the trail there is a cave. It runs through the Death. It is a much shorter route."

"Then what the hell have we been struggling out here for in the teeth of this storm?" shouted one of the older warriors, even now rubbing an aching and arthritic knee with frozen fingers.

"Because the cave leads to Ash Ul M'on," shouted Fredach, over the howling of the wind. The old man with the arthritic knee gave a gap-toothed grin and slapped a hand to the hilt of his sword.

"All I heard was a much shorter route!" he said, setting off back the way they had come. Aelrik and Fredach shared a smile, and then followed, hurrying to take the lead and find the new trail.

Rothgar was the last to file back along the trail. With a final look at the obliterated path, he hunched his shoulders and pulled his hood closer. "Bugger it," he muttered, to no one in particular.

CHAPTER 2
WOLF

Steeleye knew he was dreaming but this didn't null the dread that he felt. He was being hunted through the sleeping world, as he was most nights. He could see his hunter clearly, and didn't know how he himself remained unseen, yet that is the strangeness of dreams.

He stood upon a wall, wide enough for twenty men to stand abreast, its rim covered with a lip shoulder height and three feet thick. The wall was shrouded by a thin mist. A pale dawn light filtered through, painting the massive structure in sepulchral blue. He stood alone on the wall, save for several crows sitting upon the parapet, watching him. He felt a kinship with the birds. It seemed they followed him through the dreamscapes, always watching, black eyes fierce and intent.

He walked along the wall to the parapet, and found himself at once wearing armour, bronze plated, very stylised and ancient in design. He was looking through narrowed eye slits, and could see from the shape of his shadow that the helmet he wore bore great horns reaching out wider than his shoulders. He reached the parapet, and rested gauntleted hands upon the stone, peering across the dreamscape beyond. The wall stretched for miles to either side of him, at least fifty feet high, glowing pale gold in the morning haze. The great wall ran the width of a steep-sided valley, its rearing hills made up of granite and ice.

The valley floor drew his eyes, as he knew it would, as it always did. Sweat beaded his face underneath the helm. His dread came crashing upon him in great waves, uncontrollable and relentless. As far as the eye could see, the valley floor was littered with bones of the dead. Skeletons of men and horses, great elephants, their skulls still bearing the trappings of war. And amongst the familiar shapes: creatures that defied his understanding. Enormous ribcages sprouted from the field of death, shreds of flesh still clinging to the bone despite the ravages of time and carrion. Huge skulls full of teeth as long as Steeleye's hand, their eye sockets the size of his head, stared emptily at the vast sea of destruction. Here was the aftermath of the battle to end all battles. Where humankind had stood toe to toe, chest to chest, with the creatures of the abyss, and given not an inch.

As is the way of dreams, Steeleye didn't know how he knew this, nor if he was looking into the past or a distant future, but he knew he was looking at humankind's last stand against a great darkness.

And he knew what was to follow.

He tried to will himself awake, but as ever it was futile. He heard the footsteps. Like the beating of a war drum, echoing in the otherwise silent land, closer and closer, his hunter stalked through the valley of the dead.

Steeleye at last caught sight of his pursuer. She was still distant, yet, in the way of dreams, he could see her vividly. Tall and slim, her hair, long and pale as spun silver, moved as if caught in a light breeze. She was dressed for war, her body encased in leather and ebony mail that made her pale features glow. She wore a cloak of midnight hue that trailed over the pavement of bones. In her left hand she carried a drawn sword, its steel sharp and cruel. The fingers of her right hand danced constantly, their nails of silver, sharp as talons, and long as knives.

Step by thundering step, this exquisite beauty came towards the wall, eyes as blue as a sapphire sky searching the dead. Her pale lips moved as she murmured spells and curses, breath frosting in the cold dawn air, slim fingers dancing, clickity click. Steeleye felt his fear grow and panic surged within him. He had to wake up; he had to get away. She must never see him, must never know he was watching her in this twilight world. The huntress paused besides the skull of what must have been the father of all serpents; it was longer than Steeleye was tall, its teeth like sabres.

The huntress stood stock still, her free hand resting upon the skull. She closed her eyes, head tilting this way and that. Her fingers twitched, *tap tap* against the ancient skull. *Tap tap tap.* The sound carried to the ramparts of the wall and sent a chill down Steeleye's spine. He watched, frozen with fear, as her lips parted.

Tap.

Tap.

His heart beat faster and faster until he feared it would burst. *Wake up!*

Tap.

Tap.

Her chin lifted, as if she were catching a scent, her eyes flared open in triumph, and her voice uttered a whisper soft as silk that yet carried clearly to the battlements and its lonely occupant. "At last! I can *feel* you my brother!"

* * *

Steeleye awoke with a start, his skin soaked with sweat from the terrors of his dream. He lay still upon his simple cot and tried to slow his thundering heart. He was alone, he was in his own home, small and plain as it was. He was safe.

His cabin, one of many in this Northern settlement, nestled beneath the shadow of his Lord's Keep. His eyes adjusted to the dim cherry light given off by the dying embers of the fire in the grate.

His room was sparsely furnished: a table, two chairs, the cot he slept upon, a sideboard with wash basin and the bare essentials, all hand made by Steeleye himself, some carved with care and imagination, some rude and plain depending upon his mood at the time. As the familiarity of his surroundings began to calm him, the memory of the dream began to dissipate; as dreams are wont to do. Within moments of waking, he was beginning to calm...

Tap, tap, tap, tap.

Steeleye jolted upright, throwing aside the thick blanket and fur that kept him warm through the cold Northern nights. The nightmare had left his nerves on edge. His eyes were wide with surprise as they raked the inside of the cabin. The door was closed and barred, the window shuttered. The sound had issued from beyond the window, so as Steeleye swung out of the bed and silently padded over to the shutters, his attention was fully focused. He put his ear to the shutter. He could hear the moaning of the wind and feel the cold night upon his cheek through the rough timber. He could picture the snowbound landscape, the darkened cottages and cabins. He could see the bare trees, black and sharp against the snow in his mind's eye. He knew the lookout at the keep would be watchful, and yet his own dwelling was on the outskirts of the settlement, away from those he called neighbours, too far perhaps for the sentry to see should someone come skulking.

Moments passed.

Taptaptaptap!

Loud and insistent this time, from the rear wall of the cabin. Steeleye silently pulled on a woollen tunic, worn leather breeks, and sturdy boots. Still, he made no sound. He drew the sword that hung in its scabbard from a peg on the wall, feeling more confident as he felt the hilt in his callused palm.

Likely, it was just foolhardy children playing games with the Outlander living amongst the clan, daring one another to run up to the cabin and rap upon the wood, then scatter helter skelter into the night as the door opened. Likely...

The dream still haunted him, stretching his nerves tight. The sword felt good in his grip, and he squeezed the hilt as he padded to the door, silently easing the wooden bar from its resting place. Now the door was only held closed by a simple latch. Slowly, he reached for it, cursing himself for his fear; he took hold of the latch tentatively. The iron was cold as ice.

Taptaptaptap.

He jumped back, raising the sword, the hairs on his neck standing rigid. Swallowing his dread, he quickly reached for the latch and yanked open the door. A blast of icy wind caught him square, taking his breath, then a black screeching shape burst from out of the night, great pinions beating the air as it flew by the startled Steeleye. He fell back in surprise, abandoning his post at the door, quickly scanning the confines of the cabin.

Sat upon the back of his carved wooden chair was the biggest crow Steeleye had ever seen. He breathed a sigh of relief, all tension leaving him, for he and this bird were well acquainted. He gave a chuckle, walking over to the bird. He noticed his hand shook slightly as he reached out to lightly stroke its head. Its black eyes shone as they regarded him. Steeleye felt a fool. The dream had obviously affected him more than he had thought; it was stupid to be so overwrought by night terrors. He couldn't even fully remember why he was so afraid in his sleep. He had to dismiss the dream now, however, for this bird was no casual visitor, but a beckoning call to visit Hewla the seer.

The crow rubbed its head against his hand, seeming to enjoy contact with a human. Its name was Morrigh, and was a close companion to Hewla, an oracle, and wisest of councillors to their Lord Aelrik the Bearslayer. If one listened to the tales, Hewla was two hundred years old and trafficked in dark magics. Steeleye believed all the tales, for Hewla was perhaps his closest friend in this Northern outpost, and he had seen firsthand her power, not only at healing and seeing into the future, but her communion with the wilderness and its denizens, such as Morrigh the crow. It was Hewla who, along with their Lord and several of his faithful warriors, had journeyed to the sea, five hard days' walk away from the outpost, to find the young boy Steeleye in a small boat washed upon a rocky beach, abandoned and alone.

That had been eight years ago. Eight long hard years for the outcast boy. Though he had grown to a man amongst the Northern tribes, he was well aware that he was only suffered there by the will of Hewla and their Lord. Of how he came to the beach, or from where he set sail, Steeleye had no memory. Before seeing the party of Northerners bearing down upon him all those years ago, he could recall nothing.

His skill with sword and spear, even at such a young age, gave testament to him being brought up in some noble setting. He could read and write, could speak the Northern tongue well enough, and had obviously been tutored to a high degree. Now, somewhere near his twentieth year, Steeleye was a hunter and warrior of fierce skill, so much so that most other young warriors of the clans gave him a wide berth. The older warriors, those who had fought in campaigns long ago with their Lord, were more ready to accept his skills and good council, for they had more of an inkling that here was a true warrior, if not yet tested fully. Yes, he had friends amongst the grizzled veterans, and several of the spear maidens smiled kindly upon him.

Morrigh shivered under his hand and he looked closely at the bird. He had better wrap up and set off to see what Hewla wanted, this deep into the night. As he was about to reach for the fur upon the bed, he noted something odd about his visitor. The crow was leaning to the side, craning its head to see *behind* Steeleye. Its eyes were bright and intense, and suddenly Steeleye felt as if the whole night was holding its breath. A slow and cold shiver made its way down his spine. Slowly he turned to see what the bird was staring at.

The door was still open wide. Snow was just beginning to fall, large silent flakes drifting, almost luminous, in the darkness. Steeleye squared to the door, watching as intently as the crow. Then, out of the night, padding on silent feet, came an enormous wolf. Its pelt was black as the night that had kept it hidden.

The beast crossed the threshold into the cabin. The sword in his hand was forgotten. He felt not the slightest threat from the creature, but rather a feeling of awe as it came to stand directly in front of him. The wolf sat on its haunches and its slanted eyes met his. Steeleye caught his breath as he met the gaze; one eye was as blue as a summer sky, the other as yellow as a buttercup in spring.

The wolf sat and stared at him for several moments, then, still without a sound, it stood and circled his legs, leaning its weight into him as it sat down once more. The crow gave a raucous caw, and flew to sit by the open door, where it cocked its head and sat watching the odd pair, its beak cracked open as if in surprise. The wolf was warm as it leaned against him; Steeleye was as surprised as the crow. Tentatively, he rested his hand upon its fierce head, and the wolf nuzzled closer. Steeleye let out a breath that he had not been aware of holding. Surely the wolf was another of Hewla's wild companions? He had grown accustomed to Morrigh the crow, and he was sure he would become used to the wolf too.

"Well, if you are sticking with me, it's back into the cold we go, the three of us,"Steeleye said aloud, at last finding his voice. "We had best not keep Hewla waiting."

So saying, he scooped up his cloak, took down his belt and scabbard for the sword, and stepped out into the snow. The crow and the wolf exchanged a look, and then followed.

* * *

THE CLANS of the North were closely knit, save for exceptions such as Steeleye, where he was tolerated. Though he did his best to integrate, he was always considered an outsider, an outlander, hence the slight isolation of his cabin. Hewla was even more isolated, living almost a mile from the safety of the settlement, deep within the woodlands that were the life's blood of the clan. Here, among the towering pine and spruce, with their overpowering scent, and the animals of the wilderness, was where she chose to reside. There was no chance of getting lost, for the path from the settlement to Hewla's cabin was wide and well-trodden. Even now, as fresh snow fell fast upon the ground, settling upon existing layers, the path could be seen.

Fresh tracks of ponies and men were cut deep into the snow. A large party had passed this way, and only a short time ago. Only Hewla's cabin occupied this part of the wood, and so it had been named after her, The Witch's Wood, or as the children whispered with superstitious dread, Hag's Wood. The presence of such tracks could only mean there was some kind of gathering. Steeleye was more curious than concerned. Curious as to why he could have been summoned. Hewla would talk with him often, but rarely was he invited to a gathering.

He picked up the pace, pulling the hood of his cloak closer to him. The crow perched upon his shoulder, the wolf padded along silently at his side, so close he could feel its body heat. Every so often, he would look down to see the odd eyes staring back at him. Disconcerting. Were they amused? Did wolves have humour? It occurred to him what an odd trio they must appear, and he smiled. Now, he was certain the wolf posed no threat. He found its company reassuring.

As he slogged through a drift of snow that rose above his knees, he wondered what Freija the shield maiden would make of him and his new companions. The thought of the girl, as ever, lifted his spirits. She was his truest friend, the only one amongst the clans that accepted him fully. She would spar with him with both wooden, weighted swords, and with her wit. He cherished her friendship.

As it turned out, he didn't have to wait too long for her reaction.

He entered the clearing where Hewla had built her cabin. It was a fine affair, strong and cosy. Warm yellow light shone at each window, wood smoke curling into the night sky. Steeleye could smell the burning pine. Freija stood upon the path waiting for him, a grin upon her face, though she cast a nervous glance at the wolf. She stood as tall as he, her hair long and red, and tightly braided. Her face was delicate, almost elfin, with high cheekbones and wide set eyes as green as spring grass. Though she grinned as she stepped to meet him, she was dressed for a fight.

Beneath her heavy cloak he could see a fine mail shirt that fell to almost her knees, belted at her narrow waist. From the belt hung her broad bladed sword, its hilt well worn with use. In her left hand she carried a throwing javelin, a wicked weapon and one that she could use to deadly effect. In her right, she carried a lantern to light their way. She quickly steeped to meet him and awkwardly hugged him, not only hindered by spear and lantern, but also by the wolf which had somehow wound between them. Steeleye returned her embrace, like a brother would. Perhaps once he had dreamed of more, but over the years it had been made clear to him that Freija was not for him. And so a deeper bond had been made. They were as siblings, sharing secrets and dreams. They read together, and spoke of travels to distant lands, but more than this, they had become one: if Freija was the shield, then Steeleye was the blade. She seemed to fill a void within him.

Only after their embrace did Steeleye register the remaining company along the path, gathered outside the cabin. There were around twenty clansmen, and at least as many horses. Each was equipped not for the hunt but for war; with iron rimmed wooden shields on their backs, they bristled with spears, axes, and swords. Many carried lanterns, steel reflecting the yellow light coldly.

"Hewla and Rolf are within. The Crone wouldn't let us set off until you were here," Freija said, through a playful pout.

"Better not let the Crone hear you call her a Crone." He grinned back at her. "She would turn you into a toad!"

He took the lantern from her and she linked her free arm through his, the great wolf somehow managing to stay between them as they made their way towards the cabin. As they passed the gathering, it struck Steeleye that the party was made up of white bearded warriors, and women wedded to the shield and lance. Nowhere did he see a man's face less than thirty years of age. Several of the grizzled warriors nodded towards the pair in greeting; they looked grim of face, resolute. The women were less grim, some even laughing, relishing the chance for combat. But they were younger, had not experienced the clash of arms and the grim reality of death. Steeleye shuddered involuntarily. Where had that thought sprung from?

Freija led him over the threshold into the cabin proper. It was spacious within, and well lit by several lanterns. A large stone fireplace and chimney breast dominated one wall; the fire set therein blazed merrily, sending out waves of heat, and the pungent smell of pine. The rest of the room was cluttered by tables and sideboards, bookshelves and cupboards. Scrolls and books lay scattered everywhere, on tables, on the floor, stacked in corners and on the windowsill. Herbs and dried twigs, gathered together with twine, hung from every rafter; jars of oils and unguents sprouted haphazardly amongst the scrolls.

Sat at a table near the centre of the room were two figures hunched over, heads close as they muttered quietly. One was the white-bearded Rolf, old and long in the tooth, yet somehow all the more daunting for that. Beneath the battered scale plated mail he wore, his shoulders were still broad, his scarred hands still strong. He glanced up as the younger pair arrived, his face practically lost behind tangled white hair and wild whiskers. Bright eyes peered from beneath ever scowling brows.

His companion was Hewla the Crone, the Seer of the North, and she looked not a day over a hundred.

Hewla looked frail, ancient and withered, yet Steeleye could attest to her vigour, as she had caught him a buffet around the ear many a time when his words didn't carry due respect. She was smiling, gap toothed, as she saw Steeleye and the crow perched upon his shoulder. The smile faltered a little when the wolf came stalking into the cabin. The wolf sat when Steeleye came to a standstill, its odd eyes boring into the seated witch.

"It seems I am late grandmother," Steeleye began. "Your pets found me asleep. I had no notion of the gathering, my apologies."

The witch was still locking eyes with the wolf. Moments passed and it was the witch who looked away first. "I sent Morrigh to fetch you true enough. As to the wolf... She just sauntered into my house this morning as if she owned the place, sat in front of the fire and generally got in the way until I told the crow to fetch you. Then, up she got and trotted off without a backwards look!" Hewla sounded perplexed, which was rare. "She seems docile enough, but mark me, young buck, there is strangeness here."

The witch stood; though old, her posture was straight as a rod.

"I will be brief, young buck. I have seen darkness in my waking dreams. It seeps into the hearts of our young warriors and yet they remain unaware. Whence the darkness issues, I cannot tell. There is a power at work that I fear is beyond me, and that in itself should concern us all. I am not without power, for all my age."

"The grandmother has been rolling the bones and parting the veil," Rolf broke in. "She fears for the Bearslayer." His voice was deep and low, and as he spoke of the old one's talents, there was awe in every syllable.

Hewla rolled her eyes at the interruption. "As I was just explaining to the oaf here, our Lord has been visiting the Spring Fair to the East. He took with him both Wolfrumm and Rannulf. He took also ten seasoned warriors and a dozen or more youngsters that he felt could do with a chance to see beyond our lands." She paused to ensure she had all their attention. "In a waking dream, I saw our Lord and ten companions at the gates of Ash Ul M'on, the frozen city of the dead, the last outpost of the legendary Grimm Horde. They were beset by shadows and darkness, a power that I cannot fathom."

The witch fixed Steeleye with a searching gaze. He wondered what she saw, looking at him. Did she see a strong man, hair worn wild and free? Or did she see a brute? His hand rested upon the neck of the black wolf, an unconscious gesture. She frowned.

"The paths of the waking dreams are never as clear as one would wish," Hewla continued. "I see the future sure enough, and I can feel when danger threatens. I saw our Lord at the gate of the loathed City of the Dead, and I could feel terror. I could hear the pounding of his heart, and feel the icy breath of some monstrous evil. There were none of the younger clansmen with him, only the older men, men that have fought by his side in many wars and skirmishes, and they have the bond of blood.

"I believe that an evil has come upon the young warriors of our Clan. Not upon them all, certainly, but upon enough, and those with influence over others. For half a year or more, the Lord and I have been concerned by grumblings amongst the men. A new callousness, sidelong looks and sneers. All is not well with this faction of our Clan."

Rolf cast his eye at Steeleye and Freija. "The maidens of the Spear are unaffected, as are you, Steeleye."

Freija snorted with mirth at this. "Are you suggesting that he is more a maid than a man?" she asked, a mischievous twinkle in her eye.

"Nay, not at all," Rolf responded. "Just that he has very few friends amongst the young warriors of the Clan, and has been accepted more by the older generations and the maids than his own ilk."

"And I think he has more sense than to have any truck with dark forces," added Hewla, "hence his inclusion in this endeavour." She rested a hand upon Rolf's shoulder. "You must journey to Ash Ul M'on. What I have seen has yet to come to pass. You must be on hand at the city gates when our Lord has need of you. This shall be at the dawn of the day after the next. It is a hard journey, but you must make all haste and ensure that you are on the plain before the city as the sun rises."

"And is the threat from the Horde?" asked Steeleye. He had listened to grisly tales of the Beast men whilst sat around the hearth fires in the Long Hall at the Keep, and their attempts to overthrow the lands of humankind. There were many tales of heroes, coming together from all over the world to fight the evil Horde and their cursed warlock leader. They told of great battles as armies raged across the world, eons ago, when even the Gods themselves were called upon to take a hand in matters.

And great had been the calamity from that intervention.

The Grimm Horde and their master were defeated, but at such a cost: mountains were toppled, whole lands were engulfed and drowned in boiling seas in the Gods' fury.

A little over a year ago, Freija and Steeleye had come to the Great Chasm whilst on a hunting trip. It was miles in length, a hundred strides wide at its narrowest point, and so deep as to reach the very bowels of the Pit itself if the tales were to be believed. This was Aihaab's Gap, where the Dark Lord smote the earth and dragged the screaming Aihaab into a fiery doom. The area was shunned now. The legend went that the tortured souls of the destroyed Horde could be heard drifting from the depths, and the despair of their voices could send a man insane.

Steeleye had heard no voices, but the magnificent spectacle of the icy ravine would stay with him forever.

"I don't think the Horde are responsible for this," Hewla was saying, bringing Steeleye back from his reverie. "They are brutal killers, blunt and vicious. Whatever we are dealing with is too subtle for those creatures. They still thrive in the shadows, I am certain of that, but it has been thirty years or more since anyone tried to gather the Horde under their banner, and that was far to the South, in the Warm Lands. The Kings of the world remembered their history and gathered together to defeat that uprising. Aye, even Aelrik, our own Lord, led men on that campaign, and though the Horde were formidable, their new master was no Aihaab, and like many pretenders before him, he was crushed in battle."

The witch paused and poured herself a cup of water from a jug upon the table, she took a sip and then continued, "This is something new. Something quite evil has slithered into the Northlands, and I think taken up residence in the City of the Dead. From there its influence is spreading like a disease over the Snowlands. You will stop it, whatever it is, with steel and courage." The witch gestured to a pile of blades and armour by the cabin wall that Steeleye was sure had not been there when he came in. "There is little time to lose: take mail and weapons from here, there will be a fine bow there too, all that you could need."

Hewla motioned for Freija and Rolf to leave and prepare for the journey. When she and Steeleye were alone, she sat heavily at the table. As Steeleye was pulling a vest of fine linked mail over his head, she began to speak. Her voice was low and pained; her eyes had a faraway look. "When I journeyed to the sea to find you, all those years ago, I was *compelled* by a waking dream. But it differed from all my other visions, for with it came a command: to keep you safe, and to keep silent about any suspicions that I may have had."

"Keep me safe?" He pulled on a bronze helm with hinged cheek guards and a rather moth-eaten crest of red horsehair.

"It was as if there were plans being laid, fate was readying a board, and we were all mere counters, being shifted hither and yon in readiness." She stopped abruptly as the great wolf rose to its feet, the odd coloured eyes seeming to draw Hewla in. Slowly, the wolf took a step closer to the witch. From its throat issued a low growl. It was the first sound either Hewla or Steeleye had heard it make. The witch held up her empty hands to the beast, and smiled sadly, resigned.

"And so fate unfolds," she said. Steeleye watched fascinated. Though Hewla wasn't exactly cowed, she was clearly apprehensive; he had never seen the old woman in anything other than complete control. "Keep close to him," she said to the wolf.

CHAPTER 3
AT THE WESTERN GATE

Steeleye waited alongside Rolf just twenty paces from the west gate of the City of the Dead. At his feet several arrows protruded fletch-upwards from the snow. He held his bow already strung its weight comforting. Freija stood to his other side, as tense as the bowstring. She constantly adjusted the grip on her buckler. Her eyes were bright with anticipation. Wolf sat on its haunches, her tongue lolling from an open mouth, teeth bright and sharp. The wolf watched the gate intently, its odd eyes narrowed.

Rolf looked along the line of men and women. In the pre-dawn light, he could make out little detail, but he knew how most would be preparing, so often had he been to battle with these hardy souls. He knew Eogan would be taking a drink of strong brandy from his dented flask, for Eogan always fought better when the strong liquor was in him. The brothers Hamm and Torak, both seasoned warriors and into their sixtieth year if they were a day, would be wagering how many of the foe they would kill; it was the same every time they went to war, though Rolf had yet to see either brother actually admit he killed less than the other. Their arguments were legendary throughout the North. But both men were made of iron, with no give in them, true warriors.

The shield maidens mostly stayed together; this was how they preferred to fight, and how they were most effective. As a unit, they were shield and spear combined with the speed and the recklessness of the berserker, or so Rolf often thought. Along the line, close to the warrior women Rolf could hear snatches of an argument coming from the huge form of Gunag and the much shorter, and flamboyantly dressed Mallados, who spent as much time grooming his beard as he did sharpening the twin blades he wore strapped to his back. "You have!" exclaimed Mallados, "I can see steam coming from the front of your britches!"

"Nonsense," returned the giant gruffly. "I spilled hot wine earlier."

"Nothing to be ashamed of. I hear Torak pees himself regularly before a battle," quipped one of the shield maidens. This caused a splutter of outrage from Torak, and a huge guffaw from Hamm.

The casual baiting continued up and down the line, but now Rolf paid little attention, dawn was almost at hand. He stole a wary glance at Steeleye; his profile was impassive and calm. "Remember now Young Buck, hold back a little, and whatever comes out of that gate that's not a Northman, you feather it."

"You look a little nervous, Old Man." Steeleye was looking directly at the old warrior, seeing him chew on his beard.

"I was just wondering if we would see the Shining today," he said quietly. "I've not seen you truly *upset* since the day Aelrik, Hewla, and I found you on that pebbled beach. As we came upon you, such a small tyke sat there in your boat... well, I've not seen the like before, nor since. And it is, after all, where you got your name from."

Steeleye grinned mirthlessly in the shadow of his helmet. "Old Hewla seems to think that the occurrence may have been related to stress. In all honesty Rolf, I can barely remember my arrival in the North, certainly not how I came to be sat in a boat on a shore, miles from anywhere. And though you and the witch - and aye, even Aelrik a time or two when he has been in the cups - have told me about *the shining*, I can offer nothing more."

Freija moved a little closer, almost stepping on the silent wolf's tail. She put a hand on Steeleye's mail-clad shoulder.

"For a while it was the talk of the Clan. Steeleye, Shining Eyes, Straw Top, Short Arse. It was touch and go what the witch would call you for a while, so I am told." She jutted her chin and copied his grim posture. "Lucky for you she had not been chewing the leaves that day, or only the gods know what you would be answering to today." She flashed a grin even as Steeleye made to give her a buffet to the side of the head.

Rolf chuckled. The banter before the fray, it would never change, though the warriors did. He filled his lungs with a deep breath; it felt good to be alive. Here in the moments before bloody conflict, was when he felt at peace, when his mind was most clear, Rolf was a true warrior born. He had lived this very moment more times than he could remember, the camaraderie, the rough humour. Soon, there would be the screaming, the fury and the blood. Yes, he had lived this moment many times, and in the clamour that followed, he had never taken a backwards step.

He hoped to see the Shining today. It was the strangest thing he had ever seen: eyes like sunlight glimmering on steel. There was anger in those eyes, fury and violence. But he was sure there was no evil there, for all the strangeness, there was a purity.

As if the very thought of those shining eyes manifested something in the here and now, Rolf became aware of a gaze upon him, and he looked past Steeleye to see the slanted blue and yellow eyes of the wolf. For a moment the two simply stared at one another. Rolf suddenly felt a chill along his spine and the hair stand up on the nape of his neck.

Dawn. The sun flooded the City of the Dead with a weak and watery light, though the shadows of the gate were cast dark across the snowy plains. A heavy silence came upon the gathered warriors. As one they drew swords and axe, hefted spears and adjusted shield and helmet straps. This was the art of war, the art of dying well.

Rolf and the Wolf still gazed at one another, old battle-hardened souls the both of them. And then from within the City of the Dead there came the great tolling of a bell. Just one deep echoing sound that rolled out of the gate and across the plain like a wave.

The wolf raised its head to the sky and howled in answer.

Aelrik had found the narrow pass that ran through the mountain easy enough. It was as if an axe had been taken to the rock, slicing a narrow gorge through the black stone no wider than three men standing shoulder to shoulder. He stepped into the cold darkness, feeling the very weight of the mountain press upon him. He looked upwards and there, far and far above him there was a narrow smudge of light that he knew to be the sky. He motioned for his men to light lanterns and brands, and soon they followed their lord into the stygian gloom. The confining walls of the gorge danced with their flame-cast shadows.

Though he did not mention it to his men, Aelrik was concerned to find this pathway through the Death so well-trodden. The ground at the foot of the ravine was of frozen rock, with very little snow reaching the dark confines.

The more imaginative of the veterans fancied they saw figures, hunched and clawed stalking them amongst the rubble and debris alongside the path. Of the less imaginative, Vintar was the loudest; he grumbled it was hotter than a Viradian whorehouse within the Death, and how a tot of brandy would do them all the world of good right about now.

It took several hours of hard marching, with many turned ankles and battered shins due to the uneven ground and hidden rock formations, but at last, the company made its way from the rough-hewn cut in the mountainside to a corridor of dressed stone.

Aelrik stopped to catch his breath, and motioned for his men to gather around him, putting a finger to his lips to silence their grumbles and questions.

"We seem to be in the halls of Ash Ul M'on," he whispered, though even the whisper ran along the walls in an eerie echo, making Aelrik wince. "From here, its weapons ready, single file. We will gain the outer lanes and head through the city streets and plazas to the western gate. From there, we shall make our way over the plains and be back in the keep within two days." He looked at their torch-lit faces, old faces, scarred and weary after the hard march through the defile. But there was no time to rest, and he knew harder travails lay ahead.

All during this long march, he had been mulling over the events that had brought him here. The way their group had been divided upon the pathway alongside the Death, the sudden landslide that had stranded them on the wrong side of the mountain, so close to the mouth of the pass that would lead directly to the Dread City, the grim certainty that if they were to survive, they would need to brave that ancient place. There were no coincidences here, he concluded. This was a trap. He and his most loyal followers had been separated from the main group just as a wolf pack will separate a young deer from its mother.

Even as he turned grim eyes on the path ahead, he was forced to admit that he had been most royally duped. Of course, it was Rannulf. It was always going to be Rannulf. Ever since Hewla had made him aware of the changes in his son he had known that things would end badly, known that something disastrous would happen, but he had believed that he had time, time to try and reason with his son, bring him back to the clan. But no, there would be no more talking. If he made it back to the keep, then he and Hewla would need to discover the true nature of what Rannulf had become, and deal with it.

He cast an eye over the gathered men, nodded with satisfaction when he saw them all with weapons bared. It was Fredach, his trusty lieutenant, who voiced the question that Aelrik saw echoed in every pair of eyes, all save old Rothgar, who had only one eye, but that piercing old orb asked the same question as all the rest.

"Are the Grimm in the City, Aelrik?"

The others all nodded and turned their faces to their chief, grim and tight-lipped.

"Truly, I cannot say." replied Aelrik, with a shrug of his great shoulders. "Hewla says the Grimm are no more, that they withered and died not long after Aihabb was cast into the chasm. But Rothgar there, and you Fredach, you too Eogan, in fact most of you here came south with me twenty years ago and fought those creatures following the dark banners. I have done much research since then, and I cannot say that I see much difference between them and the legendary Grimm Horde. It may be that some of their number linger in the halls of Ash Ul M'on. It is said that many fled here when the Dark One claimed their master. Perhaps they did not all die out?"

"Those things in the South were vicious buggers," muttered Rothgar. "'Twas one of them that took my eye, and a couple of teeth too if I remember rightly"

Fredach snorted, holding in a laugh "You hardly had any teeth before we ventured south."

Quiet chuckles ran around the company.

Aelrik motioned for quiet, and then continued in hushed

tones, "I have reason to believe that evil deeds have brought us here. We are meant to perish here, in this cursed city. Be it the Grimm or the Horde or whatever the hell dwells here, I fear we are meant to be their meat."

Resolute stares met his own. Here and there a fierce grin. Nowhere did he see a shadow of fear. "Let's be on our way then. Watch each other's backs, keep an eye on the shadows, and don't get separated or left behind." With a final nod and wink he set off at a brisk march. The men filed behind him, Fredach taking his place at the rear to ensure all kept pace.

Once they entered the city proper, the Northmen gazed about them in wonder. Even though abandoned for centuries, the scale of the place was immense. Great pillars fifty feet high and so far around that at least six men would need to link arms to stretch round their girth, ran far into the distance, thirty each side of a vast avenue. Atop each pillar they could just make out statues, whether of Kings or warriors they couldn't see, as their torches and lanterns didn't give off enough light. Great buildings crowded the way, shadowy and ice- covered, glimmering with yellow reflections and crimson shadows. Here was a giant fountain, there a plinth with rubble at its crest, all that remained of the once magnificent structure.

They crossed rivers of ice by way of enormous bridges, edged with stunning filigree iron work long since turned to frozen spindles, onwards and onwards, heading for the Gate they knew to be ahead.

Soon enough they became aware of eyes upon them.

From the dark doorways and shadowy alley's, they could feel the malignant gaze. Even these stout-hearted men of the North felt a chill that was nothing to do with the cold. They picked up the pace, their mail and harness jangling in the silent streets, their footsteps loud to their ears. Yes, there, alongside that wall, and there darting behind a statue of an archer fifty feet high, movement all around them. Shambling figures, rushing hither and yon, keeping pace with the now jogging company.

Rothgar was beginning to slow even as his comrades were speeding up. Sweat beaded his brow even in this frozen City, his breath coming in great gasps. Fredach came alongside him matching his pace.

"Not far now, old friend," he whispered. "See, there, ahead at the end of this avenue? There is the gate. It is only another hundred paces or so. Deep breaths and keep pace with me."

It was true, there at the end of this once-magnificent avenue, now with its huge paving stones cracked and blackened by eons, stood the Western gateway. It stood in a wall twenty feet high, the wall still strangely intact and more imposing than ever in its coat of ice. The gateway was an arched affair, wide enough to admit five men abreast. Even in the gloom they could all see the bronze gate itself hung half off its hinges, gaping open.

Now they could hear their pursuers, their rushing footsteps, and the scrape of iron or talon against stone. More and more of the shadowy figures were converging upon them, ten, twenty, thirty, more, many more! Rothgar put a sprint in his step almost leaving a wild eyed Fredach behind. Up ahead Aelrik and the front runners of the company were nearing the gate. Thirty paces, then twenty. Aelrik was beginning to let himself hope that they would be able to reach the gate, regroup on the plain and face these flitting shadows away from the oppressive halls of Ash Ul M'on.

At ten paces, dawn broke full, chasing the darkness into confined corners and doorways. It was at this moment that Aelrik got his first true look at their pursuers. They kept pace easily with the warriors, long of arm and leg, clad in tatters of leather and armour. They brandished spears and blades of ungodly black steel. They gnashed their teeth, sharp and yellow, almost fangs, and eyes red as coals burning with a senseless hatred.

And then, rolling like thunder came the tolling of a bell!

This was the signal the creatures had been waiting for. Like a wave the savage figures left the shadows and raced headlong towards the Northmen, yelps and howls and savage cries issued from their throats. As they came closer, the companions could see leathery skin. Some bore scales, some had horns on their brow. Taloned fingers and slavering maws.

"The gate! The gate!" shouted Aelrik over the sudden din. Even as he shouted, he reached the gateway, skidding to a stop and forcing his men through ahead of him "Faster! Faster!" he roared, as his men stumbled past. Fredach ran by pushing, a stumbling and panting Rothgar ahead of him. The first of the creatures reached the gate: a huge, terrible figure all muscle and teeth and burning hate. It leapt at Aelrik with a great axe held aloft. With a blood curdling roar, it died, as Aelrik swung his sword to meet the attack, the creatures head was lopped from its neck to sail into the air in a fountain of black ichor, the jaws still snapping and frothing.

And then they were through the Gate and on the plain, staggering away from the darkness, and turning to face the onrush of howling bedlam and insanity.

* * *

EVEN AS THE wolf howled and the bell rang out, Steeleye snatched up an arrow and readied his bow. In the dawn light the great wall of the city, and its impressive arched gateway were clearly visible. The walls were old as time, strong and indomitable. He was aware of the grim legends surrounding Ash Ul M'on, and standing here, bow drawn taught, he could well believe them all.

In an instant, chaos ensued. From the gateway, several exhausted figures ran. They cleared a few yards space, then turned about to face the portal, raising shields in a defensive wall, their swords, axes and spears held ready.

"Aelrik!" shouted Rolf, his voice raised high. His chieftain's name was a battle-cry. The rest of the men and maidens of the shield took up the cry and charged forward. Within seconds they would be at their countrymen's side, yet even before they could cross the snow and ice that separated them, foul creatures burst through the gate and onto the plain. Without hesitation, Steeleye let his first arrow fly, and before it had punched into the throat of the lead monstrosity, lifting it off its feet and throwing it back amongst its kin, he had notched another arrow. He shot four in quick succession, each finding an easy target amongst the milling throng at the gate. His withering fire and accuracy gave the Northerners a few vital seconds to get their breath.

And then the creatures were upon them, sword and axe rising and chopping, spears stabbing and gouging. Shields rang and splintered under fearsome blows. Aelrik's party withstood the initial onslaught, their heels digging into the snow as the sheer weight of numbers pressing against their hastily made shield wall threatened to drive them back. All was chaos and noise, growls and screams, roaring and howling and dying.

It took mere seconds for Rolf and the rescue party to reach the melee. They added their weight to the shield wall and made the line longer in an attempt to keep the creatures hemmed in at the gate. If they could limit the numbers that could attack at one time then they might have a chance. Aelrik gave out a whoop of joy as his oldest friend shouldered his way to his side.

"I should have known you wouldn't miss the chance to get bloody one last time!" he shouted above the clashing din, blocking a savage cut from beyond the shield wall. Aelrik rammed his blade into a nightmare face.

As Steeleye began to run towards the fray, drawing his sword as he did, he could see more and more of the hell-spawn surge from the city. He saw warriors falling beneath claws and teeth, fighting even as they spat their last breath. The giant form of

Gunag went down, a spear in his chest, yet even as he fell, he lay about him taking two of the attackers to the void with him. The brothers Hamm and Torak stood side by side, fighting as one-unit, gnarled figures throwing themselves upon their swords with mindless abandon. Soon, the warriors of the North were standing in a sea of churned red snow and gore. Yet still the devils came on to die and kill.

Steeleye was hardly aware that the wolf had remained with him during the first charge of the clansmen, yet now as he neared the enemy, the great beast sped past him and leapt at the throat of a monstrous creature that was bearing down upon Freija and another maiden who had, by the looks of it, already been dealt a mortal blow. Wolf and monster rolled snarling and biting into the throng.

Steeleye was quick to follow. He was begrudgingly respected in the practice yards for his speed and swordsmanship, for all the forms and techniques he had mastered in his now forgotten young life, but that stood for little in this gateway. Here, it was a butcher's yard. Stab and hack, chop and swing. Feet sliding and slipping in snow melted by hot blood, shield to shield and chest to chest with the foul enemy.

He stood his ground next to Freija, stabbing over her shield at a snarling face. At his other shoulder was Elwyn, a maiden in her forties, hard as her blade. The three of them stood fast against the tide. Dimly Steeleye could hear the wolf snarling and growling, could hear too the screams of her victims. A great axe crashed against his helm, sending stars across his vision, Freija was quick to stab at the attacker, but there were so many he couldn't tell if she had found the correct mark. Elwyn grunted in pain and was gone, just like that, struck by a vicious blade. Before the line could break, Rothgar One Eye had stepped into the breach.

Steeleye felt a laugh striving to break past his snarling lips. He would swear the old man at his side was singing! Head tucked behind raised shield, his sword stabbing and jabbing into the foe, Rothgar glanced with his one wild eye at his young companion, and raised his voice loud in a bawdy song that Steeleye was vaguely aware questioned the morals of a seamstress in the village of Berry, and a stable-hand called Fipp.

Hack and slash. Clang and scream.

With a sudden surge, the foul creatures had broken the line. Gaps appeared as men and women of the North fell. But what a toll they took upon the creatures. Bodies were sprawled thick across the plain, piled high at the gate hindering the remaining attackers. The Northmen were forced to make smaller groups, falling back into unbroken snow to gain sounder footing.

Hack and slash. Clang and scream.

Though only minutes had passed, Steeleye was breathing hard, constantly moving, blocking cutting. His helmet was gone, chewed off his head by a loathsome creature now dead beneath his boot. He bled from a dozen scratches and cuts, his yellow hair matted and dark with blood from a cut to his scalp. Wolf was now at his side, teeth a-snarl, muzzle thick with gore, her eyes wild. Still with him were Rothgar, his one eye glaring hatefully at the gate, Freija also stood close by: he could hear her panting breath. Her mail shirt was torn, her shield gone, her sword red to the hilt.

A few paces to his left, the brothers Hamm and Torak stood, both swaying from exhaustion and the wounds they had sustained. Steeleye was suddenly aware that these brave men and women were mostly thrice his age. They were mothers and fathers, grandparents some of them. Torak spat blood into the snow; his beard was thick with it. "The last one was mine," he was saying to his brother. "The big one with the mace, you might have wounded him, but my sword killed him."

"Wounded him?" Hamm responded wide eyed, "I lopped his bloody head off! How is that wounding him?"

"He was still twitching when I struck," grinned Torak. He gave

a cough, and spat up crimson. Slowly, he fell to his knees. "Oh."
He looked surprised, his free hand digging in the snow, but his
right hand gripping the hilt of his sword tightly. "Bugger, I was
winning too..." Hamm watched his brother die outside the
Western Gate, and a rage built up in him the likes of which he had
never felt. He glared balefully at the gate and at the creatures
massing for a final onslaught.

He thrust his sword into the snow, and unfastened his helmet,
throwing it to the ground. His shield even splintered as it was,
joined it. Then he once more took hold of his sword. "Hold fast
brother," he said, casting a glance at Torak's crumpled body.
"Hamm is coming." He looked over at Steeleye, meeting his gaze
levelly. "You have done well today. Should you make it to the
Longhouse, tell the tale." He grinned fiercely, then with a great cry
he ran full at the creatures, sword raised high.

So furious was the attack, so heedless of defence was Hamm,
that he struck down one, two, three before the devils could
fathom what was happening. By that time Steeleye himself was
amongst them, though he could barely remember moving his feet.
Aelrik barrelled into the fray, striking left and right. Rolf was there
too, as ever, a shadow to his chief and friend, killing all that were
not of the clan. Drunken Eogan, Rothgar One Eye, and the vain
Mallados were quickly beside their comrades. So too were all the
remaining swordsmen and women, less now than a score in
number, but driven on by Hamm's example. Here, outside the
Western Gate of Ash Ul M'on, the warriors of the North proved
their mettle. Outnumbered two to one, still they threw themselves against the creatures of the dark. With passion and rage
they struck. No mercy was given nor asked for.

And then, from the shadows of the gate lumbered a terrible
creature, as if, as a last resort, the darkness spat its very worst at
the Northlanders. Standing fully eight feet tall, with more muscle
than a plough horse, there came a monster from the darkest of

dreams. Armoured in black plate and jet mail, its head bereft of helm, its hair long and lank, adorned with finger bones and about its throat bearing a necklace of teeth and human ears, its eyes burned with hatred and malice, and from its fanged mouth saliva drooled as if it could already taste the flesh on offer before it.

In its hands it bore a great spear, fully ten feet long and as thick as a swordsman's wrist. The blade was a wicked serrated affair over a foot in length. With a contemptuous sweep of the spear the creature opened the throat of vain Mallados before the human could even lift his shield. As the man bled out his life at the feet of the creature, it grinned at the gathered men and women, who backed warily away, exhausted and close to spent.

"I am Kleave!" the thing growled, its voice so deep it seemed to come from the very bowels of the earth, like tectonic plates grating against one another. "Who dies next?" The words were guttural, as if the throat that made them was unused to the tongue of the Northerners. But it was clear enough.

Aelrik launched himself forward, his great axe lashing out at the head of the monster, which dwarfed even the Clan chief.

Kleave caught the haft of the axe in one huge and taloned hand, wrenching it clear of Aelrik's grip. It was only by throwing himself back with desperate haste that Aelrik wasn't cut in two as Kleave returned the blow.

Aelrik landed heavily in the snow, the wind knocked out of him. For a moment he was at the mercy of Kleave, but the creature took too long to savour the helplessness of his fallen enemy, and then Rolf was suddenly there, raining blow after blow upon the monstrous form. Kleave was driven back two paces before the furious Rolf. The blows were easily turned aside, but so relentless that the monster couldn't counter strike. Again and again. Rolf struck, until his sword shattered upon Kleave's breastplate, and even then, he stabbed at the snarling face with the jagged remains of his blade.

Kleave caught old Rolf's wrist in a huge hand, and squeezed until Rolf screamed in his pain. Over the scream the shattering of bones could be heard. Not deigning to use a weapon, the monster swiped Rolf aside contemptuously. The old warrior was sent flying, landing in a crumpled heap. He did not move.

The battle was as good as over. The very last few of the creatures were now scrambling over the piles of their dead in the gateway to reach the humans. They roared and gibbered, eyes afire with hate and hunger. The Northerners redoubled their efforts, they could sense victory. Survival was tantalisingly close.

Steeleye had watched as Rolf was swatted aside.

The monstrous Kleave once more turned to the prone Aelrik, raising the great spear to finish the northern chief.

Steeleye was moving fast through the melee, his grip tight upon the sword, ducking and weaving through the remaining life and death struggles, then running full at Kleave, a roar escaping his lips. Kleave paused in his death stroke and faced this new threat, his crimson eyes growing wide with alarm. For the first time since being birthed in whatever loathsome pit had spawned him, the giant Kleave, champion of the City of the Dead felt the icy fingers of dread chase along his spine.

Running towards him was a yellow-haired warrior, sword raised high, at his side bounded a great black wolf, gore streaming from its bared teeth, its narrowed eyes blue and yellow. But this was not what sent chills through his veins, it was the warrior's eyes. They were afire! Shining and blazing like sun-kissed steel, wild and pure. Kleave felt the power emanating from the man, could feel that here was the exact polar opposite of he and his kind. Here was something new to this realm, and yet as old as time.

And then the man and his snarling companion were upon him. Stabbing again and again at the bright-eyed warrior, Kleave roared curses, the wolf darted in to bite at hamstrings and groin, then was gone in the blink of an eye. Steeleye himself hacked and chopped, ducked back then leapt in, blow after blow dealt and received. He was aware dimly that he had taken several wounds, but he was beyond pain, beyond fear. It was as if another entity were within him, shielding him from the agonies the spear inflicted, as if it loaned strength to his arm and speed to his eye.

With a brutal efficiency, Steeleye, eyes shining like balefire, and his terrible companion Wolf, tore into the monstrous Kleave. So violent and filled with rage was the conflict that those around them paused in their own struggles to watch open-mouthed. Kleave was a monster, huge and burning with violence, yet he was matched by this yellow-haired devil that seemed to dance by the great spear unmindful of cuts and stabs, to strike again and again. Every man, woman and slavering beast upon the plain watched as Kleave suddenly hurled his spear at the wolf. They saw Steeleye twist aside, his blade knocking the spear from its true course. They saw that in that split second, Kleave had drawn a wicked curved dagger from his belt, and had plunged the blade into the warrior's side.

For a moment the tableau held. Silence came over all save the gasps and rasps of laboured breathing. Steeleye staggered, fell to his knees. Kleave, bloodied and torn, barely able to stand himself, sank to his knees also. His face, savage with glee close to Steeleye's own. "I know who you are Lightbringer," the creature spat. "I have been shown your coming in dreams of death and chaos. You bring the time of fire and blood! You are the herald of the return of the Horde! The Grimm is coming, Lightbringer, and the Old Gods will follow. The true Darkness has been awakened. Too long have the faithful hidden in the shadows."

Steeleye raised his eyes, still burning with fierce light, to meet those of Kleave. Their faces were only inches apart. He could see the rage in that crimson stare. He could see the death of every man, woman, and child throughout every land in those merciless orbs. In that moment, locked eye to eye with the monster, Steeleye knew he faced an evil beyond anything he had ever imagined.

Kleave bared his teeth in a ghastly, rictus grin. "I see you Lightbringer, hiding in there." The creature made a strange cooing sound, swaying his head from side to side, almost a serpentine, hypnotic motion "Kleave sees you," he rasped, more guttural than ever. "The Mistress will favour Kleave..."

A deep throated growl stopped Kleave mid-gloat. Right there, just inches from his face, was Wolf. Lips curled back over red stained teeth in a pitiless snarl. Even as Kleave saw the wolf, Steeleye struck, with his last ounce of strength he drove his sword upwards. It caught Kleave under the chin, drove through his skull until the cross-guard of the hilt thudded into the jaw, snapping the teeth shut, biting off a chunk of tongue. Kleave fell back dead. The great body hacked and battered, bitten and gouged.

Dimly, Steeleye wondered how the creature had continued to fight with such wounds. Then, a wave of pain and weariness engulfed him. He was vaguely aware of rough hands steadying him. He could hear Freija calling his name from a great distance. He could hear his breathing ragged and loud, his heart thudding in his chest. The hands at his shoulders shook him, bringing him to his senses a little. He could see Aelrik helping a very battered looking Rolf before him, their faces creased with concern. When they saw he was conscious, they both grinned through their matted beards.

"You brought the Shining," Rolf exclaimed happily, almost childlike. It was disconcerting here, amongst the death and the bloodied snow, to see the old man so happy. Aelrik was looking about him sadly now. "We have lost some good friends today," he said quietly. "If not for old Rolf here, and you and that beast of yours, I too would be embracing Morriggu of the raven cloak." He pursed his lips as he saw the wound in Steeleye's side. "It looks like that creature Kleave has left you a scratch to remember him by" Steeleye chuckled at this, for the wound was far from a scratch and burned like the devil. It was, he feared, a mortal wound.

"Is it over?" he asked, his voice a croak. Gods, but he was parched. He was still on his knees, the snow around him red with gore. Hot blood from both the mangled Kleave and his own wounds had melted the snow until it was mush.

"Aye," replied Aelrik, casting an eye about him. "When that big one fell, the rest lost heart and scattered back into the city."

A water skin was pressed to his lips and he drank greedily, gasping for breath even as he did. When the skin was lowered, he saw that it was Freija that had brought him the drink. She watched him closely, concern clearly writ in her eyes. Though her face was bloodied and a large bruise was already forming on her cheek, from some fist or club, she was still lovely to behold, his dearest friend, his comrade at arms and as far as he was concerned, his sister. As his vision cleared even more, he saw a crow perched upon her shoulder.

Seeing him register the bird, Freija grinned widely, "Hewla is here. She must have left almost on our heels to get here this fast!"

As if the mention of her name had summoned her, the witch was at the girl's elbow pushing her aside, though gently. "Foolish girl. I left my cabin at dawn no later. I turned myself into a raven and flew with the crows!"

The old woman laid surprisingly strong hands upon the wounded young man; she muttered words beyond hearing or understanding. Wolf had silently positioned herself as close to them as she could and watched, tongue lolling from a bloodied mouth. The yellow and blue of her eyes glowed with an unnatural intelligence. Hewla was obviously aware of the beast, but continued with her mumbling incantation. For his part, Steeleye felt the pain from his wounds subside a little. He could feel heat emanating from the hands pressed to him, and with the heat came a soothing numbness. Soon, he could feel the wounds hardly at all, nor the cold of the snow through his torn and soaked garments. Darkness swam close by as his vision blurred.

"Is it night already?" he asked, his voice thick with exhaustion.

"Nay, it is still early morn, and the sun shines," Freija answered, from far, far away or so it seemed. As sleep crowded about him, he was aware of much movement about him. Then, he heard Hewla's voice loud and sharp as she took charge. "Look to the living. The dead are with the Morriggu and can be helped no more. Say a prayer for their souls as you help those that need it, for we must away to the settlement as fast as we can."

Just as sleep claimed him fully, he heard the chieftain Aelrik giving commands, "Check each and every creature. Whether there is breath or no, take off its head..."

CHAPTER 4
ENEMY

The creature that had once been Rannulf could feel his hatred of the men following him growing, hour by hour. They spoke constantly of those they had left to the mercy of the caves of Ash Ul M'on, which they deemed to be scant, if it existed at all. They planned a return to the City to find their fellows, to gather up a rescue party and trek back along the pathways of the Death. Guilt ate at them. It broke through all the dreams of glory that this new Rannulf had implanted in them so carefully, over such a long time. How quickly they forgot his promises of riches, glory, and land.

For four days he had led the men, through blizzards and gales of freezing wind. He led them at a steady pace. The nights in the mountains were beyond freezing, and they had huddled in their tents, drinking melted snow and eating dried rations, each voicing their regret at leaving clansmen, sleeping only when exhaustion claimed them.

On the second day, Einar had fallen through the ice into a crevasse; one moment the lieutenant was there, loyal to Rannulf and steady as the mountains themselves, the next he was gone.

Without a sound, save the dread cracking of the ice. After that, the men had begun to look differently at Rannulf. He caught them often gathered around young Wolfrumm, muttering in lowered voices. He caught the word "cursed" often, and smiled inwardly, if only they knew just how cursed they really were.

There were no more major distractions, but the march home was hard by any standards, and took longer than Rannulf had hoped. He was keen to begin his rule over the Northlands. He would be the spark that would ignite the new war over all kingdoms, that would usher in the rule of shadow. As he slogged through knee deep snow, his mouth watered at the prospect of strife and bloodshed.

At noon on the fourth day of their weary trek, they saw at last the final rolling plain of snow, and there beyond it was the forest that marked the boundary of Aelrik's domain. The trees were dark and looming, reaching into the clear blue of the sky like needles. Just one more mile to go, then they would be in the trees and, the going would be easier, with well-trodden paths and animal trails to guide them back to their hearths. Unbidden, the party increased its speed, the sight of the forest and the knowledge that they were almost home leant energy to their tired limbs.

Rannulf strode out in front of the party; he could smell the pine in the clear air. Somewhere deep within, the new Rannulf felt the old one screaming and railing against his imprisonment. He crushed the old Rannulf down mercilessly, locked him away in a deep, dark place, populated with all the horrors that the beast could imagine. They were many indeed.

There was no time to gloat for the imposter though, for even as he approached the tree line, from the shadows there emerged a silent host. Northmen. Geared for war, dressed in mail and scale, carrying spear, axe, and shield, many with helms adorned with horns or wings. This was a sight to freeze the marrow in the bones of any man, but for Rannulf, the fear he felt was increased when he spied the great figure of Aelrik striding from the gloom of the forest. Resplendent in his silvered, chain-mail shirt, the helm upon his head was crested with a scarlet plume of horsehair, its cheek and nasal shields hiding most of his face, but there could be no doubt this was Aelrik, the Bearslayer himself at the head of his warriors; the giant didn't look so old, after all.

Rannulf walked a little nearer, until he could see the grim set of the Bearslayer's mouth, and the fury in his storm grey eyes. The chief seemed to vibrate with barely controlled violence.

"Father!" called the imposter, "I knew you would make it back before us... why, I told the men so, did I not Wolfrumm?" Rannulf twisted from the hip slightly to catch the eye of the youngest son of Aelrik. But Wolfrumm had stopped his advance ten paces before, and now he stood with his arms spread, holding back the rest of the men. "What ails you brother?" Rannulf called. "Come stand with me little brother. Let us greet our father together, as brothers!"

But Wolfrumm did not move. Rannulf's hand strayed to the hilt of his sword. He looked to his father, the great brooding shape with his baleful gaze. Wolfrumm noted how his father's hands clenched into fists. The men behind Wolfrumm were silent too. They watched the eldest son through narrowed eyes. Though they were unsure why, over the last day or so, Rannulf had begun to fill them with dread whenever his look fell upon them.

"Your guise is a good one, but the deception is at an end now." Hewla stepped forward from the ranks by the forest's edge. The crone was still dressed in grey homespun weave, her thinning white hair pulled back severely and braided into long tails that reached her hips. She was still their Hewla, but now there was iron in her spine and flint in her gaze. She strode purposefully forward; her staff, though used for support, seemed menacing.

"Rannulf does not stand before us," she stated in a strong voice.

The imposter held out his empty hands, and looked imploringly at the gathering before him. "Grandmother," he said, a touch of a whine in his voice. "'Tis I Rannulf! You know me... You have sewn my wounds and tended my fevers when I was a child. What foolishness is this?" He began to laugh a little, nervously, like a naughty child caught misbehaving. "Father, tell her 'tis I."

But Aelrik remained stoic.

"Wolfrumm, tell them all it is I!" But Wolfrumm was silent too. "Stop this foolishness..."

"Aye let's put an end to this charade" Hewla's voice cracked like a whip over the tableau.

The imposter took a deep breath and turned beseeching eyes upon the gathering one last time and, finding no succour, relaxed visibly and lowered his head. Soon his shoulders were shaking slightly, and Wolfrumm thought that Rannulf was sobbing. For a moment, he was compelled to step forward and comfort his brother. Rannulf raised his head, and all could see that he was laughing softly. He pulled off his helm and cast it into the snow at his feet, shaking his long red hair loose. Still laughing, he smoothed his beard and fixed his eyes upon Aelrik.

"What a father you are! For months now, I have paraded about your lodge and keep. And you were never the wiser! In here..." He tapped his head with a finger... "your son has been screaming for help! For months! How does that feel, Old Man? Knowing that you as good as deserted your own blood?"

Aelrik felt the blood drain from his face as this imposter spoke. Was it true? He took a step forwards confused and full of despair. But Hewla stopped him in his tracks. "Wait," she spat, her eyes narrowing as she watched the imposter closely.

"Very wise grandmother!" laughed Rannulf. He breathed deep, rising to his full impressive height. He held out his arms wide, and looked to the sky, a sly smile on his face as he slowly turned full circle, letting all the gathering see him. "Behold! Am I not magnificent?" He made a soft cooing sound, tilted his head slightly as if listening to a voice only he could hear. Eyes half-closed, he began to sway slowly and dance. The onlookers were dumbfounded.

The cooing became louder, and words could be heard though none there could understand their meaning. Long seconds passed, and then Rannulf slowly drew his sword, letting the sun dance upon its bright length. "Are you not all afraid of me?" he asked. His voice was Rannulf's voice, strong and loud. "Am I not wondrous to behold?" With his left hand he undid the clasp to his cloak, letting the warm fur fall to the snow. "I am everything that you fear. I am the bump in the night, I am the shadow under the bed, the scratch at the door at midnight. And I am come to usher in a new age. Too long have the shadow folk hidden from the likes of you." There was a sneer in the voice, a taunt, and the watching men felt a chill that was nothing to do with the weather. The odd dance continued, slowly, slowly his steps bringing him closer to the clansmen gathered by the trees.

"Stay where you are, demon!" Hewla intoned harshly. She raised her staff in a warning gesture, and all could feel the strange power emanating from it. She seemed to grow taller, straighter. The men closest to her were suddenly unsure who posed more of a threat, the witch or the strangely dancing, capering creature wearing their beloved Rannulf's body. "Come closer and I will strike you down."

The imposter laughed at this. "You would strike down the son of your Lord?" For a moment, he stood stock still head cocked to the side as if once more listening to things no one else could hear. He put his hand to the side of his mouth, as if he were shielding his next words from prying ears, though when he spoke his voice was an exaggerated whisper that all could hear. "Rannulf is still here! Locked in the darkness." The imposter continued his charade of uttering a secret. He looked left and right pretending to spy eavesdroppers. Then, he put an open hand next to his ear, as if to listen more closely to something. "What's that Rannulf? What do you say? You love your Daddy? But your Daddy is about to drive his sword into you!"

Aelrik groaned in anguish. "Let my son go, creature, and then you and I can settle this as men."

The dance began again, slow circles, arms wide, eyes half-closed, cooing in almost ecstasy. "Let him go? Are you sure? Could you bear to see the drooling, weeping wreck that I will have left for you? His mind was gone long since to be truthful; it broke soon after I introduced myself to him. I suppose you could prop him up in a corner somewhere, and have a nurse feed him gruel twice a day; clean him up when he messes himself? Put a strap betwixt his teeth to stop him swallowing his tongue and shattering his teeth as he screams when remembering the horrors that I have shown him. Are you sure you would like me to release him to you?"

Aelrik began to walk forwards now, tears in his eyes, but resolve in his step. "If that's how it is, then I will deliver mercy myself."

"No Aelrik! I must question the beast, to find its true intentions here in the North, it must be taken alive." Hewla stepped forward to restrain Aelrik, her face contorted with grief for the dilemma that her Lord and friend faced.

The imposter was laughing full and loud now, malice and glee bright in his face.

"Come on Father, and stick a sword in your boy! Hack and stab, hack and stab, hack and stab and lop off his head!" he shouted in a sing song voice "You can do it! You have killed hundreds! What is one more to you?"

And then it all happened with blinding speed and fury. The imposter darted towards Hewla, his mouth spread wide in a rictus grin, sword raised high to strike down the witch even as shock registered in her face that she was too slow to defend herself. Aelrik broke into a run, a shout of rage as he saw he was too slow, too old to stop the attack.

The imposter pushed aside the staff with contempt, raised Rannulf's blade, and hissed "It's past time that you died, bitch..."

He crumpled to the floor senseless, toppling without a sound. Wolfrumm stood over Rannulf, breathing hard, recovering from his shock and horror; he had sprinted full at his brother and brought the flat of his sword down upon his head with terrific force.

Hewla recovered first; she pounded her staff into the snow, and cast wild eyes at the gathered men. "Bring rope, or twine, anything to bind him! Hurry before he awakes"

Several of the men did as she bid, and soon Rannulf was trussed securely, hands drawn tight behind his back, ankles and knees bound also. Once the fallen creature was fully secure, Hewla stepped forward to apply a gag over his mouth, just as she was about to cover his lower face with a cloth, Rannulf's eyes sprang open, and he snapped and snarled at the startled witch. This time, it was Aelrik himself who was the quicker; in a blur of speed the huge man ran in and delivered a mighty blow to the side of Rannulf's head. With a grunt, the bound figure's head dropped to the snow. Once more Rannulf was still.

"That was for my boy, you bastard" Aelrik spat. He stood over the figure as Hewla quickly set to and tightly knotted the gag, careful to keep her hands as far from the teeth as possible. Aelrik moaned in anguish at the sight of his beloved son so bound. He turned beseeching eyes upon the witch. "Tell me you can cast out whatever devil has possessed my son Hewla"

The witch would not meet his gaze; she hated to see her Lord and friend in such misery.

"I will do all I can, once we get him back to the Keep." Aelrik wasn't fooled by her evasiveness, and put a giant hand gently upon her shoulder. "I know you will, but even so, do you think I should prepare for the worst?"

Leaning on her staff the witch turned fully to her Lord. "I fear this is just a beginning. I fear the shadows have returned to our world, if indeed they ever truly left. This one..." She nudged the bound and gagged figure in the snow with her foot. "He is *old*. Though he is hidden well, and I fear it is true what he said, that he has been amongst us for a long time, I can feel his evil when I am this close to him. The corruption, and the malice, I see the end of days for humankind before me." She shuddered, and looked to the Bearslayer with haunted eyes. "Though it breaks my heart to see Rannulf thus, I fear greater tragedy lies ahead for us all."

Aelrik's frown was deep, his brow furrowed in a scowl. "Had I but taken you more seriously weeks ago when you said there was something wrong within the clan, perhaps we could have stopped this. Had I listened then, good folk would not have died at the Western Gate..."

"And we would be none the wiser that demons lurk within the caves of the Death" Hewla broke in sternly. "They didn't die in vain, and it was a noble end. Now we know the shadows are returned to the lands, and soon, when Spring is here and roads to the South are open again, riders must be sent to all Kingdoms. We must hope that their memory is as long as ours in the North. We must hope that our ancient allies have not succumbed to the shadows already."

"You speak as if war were coming to the Lands."

"That is what I fear. That is what I see in my waking dreams. The land covered in tides of shadow, a host of Nations standing against them."

"And do we prevail in these waking dreams?" It was old Rolf who spoke the question; he had come from the line of trees whilst Aelrik and Hewla had their heads together.

They both looked to the white bearded warrior, and Hewla

spoke to them both. "That is unclear, there is so much that can happen to change fate. But mark me, the age of peace is over, and a time of strife has begun. We have been too complacent; we didn't even notice the serpent among us."

They all looked at the recumbent form of Rannulf. A huge bruise was already forming on the side of his face where Aelrik's fist had struck. "We are behind in this game," stated the witch. "Here at our feet, is a means to learn just how far behind we are."

Aelrik's hands formed into great fists, clenching and unclenching, the knuckles cracking loudly under the strain. He chewed his beard for several moments, and conflict raged within him. This was his son. His first born. He looked to the sky, now a clear, cold blue. "I am at a loss what to do Hewla," he whispered. "Even after what the creature said, this is still my son here in the snow."

The witch sighed, not with impatience or scorn, but with understanding. Though a terror with sword and axe, where his children were concerned, Aelrik had always been tender- hearted. It had been his wife who had wielded the rod to keep the young Lordlings in check, but since her passing ten years gone now, Aelrik had softened towards his boys even more. Rannulf had ever been the apple of his father's eye, tall and straight, a hunter of skill, and a warrior born. All this and a natural leader of men...

Hewla took charge, as she always did.

"Rolf, Wolfrumm, don't just stand there gawking, get help and take Rannulf to the horses, lay him over a saddle and head for the keep. Those men who came over the Death with him..." At this she narrowed her eyes and stared fully at young Wolfrumm. For long moments she gazed at him, and the young warrior felt her stare pierce him to the bone. Finally nodding her head as if satisfied, she continued, "Make them comfortable in the keep also, but keep an eye on them until I am able to speak to each and every one of them. As for Rannulf, put him, in a cell, four guards at all times.

No one is to speak to him, no one is to take off that gag. If he so much as looks like he is thinking of causing trouble, put him down with clubs."

As the pair jumped to do her bidding, Hewla met Aelrik's eye and shrugged helplessly. "I will do everything that I can Lord. But I fear this is a demon of ancient times, with old powers that are beyond me. I have lived my life believing that the Demons of Aihabb were gone, that they were destroyed utterly when the Gods last walked the world. But now, we have here what I believe to be a captain of the Horde, and the creatures that pursued you through the City of the Dead: they were the Grimm! We are not as strong as we were when last these creatures engulfed the world."

Aelrik let out a long breath. He seemed to deflate before her very eyes. "Do what needs to be done Hewla." The words tasted of poison and bile as they passed his lips.

Northmen appeared and grabbed the creature carefully, six of them lifting him and striding off to the tree-line where the ponies were tethered, and two more flanking either side with swords drawn and eyes wary. As he watched his brother carried away, young Wolfrumm looked to his father and the seer. "What is happening father?" he asked, still confused, even though it had been his own instinctive actions that had felled the creature initially.

Seeing Aelrik was still wracked with his grief, Hewla spoke for him. "Much has been happening within the Keep and the lodges and cabins for what would seem to be several months now." She placed a hand upon the young Lords' shoulder. "Damn me for an old fool, but I had no inkling that it was this severe. Shadows and darkness have come upon the North. That creature that you just put down, the one wearing the skin of your beloved brother, he is a demon from the ancient times of the Horde. For some time, through Rannulf, he has been perverting many of the young warriors, sowing seeds of dissension and discord. Where they had loyalty to their Lord Aelrik, slowly did the creature blind the men to reason. With promises and stealth, and I have no doubt dark magic, he bound the young to him. His plan, or so I believe was to have Aelrik die within Ash Ul M'on. If that had happened, he would have been free to cause mayhem as leader of all the North."

Wolfrumm was speechless, casting a nervous look at the warriors carrying his brother. It was true that he had noted a change within Rannulf, and within those that he considered his cronies. He had seen a cruel streak that he had been previously unaware of. In the practice yards he had seen men left battered and bleeding when they sparred with him.

Now, when he thought back, there seemed to be a permanent sneer twisting his brother's lips, but the transformation had taken place so slowly that it seemed almost as imperceptible as the passing of the seasons. Only now, as he was confronted with this new and devastating news, did young Wolfrumm begin to see clearly the changes in Rannulf. From a noble, and considerate young warrior, whose fierceness in battle was matched only by the loyalty that he showed his father and fellow Northerners, he had become sly, a whisperer of secrets, and a bully, spending too much time in his cups.

Wolfrumm steadied himself, his young eyes seeking the mountain ranges, their great size and lofty reach, was an anchor to him as all else he knew seemed fragile and changeable. For several moments he stood thus. He knew his father would be blaming himself because that was the way of a father. But he would come to terms with this great loss. He would emerge from his melancholy given time. Until then young Wolfrumm knew he had to assist Hewla in any way that he could. With Rolf and several others of the older men and women, the North would fare well enough until Aelrik was once again himself.

Shaking clear of the reverie, Wolfrumm addressed the crone,

"I see old Rolf there, and my father, but how many of the others that we left upon the Death made it home?"

With a sad smile, Hewla linked her arm in that of the young Lord, gently guiding him towards the trees and home. "Not enough," she said quietly, "though there shall be a song sung for them. Your Lord and father led true men through Ash Ul M'on, and they were met by what we had come to believe were mere stories, myths and legends. But the shadows have returned to the world. And I for one am glad that it was the Bearslayer that they found first. He let them see that we can still stand tall and not give." The witch and Wolfrumm both cast a glance at their Lord. The huge figure trailed after them with his head down, an air of despondency upon him.

It was white-bearded Rolf who broke their reverie, as he buffeted the young Lord on the shoulder affectionately, Wolfrumm noted he used his left hand, the right was swathed in bandages to the elbow. "It is good to see you, young Wolfrumm." said the old man. "Your father will come around, there's no fear of that. It is the shock. He had resigned himself to Rannulf's treachery, but this... it will take time."

"What happened to the arm?"

"T'was snapped like a twig by a giant spat out of the depths of hell!" Rolf said, his face splitting in a grin. "Our outlander saw to him though! Now that is a story to tell you!"

Wolfrumm looked to Hewla to see to see if the old man was jesting, but her look was sombre and grim.

"We must make haste to the Keep for there is much to be done, and much for you to be told."

Wolfrumm felt icy fingers play along his spine as he trudged towards the trees.

CHAPTER 5

LOSS

Steeleye breathed in deep. He could smell decay, the odour of death lingered in the air even though eons had passed since battle had choked the valley floor with the dead. As in every dream, the bones of the dead shone dully in the dawn light, reflected crimson in the fiery sunrise.

He stood upon the same battlements as ever, his hands resting upon the rough stone wall. All was familiar. This was a scene he lived most nights. Here was the sunrise that he had watched his entire lifetime, there the carpet of skulls and ribs, the broken spines, the shattered limbs. As ever, he had the company of crows, their cruel beaks parted, their breath frosting in the cool dawn air.

And he knew what was to follow. And he knew dread.

Clack, clack, clack came the sound.

It was a sound like the breaking of brittle finger-bones.

Clack, clack.

There, in the burning shadows of the dawn, moved a grotesque shape. A spider, as tall as a horse, its legs many jointed and thrice as long as a man, tipped in silver spikes, clack- clacked over the skulls of the fallen. The creature was as black as a raven's wing save for its eyes; they burned with an unholy yellow fire. And there, upon its back, sat the true cause of Steeleye's dread. With silver hair blowing free, the exquisite face of the huntress was turned towards the ramparts of the castle, her sapphire eyes bright with triumph. She was dressed for war, her plate armour lacquered crimson, in her slim hand she held aloft a serrated long sword.

"The time is at hand, Lightbringer!" her voice was singsong in its joy. "You cannot hide from me forever. It is fated!"

High above the valley, behind his stone wall, Steeleye trembled. *Clack, clack, clack,* came the spider. Steeleye stepped away from the ramparts; he had to get away, had to flee, to hide. He felt panic surge through him, his heart beat so fast, so loud he felt sure the Huntress would hear it, and she would find him!

In the dream there was a whisper of sound behind him and Steeleye spun to see who was upon the battlements with him. Calm, slanted eyes stared at him. One was golden yellow, the other clearest blue. The great wolf sat upon its haunches and watched him. As their eyes met, Steeleye felt his dread fade away, his racing heart calm, his breathing return to normal.

He turned again to look over the valley, and Wolf came to his side. Together, they stared over the bones of the dead. The ebony spider had come to a stop, its slender legs twitching like fingers. The rider examined the fortress, though it was clear she couldn't yet see them. Her face, more beautiful than any he could ever have imagined, was smiling. "Still hiding?" she called. "Soon, brother, there will be no more hiding!"

Steeleye awoke, and looked into the steady yellow and blue eyes of the wolf.

It had been two moons since the Horde champion Kleave had almost killed him. The return to the Keep and the settlement remained a blur. He remembered pain, delirium, the smell of strange herbs and the sting of needles, the feel of hot irons on wounds, the pungent smell of poultice. Yet, he had survived. After a full month in the Keep's great hall, hastily converted to an infirmary, he had been able to stand, with aid. Mere days after that he had returned to his own cabin. Wolf never left his side. Freija and Hewla too spent a great deal of their time with him, checking his wounds, changing dressings.

Spring was well and truly upon the North, though that meant little save that the days were a little longer, and the snow on the ground near the Keep and the settlement was less thick. It was still cold, fires still burned in the hearths of the cabins and the homes of the Northerners. Many of his neighbours had left chopped wood for Steeleye's fire. The story of his battle with the monstrous Kleave had been told in the halls and homes, and many were grateful for the young warrior's skill in combat. Their Lord was alive, as too were many others due to the outlander's bravery.

With a groan, as half-healed wounds pulled tight, he swung his legs out of his rude cot. Even though he was well on the way to a full recovery, he tired easily, and sweat bathed him after only mild exercise. Pulling on woollen leggings and shirt, he looked around for his boots, pushing the wolf aside with his foot. The animal looked at him with reproach. Finding his boots, Steeleye made his way to the door, and let in the brisk morning air and the pale sunlight. As had become his habit over the last few days, he gathered a cloak and a walking staff that Rolf had brought by, and set off to walk to the cabin of the healer. The wolf trotted along silently at his side.

As he walked, Steeleye mulled over the news that had come to him about Rannulf. He was still a little in shock, as were most of those that knew the young lord. He was now perceived as dead, even though his body still lingered in the cells of the Keep. Steeleye expected that come full summer Aelrik would call a gathering of all the Northern clans. He was, after all, their Lord; they would come to his banner readily enough, and then they would march upon the City of the Dead and root out any more of the foul creatures. Steeleye expected that the whole city would be razed to the ground, every shadow and nook exposed to the sunlight. But that was for the summer. For now, the people still grieved their losses, the keening laments and the funeral rights were over, but still a deep sorrow lay in the hearts of the Northerners.

From what he could gather from speaking to Freija, one of those tasked with standing guard in the cells, the creature that now bore the shape of Rannulf had indeed come from Ash Ul M'on. And there were still others. According to the creature their number was endless, and not only in the North, no, they were spread far and wide, they had awakened and they hungered for the blood of humankind.

Freija had come to sit with Steeleye often as he lay swathed in bandages, and had told him of the goings on in the cells. The creature had at first been reluctant to say much other than taunts and vile threats to his captors, but as the days drew on, things changed. Hewla was chief amongst the inquisitors, and she would sit close by the bound demon. She had drawn glyphs and runes upon his skin and crooned in a soft, wordless whisper as she worked. The defiance and bluster left the creature then, though not his hate. Still, his eyes promised nothing but pain.

Once Hewla was done with her spell casting, she had begun her questioning, hour upon hour of questions. She was tireless, Freija told him. The guards were organized in groups of four, changed three times through the day and night, and often as Freija and her company of guards went off-duty, and subsequently returned, Hewla would still be there, hunched next to the creature, as if she had not moved.

But Hewla's persistence paid dividends. The imposter had a name. On the third day of questioning, the guards and the healer heard his true voice, a sibilant whisper that froze the blood in their veins. "My name is Khuur'shock," he said. A slow smile then spread over his face. Freija had said in that moment there was nothing left of Rannulf, only the demon, only Khuur'shock, and the warrior woman had felt a fear unlike any other as the demon's eyes had lingered on her.

THE CABIN of the witch came into view at last, a thin plume of smoke rising lazily into the clear sky from a small chimney set in the thatch. The window shutters were open, and Steeleye could smell bread baking, the delicious aroma causing his mouth to water, and reminding him that he had not broken his fast that day. *Where did the witch find the time to bake?* he wondered idly as he approached the door. He was also wondering how could he be here, in such idyllic surroundings, with birds in full song in the early morn, when less than a mile away a creature named Khuur'shock sat behind the bars of the Keep's only cell, promising death and destruction with his every glance.

As Steeleye made to rap his knuckles upon the door, the wolf nonchalantly pawed at the wood, pushing the portal open and wandering in without pause. Steeleye dropped his hand, and then followed his nose and the wolf into the cabin. The smell of baking was stronger here, a good clean smell that somehow made Steeleye feel right at home and at peace. The interior of the cabin was, as ever, full of hanging herbs and stacks of books and rolled parchments. Upon the table in the centre of the room were set four places; wooden bowls filled with a rich stew that vied with the smell of bread to set his taste buds a-dancing. Sat at two of the placings were Aelrik and Rolf, both paused with spoons full of stew half way to their mouths. The wolf strolled by and wandered to the hearth, where Hewla was busy stirring something in a pot hanging over the flames.

"I'm still not used to that beast just wandering around as if she owns the place," said Rolf around a mouthful of breakfast His injured hand rested on the table, its dressing clean and fresh. "Not that I'm complaining mind" he added hastily, "if it were not for you two, I doubt that I would be sat here now enjoying this repast!" He waved his spoon in the vague direction of Steeleye and the wolf.

Aelrik tore a chunk of bread from a small loaf at his elbow. As he dipped it into the stew, he nodded agreement with his oldest friend. The days and weeks since they had confronted the demon had given the great Lord time to recover somewhat, although it seemed to Steeleye there was more white hairs in his beard, and the lines on his face ran deeper. His eyes though were clear and his shoulders straight. He popped the bread into his mouth and chewed with relish.

Hewla came to the table and set a dish of stew in front of Steeleye, and a small loaf so fresh its crust was still cracking. Then she sat herself down opposite Aelrik and motioned Steeleye to join them. He did, and set to with gusto; this was far better than the fare that he managed to prepare for himself, better too than the table set at the Keep every so often for gatherings of the Lords and their swordsmen.

"You will have heard the news of the demon, I take it?" she asked him directly, even as he spooned stew into his mouth. He chewed hastily, relishing the flavours, and swallowed. "Freija has told me the odd snippet," he replied, "Was she wrong to do so? I'm sure she meant no harm."

"Nay, it is common knowledge lad," joined Aelrik. He paused

to compose himself. "My son is dead. The gods only know when Rannulf was taken, but this entity, this *Kuur'shock...*" He spat the name, his eyes hardening. "...He has played us for fools long enough. Our settlement is not great in number, the Keep is open to all, it is there for us to gather inside during raids or the most severe of weather. It would have been nigh impossible to keep a secret such as the creature in the cell. Better all know what has been going on in the settlement. After all, it effects every one of us." Aelrik broke more bread, then put it aside, apparently his appetite had gone.

"Once the vile creature began to talk, we couldn't shut the bugger up," Rolf joined in. He still chewed enthusiastically; it took a lot to put the old warrior off his food.

"I put many spells upon the devil," Hewla said. "I tried everything that I could think of, all to no avail, and then, just like that, as if he knew that I had tried everything and failed, he began to speak. The Horde from eons past has returned. Not only those that have been hiding in the shadows, in places like the City of the Dead, or the caves that run through the mountains to the east or the steaming jungles in the south beyond the great desert..." She blew upon a spoonful of stew, her eyes sharp as flint. "Someone has read from the Book of Aihabb." As she said the words, it seemed shadows grew from the corner of the cabin, the flames in the fire seemed less bright. Even Rolf stopped chewing and looked about him nervously.

"A doorway has been opened so says Khuur'shock, and the brethren of the horde are slipping into this realm. Not as before, in the time of legends, when they came as an army, flooding the lands in their thousands. No, this time they have been crafty. This time they have come upon our world in stealth. For ten years, they have been stealing through this doorway to gather and mass in the secret corners of the world; in the shadowy lands of the sorcery-riddled cities in the south, their generals and princes keeping their profile low until their numbers are great enough to prove a match for the armies of humankind.

"That time seems to have come. This Lord of the Horde, this Khuur'shock, has become impatient and has shown his hand, because of you." Hewla pointed a bony finger at Steeleye. "Oh yes, he talks about you quite a lot." The old seer paused to slurp stew from the spoon. "This could have done with a tad more salt," she mumbled, distracted for a moment.

"Me?" Steeleye was aghast. "What could a demon possibly know of me?

"Whatever my son knew, now the demon knows," broke in Aelrik. "He knows that you came to us by strange means. He knows that you are gifted beyond the norm with a sword and shield, and he knows about the Shining!"

"Lightbringer, he calls you," Hewla said. "And it's hard to tell if he is more scared or exhilarated to have found you here."

Now it was old Rolf's turn to add to the story, "Remember that big bugger, Kleave? He called you Lightbringer too, and he mentioned a mistress..."

For a split second, the vision of a silver-haired beauty, bedecked for war, sat astride a monstrous arachnid, flashed into his consciousness. It was but a dream. He shook off the feeling of sudden dread and leant his concentration once more to the trio around the table.

"...things are happening at such a pace," Hewla was saying. "The Horde, then this Captain of darkness, omens coming thick and fast in the waking dreams that beset me. The world is not as strong as it once was, I fear. The great cities have become placid and bookish. The Great kings and Lords of old are no more. Now most people are ruled by weak men and women, who cannot see the world for what it truly is. They strive only for decadence. They seek pleasure for themselves first and foremost, their people a distant second. Their armies are great in number, but many are filled with braggarts and bullies suited for tax collecting and guzzling. Gone are the Host of the West, those brave souls that thundered to the aid of the world. Gone are the Kings of the world that would stand true in the face of evil. We have become weak..." She finished with a sigh, her bony fingers trembling a little, eyes lost in a past that only she could see.

"Here, at least, we live by the old ways," Aelrik asserted. "We have not forgotten the sacrifices of our ancestors. We stand ready as ever, and I think it is time that I called upon the other northern Lords, and we shall clean out the serpent's lair in the shadow of the mountain."

Hewla seemed to revive somewhat at Aelrik's words, her sharp eyes pierced the three at the table. "That would be a start, right enough. You are the High Lord of the North, Aelrik Bearslayer, son of Brinn. The Lords of all the Northern lands will come to your banner. Gather the shields then, send runners to all. And runners too must be sent to all the kings of men. It is time to put aside petty thoughts and ambitions, it is time for all to join together, or I fear the days of humankind are numbered."

Rolf set down his spoon, his bowl all but empty and began to mop up gravy with the bread. "Is there perhaps a mug of ale to go with this stew?" he asked the witch hopefully, as if for all the world their talk around the table had been of a neighbour's yapping dog and not the possible end of the world as they knew it. Hewla fixed him with a steady eye, and Rolf shrugged his great shoulders and smiled weakly, abashed. "I understand the import of what we are talking about," he explained, "but for this old man, picking up the spear and heading off to war again is a cause for celebration. Dying in my bed seemed to be a realistic prospect. What kind of a death would that be for an old fool such as I? My wife has been waiting for me in the afterlife for more than ten years, can you imagine the scolding she would give me if I joined her by dying of old age?"

Hewla's gaze softened. She had known Rolf's wife well for many years, a fierce woman as much at home with axe in her hand as a loom. It had almost broken Rolf when she died of the wasting sickness. They had been together for over thirty years, had raised two sons, had both gone to war in the South with their lord. She could almost imagine her waiting in the afterlife with a scowl upon her face should her husband not be ushered into the Halls of the Dead with fanfare. The image brought a smile to her face.

"And you, Lord Aelrik, are you for celebrating too, to see such a threat creeping into the lands?"

Aelrik grinned, perhaps the first since the taking of his son Rannulf. "I am old Hewla. If I can stem a tide of evil then perhaps my life will have meant something. I am a vain man, I would wish the world to remember my name with fondness, perhaps one last enemy to defeat, one more bear to slay." He paused to slap Rolf upon the back. "Fools such as we were not meant to sit in our Keeps and cabins, the only time that we truly come alive is when we are facing death. Bring the ale, Hewla."

The witch turned from the table, and beckoned Steeleye to join her as she wandered to the door. The ale, she said, was outside in the lean-to, and she would need his help. Steeleye scooped up more stew, and then moved to follow; Wolf was at his side, a soundless shadow. Once outside, the trio gathered at the door to the small shed that sat upon the shoulder of the cabin, but Hewla made no move to open the door. Instead, she rested a hand upon the frame and sighed deeply. Suddenly she looked all of her years, old, frail, and quite lost.

"There is more to tell," she said softly. Wolf shifted, though she still sat upon her haunches; the animal seemed to be weighing the witch's every word. Hewla waved a hand at the wolf dismissively. "Hush you," she said, her back straightening a little. "I have an idea who you may be..." She poked a finger at the wolf.

"And I know my place, well enough." Wolf suddenly lay down and relaxed, her side pressing close to Steeleye's leg.

"She likes you," Hewla said, nodding at Wolf. "Have you wondered why she is here?"

Steeleye grinned, even as his fingers absently scratched Wolf's head. "I think of little else. It is more than strange, how she just... turned up, but I cannot imagine being without her now. She feels *right*. I somehow know that we are meant to be together. I feel safe with her..." All he said was true, but it went deeper than that. Ever since the animal had entered his cabin, he had felt at ease with himself. He had no memory of who he truly was; he had no one to talk to save Freija and Hewla about the fears that he harboured, about the Shining, about where he came from. He could speak several tongues, could read ancient scripts, his swordsmanship told of expert training well beyond that of a common soldier or even the warrior caste, but from whence the skills came he could not fathom. When he tried to look into his past, there was naught but darkness, a wall of impenetrable nothingness. His life had effectively begun on a cold deserted beach ten years ago, when he had awakened and looked up to find Aelrik, hair blowing wild and unkempt in the sea breeze, staring down at him.

And now here he was grown to manhood, with mystery upon mystery piled upon him, but the very presence of Wolf calmed him in some way he could neither understand nor articulate. Throughout his years with the Northerners, he had always been an outsider, his eyes and the manner of his coming into their world had set him apart. If not for his martial expertise, he doubted he would have been accepted so much as he had, but he'd always suspected he would never be fully trusted by most in the settlement.

The arrival of Wolf changed everything for him.

He was brought out of his reverie by Hewla as she pulled open the door to the lean-to. Within it, Steeleye could make out several small casks. She motioned to one absently. "Take that one." As Steeleye moved to comply, the witch continued to speak. "The gods have given me the gift of the seer, but not everything is clear to me. The arrival of the wolf took me aback. I did not foresee that. In fact, my gift seems shrouded of late, perhaps the wizards of the Horde are casting spells?" She paused as Steeleye stood with the indicated cask of ale, liquid sloshing within. "That was brewed by Bevan the smith and gifted to me last year." She chuckled a little, "Bevan was never the best brewer, but I'm sure it will suffice to wash down the stew for those two old mules."

Steeleye hoisted the cask onto his shoulder easily enough, and waited as Hewla closed the door. "Where was I? Ah yes, I have glimpsed the future in dreams; Aelrik and Rolf may well get to build their legends yet. I see the world at war. I have dreamed of the land trembling beneath the hooves of ten thousand chargers, a sea of steel as the warriors of the world unite to face the shadow. Banners of a thousand houses will unite upon fields of battle. It will begin soon I think, Aelrik will strike the first blow for humankind in the City of the Dead... but I cannot see you there in the ranks of the Northerners, Young Buck."

"Where else would I be?" Steeleye demanded, "I am tried in battle, I have proved my worth." Hewla calmed him with a hushing sound.

"This is what I was saying to you. The future is unclear where you are concerned. Thrice now have I dreamed the dream of your future, and every time I see the same. You and the wolf, standing by a bridge that seems to be made of glass; it spans a terrible chasm. Beyond this bridge is your destiny, that much I can tell, and the wolf will lead you, she will be your guide upon the path." She shrugged. "And crows, I see crows more than I have ever seen..."

"So, the wolf is a good omen? he asked.

"An omen of sorts, yes. A messenger and a guide. I feel the two of you are bonded in a way that is unclear to me, but what is clear is that your future lies not with us here in the North, but with this creature beyond the Bridge of Glass."-

Suddenly the still air was rent by a great clanging, the urgent and insistent ringing of the Keep's alarm bell. Its strident call rolled over the snow and through the forest. *Clang! Clang!* Great flocks of birds took flight from their roosts in the trees, their screeching calls adding to the cacophony. The bell rang on and on. Steeleye was still besides the witch, and he saw her eyes roll into her head, could see her frail body begin to shake and tremble. He knew there was a vision upon her. Seconds passed, and Steeleye stood indecisive. The door to the cabin burst open and Rolf and Aelrik came charging out. They barely paused before hurrying off through the forest towards the Keep and the urgently ringing bell.

Steeleye and Wolf stood by the witch. He still held the cask, now forgotten, resting on his shoulder. He watched Hewla closely, concerned she might bite off her tongue, so violently was she trembling.

The colour drained from her face, and he saw her eyes clear and focus, the terror and pain dawn upon her. She grabbed his arm in a claw-like grip, her nails digging so deep they almost drew blood. She looked at the young warrior with frantic eyes, a low keening sound issuing from her bloodless lips. She clawed at his arm, and threw back her head, the tendons in her neck stretched so tightly he feared they would snap. At last, he could hear her words, and darkness threatened to engulf him.

"The Keep! I see the Keep! And blood, so much blood! Freija!"

At the sound of her name, Steeleye threw the heavy cask aside, it shattered and splintered on the ground, its foaming dark contents quickly drunk by the snow. Steeleye was gone, dashing towards the still ringing bell, his panting breath tearing his throat. He entered the forest at a dead run, ignoring the branches that tore at his face and hands, tripping and sliding as he ran. He stumbled and fell, rolling back to his feet, hardly feeling the wounds that reopened and splashed the snow crimson; on and on he ran, the sleek lupine form of Wolf easily keeping pace. Twice more he fell, each time he surged to his feet and ran on, panic gnawing at him, fear twisting his innards and leaving them cold as ice. Freija! What had Hewla seen in her waking dream?

He burst through the tree line and the bell clanged on. Ahead he could see the black stone walls of the Keep, the squat tower that housed their Lord and his retinue, where he had dined and danced with the people of the settlement, with Freija. Running ahead of him he could see Aelrik, a little behind was Rolf; judging by his staggering gait, he was obviously exhausted, but he, like Steeleye, pressed on beyond his own endurance.

Now there was a cleared pathway to the gate of the Keep, and Steeleye pressed harder, his heart hammering loud in his ears, drowning out even his gasping breath. He drew abreast of his Lord as they reached the arched gateway, the portcullis was raised, and within the yard chaos was unfolding.

Armed men ran hither and yon, their shouts and bellows mingling with the insistent clanging of the iron bell, mothers keening, their voices loud and shrill in the morning air. Steeleye caught the arm of a warrior as he ran by, almost pulling him from his feet, the man's eyes were wild with panic, and with fury.

"What has happened here?" Steeleye demanded roughly, bringing the man to his senses. For a moment, the warrior was still. He blurted, "the demon is loose! It has killed the guard at its cell, and more, it has killed whole families in their beds!" The man pulled free from Steeleye's grasp. "Come, brother," he panted, hefting his spear. "We must find the creature..." and the warrior swirled away into the chaos of bodies running to and fro, to check upon loved ones, to find comrades, and to search the Keep's every dark corner. But Steeleye did not follow the man. Instead, he turned his feet towards a structure strongly built against the West wall; the cell's thick stone walls, a stout oaken door now ajar.

With feet of lead, Steeleye trudged towards the doorway. It was as if the door were at the end of a tunnel, his only focus, all about him a swirling blur save the dark doorway before him. Even as Rolf caught up with him and put a hand upon his shoulder, Steeleye didn't pause. Shaking off the hand, he walked into the cells as if he walked to the gallows.

Stepping over the threshold, Steeleye became aware of the strong stench of death, the coppery smell of blood and the stink of fear. Within the cells, it was a charnel house. His feet splashed through a pool of blood and he put his hands to the wall to steady himself; the cold stone of the wall was also slippery with blood. There were eight bodies in the guards' area of the cells. In the dim light Steeleye could see they had been hacked and bitten, chopped and butchered, organs torn from bodies, entrails strewn across the paved floor.

He found her amongst the dead. Her beautiful face was white as snow, a savage bite had torn out her slender throat, blade and teeth had ripped at her body and had broken her bones. Like a doll, Freija lay dead and torn amongst her fellow guards.

Steeleye fell to his knees beside the girl that was as a sister to him. With trembling hands, he cradled her head to his chest, her body was cold, beginning to stiffen in death. Dimly he was aware of others entering the room, of torches casting grisly shadows as loved ones came to find their husbands, their wives, their sons and their daughters, all mauled and lifeless.

Steeleye was aware that he was moaning softly as he rocked Freija gently. The sound was unbidden, a raw utterance of broken misery. Tears streamed down his cheeks. He lifted his head as strong fingers dug into his shoulder, his moaning becoming a sobbing that wracked his body. Hewla stood with him, her eyes, reflecting the light of the lantern that she carried, hard as flint.

"I have seen carnage throughout the Keep." Her voice was little more than a whisper. "I was complacent, and these poor souls have paid the steepest price."

There was the sound of footsteps, heavy and forlorn, and Aelrik and Rolf crowded in to the cells. "May the Morriggu guide their souls to rest in her Halls," the great Lord said softly. He looked about him with grim resolve. "I have spoken with the trackers," he said at last, "and I have an idea of what transpired. It would seem that as the guard was changing, a group of those creatures from Ash Ul M'on burst in and wreaked this havoc, freeing Khuur'shock. Once free, the creatures began to attack wantonly, entering cabins at random and slaying folks in their homes. But many fought back; we have found the bodies of six creatures amongst their victims, brutal looking and huge. They have gone now to whatever hell will have them."

"And Khuur'shock?" asked Steeleye. He ceased his rocking and gently stroked Freija's face. "Was the demon found amongst the dead?"

"No, it looks like he made his escape. He is probably well on his way back to the City of the Dead," said the Lord

"Men are getting ready as we speak," broke in Rolf. "We shall enter the damned city and root out every vile creature. We shall repay this deed a thousand-fold."

It was then that Hewla raised her lantern to the walls, and there in the darkest corner, she found strange writings, scrawled in blood upon the stone. "He has not returned to the city, I fear," she said. She squinted at the brutal markings on the wall. "This script is arcane and strange, but I can make out the odd word..."

"It says 'I shall await the bringer of Light and Death at the Stone Gods'." Steeleye said.

"You can read this?" Hewla asked incredulous.

"As clear as if I had written the words myself." He laid Freija's head gently back on the flagstones, then wiped away tears with his forearm. He looked one last time upon her face, now calm and at peace in death, and then stood to face the three gathered there. "I will need a sword; mine broke at the Western Gate."

"You can have mine," Rolf said at once. "I will be using an axe on these bastards from henceforth." He unbuckled his belt and passed the sword and scabbard to the younger man.

"The Stone Gods are a full day's hard march to the South and East from here," Hewla said in a sombre tone. "We have bodies to prepare for their funeral rites, and a dirge to sing for our loved ones' passing. We shall take a full war party, and leave before dawn. With luck, the demon will have been eaten by a bear, or frozen to death."

Steeleye left the chamber and walked back into the bright sunshine, Wolf was waiting for him. Once away from the stench of death, he breathed deep of the cold fresh air. "I hope not, Hewla," he said, in a voice so low that only the wolf could hear. "I want to take off his head myself."

CHAPTER 6
STONE GODS

As the first pink rays of the dawn crept over the horizon, tinting the sparse clouds with mauve and violet hues, the Northerners came upon the Plain of the Stone Gods. A huge blanket of snow stretched out before them, from the pine forest at their backs to the ominous Aihaab's Gap, visible to the naked eye and several miles distant. The fabled chasm could be seen as a jagged black scar running from East to West, testament to the apocalyptic power of the supernatural forces dwelling in this place.

Aelrik had led his one hundred strong band of Northerners on a hard march through the night. They had forced their way through deep snow and covered forest trails, startling the nocturnal beasts of the wilderness with their clanking armour and jangling war gear. Many used spears as staffs to help with their unsure footing, some of the older and less able of the band were helped through the more difficult drifts by their companions, yet none complained, nor thought of turning back. Even though the bitter cold of the night numbed their feet and hands and set their teeth on edge when they took a breath, none would ever have considered returning to the Keep without seeing through this mission.

Far, far behind them, the settlement around the keep still rang with keening wails for the dead. The bodies of the victims of Khuur'shock and his rescuers were laid out in the Great Hall for all to see and bid farewell. Women and children, warriors, and the elderly alike were all set out in funeral finery for their journey to the afterlife. The Mistress of the Crows, the Soul collector Morriggu, would reap the spirits of the fallen and take them to the halls of plenty once the rites were done. The bodies would be cremated upon pyres the following dawn, though it was unlikely that this party would return in time for the solemn event, so each had bid farewell to their loved ones, their comrades at arms their friends and neighbours before gathering at the gate of the Keep to volunteer for this grim trek.

STEELEYE HAD SAT for a long while beside the supine form of Freija. She had been dressed in a white gown, high necked and woven of thick material to hide the grotesque wounds that laid her low. Her face was at peace, serene and beautiful. Her fiery hair had been combed out and carefully cleaned of blood, then teased and tied into an ornate design, bedecked with thin chains of silver and pins headed with semi-precious stones. Steeleye had been struck with the thought that Freija would never have let herself be seen dressed like this. He would remember her with her braids, with a fierce grin, and a shield upon her arm.

As men and women were gathering for the pursuit of the murderous demon, he stood and gently placed his fingers upon Freija's cold lips, silently promising that they would meet again beyond the veil. As he did this, he was aware of several women decked for war standing with him. Old Breen, a warrior-woman of fearsome courage and skill, now dressed in mail and plumed helm, had rested a hand upon his shoulder.

"She was the finest amongst us," she had said, her voice was soft, like music, a stark contrast to her warlike demeanour. "She would often tell us that you were her sword arm, as she was your shield. Weep not for her, for she is assured a place in the Halls of Plenty."

"She was my friend." He had shed a river of tears for her, and now had no more tears to give. His grief was giving way to anger like he had never felt; it was beyond rage, beyond fury. It coursed through his veins like poison.

With a nod to Breen, he had stepped away from Freija and walked out into the evening air.

* * *

AND NOW HERE HE stood upon the Plain of the Stone Gods. As Aelrik had been quick to point out even before they set off from the Keep, Steeleye's wounds were far from healed. Even now, as he breathed deep of the dawn air, he could feel the damp blood on his shirt beneath the mail that he wore. The stitches that Hewla had so carefully sewn into his skin had burst only a mile into the journey. But with stoic resolution, he had kept the pace, at times even pulling those getting on in years from drifts of snow, or helping them over fallen trees as they pressed on through the forest.

Steeleye had ignored all warnings from his Lord, and it had been wise old Hewla that came to speak to the pair of them.

"It must be Steeleye that enters the Stone Gods' circle," she had said, matter of factly. "The challenge was writ clear, and in blood. The demon awaits the Bringer of Light and Death on the Plain of the Stone Gods. Such a challenge must be met, it is the way of the North, a trial by combat has long been our creed, Aelrik. He is the Bringer of Light and Death, according to that foul creature that wears the guise of your first born, so it must be he that answers the challenge."

And so that had been decided, Steeleye had gripped the hilt of his borrowed sword tight at the words of the witch, and it was with a grim smile that he had begun the night's march.

* * *

THE STONE GODS was a wondrous sight; A huge circle of stones, twenty or more in number, each thrice the height of a tall man. According to legend, the goddess Narissa had carved the great stones to replicate all the gods that came to this spot after the Great War so many eons ago. Here, within easy view of their brothers' violence, the chasm that rent the earth and fell away to the underworld, the Gods, led by the mighty Eros, King of the Immortals, had met and agreed that no longer would they bare arms upon the world of men. To commemorate the gathering, Eros had commanded that the circle be built, to act as a reminder to all of the wisdom and power of the gods.

With the rising sun behind them, the giant monoliths cast great shadows over the snow-scape. At this distance, and to Steel-eye's naked eye, the monuments looked like nothing more than massive black stones though he knew from stories told to him by the other Northerners that beneath the thick coating of ice and the centuries of erosion there was still glorious detail to be seen.

But for all the wonder of the Stone Gods, it was not the monument that drew Steeleye's' keen attention, but rather the solitary figure that could be seen standing at the centre of the circle. Khuur'shock the Demon waited. Khuur'shock, the murderer and the bane of the North, the Stealer of Joy.

Without hesitation, Steeleye set off across the Plain. The snow was to his knees and every step was a torture upon his battered body, yet he ploughed forwards nevertheless, his teeth bared in a savage grin, his eyes narrowed with their focus upon his enemy. By his side, the great wolf stalked. Hewla followed. Though old beyond reasoning, she had kept pace with the party through the night march. She used a staff to assist her through the snow, a branch of oak longer than she was tall, well-worn and wrapped around with mistletoe.

The rest of the one hundred marched on too, spreading out as they neared the standing stones, forming a perimeter, making a circle of muscle and steel around the circle of stone.

At last, when the sun had lifted a full hand's breadth over the Eastern peaks, and a chill breeze picked up from the North, Steeleye came to the Stones.

The daemon had cast aside his tunic, and stood bare-chested in the freezing morn. His hair, when he had been a son of a Lord, had been long and thick, the envy of many women of the Keep. It now hung lank and filthy. His upper body, all muscle and veins, covered in Hewla's tattoos, looked more that of a beast than a man. The face behind the matted beard was grotesque in its hatred. Slowly, the daemon focused upon the approaching Steeleye, and a grin split his features.

"I was worried that my boy Kleave had done for you, Lightbringer." He sounded relieved that the young warrior was whole and standing. For a moment, he chewed his beard, and ground his teeth, then continued. "This is betwixt you and I agreed? No devil wolf!" His eyes flickered to the great lupine shape at Steeleye's side. "No Bearslayers or witches within the circle, yes?" In his right hand, he brandished a stained broadsword; he swung it to and fro, its edge cutting the still air with a keening sound.

"Agreed," Steeleye answered. He unclipped the broach, a simple gift from Freija that held his cloak in place, and let the fur fall to the snow.

"Although you dullards have no notion of it," the daemon raised his voice so all the gathered Northerners could hear. "This is a momentous day! This has been foretold in prophesy amongst the ranks of the Horde for a thousand years and more. The Bringer of Light shall bring forth the Bringer of Death. And here is the Lightbringer! He has hidden amongst you, hiding behind your walls and spears, and when I take his head momentarily, then shall my mistress be free to stalk this world of Men. Then there shall be a great feasting for the Horde as the Bringer of Death shall lead us, and we shall ravage this world!"

"Enough talk!" snarled Aelrik, his face like thunder. He turned to Steeleye. "Get in there and finish this." Aelrik looked directly at the daemon wearing the guise of his first born, and his eyes turned to flint.

Steeleye wasted no more time. Cutting the air with the blade to loosen his shoulders he strode into the circle of Stone Gods. Khuur'shock came onwards too, his gait brisk and confident. Each lengthened their stride as they closed until they were near running at one another, their faces contorted with rage and hatred, swords held high in a double-handed grip.

And then they clashed.

The Northerners were well used to swordplay. Each gathered had stood against foes bearing steel, and knew well the rhythms of combat. They watched as the pair within the circle struck again and again. The clang of steel upon steel rang loud and fierce in the still and frigid air. There was no fencing skill on display in this first clash, just a brutal, hateful attack upon one another, the swords whined through the air and met with sparks, leaping apart and then surging back together. Six times did each swing for the head of the other, only to be met by a responding blade. At last, the initial fury spent, and the measure of each other taken, the pair stepped apart, their breath ragged and short. Steeleye's habergeon was leaking blood through the chain links, it dripped upon the snow red as rose petals.

"I see Kleave left you with a memento then?" Khuur'shock panted, nodding at the widening stain at Steeleye's side.

Steeleye gritted his teeth against the pain. "A scratch, it won't stop me putting you down"

"Very well then, let's have at it!" the daemon said. He wove a slow pattern of steel before him. Steeleye mimicked the styles; he was well used to each form that the daemon presented, and instinctively he flowed from one move into the next. His initial fury was spent. Now, he wholly let his training take over, becoming far more than a Northern warrior. His companions watching every move were well aware that here they were seeing a very different Steeleye. Many had spent hours with him in the training yards, swinging weighted wooden blades, but few had been able to push Steeleye's abilities to their limit. Further, this was a swordsmanship very different to the hack and slash of battle, with each combatant moving through forms and counter forms, seeking and blocking any advantage.

Steeleye surged forwards, his blade slashing at Khuur'shock's naked breast. The daemon pivoted to one side, kicking up snow in a great plume. Like a striking cobra, he returned the attack and both stepped back, weaving steel before them. The creature now sported a cruel cut just below his collar bone, dark blood mingled with the tattoos and sweat.

The daemon looked a little perplexed. He was a Captain of the Horde, and his swordsmanship was sublime, yet here he stood giving first blood to a mere human. Again, they set their feet, each looking for an opening.

This time it was the creature that struck, fast and hard. Once, twice, and yet a third time. His speed was blistering and the on-looking crowd was hard pressed to keep track, but Steeleye met the attack and after the third lunge, he locked their swords tight against their breasts and smashed his forehead hard into Khuur'shock's face. With a grunt of pain, the daemon staggered back, broken nose spraying blood, but Steeleye was once more upon him.

Again and again they struck, whirling and dancing, steel flashing bright. The sound of blade upon blade became almost as music to the pair as they flowed from form to form, attack and counter-attack. It happened suddenly, a shoulder too low, a reaction a shade too slow, and a fountain of crimson splashed upon the snow. Steeleye staggered back, chest heaving through the effort, his face twisted with pain. The daemon stood before him, huge and menacing, but the life was gone from the eyes. Steeleye had struck true, his blade cutting through the creature's' neck, almost decapitating him. Blood bubbled and welled from the wound, and slowly like a great tree, the Captain of the Horde toppled dead into the snow.

For long moments, all was still. Steeleye felt empty, he had no rage left, and that had seemed to be all that had kept him going over the last days and hours. He slowly sank to his knees, letting his borrowed sword fall from his fingers. He had lost a lot of blood and his vision swam. The white of the snow and the clouds building to the West seeming to blur and spin. *What now?* he wondered. All his remembered life he had waited here amongst the clans of the North. He had been content, not fulfilled, but content to live and train and hunt with these folks of such stern demeanour. To laugh with Freija and listen to her as she told him secrets of her plans for a future in the warmer climes; she'd had a whim to travel and to see the wonders of the world beyond the great chasm. All those dreams had ended in the Keep's grim dungeon, snuffed out like a candle-flame by the now vanquished Khuur'shock. The world would be a duller place without Freija's boisterous spirit. To Steeleye, it seemed as if all the joy in his life had centred on the fiery-haired maiden, nearly every happy memory he had seemed to feature his sword sister, the maiden of the Shield.

What now?

The gathered Northerners began striking sword and axe against their shields in a steady rhythm; it was at once a celebration of his swift victory, and a farewell to their lost brother in arms Rannulf. *Thud. Thud. Thud.* The noise rolled over the barren landscape,

Steeleye became aware that he was no longer alone within the Circle of Stone Gods. Wolf had approached as silently as a shadow and sat beside him. The odd eyes were focused upon the distance, where Steeleye knew the great Aihaab's Gap waited. It seemed that his silent companion was giving him an answer. There came a flapping of great pinions and a huge crow alighted upon the nearest Stone God. Vaguely, through eons of ice and snow and the erosion of wind and sleet, he could still make out details of the ancient carvings. A cloak of jet feathers falling from slim shoulders. This, then, would be Morriggu, the Keeper of Souls.

Though hardly in his right mind from grief and fatigue, from the constant pain brought on by his wounds and the loss of blood suffered from their reopening, Steeleye was granted clarity of thought. What now? Now he would venture to the Bridge of Glass, and he would let the Wolf, his seeming guide, show him the way. With a shake of his head, he broke his reverie and slowly gained his feet. Without turning, he knew that Hewla had approached and stood now watching him. He could feel her keen gaze as he could feel a winter's chill.

"It is done then," he said simply.

"Aye, and done well. No shining, just a man and the darkness. It gives me hope that we can stand firm in our future trials, however grim they become." Hewla's voice was soft and tinged with sadness. "But you will not be with us I think?"

At this Steeleye turned to look full at the Crone; as old as the mountains she seemed, yet still standing straight, indomitable. "Your visions are seldom wrong, grandmother, and more, I feel that my path leads elsewhere. I shall follow Wolf, and see where she leads me, to the Gap and its bridge, or wherever."

He watched as several Northerners rolled the corpse of Rannulf into blankets and tied them secure. He was Rannulf again now, the creature that he had become was dead and gone. Aelrik, with Wolfrumm beside him, watched as his son was prepared to be taken back to the Holdings, there to be given proper funeral rites.

Once satisfied that his son was secured, the great warrior walked over to where Hewla and Steeleye were standing. Old Rolf sidled up to them too, a mist of sadness in his eyes. "You will be going with the wolf, then?" asked the white-haired Northerner. He fidgeted a little as Steeleye nodded. Rolf was a simple man; long protracted conversations were hardly his forte. "I have packed a little food to start you off on your journey," he said at last. He handed Steeleye a leather satchel that bulged with provisions. "There is also a drop of brandy wine in there, to keep the innards warm." He stroked his beard reflectively and stared at the distant chasm. "We shall miss your skill when we venture back to the City of the Dead." With that he patted Steeleye upon the shoulder, turned and walked back to the edge of the circle, where the rest of the clansmen were preparing to depart. "Keep the sword," he called. "It was never used as well as it was today."

"I'm not sure that you will even make it to the bridge," Hewla stated flatly.

Steeleye smiled at this. "As ever you instil me with confidence, grandmother. But I will endure. For the first time in as long as I can remember, I seem to have a purpose. I was waiting for this day all the years that I spent amongst the Northern folks and didn't realize it until I felled Khuur'shock. This is the first step upon my journey."

"I wish you well then Steeleye, Son of the Sea. Stay true to the Light, defend the weak, and champion the Just. And remember you have friends here in the Cold Lands. I see great conflicts ahead, and we of the North shall be wherever the fighting is thickest, look for us there should you need us." She patted his arm fondly, then using her staff to aid her way, she turned and began to walk towards the Stone Circle's edge, and the forest beyond. "Hurry up you, old simpleton!" she snapped at Aelrik, though there was kindness in her eyes as she glanced at the warrior over her shoulder.

The Northern King grinned through his beard at the rebuke. "We shall meet again on the field or in the Halls of the Morriggu!" he said to Steeleye. He then held out a staff, topped with a brass lantern. "Take this, 'tis filled with oil. It will burn bright and sparks up easily with flint. The chasm is a cold place, boy. It is as if the very frost of winter comes from its depths. Many of our hunters trek along the Gap, and every few miles I have had shelters built. They are simple affairs, stocked with wood for a fire, some with a bed, though most not. Keep an eye out for them; they are nothing fancy, but can keep a man alive through the cold nights."

Steeleye took the staff gratefully and nodded his thanks. "I am sorry about Rannulf," he managed at last. Now it was Aelrik's turn to nod, though he did not answer. Instead, he looked directly at the wolf. "Keep an eye on him," he said, then turned to the Stone Morriggu and the resting crow, "And you too." Steeleye wasn't sure if the chief was speaking to the bird or the effigy.

Aelrik turned and made his way through the snow, following the muttering witch.

Steeleye stood beside the stone Morriggu for long minutes. He watched as his companions reached the distant tree line, and then they were gone. Save for Wolf, he was alone with the Gods of Stone and the distant mountains. He breathed deep of the frigid air and looked to the sky. It was not yet midday and that gave him a good few hours in which to make a start on his journey. How far to the gap? Twenty miles? Thirty? More than he would walk today that was for sure. Could he survive a night out here on the ice and snow? When in full health, he had no doubt that he would, but wounded as sorely as he was...?

He retrieved his cloak, throwing it around his shoulders and fastening the pin. His fingers lingered upon the broach and he silently said a prayer for Freija, and hoped the gods saw fit to give her Khuur'shock as a plaything in the next life.

"Lead on then Wolf," he said to his silent companion. "And let's see just what you have in store for me."

CHAPTER 7
THE MISTRESS OF CROWS

Steeleye had walked for an hour or more, struggling through the deep snow. Behind him, the Stone Gods were no more than a dark smudge against the white landscape, the forest beyond them a stark line of dark greens and browns beneath a clear cold sky. Ahead, he could just make out the great chasm that was Aihaab's Gap; it cut through the snow and ice like a jagged lightning bolt. Still an hour's walking distance, due to the gradient of the terrain, he could see already the shadowy crevasse to the South, and its size beggared belief. It stretched as far as he could see to East and West on and on, a great tear in the tundra.

His plan was simple enough; he would follow Wolf, his guide, and Wolf was making directly for the Chasm. Once there, Steeleye presumed his lupine friend would head West and continue until they reached the bridge. A simple plan, but as he was already wracked with fits of shivering, the cold biting deep into his abused body, he had to wonder if in fact he would reach his destination, and if he did, what then? Already he felt as weak as a kitten and the muscles in his legs ached fiercely.

There was no natural sound on the tundra, just the crunch of the snow as Steeleye blundered one step after another. Wolf padded ahead seemingly unaffected by the cold or the harsh environment. She would wait patiently as her companion slowed, or, as he did several times, stumble and fall to his knees. Steeleye's breathing was ragged and came short, the cold air burning his lungs, even setting his teeth on edge. Gods but he had never felt this cold! He stumbled again, managing to break his fall by flinging out his hands. The impact jarred his side and a lance of agony seared through him. He gave an involuntary gasp as the pain enveloped him. For several seconds, he stayed on his hands and knees waiting for the pain to subside, his head hung low, eyes creased with pain.

Slowly, the agony decreased and Steeleye was able to lift his head. Wolf was mere inches from him, her yellow and blue eyes enigmatic as they met his own. "I will be ready to go on in a moment or two," he croaked, his voice little more than a whisper. The wolf sat on its haunches to wait. Steeleye used the lantern staff to get to his feet. He stood blowing and swaying for a moment, then gritting his teeth, gestured to the wolf with his chin that they should continue. And so it went. On and on they trekked.

As the day wore on, Steeleye stumbled often, many times he would crash into the snow headlong. Each time it took him longer and longer to regain his feet. Behind him, the snow was stained crimson. He sipped from the flask that Rolf had given him, the fiery contents seeming to lift his spirits a little. In the satchel he found strips of dried meat. He chewed without enthusiasm, he needed nourishment but was too exhausted to really care.

The light began to fade. At first, he thought that he was losing consciousness, then realised the North's short daylight was almost spent. He smiled. His body could do with a rest, he thought, just a few minutes, to close his eyes and gather his strength. But should he stop here, exposed to the frigid night, he knew there was little chance of him waking again.

He scanned the barren landscape as he plodded on, searching for one of the Hunters' havens that Aelrik had reminded him of, but found none. Soon, his view was limited to but a few yards by the gathering darkness. He almost walked past his companion in the gloom, for the wolf had stopped before a small mound of snow and was digging with her forepaws, industriously clearing a ditch before the mound. It took him a moment to understand what she was up to, and then he grinned painfully as realization dawned upon him. The wolf was creating a crude shelter for them from the very landscape that would otherwise mean his death.

Awkwardly, he fell to his knees and set to helping the wolf, his hands were already frozen and so he hardly felt any worse as he scooped great armfuls of snow and pushed it into a makeshift wall before the mound. Exhaustion fell upon him, but he continued on, packing the snow tight and then digging out more. His vision began to blur even as full night fell upon the tundra. He was on his knees with his head bowed.

"I can do no more." His voice was little more than a whisper. The night sky seemed to tilt and spin as he collapsed into the ditch.

Steeleye shook uncontrollably from the cold in his unconscious state, though at the same time a film of sweat covered him. He spasmed violently, his body wracked with pain.

Wolf padded to his side, her keen sense of smell easily picked up the corruption in the wound in his side, her senses attuned to more than human spectrum. Wolf knew Steeleye was close to death. With a soft whimper, the great beast lay down beside the man, wriggling close to share her body heat. Her odd eyes cast about the darkness; they glowed faintly like amber and steel kissed by torchlight.

She was coming!

The night air was already still, with barely a breeze, but now it was as if the very night held its breath. Wolf watched the darkness, keen and intense, she, like the night itself, was frozen in place. Slowly, silently, out of the night came the Morriggu. Terrible in her beauty was the Collector of Souls. Tall and supple as smoke, she glided over the snow, leaving not a trace of her passing. Her face was almost elfin in shape, her skin as pale and smooth as milk, and her eyes, slanted and long-lashed were as grey as a storm-tossed sea. Those unblinking eyes were now fixed upon the still form of Steeleye and his lupine companion; they were filled with knowledge beyond the ken of humankind. They had seen ten thousand years, more, and they had gazed beyond the stars and into dimensions undreamed of.

Her lips, perfect in shape and the colour of freshly spilled blood, parted, and she spoke in a soft breath of a voice. "You have done well thus far, my young pup." She spoke directly to the wolf and the creature looked on her mistress with attentive adoration. "I shall see to it that our young friend here survives the night, but that is all the aid I shall give you. Another day and a night and you shall both be at the Bridge of Glass, and then..." A breeze moved her long, midnight tresses, stirring her cloak, which shone a glossy black and was made entirely from the feathers of crows.

Slowly the dark figure lifted her arms, and her cloak rose with them until it blotted out the stars. The wolf watched, and Steeleye lay shivering and unaware, as a huge crow fluttered from out of the shadows of the cloak. It landed upon the rampart of heaped snow and looked fiercely at the figures in the shallow hole. Then with a chilling caw, it hopped upon the chest of the young warrior, and spread its wings protectively over him. A moment passed, and then another crow emerged from the cloak and once again shook out its pinions and spread them over the man. Another and another followed, then more, until the two still forms in the snow were soon covered by a murder of the dark, glossy-winged shapes.

The Morriggu let her cloak fall, surveyed the mass of winged shapes before her, and gave a slight almost imperceptible nod of her head. "It begins, brother," said the goddess. "Soon the Seven will be writhing in your fires, and your beloved... My sister will rise again." As silently as she arrived, the Mistress of the Crows faded into the night, and beneath the warming murder of crows, Steeleye slept on.

* * *

STEELEYE AWOKE as the sun broke over the banking of snow that he and Wolf had built the night before. The early morning sky was a pale ethereal blue, and he wondered at the fact that he was alive at all to see it. His bones creaked and cracked alarmingly as he shifted position, gradually sitting upright. His muscles screamed with the effort and his vision swam as he came close to passing out. He reached out instinctively to steady himself, his fingers curling in the warm fur at the nape of his silent companion. Wolf was with him still, her strange eyes showing almost human concern.

Slowly, he gained his feet, and as he did three large jet-black feathers fell from his chest to the compressed snow at his feet. He looked at the feathers, and then at Wolf. "Can you explain this?" he croaked. His throat hurt, and Wolf merely stared at him with her odd coloured eyes.

Steeleye took a drink from Rolf's flask, gasping as the liquid burned his throat, then he retrieved his staff lantern and clambered out of the ditch. He felt a little better than the night before, but was under no illusion that he was in any way recovered. With every breath that he took, the wound in his side felt as though a hot poker were being pressed against his skin. The stench of putrefaction assailed him, and he was quite sure that the blow Kleave had dealt him at the Western gate was slowly and painfully killing him.

All thoughts of the feathers were chased away by a new wave of pain, which bent him double. Grasping the staff tightly, he breathed deep. "Come then, Wolf, let's get this over with." He lurched into a shambling, swaying walk in the direction of the great chasm in the ice. For a moment or so, Wolf merely watched and then in her loping gait she trotted into the lead, once more his guide.

By midday Steeleye was once again spending as much time sprawled in the snow as he was struggling through it. His breathing came in great ragged gasps, and though his body was wracked with shivering convulsions, he felt as though he were burning up; sweat ran freely down his face and his yellow hair was lank and plastered to his scalp. When the snow began to fall, he barely noticed it, nor when the wind picked up and began to howl across the tundra. He was beyond rational thought by this time. His body was moving automatically, almost of its own violation, step after step, yard after agonising yard.

Soon, the sweat upon his face was frozen in the icy wind and frost had formed in his hair. The swirling snow buffeted him this way and that, and often he would lose sight of his ferocious guide. But always Wolf would come to find him in the maelstrom, always she would return to him, to tug on his cloak with her powerful jaws, or to lick his face with a hot rasping tongue should he be sprawled in the snow. Again, and again the wolf would hurry him along, and Steeleye soon became totally dependent upon his guide, for the snow fell so thick and the wind was so strong and cold that Steeleye could barely see his hand before his face.

He was so blinded by the weather, that he almost walked into the hunter's shelter. A shelter was all that it could be called, certainly not a cabin. It was a simple A frame structure, some six feet tall at its apex, perhaps ten feet square at the base, roughly constructed, meant to give succour for a night or two, certainly not for permanent habitation. Rough and lowly as it may be, to Steeleye at that moment it was a palace, a safe haven where he could perhaps rest out the storm. Silently he gave a prayer to whatever god had seen fit to guide Wolf here.

Steeleye found the door, a rude affair of planks, and set to clearing the snow from around it so he could at last pull it open. For a moment he thought it would fall from its warped frame, but the leathern hinges held fast, and he staggered into the comparative safety of the shelter. Wolf followed, her form snaking through the gap as he pulled the door to, shutting out the swirling snow. Several cracks in the roof let in dim light, and Steeleye was able to see a small cot against one sloping wall. At the opposite wall to the door, there was a simple flue built into the wall and roof; at its base stones were set in a circle, almost like a camp fire. There were logs and kindling laid there, and more wooden logs stacked beside it.

Steeleye sat heavily upon the cot, which creaked beneath his weight. Next, he took the lantern from the end of the staff, and, after a moment's scrutiny began to thumb a small wheeled device built into the lanterns oil chamber. His fingers were cold and fumbling, but on the third attempt the device struck a spark from flint, and the oil-soaked wick was lit. The lantern lent the insides of the shelter a cheery glow, but more than this, a means to light the fire laid before him. Steeleye grinned. The ice that layered his face cracked, his blackened lips splitting painfully; he could taste coppery blood. But still he grinned. It was quick work to ignite the kindling from the flame of the lantern, and before long he was crouched before the small fire, feeding thin sticks and twigs until it really took hold and he could feel the heat bathe his face and hands.

The pain that came with the heat like needles pricking into his skin, making him grimace and wince, but still he added more of the wood stock, until he was driven back on his heels. Slowly, little by little, his breath ceased to frost in the air, and the temperature in the little shelter became less and less cold, almost warm. Wolf had thrown herself upon the floor, which, by the lantern and fire-light, Steeleye could now see was covered with hide. A pile of old furs had been laid at the foot of the cot and precariously perched upon the top of the pile was a small iron pan. *My blessings are unending,* he thought. He quickly took the pan to the door. Shouldering open the rough portal, he scooped up snow with the pan, then once more pulled the door shut, a flurry of snow accompanying him inside.

Taking his treasured pan of snow to the hearth, he carefully balanced it upon the burning logs. Next, he fished through his satchel, finding strips of dried meat and a small bag of herbs. The meat he added to the melted snow, a sprinkling of herbs too. He didn't wait for the water to boil, merely to warm through the meat, then, using his cloak to save his hands from burning, he poured the hot water into the now almost empty spirit flask. Taking a long pull from the flask, he revelled in a different heat to Rolf's welcome spirit.

He scooped up a strip of meat from the pan and tore into it. It was tough and would normally not be anyone's idea of nourishing fare, but at that moment, it was a feast. He quickly devoured the first strip of meat and scooped up a second; this, he offered to his sprawled companion, but the Wolf merely rolled her eyes and made a snorting sound. Shrugging, Steeleye finished the repast, and was able to drink the still warm water from the pan.

A wave of lethargy swept over him. It was all he could do to pile up a couple more logs upon the fire, then, pulling the furs from the cot he lay down upon the floor next to his companion. In moments, he was in a deep sleep, the sleep of exhaustion, so complete as to be next only to death.

Outside the shelter, the wind howled and the snow swirled. The light of day faded and a cold night fell upon the tundra. The shelter had stood here for several years, often repaired by hunters and travellers alike, its wood stocks kept high by all that had the time and opportunity.

Steeleye slept on, unaware that had the night been clear, he would have seen the strange Bridge of Glass but twenty paces distant.

* * *

IN HIS FEVERED DREAM, Steeleye stood upon the battlements of the castle at the head of the valley of death. Crows wheeled in the pale dawn sky, hopping from stone to stone along the castle walls; they skipped at his feet, their ebon wings stark and black, like shadows. Never had he seen so many crows. Wolf sat beside him too, and Steeleye for once didn't feel the numbing fear that usually held him at the wall.

When the Huntress rode the Great Spider over the causeway of bones, he didn't shrink back into the shadows, but instead leaned forwards to get a better look at this dread rider that called him "brother". As ever, she wore the crimson plate armour, sitting high in the saddle of the nightmare creature; her hair, as delicate as spun silver, moved in the breeze like an exquisite banner. When she looked up at the parapet, her perfect lips parted in a wide smile. "There you are, my brother!" she exclaimed happily, "The time draws near then? Have you accepted who you are and pledged to the Light?"

Even as Steeleye made ready a reply there came a low growl from the throat of his lupine friend, a growl so deep and menacing that the hairs upon Steeleye's neck stood on end. The crows began to caw and screech in an unholy din, their wings beating loud and furious in the chill morning air.

Steeleye awoke in the crude shelter, as yet unknown to him, only a short distance from the bridge that he sought. He was shivering from the cold, yet sweat bathed him in a greasy film. The pain in his muscles and bones was nigh intolerable, but it dimmed to naught compared to the corrupted wound in his side. From that dread wound radiated an agony that wracked his whole body.

The fire had burned out sometime in the night, but he was able to see about the cramped space well enough due to the cracks in the planking of the A-frame. Snow drifted through the cracks too, along with columns of wan daylight. Steeleye became aware of the sound of the wind; it howled and clawed at the roof of the small shelter, the very noise of it chilled him even more. Wolf sat at the foot of the cot, her eyes on the door, making it clear where she wanted to go.

With much groaning, and fresh sweat starting out upon his brow, Steeleye managed to get to a sitting position. His mind seemed a little dull, like his thoughts were wrapped in wool. Why not light the fire and stay here awhile? He thought this was a sensible idea; he could recoup through the day, ease the chill, and perhaps doze a little. His eyes were heavy with fatigue and his chin fell to his breast, exhausted sleep claiming him in an instant. The hot breath of the wolf upon his face woke him with a start. He had to move on, use what little strength that he had left, to cross the gorge, to find help beyond the bridge. If he were to stay here much longer, he knew the long sleep would claim him.

"I am awake, my friend" he rasped to the beast, their faces but an inch apart. "Lead on, I will follow as best I can." With that he heaved himself to his feet, crying out with the pain from his side, the putrid stench from the wound filling the little cabin, making him gag. Wolf pushed open the door, and snow came tumbling in, along with the freezing cold Northern air. It was only now that he realized just how much protection from the elements the Hunter's Refuge had afforded him. The wind howled gleefully through the door, and he had to bend almost double against its force to make his way outside. The snow was like a wall of stinging, biting white needles. It tore at his cloak, scratched at his face with icy fingers.

He stumbled out of the refuge, the shape of his guide an indistinct blur in front of him. Steeleye blundered forwards into the knee-high snow, wave after wave of nauseating pain beginning to swamp him. Through frozen eyes, he caught a glimpse of his fingers clamped around the lantern haft. They were black, the skin cracked and bleeding, yet he could feel nothing at all. For what felt like an eternity, he fought his exhaustion and the elements, but he would not give in. A natural stubbornness had surfaced within him, something that Freija would chide him about. He had set his sights upon reaching the bridge and then the South, and so long as breath remained in him, that was what he would do.

The thought of Freija, her sweet face frozen in death, even now brought a wracking sob to his throat, and with it a pain that cut deeper than any sword. It was with the thought of his friend and companion at arms swimming in his mind's eye that he became aware that the blizzard's fury was lessening. It was as if it had spent its energy trying to keep him from his goal, realising its failure had become spent. As visibility cleared, he saw, no more than twenty feet before him, Aihaab's Gap.

The spectacle was staggering. This was a narrower part of the great abyss, and yet it was still a hundred paces wide if not more. In fact, the far side was so distant that even now, with visibility clearing, he could barely make out its features. This was what the fury of a god looked like. It was remnant from the days when those unfathomable beings strode the lands, when their power was unfettered and not held in check by oaths. This great tear upon the land was a grim and stark reminder that there existed powers far greater, far wilder, than any wielded by mortal man, whether wizard or warrior.

And yet, there was a bridge.

This was a marvel not of the raw power and brute strength of a god, but of the inventiveness and resourcefulness of humankind. The builders were long lost to the memory of subsequent peoples, yet here the bridge stood, a testament to their determination and skill. The origins of the bridge had been lost through the ages; it was spoken of in sagas a thousand years old, and even then, it was called the Bridge of Glass, due to its planking and chains being covered in a thick sheen of ice, ice that would never melt no matter the season, due to the freezing cold air that billowed up from the depths of the abyss.

The deck of the bridge was but two paces wide, shimmering and glittering in the sunlight. The bridge bowed in the centre due to its great weight. Ropes had once been secured by chains every few paces, to provide hand-rails. These ropes, like the planking, were as polished glass, shining blue and silver as the sun reflected off their surface. Icicles, as long as Steeleye was tall and as thick as his thigh had grown over the years, pointing into the depths from the footway.

As Steeleye drew nearer he could see that the whole affair was anchored to great stone columns sunk into the edge of the abyss, and they, like the bridge itself, had been turned to ice long ago. He stumbled towards the nearest column. Though now almost blind from the dazzling snow, he could dimly make out the tear in the tundra. His tears had frozen upon his lashes, and the bright reflected light of the sun off the snow stung and made his eyes water all the more. Groping like a blind man, Steeleye reached for the next column, leaning gratefully upon the sturdy structure.

All reason had fled from Steeleye's exhausted thoughts. His obsession was to cross this seemingly fragile structure, to gain the far side of the abyss and there his thoughts ended. He could no longer picture in his mind's' eye what could follow.

Tentatively, he put a foot upon the gleaming structure. Holding fast to the left rail of ice, unable to feel the keen bite of the cold, as his arm was numbed to the elbow, he slid his foot forwards. One sliding step, and then another. The cold that came from beneath the bridge was unlike anything he could have imagined, as sharp as a razor's edge it cut through his furs, sliced through his skin, and froze him to the marrow.

He had slipped and slid a dozen paces and was not yet anywhere near a quarter of the span. When he dared a look over the rail, a crippling vertigo sent his senses swimming. Beneath him, there was nothing but a billowing white mist, and that did not start before a long bowshot. It seemed the depths of the abyss were endless and Steeleye was perched precariously over the great space on the ancient and long untested bridge.

Wracked with uncontrollable shivering, his teeth chattered so fiercely he feared they would chip and shatter. Six more hesitant steps and a wind came howling from the depths, near turning the very air to frost. Steeleye looked back along the way he had come. Wolf sat between the support posts. She had not advanced upon the bridge. Her eyes bored into him, her head stretched forwards, so intent was her concentration. It was as he looked back at his companion that a harsher gust of the wind sent Steeleye's feet skidding from under him. His frozen fingers lost their grip and he crashed to the icy planks. Instinctively he threw out both his arms the impact drove the breath from him in a painful grunt.

He sprawled on his back. Fingers and heels tried to dig into the unyielding planking, and for a moment Steeleye thought the worst was over. But as he caught his breath, he became aware that he was slowly, ever so slowly sliding to the left. He tried to stop the slide by rolling onto his side, giving him more purchase with his arms, but to no avail. If anything, his slide seemed to accelerate. He became suddenly aware that his feet were no longer on the bridge and frantically he twisted onto his stomach. His knees and then his thighs slipped over the edge and, with a cry, Steeleye lunged for a supporting chain rail, fingers curling around the frozen links even as his waist went over the edge of the bridge.

With a desperate effort, Steeleye wrapped his arms around the supporting chain, momentarily halting his slide. He gulped in the frigid air. He could see back along the bridge to where his companion sat, her head cocked to the side. He wondered if she would venture onto the bridge and help him? The strange beast had been at pains to ensure his survival thus far. Even as these thoughts flitted through his tired mind, and the realisation that he didn't have the strength to regain his footing on the bridge, dawned upon him.

Wolf raised her head and began to howl.

The sound carried over the tundra, rolling like a tide over the snow, a melancholy, anguished cry that sent shivers along Steeleye's spine. Again and again, the beast let out the howl, until its echoes blended with the howl itself and the air was rent with a continuous eerie wail.

And then, as suddenly as she had started up the noise, Wolf fell silent. The very wind seemed to pause in its violence too, it was as if time held its breath, waiting in anticipation. Several heartbeats passed. The only sounds were Steeleye's gasping breaths. The effort of hanging onto the chain was like nothing that he had ever experienced, as if he held up the world, not just his own weight. And then, he heard it.

Far below him, lost in the swirling mists, there arose a terrible din. With wide, panicked eyes, Steeleye looked beneath him. The sound was so loud now it seemed almost tangible, filling the abyss with furious volume. And then, they burst from the mists.

Crows!

Hundreds, nay thousands, of the night black creatures, spiralled up from the depths, their beating wings and grating, cawing voices so loud they hurt the ears. They headed straight for the bridge, their claws and beaks a maelstrom, their ebony pinions beating at him like clubs, their fierce talons plucking at his fingers. Their numbers blotted out the sun as they dove and swirled and screamed about him.

And then they were gone. Just like that, the great birds passed over the tundra.

But the damage was done. Steeleye could feel the very last ounce of his strength and resolve leaching away, his fingers slipping slowly from the chain. He had no stamina, his muscles were as water, and his will had deserted him. He locked eyes with the wolf, still sat so proud and aloof at the entrance to the bridge. Her eyes were unfathomable, pale sky blue and yellow as spring daffodils.

Without a sound, Steeleye slipped from the bridge, into the chasm, lost in the swirling mist.

CHAPTER 8
THE PACT

S teeleye gazed upon an endless meadow of buttercups and bluebells, the lush grass they peppered a vivid green, the yellow and blue of the flowers striking. Like an ocean, the colours gently waved to and fro in the warm spring breeze. The air had a heady floral scent and he breathed deep, filling his lungs. He could smell wood smoke too. Pine, he thought. Turning on his heel, he could see a cabin in the near distance. The smoke he detected rose from a chimney in the roof. It too moved and flowed in the breeze.

The sky was a deep and peaceful blue, errant white cloud slowly drifting across the azure canvas. Beyond the cabin he could see the tree line of a pine forest, the deep greens and ochre calming him. He found that as he walked to the cabin, his feet were clad in well-made sandals, and he wore trousers of home-spun wool, with a tunic to match. Steeleye didn't know who he was, nor how he came to be walking through this perfect meadow, nor was he curious: he was content and at peace.

He reached the cabin faster than he expected, the spring sunshine warm on his shoulders. He smiled as he reached the structure, noting it was well made and sturdy, without hesitation he pushed open the door and stepped inside.

As he crossed the threshold, his sandalled feet came to rest upon great marble tiles, and he was not in a cabin but in a cavernous hall. The marble floor was white and veined through with pale blue seeming to glow with an inner light, to stretch on as far as Steeleye could see. To his left and right there were row upon row of great arches, so high that they were lost in shadow. Again, he could see no end. He slowly turned in a full circle, finding that there was no cabin doorway behind him, only more of the wondrous hall.

He knew that he ought to be alarmed, yet he felt only a dreamy contentment. This was the most natural thing in the world, and so he continued to walk across the tiles. The tread of his sandalled feet upon marble the only sound. And then he saw his destination. Still a-ways before him there was a plinth of great stones set upon the marble flags. The dais was made of jet. Colossal, and sitting atop the great structure, was a high-backed seat, black as a mid-winter's night. Drawing nearer, he saw the great throne held an occupant. His feet slowed, for seated upon the chair there was a woman of devastating radiance and beauty.

Skin pale as alabaster contrasted starkly with her sable hair and smiling ruby lips. Eyes grey as thunderheads stared at him from beneath lashes so long, they seemed to brush her high cheekbones. From her slim shoulders fell a glistening cloak, made all of feathers and which shone slick as oil. Steeleye stared in awe of the woman, her beauty was such that it bordered upon the terrible. So otherworldly that he dared hardly look upon her, yet so entranced that he dared not look away.

At last, Steeleye came to the foot of the ebony plinth, and instinctively he went to his knees. He tore his gaze from the beauty on the throne, and looked upon his hands, fingers pressed on the white marble floor. A shudder ran through him. Where was he? Who was he? And who was this figure upon the throne? The fog inside his head was thick, he couldn't *think*. "Questions." It was the ebon-clad vision that spoke, her voice as rich as honey yet soft as silk, the very sound of her voice made every nerve in Steeleye's body sing.

He dared to look at the woman. Though still unnaturally beautiful, her perfect brow arched, showing the faintest amusement. "This must be very confusing for you." Her white hand rose to her face, a slender finger tipped with a scarlet nail gently tapped upon her perfectly white and even teeth. "There are not many that come before me once they have passed." With a swift movement a small scythe, silver and as keen as the northern winds, cut the air before her. "That," she said, looking fondly at the scythe, "is usually the last that the departed and I have to do with each other." Her eyes bored into his, though he felt no threat, only awe. "I am the Collector of Souls," she said at last, "in the Northern lands they call me the Morriggu, in other climes I have other names, but always I am the Collector of Souls, and I ferry the dead to their next life."

Steeleye was aware that his jaw hung open, but was unable to snap it shut. The vision upon the throne smiled at his confusion, though not unkindly. "I understand that you are struggling to comprehend what has befallen you: can you remember your name?" Steeleye shook his head slowly, and then answered, "I don't remember... anything"

"That won't do," said the Morriggu with mock severity. "I need my blades sharp, not dull witted." With that, she stood, and made a beckoning gesture to the back of the throne. "Mayhap I can refresh your memory?" she said softly, though her eyes were suddenly keen and bright. Steeleye felt a chill as a shadow detached itself from the ebony throne, and silently padded into light. The shadow soon became clear to Steeleye. A wolf, though no ordinary wolf, it was midnight-hued and huge. Its savage head held low, it padded towards the platform steps. Steeleye saw the eyes then. One was as yellow as spring flowers, the other as blue as a summer sky.

And Steeleye remembered. His memories came crashing in on him like an avalanche until he floundered beneath the weight of them: Hewla the Seer, so old yet wise and kind; Aelrik, so proud and just; Rolf, his Lord's trusty shadow. Faces and events beat down upon Steeleye. Wolf entering his cabin for the first time, and once again feeling the thrill of the supernatural. Again, he accompanied Rolf and the clan to the Western Gate; he fought the Horde and saw his friends die in the crimson snow. For a second time he felt the bite of Kleave's poisoned blade.

Lightbringer!

And Freija: once more he held her lifeless body in his arms, and gave a cry of grief.

He remembered the rage as he trekked across the tundra to the circle of Stone Gods, and Rannulf. He remembered the son of his friend as a friend, and as the foulest of enemies. He felt again the euphoria of the killing blow, and the agony of the struggle through the drifts of snow to the Gap. Wolf was a constant; she had been there by his side since the moment that she had entered his cabin, even in his nightmare dreams, Wolf had been there to calm and reassure him.

And upon the Bridge of Glass, Wolf had been there to watch him fall to his death...

* * *

"I REMEMBER NOW." Steeleye said softly, his gaze locked with that of the wolf, and it was to his erstwhile lupine companion that he spoke. "You led me to my doom on that bridge didn't you, Wolf?" Steeleye's gaze hardened, and the beast seemed to flinch, abashed. "I think that you knew from the first that I would not make it over that damned bridge." The wolf sank to its belly, whimpering miserably.

The Morriggu stepped forward then, to stand beside the prone beast. "None of this is the fault of hers, Steeleye Lightbringer," said the Collector of Souls, and there was power in her voice, command and steel. "It has long been writ that you would enter my domain from the Bridge of Glass, though what will happen next remains cloudy, even to me. The writers of fates have seen fit to be less than forthright." Her wondrous lips pursed, and her brow furrowed. Again, she tapped upon her teeth with that perfect fingernail.

"I took your soul as you fell from the Bridge of Glass," as she spoke, with one alabaster hand she brought from the folds of her feathered cloak a small vial, stoppered with a silver cap. Within the glass vial Steeleye could see a tiny spark. As he watched he became aware that the tiny light pulsed brightly, as he watched longer, he became uncomfortably aware that the pulsing spark seemed to be in rhythm with his own heartbeat, which now beat loud in his ears.

"With my silver scythe, I cut from you that which makes you what you are, that which separates you from the creatures of the dark." As she spoke, the Collector of Souls gently shook the vial, her unearthly gaze intent upon its contents. "This tiny spark..." her voice was soft as a breath, "This fragile thing is the real you Steeleye Lightbringer."

Once more those stormy eyes locked upon him. "You are mine now mortal, as are all men when their time comes, mine to pass on to the next life, be that a joyous reunion with friends and loved ones, or a never-ending torment, writhing in the fires of the Pit. What do you deserve, Lightbringer? Has your life been well spent? Have you filled your days earning eternal bliss?"

Steeleye was unable give an answer. He could barely think straight and his memories were still a jumble of colours and sounds, emotions and sensations. But not all his memories had returned. He remembered a small boat upon a pebbled beach. Waves that left a trail of frost in their wake they were so cold, had deposited him upon that barren shore just as the sun rose. A cold and bleak dawn for the young occupant of the tiny craft, until he spied, walking over the shingle, an ancient woman, striding towards him like she was in the prime of life. And with her were a fearsome group of giants, though they grinned whitely through their frosted beards.

But before the pebbled shore there was only darkness. A void, as if that had been his birth, spat out by the ocean upon the Northern shore.

The Morriggu relented from her questioning, and though her eyes were still intense, her lips smiled kindly. "I see the deeds of all mankind," she said softly. "When in a fleeting moment, I sever the soul, I see all. I have seen... all. Auras as bright as a sun and pure and clear as a spring morning, and I have seen those that are rank with corruption, those are the auras of the greedy, the cruel, the betrayers and vile, and those that have turned their backs upon their fellow man. They are the murderers and the kin slayers, those who are blind to mercy." Absently her free hand scratched the great wolf behind the ear, its eyes narrowed in pleasure.

"Your tale need not end here, Steeleye. Lightbringer. *Grimmsbane*." Those bewitching eyes held his, and it seemed the great hall dimmed, faded, until there were only those grey, stormy eyes, lambent and watchful. "It could be that you may yet return to the world, to live out your life. How does that sound to you, Grimmsbane?" Again, she gave him a title that he did not understand, yet before he could ask her its meaning or even respond to her question, she spoke again.

"I can offer you the chance to return to the world, to feel the sun upon your face and the breeze upon your skin. I can give you the chance to stand by friends in need, to finish that which has begun. All you need do, is serve me."

Steeleye stammered, his speech clumsy, "Serve?"

"Aye, serve me, serve the Gods. Help us to put right that which has been done wrong." The Morriggu arched her brow and tilted her head. "Will you walk with me, man? Will you let me show you the Hall of Heroes? Will you walk beside me, and will you see wonders?" She smiled gently. "Of course you will. You are the Grimmsbane, you are the Lightbringer. You were born to be here before me, born to be my foil in the mortal world." With that, the Morriggu turned upon her exquisite heel and began to walk into the shadows, with a slim white hand she beckoned. And Steeleye followed.

* * *

THE MORRIGGU TOOK him deeper into the great hall. They walked for an age, and Steeleye's footsteps rang hollow upon the marble floor, whilst the Goddess was utterly silent, as though her dainty feet hardly touched the tiles. The great wolf too followed her mistress, claws ticking and scratching rhythmically upon the marble with each step.

Steeleye was agog with wonder: how was this structure possible? Its size defied all logic. He could imagine the whole of the Northlands, mountains and all, getting lost within this great hall. At length, the Morriggu led her charges between two of the enormous pillars into a wide corridor. Steeleye's mind reeled at the thought of such corridors between all the pillars that he had seen within the hall, and though he had not had the presence of mind to look, he the felt such would be the case.

And now he saw that the corridor was host to doors along each wall. Each door was identical, plain and tall, made of what Steeleye thought might be oak. The corridor led into the distance, seemingly endless, the number of doors infinite. If each set of pillars within the great hall did indeed contain a similar corridor, and each corridor had its walls filled with doors...

The Morriggu was looking at him, amusement writ upon her lovely face. "These are the doorways to all the realms of creation," she said, her hand waving towards the nearest door. "Beyond each doorway lies a different destination, with a turn of the handle and a step, we could be anywhere in the world, in any world, any possible dimension." Seeing his confusion, she moved soundlessly to a random door.

"Shall we see what lies beyond this door?" she asked softly. Her hand moved slowly to the handle and for some reason Steeleye felt dread steal over him. He felt sweat break out upon his brow, and the hairs on his nape stood stiff. He was aware that Wolf was beside him, and he gratefully rested his hand upon her head. Grounded.

Slowly, the Morriggu turned the handle, and with a gentle push, opened the door. Steeleye gave an involuntary start as he saw that the doorway led out onto a parapet of rose-tinted stone. It was wide and well flagged, though of obvious great age. Beyond the crenulated wall, from the safety of the corridor, he could see that dawn was breaking, the sun rose pale and cold, filling the valley beyond the great wall with revealing light. Steeleye shuddered. Wolf leaned into his side, feeling his dread, and sharing it.

"I know this place." Steeleye's voice was a hollow whisper, as he peered through the doorway at the scene beyond. "I have *dreamed* this place before."

"This doorway leads to the citadel of the Fae..." The Morriggu's voice was as soft as his own, and he gave a start as he felt her breath upon his ear, for she had come silently to stand at his shoulder. "Shall we take a stroll upon the ramparts and watch the sunrise?" she waited a moment for a reply, then continued, "it is quite safe; this is the here and now. Well, the there and now in truth. *She* will not be searching for you here, today." With that the Morriggu stepped through the doorway and onto the stonework beyond. With only a moment's hesitation, Wolf followed. Steeleye stood a little longer, alone in the endless corridor, and then he too stepped over the threshold and onto the familiar battlements.

At once the morning chill bit deep, giving him cause to shiver. As he took a step forward to stand with the Collector of Souls he glanced over his shoulder and was both relieved and startled to see that a rectangular aperture leading into the corridor hung like a canvas in the air. He turned once more to see the rising sun bathing the familiar valley.

"What is this place?" he asked, peering cautiously over the parapet of stone, and shuddering as he saw that the valley floor was indeed carpeted with bones. It was the valley of his nightmares, true enough. There he could see a huge serpent skull, all sabre long teeth and eye sockets as wide as the span of his arms. There, a tattered standard that was familiar, gently moving as a warming zephyr caught at its folds. He felt a great sadness envelop him as he looked out upon the endless field of sun-bleached bones. Death upon such a scale was awful to contemplate.

"We are standing upon the walls of the Citadel of the Fae," said the Morriggu. "In its prime, the Citadel was wondrous to behold, its walls as long as the valley is wide, and so high that none could assail them." Her voice took on a wistful tone and those storm grey eyes seemed to see other than that which Steeleye saw. "The Fae were a beautiful people; their arts and music surpassed all other races for wonder. But even so it fell to them to stand against the Grimm like all the other peoples of this realm. Though peaceful by nature, the Fae were fierce once roused to violence, and the Grimm Hordes and all their dark allies broke upon these shining ramparts. Like a great tide the Horde filled the valley and rushed headlong at the walls, as if their numbers alone could bear down the stones and vanquish the Fae and their human allies. For a year the Fae fought the creatures of darkness, they were a wall of not only stone, but sinew and bone that stretched over the valley, denying the Horde progress into the lands beyond." Again, the Morriggu cast her saddened eyes over the valley. "All are gone now," she said.

"There are so many that have fallen to the Grimm, and to the Darkness and its thralls. The Fae would call me the Lady of the Long Sleep, one of my more poetic titles, I always thought. And I miss them terribly. They were a long-lived folk, one lifespan was tenfold that of a human, their art and culture a delight." She sighed, wistfully. "All are dust though now, swept away by the Darkness, by the Horde and their ilk."

Steeleye was at a loss how to react, to see so powerful and frightening a being as the Morriggu pondering and reflecting upon the past was not how Steeleye had ever expected the Gods to behave, if ever he had mused upon such a thing.

At that moment, a great crow landed upon the parapet next to the goddess, breaking her reverie. She cooed to the fierce looking bird, and held out a slim arm, which the crow dutifully hopped upon. "Enough gloomy talk," she said, "let us return to the corridor, and be off on our way to the Hall of Heroes. There is much for you to be told Grimmsbane." With that, the Morriggu turned away from the valley of death and stepped through the doorway. Steeleye hurried after her, worried that the door would close and leave him alone upon the ramparts of the citadel.

Soon, the three of them were once more walking along the strange corridor, and Steeleye's thoughts were slowly beginning to straighten out. He began to understand what had happened to him, and with that understanding came a new worry: what did the gods want with him? And why did this strange, beautiful creature insist upon calling him Grimmsbane? As he continued to try and make sense of it all, the Morriggu stopped suddenly, and tapped a scarlet nail upon a door, a door that was identical to the hundreds, nay thousands of others. "Here," she said over her ebon-clad shoulder, "here is where it all began, or ended, in so far as the memories of humankind are concerned."

The Morriggu fixed Steeleye with a piercing stare, and for a moment the corridor, Wolf, and the doors all seemed to recede into shadow and were gone, leaving only the hypnotic grey eyes. "Behind this portal lies the most tragic of tales, Grimmsbane Lightbringer. Here are the very best of all the realms, the brightest, the boldest, and most canny. All the Heroes that fate has spun into our fabric are here, they rest here, their trials at an end. Here they stay to guard she whom we gods cherish most. She who fell at the hands of the Seven, and at the hand of their foul master, Aihaab the Accursed." Gently the Morriggu pushed the door ajar, stepping aside so Steeleye could enter.

"Here lies my sister, Arianna, beloved of the Gods, and she that holds the heart of the Dark One."

Steeleye paused mid-step at that last comment, his foot hovering over the threshold. "Fear not, Hero." The gravity in the Morriggu's voice was gone, replaced by gentle laughter, like silver bells. "The Dark One is not within. He cannot abide the grief it brings to see Arianna thus."

Slowly Steeleye moved through the doorway, his hand straying to the nape of Wolf, his fingers curling in the sable pelt. The eyes of the Morriggu flickered to that hand, and for the briefest of moments, a puzzled frown marred her perfect brow.

The room was beyond vast, so high that the ceiling was lost in stygian shadow, so long and wide that the walls were a mere suggestion upon the horizon. He caught his breath at the scale of the hall. The world of the Soul Collector was so strange and enormous that its very strangeness and enormity were becoming the norm to Steeleye. At first, he thought that he was looking upon a great host, an endless throng of men and women, gathered under the shadowed roof. After a few moments, he realised his error, instead he was looking upon an endless array of statues, every one carved with such lifelike precision as to fool the eye, even under scrutiny. Still gripping the fur of his lupine companion and erstwhile guide, Steeleye stepped to the nearest statue, and gawped like a child seeing his first puppet show on the village green.

The statue stood upon a plinth of polished marble, and as he looked about him, Steeleye saw such was the case for each figure. This nearest masterpiece was that of a man of middle years, his face hard and grim, sporting a beard shot through with grey. He wore strange looking armour, a cuirass of burnished gold embellished with intricate designs inlaid in mother of pearl and green quartz. A long flowing scarlet cloak fell from his broad shoulders, its pleats and folds replicated perfectly. In his strong hands the statue held a spear longer than he was tall, its blade over a foot in length looking as sharp and keen as a frosty morning.

Next Steeleye saw a fierce-looking woman, her skin ebony hued, eyes like stone. She wore mail, the scales of which were many coloured, each lacquered and polished to shine and dazzle. Like some resplendent serpent. She held in her hand a bow, strung and ready.

Steeleye took another step, then another, and came alongside a giant of a man, all shaggy hair and matted beard. This huge beast of a man was decked out in furs the likes of which Steeleye had never seen. In his great paw of a fist, he gripped a club, like a young tree and near as long as Steeleye was tall. Even Aelrik the Bearslayer would have been dwarfed beside this titan.

He passed figure after figure, and not all were of human shape. Here, a lizard like creature, there an amorphous shape that made his eyes ache. Men, women and creatures of every creed, culture and nightmare were collected here, their numbers beyond counting, and each faced inwards, weapons ready, faces grim and proud. At least. those that had recognizable faces. For all that he had been amazed and in awe since his fall from the Bridge of Glass, here within this great Hall of Heroes his mind and his sensibilities were stretched to their utmost.

"These are my champions," said the Morriggu with pride, her chin lifted as her stormy eyes surveyed the vast army. "Each of these gave their all to try and win back sweet Arianna her life." The Soul Collector ran her fingers along the arm of a striking maiden. Clad in leather and mail, a winged helm atop her tawny tresses, this woman, this statue was beautiful, a fierce joy captured in her features. With a sharp pang Steeleye was reminded of Freija. They shared the same vitality, the same abandonment when the battle song was sung.

"Gathered here, in this great hall, are the images of those who stood against the darkness, the corruption that would engulf the realms." The Morriggu, looked at Steeleye squarely, her face grave and sombre. "Arianna was felled by the Seven, and by Aihaab the Weak, but she is immortal, and so cannot truly die. The master of the Seven is dealt with, my brother sees to that. He writhes in never-ending torment. The fate of that madman is terrible indeed." The goddess showed her teeth in a fierce smile. "But the Seven.... those Daemons from beyond our realms, from whence the Horde sprang, they are still here. They hide in the shadows, and they manipulate, they guide the weak, they coerce the greedy, they ally themselves to darkness, and there is a darkness spreading throughout the lands of your realm, Steeleye Grimmsbane. It is a darkness that threatens to engulf all."

On and on they walked. Steeleye could feel sweat upon his back, the homespun tunic sticking to him uncomfortably, his sandals scuffing upon the floor no matter how quietly he tried to walk. The slight sound loud to his ears amid the silence of the gathering of heroes. The steady tick tick of the Wolf's claw like nails upon the tiles was the only other sound, save for the hammering of his heart, that seemed to beat so fast that it might burst from his chest.

They were approaching what Steeleye assumed to be the centre of the chamber. He could see a huge stepped plinth, and it was towards this that each of the figures was facing. He came nearer, and could see that the plinth was made of a startling white marble, veined through with twisting patterns of gold.

The steps were low, and easy to climb, though there were plenty of them, and one at a time, Steeleye, Wolf and the Lady of the Long Sleep made their way to their top. The surface of the plinth was again made from the glorious marble, and the rich golden veins even more pronounced. And there, in the centre of the dais, was a great crystal casket. Set upon legs of exquisitely carved scarlet wood, the casket was at least three long strides in length. The crystal was clearer than any glass Steeleye could imagine, letting them see the supine figure resting, as if asleep within.

Arianna!

The gentle consort of the Dark Lord himself, lay as if asleep upon a velvet couch, so deep a blue it could be a twilight sky. Her hair was carefully arranged upon the pillow. It spread out like a pool of molten gold, framing a face so serene and gentle in its beauty that Steeleye near wept to look upon it.

The Morriggu rested her slim hand upon the crystal. Her eyes softened, misted as they looked at her sister laid before her in death, or as near death as it is possible for Gods.

"Here is the very best of us," the Morriggu said sadly. "When Arianna fell to the Seven, all those millennia ago, everything changed in an instant. A god's wrath was unleashed in a manner unseen before. My brother, the Dark Lord, the Keeper of the Dead, was broken that day as well as the land of the Northern Kings."

Steeleye stepped hesitantly to the side of the Morriggu and looked closely at the figure within the casket. Arianna was dressed in simple white cloth, her slim hands resting upon her breast. She was bereft of jewellery save a slim torc of mistletoe twined about her flawless brow. He expected to see the rise and fall of her breast, to see the long lashes flutter upon her cheeks, those full and half smiling lips to part and take breath.

So strongly did the sight of Arianna effect Steeleye, that the Morriggu gently took his hand within her own, and squeezed ever so slightly.

"Now do you see why there is no shortage of champions for the fair Arianna?" breathed the Morriggu. "With the Seven slain, Aihaab's curse upon them will be no more. We will be able to revive our sister and she will once again sit beside my brother, and calm his fury. Arianna is the breath of contentment to we immortals. Though not so powerful as others, her very essence, her spirit of purity, makes her the very best of us. We need her amongst us to be the best that we can be."

The Morriggu turned and looked upon the great Host of Heroes gathered about the plinth. "Each and every one of these brave souls sought to vanquish the Seven. Some have fallen to the Demons, others fell before they even found them, for the creatures are scattered throughout your Realm, hidden in the shadows, cloaked in darkness." She frowned, and her voice lowered, "and they have gathered about them armies of weak willed and dark acolytes. But the Seven must be destroyed, and we cannot do the deed ourselves for we swore to stand back and not interfere directly in the affairs of the Realms, save to gather Souls, to instil courage and kindness, knowledge and determination. Our roles have changed over the eons, but still, we can guide the worlds indirectly." The goddess paused, as if choosing her next words with care. "We guide the worlds through the noble souls that you see gathered here."

The grey mesmerising eyes once more pinned Steeleye, "And through such as you, Grimmsbane."

Steeleye shook his head a little, as if to clear a fog from his thoughts, for in truth his mind struggled to take in the cosmic scope of what the Morriggu was saying. He was aware of Wolf pressing against his leg, as if offering comfort. His heart continued to hammer in his ears.

"This is what you were born to do, Steeleye Lightbringer."

Steeleye stepped back a small pace. He could feel panic surging through him, like talons gripping his throat, squeezing his heart until he feared it would burst, a great weight bearing down upon his lungs until he could barely breathe.

Once more, the Morriggu took his hand, and comfort flooded through him.

"You were born for this, your fate and that of Arianna, of the Realms, of all of us, is tied with knots that will not loosen." Her voice was soft and close to his ear. He could feel the warmth of her sweet breath and as she spoke, his fear dissolved.

"At this moment in time, the Realms face their greatest threat since the old times. There is a new evil let loose, and I think that you know of whom I speak."

Steeleye steadied himself, once again looked at the matchless beauty lying in the casket before him. "The woman in my dreams?" he asked

"The woman in your dreams." The Morriggu affirmed. "The Seven are aligned with her, and she brings powerful allies with her from beyond, the likes of which even we, the great and the good have not seen before."

Wolf shifted against his leg; her strange eyes lambent.

"You are asking me to hunt down these creatures for you?" Steeleye asked, and was surprised that his voice sounded calm. It was almost as if another spoke through him, as if he were a mere spectator, watching as a scene unfolded in some play.

"I am offering you a pact," corrected the Morriggu. "Hunt down the Seven, do that which the solemn word of the Gods prohibits us from doing ourselves." Her voice though still soft was now intense. "Kill the Seven, free Arianna from Aihaab's wretched curse, and your own life will be restored to you in full." The Morriggu leaned forward, her eyes boring into him. "Whilst the Seven roam the Realms, Arianna cannot be brought back." She gestured at the casket. "She was taken from us too soon, and she has so much still to offer... as do you Steeleye. It would be a shame indeed if your path were to end here and now, when there is so much wonder for you yet to see, so much life to yet experience." And now the Goddess lowered her voice even more, hardly more than a breath, "...so much for you to yet discover about yourself."

Steeleye knew he had little choice. He certainly didn't wish to die, as the Morriggu had just said. He yearned to know more about his life before the Northmen took him in. But there was a stubborn streak in him yet, and he felt anger bubbling deep in his chest, threatening to drown out the fear and the awe that he had been feeling ever since he first awoke here in this strange place.

"What makes you think that I can succeed where all these..." He gestured at the forest of figures around them, "...have failed? Surely many amongst these were stronger, more capable than I?" As he spoke, he drew away from the casket. He found the unearthly beauty of Arianna too clouding. "I am only one man."

Now it was the turn of the Morriggu to step away from the casket and survey the champions set about the plinth. She considered her words carefully, her perfect brows drawing down, a slight purse to her lips. "There is more at stake here than Arianna, than uniting the Dark One with his beloved. There is a great darkness making ready to engulf your realm, nay every realm. It will spread like a cancer throughout all the plains, all the realities, until there will be nothing but darkness. This darkness is Old, and I feel it is you, Lightbringer that will play a part in thwarting its rampage. There is too much falling into place for it to be mere happenstance that you are here at this moment in time.

"There is a Realm, where my sister, Narissa, the greatest smith, the most skilled artisan ever to bless the worlds, built a temple, and this temple is built from metal that came from the farthest reaches of the universe, and to this temple, comes but once in a millennium, the Stormchild."

Steeleye was lost. He had heard of the Great Smith of course. She created the circle of standing stones in the Northlands known as the Stone Gods. Legend said that she sculpted the Great Pinnacle, the needle of stone that towered above all the mountains in the lands of the North, where the Gods resided to watch the goings on of men. But metals from the ends of the universe? The Stormchild? These things he knew nothing of, and his confusion was clear, because the Morriggu placed a hand upon his shoulder in sympathy.

"You are fated, methinks, to journey to this temple, and to take from the Stormchild that which was made for just such a purpose as this. The blade that the Stormchild carries is capable of slaying any and all living creatures, whether mortal, demonic, or even divine." Her hand upon his shoulder gripped tighter. "This blade could be the very weapon to at last succeed in vanquishing the Seven."

Steeleye countered, "If the weapon is so mighty, then why has it not been sought before? Surely some of these here could have fetched the blade?"

"In truth, many have tried to bring the blade here," the Morriggu said. "Though the Stormchild is a keen guardian. He was made for no other reason than to keep the blade safe from any hands but his. Remember, this blade has the power to kill even the Gods." She smiled. "Why, the Stormchild is a threat to even us, the immortals, as would be anyone that gained control of the blade."

"Then why are you telling me about it?" he asked. "Why have you knowingly sent others to gain control of such a weapon?"

The Morriggu smiled. "These are desperate times, Steeleye, and they call for desperate measures. Only those worthy of the task are sent to the Temple of the Stormchild. Only those that we, the Gods, are sure will not try to usurp the power of the blade for their own ends are chosen to try their hand."

Quite suddenly, the Morriggu straightened, and strode from the casket, weaving her way through the heroes, her ebon-clad feet soundless upon the marble tiles, the great cloak of crow feathers billowing in her wake, like a cloud of ink. "Come with me now, Steeleye, for even if you don't know it, your mind is made up, you are now a servant of the Morriggu!" She looked over her shoulder, a wide grin upon her face, eyes sparkling "I have a good feeling about you." Her voice was quite merry. "You have taken the first step, even if you don't know it, and that means that my sister is one step closer to returning to us. That the darkness is a little closer to being thwarted!"

Steeleye hesitated only a moment. He looked at Wolf, as if for help. The great beast merely stared back at him. That was it then, he was decided it seemed. He was to enter into a pact with the Soul Collector, fetch a magical blade from another dimension, besting its fearsome protector, then return and hunt down and slay seven demons that had run wild across the world he knew since the very breaking of the land by the Dark Lord. Along the way, he would come up against the terror that stalked his dreams, for it was she that held the leash of the Seven and their ilk... He decided it was better not to think too much about that part: one step at a time. The prize rested in the folds of the Morriggu's cloak, in a tiny vial no bigger than his thumb.

His very Soul.

Steeleye was once more with the Morriggu striding along the never-ending corridor of doors. It seemed only minutes since they had been standing amongst the gathering of the heroes, yet things were now very different. Firstly, the Morriggu moved with a purpose. She glided quickly past the innumerable doors glancing neither left nor right, Wolf padding along at her heel, tongue lolling like any domesticated hound, rather than ferocious killer.

Secondly, Steeleye was now dressed in new and more appropriate attire. From the solid and well-made leather boots upon his feet, comfortable buckskin leggings, to a quilted tunic over which he wore a half-sleeved mail shirt, all new and fitted as if made for him. About his waist, he now sported a belt, from which hung a fine blade, encased in a wooden scabbard. His hand rested upon the plain pommel as they walked to stop the sheath slapping against his leg. From the other side of the belt hung a quiver made of fine black leather. The quiver was filled with exquisitely fletched arrows, arrows that he was sure would fly true from the bow that was slung over his shoulder. He had no recollection of having dressed in this way, or having received the fine weaponry, this was just the way of things in the company of the Lady of the Long Sleep.

He rushed along in the wake of the Goddess and the wolf, his new boot heels ringing upon the marble of the floor. Ahead, the Morriggu glanced over her shoulder and nodded with satisfaction. "Now you look more like a champion of mine," she said. "I understand that this is all very strange for you, but be assured, I am certain that you are capable of completing this task. You will, I am sure, bring the Godsteel blade into this realm."

"Did you say that to all the others that have attempted to fetch the blade?" he asked, "to all those that are gathered in the Hall of Heroes?"

Again, she glanced over her perfect shoulder, a wide smile lit her face. "Of course not," she chided. "Many of the Heroes were sent on different paths, not all braved the Stormchild." Her laugh was gentle, though filled the corridor. "And less than half of those that were sent to the temple ever reached it to meet the Stormchild. That land has many perils, the path to the temple can be perilous by itself, but you have a look about you Steeleye Lightbringer, you are the one I'm thinking that will wrest the blade from Narissa's creation." Her voice was so filled with good humour and confidence that Steeleye found he was ready to believe that perhaps he could do as he was being asked.

The door they eventually stopped at was no different to any of the others, but the Morriggu placed her hand gently upon the handle and then paused. "Time is short, Steeleye. In the lands beyond this door, a storm gathers, a great once in a generation storm that will deliver the Stormchild and his dread blade to his Temple. It is of the utmost importance that you are at the Temple before the storm breaks fully. You must follow the path that is set, don't deviate from the path or you will be lost to us." Her voice was suddenly urgent, her words as nails hammering into his mind.

Steeleye faced the door and squared his shoulders. "So, I reach the Temple, I take the sword from this Stormchild, and my Soul shall be returned to me?" his voice was surprisingly steady.

"Not quite," chided the Morriggu. "Reach the Temple, take the sword, then and only then can I come and bring you back to this realm of yours. Then shall you hunt down the Seven and send them to the Pit. Once the seventh of the creatures is writhing in the Dark Ones fires, *then,* shall I return to you your Soul."

"I have your word upon it?"

"You do."

"And my soul is safe? I will be able to reclaim it and be on my way?"

"Just so. You will hardly notice that it is missing." And with that, the Morriggu opened the portal to the world of the Stormchild.

CHAPTER 9
STORMCHILD

As Steeleye stepped through the doorway, newness and strangeness assailed him. Above, the sky was vast, tinged with green rather than the blue of his home world. The clouds that scudded over that strange sky were violet and pink, though they seemed fluffy and ethereal as any of the white clouds he was used to. Squinting against the glare, he looked towards the sun, and for a moment he couldn't understand just what he saw. Slowly, realisation dawned upon him, there were two suns sharing the odd green sky. And more, he could see great moons, three of them looming in the sky, each a dozen times the size of his own world's single satellite. The largest moon, though pale as if seen through dirty water, sported strange rings about its middle.

Steeleye gaped, dumbstruck.

"There is little time to dawdle, Grimmsbane," the voice of the Morriggu came from behind him. Steeleye glanced over his shoulder and was shocked to see the trunk of an enormous tree, and there in the trunk was the sharply defined outline of a doorway, beyond which was the corridor of doors. The Morriggu and

Wolf stood at the threshold, watching him with what may have been amusement. Steeleye craned his neck upwards to see the height of the great tree, stretching into the strange green sky, He surmised it would take him the turn of a glass to walk around its girth.

The Morriggu raised her hand to stave off any questions, "I will tell you of the great tree another time, champion. For now, take heed: do you see the path?" Steeleye turned from the Goddess, and raked the land with his keen eyes. He was standing upon vast desert, though now the sand was hard packed and baked so dry as to have cracked like the shell of an egg. The colour of the landscape was near orange, and there, running straight and true over the surface, Steeleye could see a well-worn path.

"I see it," he said. As he turned back to the tree, the Morriggu was holding out a water skin, and there was dew upon its surface. The water inside sloshed invitingly. "Take this" she said sombrely. "Do not eat or drink anything from this realm, follow the path, you will come to a forest. Within a clearing in this forest, Narissa built the Temple for the Stormchild. When the storm breaks, he will come. He knows no mercy, Steeleye, do not underestimate him. He was created by my sister to hold that which we the gods most covet and fear."

Steeleye took the water skin. It was reassuringly heavy in his hand, and he could feel its coolness, as if it had just been drawn from a mountain stream. With a nod to the Morriggu, and a gentle touch to the head of the wolf, Steeleye set his feet upon the worn path and began to walk. He took a dozen steps, then looked back over his shoulder, the pair still watched from the corridor. "I will be hoping for answers when I return," he called.

The Morriggu smiled, lifting his spirits with her beauty. "If you return with the Godsteel blade Steeleye Lightbringer, I will strive to answer any questions you care to ask. But for now, remember the storm, for the Stormchild will ride the lightning, and you must be at his temple before the storm breaks."

With a nod, Steeleye turned his attention back to the path and quickened his pace. The miles went fast as he strode over the burning orange sands, beneath the many mooned green sky. He had hurried along for over an hour when he glanced behind him, and there in the distance, huge and dominating the horizon was the great tree, the spread of its branches vast and dark. Steeleye once more looked to the path and hurried up his pace. There would be time to consider the tree once he had gained the blade that the Morriggu seemed so wary of.

Dry dust kicked up with every step, and Steeleye soon began to feel the heat of this scorched place, sweat running freely, soaking his yellow hair to his brow. The water skin would be needed soon, he thought. But onwards he tramped, the moons and the suns drifting across the green sky beyond the violet clouds. He smiled and shook his head ruefully at the strangeness of it all, then his smile grew wider: at least he was alive!

It was near impossible to judge time, as he had no idea of the length of the day, but he was sure that the suns were sinking to the horizon, so he expected darkness to soon come upon the land, and with it he hoped, a drop in the baking temperature. But such a hope was soon dashed, as just when the suns began to bloat and disappear, a new and even bigger sun began to rise to Steeleye's right. Unlike its sister suns, this new one was bright and fierce and tinged with blue. As it rose, the sky lost much of its green aspect, and instead became tinged with a dirty yellow colour.

Steeleye paused to raise the water skin to his lips, relishing the cold liquid as it soothed his parched throat. Whilst he replaced the stopper, he squinted along the path. There in the distance, by this new sun's light, he could make out a dark line upon the horizon. He could also see great mounds of rock, piled high, disrupting the flat emptiness of the baked landscape.

He walked for a good while and began to get closer to one of the great piles of rock. It stood but a hundred strides from the path, so he could see clearly as he came alongside it. Much to his surprise it seemed to be made up of slabs of reddish stones all piled together, one upon another. Surely this was no natural occurrence? But who could have constructed such things and why? Steeleye had seen neither a bird nor a bug since stepping through the portal in the great tree, and even the most desolate of places in his home realm would contain some slight signs of life. Not here, it would seem. Steeleye was tempted to wander to the nearest of the great piles of rock and see for himself just how they came to be, if they were indeed natural, or had, in times past, someone, or something piled the rocks thus. But even as his feet veered from his straight path, he was reminded of the words of the Morriggu, not to stray, that there were indeed dangers here in this world. With a conscious effort he ignored his curious nature, and once more lengthened his stride, heading towards the dark line upon the horizon.

The sound, when it came, was as much of a shock to Steeleye for its suddenness, bursting the silence, as it was for its ferocity and volume. It came from the nearest of the stone piles, a great roar of animal savagery. Before Steeleye even thought of a course of action, his trained body had already reacted, the bow was in his hand, arrow nocked, the fletch resting against his cheek as he drew the string back, turning to the nearest pile of stones. This was a war bow that the Morriggu had provided, and the poundage was immense. Steeleye drew back the cord even further, feeling the strain in his shoulders.

His keen eyes raked the rocks, and soon enough he saw movement atop the pile. To his left there came an answering, bestial shriek. Steeleye didn't take his eyes from the nearer target, and before long he was rewarded with a clear view of the creature that had had let out such an awful scream. The distance to the rocks was now only fifty paces, so Steeleye could see clearly as the figure seemed to haul itself from within the rocks. There had to be an opening at the top of the pile, and the formations must in fact be hollow. Long of arm and wide of shoulder, its sloping head rested upon a thick, muscular neck.

The eyes the figure fixed upon Steeleye were tiny, blue as the great sun, and filled with hunger. The face suddenly split almost in two as the creature's mouth stretched wide to once more let out a great roar, its teeth yellow and dagger-like, the lolling tongue red and bloated. Covered entirely in coarse white hair, the creature resembled an ape from the southern jungles of Steeleye's own realm, but it was bigger, much bigger, and it was now scrambling down the side of the rocks, its deep throated roar a blatant challenge to the man upon the pathway.

As the ape-like beast leapt to the desert floor, it beat its huge fists into the baked earth, smashing the sand like pottery in its fury. Even as Steeleye sighted along the arrow, he was aware of a second creature clambering out of the rocks, and of the sound of yet more of the savage beasts to his left. Steeleye kept his calm, and drew a bead upon the hairy chest of the first monstrosity, as it lumbered across the sand towards him. Saliva trailed from its grisly maw; ravenous eyes fixed upon its prey. Steeleye let fly, inwardly cursing for not wearing a guard as the string thrummed over his wrist. The bow was indeed made for war, its arrows capable of punching through mail or bronzed cuirass. The shaft flew true, taking the ape thing in the chest, left of centre, the force of the impact stopping the charge dead, and throwing the creature back several feet.

Steeleye had another arrow nocked and drawn back before the beast hit the ground. This time his arrow skewered the back of the second creature as it was scrambling down the piled rocks. It screamed hideously as the shaft exited its chest in a spray of gore, striking sparks from the rocks.

A third arrow was fitted to the string as Steeleye spun to his left, and not a moment too soon. Only a dozen paces away was another of the beasts, jaws gnashing in anticipation of rending his flesh. Steeleye let loose his arrow, the shaft taking the ape creature in the throat even as it leapt towards him. The impact caused the beast to somersault in mid-air, a great arc of gore spraying, following it to its crushing demise upon the scorched land.

Steeleye turned on his heel as he drew and nocked a fourth arrow with smooth efficiency. He counted four more of the white-haired apes, all closing fast, all powered by terrible fury and sinew. He had time for one more shot, and it flew true, punching a creature from its feet and hurling it back like a thrown rag doll.

He snatched out another arrow with his left hand, but there was no time to use the bow, as the nearest creature leapt upon him, its great jaws snapping shut an inch from his face, its breath foetid and overpowering, the light of fury died in its eyes, the arrow thrust like a dagger under its jaw into its fevered brain. Steeleye stepped nimbly aside as the dead beast crashed to the ground.

Then his sword sang into the air as he turned to face the remaining two colossal beasts.

Steeleye sprang forward into the attack, feinting for the ape to his left, but instead darting at the one on his right, the sword slashed at the neck of the creature, but it proved too fast, leaping aside. With a snarl it came back faster than ever, the knuckles of its huge hand crashed into Steeleye's mailed chest, sending him flying, landing heavily upon the hard packed sand. Within an instant, the creature was upon him, great fists raised high, muscles straining in fury. Steeleye met the ape with a fury all of his own. He powered the sword forward, teeth bared, and his eyes were beginning to burn with a fierce light, as if there were a bright star within his skull, exploding with brilliance through his sockets. The ape's own momentum skewered it upon Steeleye's sharp blade, and gore erupted from the beasts' maw, black and stinking splashing upon Steeleye's mail shirt. He rolled aside, dragging his blade free of the great beast now dying to the sand.

Surging to his feet, eyes blazing, Steeleye ran to meet the final ape. His first swing missed its mark, though was so close to the beast's head that it sliced off its ear. The backswing lopped off the creatures reaching arm at the elbow. With a shriek of pain, the beast caught Steeleye about the throat with its remaining hand, lifting him clear off the ground, iron hard fingers crushing his throat, black talon-like nails threatening to tear his head clean off. Choking, Steeleye struggled to prise loose the fingers with his left hand, all the while pushing his sword into the stomach of the ape, forcing the steel up into the chest cavity, and then, as his vision began to dim, and the light in his eyes began to waver, he exerted all his strength and the blade split the hairy beast's heart in two. The ape convulsed, throwing Steeleye aside like a discarded toy. For several seconds, the creature stood glaring hate at its slayer, the haft of the sword and six inches of steel protruding from its chest. Slowly, the burning hate and hunger died in the deep-set eyes, and without bending, the beast toppled onto its back, dead.

Steeleye lay gasping for breath, the shining in his eyes had died along with the threat to his life. He groaned as he struggled to a sitting position, his throat burning horribly with every inhalation. He could still feel the fingers choking the life out of him. His chest ached too, even though protected by his mail, Steeleye knew that his body had been battered and bruised during the brief and violent encounter.

Very much aware that more of the creatures could be nearby, in any of the dozens of jumbles of stones, Steeleye, got slowly to his feet, then made his way to the final beast he had killed. Using both hands, and bracing his foot on the hairy breast, he pulled his sword free. He cleaned the blade as best he could on the body of the beast, and returned it to its scabbard. He then retrieved his bow, and was able to pull one of his arrows from the throat of an ape. As this could still be used, he wiped it clean on the slain creature and returned it to his quiver. Done at last, he hurried towards the forest upon the horizon.

His eyes roved the surrounding rock piles for any signs of life, his ears keen for any sound other than the pad of his booted feet and the sighing of the warm zephyr that came from across the parched sand-lands. Satisfied that for the moment he was safe, Steeleye picked up the pace, and was soon running at an easy mile-devouring lope.

The darkness at the horizon soon proved to be a tree line, and none too soon either, as in the distance, dark bruising storm clouds filled the putrid yellow sky. The clouds roiled and rolled across the heavens, a heavy and oppressive atmosphere came with them. Steeleye slowed his pace as he neared the trees. Twisted and gnarled affairs, reaching for the sky with sharp grasping branches, like tortured souls.

High above him, the sky brooded. The forest ahead had become forbidding. There was the sound of thunder off in the distance, a great rolling bass that vibrated through ground. Steeleye was aware that the Morriggu had told him to find the temple before the breaking of the storm, so he dared not hesitate too much, but the forest was a terrible looking place in the gloom. Though well-armed, and of considerable skill with both bow and sword, Steeleye still felt the prickling of fear as he looked upon the dense wooded barrier before him. Like living things, the trunks of the trees seemed to writhe and twist from the ground; the zephyr had intensified, and now those grasping, taloned branches shook and swayed.

Steeleye took a drink from the water skin. Aware that he was wasting time, but his feet reluctant to move into the shadows. His heart hammering. Upon the desert plains, he had come close to being killed by the ape like creatures, what terrors awaited him here amidst the melancholy gloom of the trees? He was alive only by the grace of the Morriggu, yet she held his soul, safe but still captive. For the first time, it dawned upon Steeleye what a quandary he was in. No matter the odds he faced, he was out of options, he was unable to turn aside, to decide that the risks were too great or that his skills and courage would not see him through. His dice had been thrown, and to falter would mean his death. Permanently.

Thunder boomed. The storm was closer now, the sky seeming to boil and churn, the great clouds shot through with crimson, like fiery blood. Slowly, Steeleye started to walk once more. He held the bow strung, an arrow in place tight between his fingers. Heavy droplets of rain began to fall, hastening his steps. By the time he reached the forest and plunged into the shade, the rain was a continuous driving sheet making visibility even poorer. He paused just a moment, peering through the gloom, his teeth gritted so hard they hurt. He felt a hundred unseen eyes watching him, his skin crawling, as if covered with a thousand spiders. The forest exuded terror, it breathed fear and woe, and Steeleye's sword and bow were no match for it.

He was shaking as he moved along a faint path, and not only from the fear of the surrounding trees, but from cold too. The driving rain was icy. Even here beneath the canopy of dread branches there was no refuge. The wind was now a howling, living thing that bent the twisted boughs and threatened to push Steeleye from the path. On and on he struggled, leaning forwards into the teeth of the gale. His long hair was plastered to his scalp and face, his clothes soaked. Had fallen into a stream, he could have been no wetter. He could no longer feel the bowstring in his fingers, it had become so cold. In his own realm, only the northern winters would compare to this. He grimaced, remembering all too vividly his trek across the frozen Northern tundra, and how well that had ended for him.

Lightning pierced the darkness, a great jagged spear of blinding fury that lit the forest for the briefest of moments, and Steeleye felt his blood run as cold as the driving rain. The trees! The trees were moving! Not swaying to the force of the icy wind, but writhing in their own sinuous dance, bending and stretching, their sharp branches undulating with a fevered life all of their own. Steeleye cast aside his bow, and with numb fingers drew his sword, every instinct within him told him to turn and run, to escape the terror, the grasping claw-like branches that even now came at him like black serpents.

Steeleye ran, but not to escape the trees. Instead, he plunged along the path, deeper and deeper into the wood, his sword lashing about him in wild desperate arcs. There was no sword skill here, no patterns learned in the sword yards, only blind panic and terror. Again and again, a grasping branch would dart from the darkness, the sharp talons tearing at his mail and flesh. The sword hacked and chopped, and branches splintered and flew, the rain intensified, the thunder cracked louder and louder still, and on Steeleye ran.

The path became waterlogged, his fine boots splashing with every step, soon turning to treacherous mud, so he now slipped and slid, almost pitching headlong. Forks of bright lightning tore across the heavens, and within seconds there came the crack of thunder, so loud it made Steeleye flinch. Hack and slash. Putrid wood shattered and flew into the air. Again, there was a bright flash, and the whole forest was lit up. It was only for an instant, but it was enough for Steeleye to see that ahead the forest thinned and ended in a glade. Within the glade he caught the briefest sight of a structure. It must be the Temple!

He redoubled his efforts, pulling free as a twisted branch caught in his hair, swiping out with his sword as if it were a woodsman's axe and not finely made steel. Another branch caught at his shoulder, and the mail gave a little under the strength of the blow. Steeleye reeled. It was as if the tree knew that he was nearing his goal and so attacked him with ever more fury. Like whips, the trees lashed his face and body, and for each cut and splash of blood that was drawn, the branches seemed to become more and more frenzied, as if the sight and smell of his blood drove them mad.

And then he was free of the shadows and the trees. The rain drove harder once he was away from the canopy and he was forced to pause and collect his bearings so impaired was his vision. As he stood, chest heaving with the effort of catching his breath, hand raised to shield his eyes from the needles of rain, a twisted root slithered and lurched from the undergrowth. As quick as a striking cobra the root wrapped about Steeleye's ankle and yanked him towards the forest. Steeleye fell onto his back with a great splash, the wind knocked out of him. He gave a gurgling scream of pain and fury, the rain striking his upturned face so hard and fast he thought he was about to drown.

As the root was dragging him over the edge of the glade, back into the tangles of thorns and spikes, Steeleye roared wordlessly and struck with his sword. Again and again, he struck at the root, the branches, and the great twisted trunks of the trees themselves. Hack and chop, hack and chop, Steeleye grinned mirthlessly as the branches split and shattered. He struck until at last the grasping tendrils withdrew, as if in terror themselves of this sword-slinging madman. As he felt the root release, Steeleye scrambled, slipping and sliding, to his feet, and whirled about to once again plunge into the clearing.

Lightning crackled across the sky. The rain drove down harder, the wind howling. Narrowing his eyes, Steeleye risked a look at the sky; the great blue sun was completely obscured by the crimson clouds, which now seemed to race through the heavens in a great spiral, boiling and spinning ever faster and faster. Great jagged forks of lightning were constant, as were the ear-splitting cracks of thunder.

Through the veil of rain, lit by the intense lightnings, Steeleye caught a sight of the Temple of the Stormchild. A great bulk of a structure that squatted but two dozen strides away. Nevertheless, seeing his destination so close lent new strength to his limbs, and Steeleye hurried forward. His leg almost gave way as his ankle turned upon the saturated sward, and he knew that the last grasping root had done damage even through his fine strong boots. Limping he reached the cover of the temple. Seeing its great stone lintel above a doorway five paces wide, he silently gave thanks to any and all gods that may be watching for his deliverance thus far, and fervently hoped they would continue to keep watch. He leaned heavily upon the great frame, and peered within.

Steeleye had not given much thought of what he would see within the temple. From plummeting from the Bridge of Glass to awakening healed of all wounds, yet deprived of his soul, all had passed in a blur, he had been shunted hither and yon with barely a moment to gather his thoughts. Thunder boomed almost overhead, and Steeleye flinched as a great spear of lightning tore out of the sky and exploded amongst the trees not far distant. He hoped the forest burned. Sheltered from the worst of the wind and rain, Steeleye wiped his hands upon his sodden trousers. He was not overly surprised to see blood running from several wounds upon his arms and hands, and that his leggings were ripped and ragged, his flesh beneath torn and shredded. Biting back the pain, he walked over the threshold, and entered the temple.

There was no roof, just four walls each around fifty feet in length making a square chamber; the only entry or exit was the one in which he now stood. The walls were made of a dully reflective metal, the floor was covered with strange square tiles a stride across. The tiles were set up like the game boards that he had seen the elders in the North playing on through the long winters' nights; half the squares were gleaming black; the other half were the same dull silver colour as the walls. High above the temple, the sky continued to swirl and billow, lightning arced through the crimson clouds. Though there was no roof, no rain fell within the temple, nor was the continuous crash of thunder quite so loud.

In the farthest corner, seated in the only chair in the room, was a man, clad entirely in ornate bronze armour. At first, Steeleye thought the figure to be a statue, it was so still and of such stature. But slowly the great helmed head lifted. The helm fully encased the head and face, with only dark eye-slits breaking the metal sheen. Great horns rose from the helm, curved and carved with runes. The armour creaked as the figure rose to its feet, a towering colossus. His shoulders were a yard wide at least, and the armour added to the span with spikes and flares. This great warrior dwarfed even Aelrik the Bearslayer, and Steeleye stared at the gauntleted hand that gripped the hilt of a sword as long as he was tall. The plated bronze looked incredibly heavy and cumbersome, but as Steeleye looked closer, he could see very few weak spots. Between the great plates was finely worked bronze links of mail. Steeleye wondered at the weight of the gear, and the stamina and strength of one that could wear it into battle.

"Welcome to the Temple of Narissa." A deep and powerful voice rumbled from within the helm, "I am Sir Gavynn of Gwyn-nett, champion of the King of the Eastern Empire, and Knight of the Lady of The Long Sleep." Steeleye felt himself relax a little. If what this great colossus said was true, then the two of them were on the same side, which Steeleye would be grateful for, because the more he studied the great warrior before him, the less he fancied his chances in one-on-one swordplay.

"Are you here to champion the cause of fair Arianna?" the voice boomed.

"I am," Steeleye replied, conscious of his battered and tattered appearance beside that of the resplendent Knight. He dragged his soaked and bedraggled hair from his face and steadied his breathing as he walked into the temple proper, his boots ringing upon the tiles. "I was beginning to think that I would be late for the Stormchild's appearance, that damned forest almost had the best of me."

The great Knight nodded. "Then the forest still stands? Even in full armour, it gave me more than a little trouble, this is indeed a realm of terrors." As he spoke, the Knight walked with a loud tread to the doorway and peered without. It was as he passed by that Steeleye for the first time saw the back plate of the armour. There was a great tear from left shoulder to right hip, the mail beneath rent and ragged. A mortal wound.

As if aware of Steeleye's scrutiny, Sir Gavynn of Gwynnett turned, and the dark eye holes of the helm looked over him. "The Stormchild comes here but once every hundred years. I have been in his terrible presence six times since he bested me. Six times I have seen this great storm swirl above the temple, and seen Narissa's most cruel creation ride the lightning to stand and gloat before me. The warrior paused, and then walked back to his corner. "I hope you fare better than I did. But whether you win or lose, I thank you, for you to just be here will release me from the guardianship of the temple."

"What do you mean by that? You lost to the Stormchild, and yet you are still here? I don't understand."

"I was the greatest swordsman of my age," he began, his voice a low rumble. "I was champion to kings and emperors, and aye, like yourself, eventually even the Gods themselves. I have slain the Great Worms of the Sandakas Plains. Singlehandedly I breached the fortress of the Robber Barons of Gwynnett, and killed the six brothers therein. I have faced the remnants of the Grimm and walked away unscathed." The knight let out a sigh, and continued his weary way to the single chair, though his voice came to Steeleye's ears clear enough. "I prayed at the Temples of the East for a challenge worthy of me, for my vanity knew no bounds. I dreamed of glory beyond all men. And the Collector of Souls heard my prayers and offered me the chance to take part in the ultimate quest... how could I refuse? How could I have known that here, in this terrible realm, there would be one so fast, so cruel and skilled that even I, the greatest Knight to ever Champion the Eastern Empire, would fall like chaff before the blade that I had come so far to steal?"

Steeleye was speechless, he looked at this huge mountain of bronze, saw the great killing wound in the figures back, and felt a new dread gnawing at him. But Sir Gavynn wasn't done with his tale just yet. "The Stormchild and I fought, long and hard, but he is as devious as he is skilled, and he struck me down. That damned God forged blade tears through armour and mail as if it were cotton. I died here. There were no funeral rights, none knew what had befallen the greatest of Knights; there will never be a song sung of my exploits here in this accursed place." The chair creaked alarmingly as the Knight lowered his great weight into it. "And here I have stayed since, watching the many suns and moons pass overhead endlessly, again and again the great Storm comes, and with it the infernal creature that guards the blade."

Steeleye found himself walking towards the knight. "But why are you still here?" A clap of thunder sounded, the crimson clouds above the temple seemed to writhe ever faster.

"I am the guardian of the Temple," replied Sir Gavynn. "It is the duty of every champion that falls before the Stormchild to await the coming of the next, to keep vigil here in this unholy place, where the Gods themselves dare not tread for fear of their own creation." The gauntleted hand gripped the hilt of the massive sword, and the dark eye slits peered intently at the young warrior. "You have freed me. At long last I will take my place in the Hall of Heroes. Should you wrest the blade from the Storm-child and thus continue with your quest to slay the Seven, or should you fall before the blade you have come for, and take up the vigil of the temple yourself, either way, my time here is at an end." With that, the Knight of Gwynnett looked up to the churning sky, where great arcs of blinding light played through the crimson clouds, thunder like war drums beat in time to the fierce lightning. "He comes!" shouted the bronze figure over the tumult. "The Stormchild is here!"

Steeleye instinctively drew his sword. The comfort that the heft of the weapon would normally bring was absent, and he felt small and insignificant before the storm. He followed the knight's gaze to the violent sky, and saw a ball of lightning hurtling through the heavens, closer and closer it streaked, growing bigger and bigger, and then as thunder crashed impossibly loud, seemingly within the temple itself, the lightning ball struck the temple floor, the violence of its impact sending Steeleye staggering so he lost his footing and fell sprawling upon his back.

He lay there for long moments, his eyes near blinded by the brightness of the lightning ball, and for a second, he thought that he had gone deaf, as the sound of the storm had gone. He fisted his eyes and looked about the temple and saw it was empty save Sir Gavynn and himself. He he glanced at the heavens, the crimson swirling clouds were dispersing, and once more he could see the sickly yellow of the strange sky.

Steeleye regained his feet and cast his eyes about, but still there was just the two of them present. He gripped the sword tighter, his heart hammering. "Where is he?" he called to the knight. "Is he here? Is he invisible?" Panic surged through Steeleye, and not for the first time he fervently wished that he had stayed in the Northlands, and had never followed Wolf to the Bridge of Glass.

The Bronze figure in the corner lifted a ponderous arm, and

with a gauntleted finger pointed at the wall to Steeleye's left. The knight spoke no more, and the heavy arm dropped. Steeleye didn't see this, nor did he pay the knight any more attention, he was gazing with trepidation at the indicated wall.

Like the other walls of the temple, it was dull and metallic, almost silver. Unblemished, it cast no reflection, rather seeming to absorb light. Seconds passed, and Steeleye's nerves, already frayed, began to wind tight, his throat constricting with fear and dread. His soul was at stake; he could spend an eternity here in this temple if he should lose the coming duel, an eternity alone in this terrible place. He should have said no to the Morriggu, what had he been thinking? What possessed him to accept this ridiculous task? Even as doubts assailed him, there was a flicker of movement within the wall.

Like a fleeting shadow, an unfurling pennant, something moved. And then, slowly, silently, a questing hand emerged. It was hard to see, as it seemed made of the same metal as the temple wall. Steeleye was riveted by it. The long fingers of the hand flexed and fisted, flexed and fisted, as if cramped. Next a wrist followed the hand, then a forearm and elbow came from the wall. The limb was long and spindly, reminding Steeleye of spiders. He felt his flesh crawl at the thought. Soon, the rest of the arm had come from the wall, and to Steeleye's fascination, there now appeared a foot, dull silver and naked, the toes wriggling as had the fingers. There was a pause, as if the hand and the foot tasted the air of the temple, like a child would dip its toe into a river to see how cold it was before taking the plunge. The pause seemed to stretch on and on, and then without fanfare or commotion, the Stormchild walked from the wall.

Steeleye was dumbstruck. He had no idea what he had expected, but this was certainly not it. Standing over seven feet tall, the Stormchild was a gangly, spindly, awkward-looking humanoid figure made all of dull metal, naked and sexless. Its head, perched upon a long thin neck, a featureless oval shape. For several heartbeats the creature stood before the wall, its limbs moving with sharp jerky movements, almost like a marionette. The tableau held longer still, and then it was Steeleye, much to his own surprise, that moved first. Raising his blade in a two-handed grip he took a tentative step forward.

As Steeleye's booted foot took its first step, the Stormchild swivelled its ovoid head in his direction. Though it had no eyes, Steeleye knew that it saw him clear enough, as the chin jutted out on the long spindly neck, and the long grasping fingers shaped into claws. Steeleye picked up the pace, committed to the attack, letting his training take over, fighting his fear with every step. The metallic figure suddenly thrust its hand into the wall from whence it had emerged, when it withdrew the appendage, it held a dully shining blade in its fist.

The guardian of the blade was faster than its ungainly stature appeared. Steeleye's rushing attack was easily countered, the blade knocking his own sword aside, and then a return swing so blindingly fast that it took Steeleye's panther like reflexes to avoid the being cut in two. He fell back several steps, and raised is sword once more. He felt a sting in his side, a hasty glance showed him that his mail shirt was damaged, the links torn as was the quilted undershirt, a shallow cut below his ribs was evidence of the Stormchild's speed and strength.

The strange creature tossed the Godsteel blade from hand to hand with nonchalant ease, the featureless head tilting upon its neck, as if it regarded some interesting titbit set out upon a plate. It swung the blade easily, the keen edge cutting the air, making it moan as if in pain. Though there were no eyes to see, and no mouth to speak, the posture of the Stormchild showed its confidence clear enough. Here was a vile creature, every angle and point of its elongated body spoke threat and malice. The lack of a face seemed to make it all the more terrifying to Steeleye; there were no tell-tale signs to give warning of an attack, there would be no look of surprise if he should react unexpectedly, only the featureless blank oval shape.

The strange creature came on suddenly, its awkward stilted posture should have been clumsy and slow, but the very opposite was true. The Stormchild lunged forward, the Godsteel blade a blur as it plunged towards Steeleye's face. Lurching aside, the young warrior was able to avoid a killing thrust, but the edge of the blade kissed his cheek, drawing blood. Wincing, Steeleye spun away, his own sword flicking out even as he retreated. His sword shuddered as it struck the Stormchild's arm, but left no mark. It was as if he had struck an iron post.

Again and again, the gangly creature came on, relentless and tireless, switching the blade from left to right hand and back again. There was no rhythm to the attacks; wild hacks, precise lunges, the point, the edge, from one side then the other. Steeleye fought as he had never done before. He moved faster than he ever had. He parried and cut in frenzy. His defence was like a wall of whirling steel between him and the Stormchild, yet still he bled from a dozen cuts. His breath came in ragged gasps as again he was driven back, towards a corner. He became more desperate with every cut. He knew if he was cornered then this duel would be over. Wildness crept into his defence as he was forced to abandon any caution; he knew without a doubt that he was out of his depth here, all thoughts of slaying the creature fled from his mind. Now he fought for survival, every twist and turn, every parry and duck were forced on him to stay alive.

As Steeleye was almost pushed into the corner, with a last desperate effort he grasped his sword hilt in both hands, and leapt forwards swinging at the Stormchild's head with murderous rage. So fast and unexpected was the strike that the Godsteel was a fraction slow coming to parry, and Steeleye's blade hammered into the temple of the blank oval head. The Stormchild staggered back, tilting its head from side to side as if clearing a bout of dizziness. Steeleye was quick to take advantage. With a beastlike snarl he once again hammered the edge of his blade on the top of the metal head. His sword shattered six inches from the point, but again the Stormchild was driven back.

With a scream of triumph and fury, Steeleye plunged forwards, his shortened sword swinging in a vicious arc, but the Stormchild was gone. Steeleye's blade cut through empty air, spinning him off balance so that he crashed to his knees. With a blind animal roar, he clambered back to his feet, turning his head left and right looking for his adversary. Besides himself, only the still and silent figure of Sir Gavynn was present in the temple room

Warily, Steeleye walked to the wall from which the creature had first emerged. He ran a hand over the smooth unyielding surface. It was solid, so how had it come from the wall? And where had it gone?

The attack came fast and brutal, a searing pain in his side as the Godsteel blade kissed his mail, slicing through the links. Steeleye spun about, his own shortened sword a blur as he aimed at the Stormchild's head height, but there was only empty air, and once again Steeleye was off balance and staggering. Yet another wound, blood running freely.

Steeleye pulled himself together and once more raised his sword. He slowly turned in a circle, his breathing ragged, the pain from the wounds burning like fire. Again an attack, this time from his left. He briefly saw the figure of the Stormchild speeding towards him, the ungainly figure spiderlike in its movements. Steeleye turned quickly but a silvered fist caught him up the side of the head, knocking him backwards. By the time his spinning vision cleared, the Stormchild was gone.

Over and again the gangling creature seemed to appear from nowhere, using fists and feet to inflict pain and damage on the young warrior, as if Steeleye's prowess had proved unworthy of the blade he had come so far to steal. Pummelled brutally, he was sure he felt bones crack; his nose, his cheek, and his ribs. But still, he tried to face the creature, he got back to his feet again and again.

He was on his knees, struggling to rise for perhaps the tenth time, when from the corner of his eye, he saw a hand emerge from one of the silvered floor tiles. The hand was quickly followed by the rest of the Stormchild, as the monstrous figure pulled itself from the floor. With a nonchalant ease it sped in and lashed out with a vicious kick which caught Steeleye under the chin. Had he not seen the attack coming, he was sure the kick would have broken his neck. As it was, the blow nevertheless sent him reeling onto his back, but still alive, and he watched with dread as the Stormchild hopped *into* another pale metal square, and vanished.

Tactics.

Steeleye needed a plan. He needed a plan to survive, to overcome and to kill this bizarre creature. But as to how, his fuddled, pain wracked mind was at a loss. He did know one thing though, that his body couldn't endure much more of this terrible punishment. Three times more, the horror appeared from the floor or the wall. It no longer struck from behind, as if it knew that such stealth was no longer necessary, it now flaunted its ability to merge with the temple, as if saying to the battered warrior, "Look at me! Look how wondrous I have been made!" Though of course it had no voice, there was no sound at all from the elongated, metallic foe.

Steeleye was beaten, and he knew it, but still a primal spark within him refused to give up. Deep within him a fire was lit, and it slowly spread throughout him, like a warming blaze on a chill evening, the spark brought with it a strange comfort and confidence.

The Stormchild appeared. This time it leapt from the floor

right in front of Steeleye, its hand like a blade lashing viciously at his face; the impact would surely crush his skull. But the blow passed through empty air, as Steeleye leaned away at the final moment. He felt the wind of the killing blow as it passed a hairs' breath from his chin. He felt the fire light in his eyes as he was overcome with the Shining and the strange calm, the controlled fury, that came with these rare visitations. Steeleye struck hard and fast, his broken sword stabbing into the featureless face. Though there was no damage done, the sword breaking even further, the Stormchild was sent reeling back to the wall.

It merged with the wall.

Steeleye blazed. White, blinding light shone from his eyes like a supernova. The pain from his injuries faded, and he stood tall.

Waiting.

The Stormchild surged from the wall, all sharp angles and speed. Again, Steeleye swayed aside, the Godsteel blade slicing the air by his throat. Steeleye struck the head with his open palm, jarring the ovoid on its spindly neck, and as the creature sank once more into a silvered tile, Steeleye's elbow hammered into where the face should have been.

Steeleye felt his confidence growing, the strange light within him adding to his strength and speed, bolstering his courage and dulling the pain from his wounds. The Stormchild could show no emotion, but its attacks became more tentative, less sure, and at the same time more deadly, as if it wanted the fight to be done with. Gone were the punches and kicks to cause pain; now the Godsteel sang and whirled with the intent of a killing blow. Steeleye was almost dancing, moving from black tile to black tile with fluid grace, for the ebony squares seemed to be resistant to the Stormchild, making them safe haven for Steeleye as he waited for the next attack. Though he was hardly aware of it, Steeleye had devised a plan.

Twice more the Stormchild came from the tiles, leaping from

the floor, the sword howling for Steeleye's head, then landing once more upon a silver tile, and sinking into the metal. Both times Steeleye swayed aside unscathed, and upon the third attack, he struck. Even as the Stormchild launched from a tile to Steeleye's left, the yellow haired champion threw his damaged sword into the blank face, and fast as a snake grabbed hold of the wrist of the creature, barrelling into its chest with his shoulder. His impetus and weight toppled the Stormchild over, and it fell into a dully shining tile. But Steeleye still gripped the sword hand, and he hammered it into an ebon floor tile with all his might. The silvered fingers spasmed and sprang open releasing the Godsteel blade, then disappeared into the floor.

Steeleye snatched up the blade, its weight and balance perfect in his hand. In one movement, he pivoted, raising the sword. The Stormchild was right behind him, and had it had eyes, Steeleye was sure they would have been wide with surprise as he brought the Godsteel blade down. The keen edge of the blade hit the crown of the Stormchild's head, and unlike his own good blade which had shattered, the Godsteel clove the featureless oval to the chin. Steeleye yanked the blade free, and was ready to deliver a second blow, but the Stormchild lay still. Unmoving. There was neither blood nor gore, the head was merely split, like a log by a woodsman's axe. A second passed, then another, and then without sound or ceremony, the Stormchild merely melted into the silvered tile and was gone.

Steeleye swayed, aware that the shining light that had possessed him had once more gone, and with it the borrowed stamina. The pain of his wounds washed over him, and he gritted his teeth to deny crying out. Blood dripped steadily onto the tiles, pooling about his booted feet.

"That was a feat the likes of which I have never seen." The voice of Sir Gavynn rumbled from the corner of the chamber. "You are indeed a champion worthy of this great endeavour. I salute you, Hunter of the Seven, and I wish you speed and good luck." The great bass voice paused, "ah, at last I see M'Lady..." and as his voice trailed away, so did the bronze armour slip from the chair and scatter upon the temple floor, empty.

Steeleye sank to the floor himself, unable to stand any longer. He gripped his prize fiercely, The Godsteel Blade, the key to regaining his soul, to killing the Seven and awakening the lovely Arianne. He looked at the length of steel in his hand, plain and unadorned, almost like an apprentice piece cast from a single mould, but the feel of it, the perfection of its weight and balance, this spoke of the work of a smith unlike any other. He gazed at the blade for long moments, feeling himself slipping into the dully glowing metal. It seemed to be almost like liquid, inviting.

"Do not lose yourself to the glamour of the blade, champion." The voice of the Morriggu brought him out of his daze. She stood at the entrance to the temple, her raven-feathered cloak stirring in the breeze, her lovely face so fearsome in its beauty, but Steeleye could sense a change in the demeanour of the Soul Collector; uncertainty perhaps? Did he see a glimmer of fear in those cool grey eyes as they fell upon the Godsteel Blade in his fist?

"So many have come here and fallen to my sister's creation, I was beginning to think that none could stand against the Storm-child, and yet... here you are, victorious!" She took a step closer, a hesitant step, and Steeleye realised that he held in his hand a means to bring death to even so powerful a being as the Morriggu. With a sigh, he let the blade clatter to the tiles, and saw new confidence surge in the Morriggu. Her red, red lips smiled widely seeing the untended blade, and the eyes were soft and gentle as they fell upon Steeleye's battered and bloody figure. "I shall make you whole and well again, Steeleye Lightbringer, and I shall return you to your own realm." She walked soundlessly across the temple floor and knelt before him, careful not to touch the metal of the fallen sword. Her fragrance filled his nostrils, a heady, dizzying scent, and the touch of her palm upon his cheek sent a shiver throughout his entire being.

A great tiredness came upon Steeleye then, and he could barely keep his eyes open. Darkness enveloped him in a comforting shawl, pulling him towards sleep. As oblivion claimed him, he heard the Morriggu whisper, "And lo, the Hunt begins. Let the Darkness tremble before the coming of the Light."

PART TWO

CHAPTER 10
MORINAE

Morinae awoke cold and stiff-boned with the first light of day. It had been more than thirty days since her captors had spirited her away from the palace of her father, Rodero, the King of Asgulun. Though terrified by her predicament, and weary from the arduous horseback travelling, Morinae's first thought upon waking was of escape. Lying there under her blanket, beneath the vast skies of the Plains of Loss, for the thousandth time she tested her strength against the slim silver chains that bound her wrists and ankles.

A boot nudged her back unceremoniously as the Captain of the Slavers walked by. "Still trying to break the chains eh, Princess?" Morinae turned her head and squinted at Captain E'bok, a tall and powerful man with a fine oiled moustache and beard.

"Let me loose, and my father will pay you and your men double whatever it is that you have been paid to abduct me." Morinae had made the same offer a dozen times each day as they rode farther and farther away from her home. Usually she was ignored, but on this bright and cold morning, E'bok squatted down beside her blankets, his knees cracking. Up close Morinae could see that E'bok was older than he first appeared, and that his lustrous black hair was in fact dyed; grey showed through at the roots and temples.

"Princess." He spoke quietly, not unkindly, but his eyes were flat and showed no remorse at her bondage. "You are a great prize for my master, amongst the dozen slaves that we take back to the southern markets, your price will be a hundred times that of the others combined." He ran his fingers through her golden hair. Even on the trail, it was kept fine and clean by the other slaves, so the Slave Master, Azif Bae, had ordered.

Morinae tugged her head free from E'bok's fingers, which she noted were manicured and spotlessly clean. Her green eyes flashed in defiance. She was storing the knowledge of the captain's vanity, should she have the opportunity to use it at some later date. E'bok laughed and pinched her chin between his thumb and forefinger, hard. "Such a pretty thing as you, and royalty no less. Oh yes, you will bring a steep price up on the block." His fingers tightened, became brutal until she winced in pain.

"Your master wants me unharmed," she reminded the captain, even as tears sprang unbidden to her eyes. "I bruise easily."

"Bruises fade, Princess," E'bok replied, releasing her chin, and with the same hand casually struck her cheek in a backhanded blow. Morinae felt her teeth rattle against each other. Her head slamming back onto the cold hard earth, and for a second all went dark and sparks and lights danced in her vision.

As she lay dazed, Morinae heard the piping voice of fat Azif Bae screeching over the camp site. "She is to be unharmed E'bok, you simpleton! Do you understand? Unharmed! By all the gods of Coin, a cracked bone in that perfect face would render her useless to the High and the Mighty of the South." Azif Bae himself followed his voice across the camp, pampered and gross, dressed in bright silks and fur trimmed-boots of the most exquisite green leather.

A dandy, thought Morinae. He clutched a gnawed chicken leg in his fist. The slaver waddled to the prone Princess, and with greasy fingers turned her face this way and that, looking for blemishes. Next, he pulled at her full lips to better see her teeth. "Open your mouth, slave," he commanded, and she did, so he could inspect her perfectly white and even teeth. "No damage done, no damage done." The slaver wheezed with obvious relief, though his eyes, so dark as to be near black, and almost lost in folds of fat, glared venom at the captain.

His inspection complete, Azif Bae ignored the girl completely, and returned his attention to the chicken leg, grease smearing his jowls. "Come, E'bok," he said. "Come break your fast with me and we shall plan our days route." Just like that, the slavers mercurial temper was calmed, and he led his Captain towards the cook fires where a slave was busy over the flames with spits and pans.

Morinae shook her head slightly to clear her thoughts. She fought back the tears that swam in her eyes, more from frustration and impotent rage, than fear or pain.

The sun was now full up, and its warming rays began to dispel the chill of the night. Awkwardly due to her shackles, Morinae got to her feet, and was at once greeted by three of her fellow slaves. The girls were quick and attentive to her needs, a grim parody of the life to which she was used, when maids and ladies in waiting had been at her beck and call.

The sisters Briss and Brissett, both simple girls, perhaps in their late teens, were kind hearted and in wonder that they waited upon a *real* princess, even if that princess were a fellow slave, chained and bound for the same market and uncertain future. The third slave was well known and loved by Morinae, Sha'haan. She was a lovely young woman, with eyes of sapphire blue, and glossy black hair now tangled a little, and no longer flowing in the exquisite ringlets that she'd worn at the Court of Asgulun. She was in her early twenties, just a little older than Morinae herself, and had been a close friend and confidant since the Princess was a child. Sha'haan had been sat reading in the enclosed Palace Garden with Morinae when E'bok and several others had stormed in, and before they could even cry out in alarm, had been restrained, bound and gagged, with silken bags tied tight upon their heads.

Now, Sha'haan shared her captivity. While Briss and Brissett fetched water and a meagre breakfast of porridge, Sha'haan took the opportunity to speak quietly in the ear of the Princess, taking out a brush and beginning to comb through the tangles of Morinae's golden hair.

"You must be careful, Morinae," she whispered. That she used her name rather than her title gave testament to their closeness. "Do not push E'bok too far. He is a brute, though he has an educated tongue. I think perhaps he is high born, but he has no morals whatever."

Morinae nodded numbly. She could see the bruises around her friend's eyes, the cut to her lip from speaking out of turn two days past. And now for the first time, she saw the rips in Sha'haan's once rich clothes, the mark of the birch clear upon her shoulder. Morinae reached out tentatively to offer solace to her friend, but Sha'haan shook her head and gripped Morinae's hands in her own. "Do not worry about me. I am worth more in ransom than upon the slavers block. Already I would think that my father has been contacted, and a price for my release set. I can endure a little hardship, knowing that my release is all but assured." Now those striking blue eyes filled with a new concern, and as she ran the brush through Morinae's hair, she spoke on, softly.

"I have heard much over the last day or two. These guards that escort the slave train talk a little loudly when in their cups, and one of my duties is to keep those cups filled." She smiled at her friend's shocked expression. "Relax, they are none the wiser that I add less water to the wine than I've been told to." Sha'haan continued to comb Morinae's hair; to any casual observer, all her attention was upon that task. But Sha'haan was as canny as lovely, and she spoke softly so none but the Princess could hear.

"I overheard the cook bragging to the men, of how he had been there when a fellow from the Palace of Asgulun had approached Azif Bae, and promised a casket of gold to ensure that you were taken in secret, and that you were slain and your body never to be found. The cook also told how Azif Bae had taken the gold, the casket bigger than his head, then, along with Captain E'bok and a small crew of slavers, he had been let into the palace in the dead of night by the same fellow. Their guide led them by secret ways to the gardens to wait for you, before leaving them to get on with their dark deeds. The rest you know as well as I, capture and a midnight crossing of the Sea of Storms and then a forced march this many days through the Plains of Loss. I no longer even know what land or which country we are in."

"Who would have access to the palace? Who could possibly get armed men through the halls to the gardens?" Morinae was shocked, though she didn't doubt the information that Sha'haan gave her. "Who could do such a thing?"

"There were no names mentioned, Princess," Sha'haan cast a wary look over her shoulder to ensure that there were no eaves-droppers. She saw E'bok by the cooking fires, helping himself to a ladle of porridge; most of the guards were sat around eating breakfast, or sewing their socks, mending harness or seeing to the edge of their blades, the endless mundane tasks of armed men on the road.

The majority of the slaves sat in abject misery, both men and women, most sold to the slaver to pay for crimes or bad debts to money lenders, or worse, to appease the blood-sucking banks of the cities. Of Azif Bae, Sha'haan could see no sign. The slaver was probably in his tent, dreaming of his profits, even as he filled his face.

"No names," continued Sha'haan, "but the cook did mention that their palace paymaster wore a necklace of golden links, so thick that if sold it would bring enough coin to buy a ship! Also, that his hair was as black as pitch, as were his eyes, and he carried himself in a haughty way that set everyone's teeth on edge." she ran the brush through Morinae't

"Juvaal!" Morinae blurted in shock, for she knew well whom had just been described, then quickly covered her mouth with her hand, the silver chains of her manacles rattling, her green eyes wide at the revelation. "That is my half-brother," she said quieter now, but no less impassioned. She recognised him from the description, his haughty manner, the vanity for gold. She had seen him many a time wearing that great golden chain. "We have been sold into slavery by my own blood." Her voice quavered, and then her brows furrowed as she digested the news. "But if I was to be killed, why am I here, being pampered and on my way to the gods know what sort of fate in the South?"

"That is the doing of Azif Bae," replied Sha'haan. "He has taken the coin from Juvaal, and now he will take more coin from the kings and princes in the Southern climes, when he sells you there. Your beauty is famed worldwide Princess, as is your wit. It is no secret that your father has relied upon your council for the past few years, and that your council has been sound and brought prosperity to Asgulun. You will be a prize indeed for any with the coin to meet the slaver's price."

Morinae found herself grinning a little. So Juvaal had sold her, so he could take her place as advisor to their father, no doubt. And then in turn had met treachery in the form of the slaver Azif Bae. Vipers, the pair of them, she thought.

The road to the South was long. There would be time enough

to win her freedom, and then return to Asgulun. For now, she would content herself with thoughts of the retribution that she would mete out to her half-brother.

Sha'haan finished with her hair and packed away the brush with their other belongings, all donated by the slaver, not out of any charitable notion, but to ensure that his goods were kept as pristine as could be whilst on the trail.

Morinae took a moment to survey the camp. She counted twelve guards including E'bok; of the master of the slavers there was still no sign. There were several fires, around which lounged men dressed in scraps of mail and boiled leather, hard men well used to giving out beatings to their bound charges. Over twenty horses were hobbled close by, cropping on the rich grass that grew thick and lush on the Plains of Loss. As she looked beyond the camp, the grasslands stretched on, seemingly eternal. They were headed roughly South-East. She shaded her eyes against the newly risen sun to look that way, and in the distance, she could see the dark smudge that resembled a tree line, and then, she had no doubt, there would be tougher terrain, perhaps rivers and streams, much more cover to mask an escape.

The sisters returned with her porridge, bowing and giggling before departing upon other errands. Some slaves were given quite a bit of freedom in the camp. After all, where would they go? How far could they get, shackled as they were, before a horseman could ride them down? Lost in thought, Morinae began to eat. She would be careful, as Sha'haan advised. She would eat to keep up her strength, would do as she was told, and act the good little slave.

Until the chance came for freedom, then she would be gone from this foul company, and if the chance came to slit the throat of E'bok or even the slaver Azif Bae as she made her escape, so much the better.

As the camp broke and made ready to press on to the distant

tree line, it was a grim and resolute Morinae that mounted the proffered horse. Once the chains were removed from her ankles, her wrists remained shackled. A bored looking guard kept a tight hold of the reins, leading her into the line. She was the only captive allowed a horse, Azif Bae was as concerned for her feet as he was for her hair, it would seem.

The Princess rode in the middle of the caravan. Ahead, at the front of the line, was E'bok riding side by side with the gross peacock, Azif Bae. Walking beside Morinae was Sha'haan. Outriders came and went often; this was after all a slave train and the goods being transported were valuable. Had it not been for the chains at her wrists, and the oaf leading her, Morinae could have almost believed that she was at home, on her fathers' country estate.

Outwardly, the Princess seemed relaxed, resigned to her fate.

Inwardly she seethed. They would all rue the day they had sought to sell her off like a prized cow.

* * *

MIDDAY CAME and went without incident, save a brief stop to snatch cold rations. The outriders returned, and it seemed all ahead was clear, and soon they were once more heading off. The trees in the near distance were visible now. They were approaching the outer edge of a huge forest. Morinae could just make out ancient oaks, their great branches spreading wide, twisted elms so high that they must have been centuries old.

It was just what Morinae had hoped for.

Soon enough they were moving steadily through the trees, The vanguard led the train along what may have been a pathway, or a game trail. Whatever, it wound its way around great trees with branches so low that Morinae was forced to lean over the neck of her horse to save being scraped out of the saddle. They travelled up great mounds of moss-covered earth and into dips filled with nettles and brambles. The sun began its descent into the western sky, and Morinae was aware of birdsong, and the rustling of leaves and branches high above in the verdant canopy. She caught a glimpse of a fox, peering from the undergrowth upon the trails verge, its keen eye's bright and alert.

The motion of the horse, the creak of the saddle leather, the warm afternoon breeze upon her skin, all lulled the Princess. It was all she could do to rouse herself when Sha'haan began to speak to her, still walking easily beside the horse.

"Do you think the troubles with Ashanarr will have escalated whilst you have been gone my Princess?" she asked.

When Morinae looked down at her friend, she saw the concern writ clear in her eyes, and the way she gnawed at her lower lip. She knew full well what she meant of course; Ashanarr had always been a peaceful neighbour, a mere twenty leagues distant over the Narrow Sea upon Asgulun's Eastern shore. Peaceful that was, until half a year past when with autumn there came a new Queen to Ashanarr, following the sudden demise of good King Betod's first wife. With this new Queen came tensions. First it was arguments over rights of fishing in the Narrow Sea where before, there had always been fish aplenty for both nations. More followed.

Soon, it seemed Asgulun could do no right by its neighbour, and then came word that Ashanarr was building a fleet of new ships, and not for the purpose of fishing. Reports came through to Asgulun that soldiers were massing across the sea, that mercenaries were being hired, that an army was gathering, and it was not only Asgulun that Ashanarr was facing off against. Its neighbour by land, Ish, had also come under a baleful eye. Ish was a tiny nation, hardly three days ride across, a land of peace and plenty. Ish had petitioned the King of Asgulun for aid, and Morinae's father had agreed to help due in no small way to the suggestion of the Princess.

It was Prince Bryann, the bastard son of a favoured concubine, who had been given the task of preparing the Asgulun for war. It had fallen to Morinae to seek a peace with ambassadors from both little Ish and Ashanarr, though for all her skills in the political arena, it was to no avail, war seemed inevitable. Bryann was the perfect choice to lead Asgulun, much to the chagrin of the prince, Juvaal, for Bryann was loved by the people, loved by the court and by the army, which he commanded as general. He was also loved by Sha'haan, though that love was unrequited, for her station was too high to marry a bastard, even if he were the son of a king.

"I am sure that my dear brother Bryann is safe and well just yet, Sha'haan." She saw a blush in her friend's cheek, and smiled sadly. "There is a way to go yet before a war is declared. Surely even Betod and this new Queen of his must see the folly of war. There are never any true victors in warfare: casualties, loss of crops, the cost of paying and equipping an army...the list goes on and on." Morinae reached down and squeezed her friend's hand reassuringly, "and let us not forget that my brother is a brilliant tactician, and a great soldier. No, there is no need to fear on that score." She smiled and hoped she looked more confident than she really felt. This new Queen of Ashanarr had so far proven unpredictable to say the least. Nay, thought Morinae, she seemed vindictive and manipulative, and rumours of her outbursts in her husband's court had reached even the shores of Asgulun.

Even as she ducked beneath a leafy bough, laughing a little as a hare bounded across the trail, she thought only of escape, of her beloved Asgulun on the brink of war, and her Father at the mercy of his own scheming Queen, the mother of Juvaal. She must return at all costs. Her father was far from his best, his mind often wandered, and he had begun to doze off at a moment's notice, at council meetings, whilst speaking to the merchants' guilds and even whilst eating. Morinae dreaded to think what mischief Juvaal would be up to in her absence.

She became aware that the vanguard had stopped. Standing in her stirrups she could see that they had arrived at a natural clearing. A stream some ten paces across chuckled merrily over pebbles and stones. Great willows bent their majestic heads to the water, their boughs trailing in the stream. The escort motioned for her to dismount, and she was more than happy to oblige. Standing on her toes, stretching her long legs to work the muscles unused to long hours of riding.

The slaves were ushered to the stream, where many fell onto the riverbank, relieved that the day's long march was at an end. Morinae and Sha'haan watched the poor souls as they scooped the cold water to their faces. The Princess could only wonder at what was to become of them. The prettiest of the girls might end up at pleasure houses, not a kind fate, but then Morinae had to admit to herself that she wasn't privy to each slave's circumstances. Perhaps a pleasure house would not be so bad for some of them?

As for the sisters Briss and Brissett, who even now were giggling together as they filled water skins for the cook, very likely they would become house slaves, working in a kitchen or somesuch. Their lives probably wouldn't change that much. Maybe it would be an improvement for them? Morinae had heard them talking between themselves, and it seemed that their father had been the landlord of a flea-ridden tavern, he had used his daughters as skivvies, and was not slow to beat them if he thought them tardy with their chores. He had drunk himself into an early grave, and left his daughters in such debt that they could never be free of it. Perhaps the magistrate that closed down the tavern and put the sisters into slavery as punishment for their fathers' shortcomings had done them a service. Morinae watched the pair splash water over each other, laughing like children. She hoped they would find kindly masters.

It didn't take long for the camp to take shape. Tents were pitched, fires lit, and horses hobbled close by, with bags of feed hung on their noses. It was an efficient camp. The guards took the main body of the slaves nearer the horses, where long spikes were driven deep into the sward. Soon the slaves were shackled to the spikes, and their bondage secure.

Morinae, being a favoured slave, along with Sha'haan, was allowed a blanket near a fire. Had it been raining, then a rude tent would have been offered, but as the evening was quite warm and the sky cloudless, she would be expected to sleep under the stars. She knew E'bok would have guards watching her, so for now she would play a dutiful slave; she would yet have them thinking that she had accepted her position, she would let them think that her spirit was broken. Then when they least expected it, she would be away. The forest was huge and dense. She would only need a few minutes' head start and they would never catch her, even shackled as she was.

It wasn't long before Briss (or was it Brissett?) brought her a bowl of thin soup and a crust of bread. Tasteless fare, but the Princess ate every morsel and drank every drop. She had to keep up her strength, ready for when the opportunity of escape presented itself. She was pleased that Sha'haan too finished every crumb. Morinae would ensure that her friend came with her when she made her escape; the thought of leaving her behind had never occurred to her.

For now, there were too many eyes upon her, the guard's vigilance was too keen, this being the first night in the forest. But *soon*, she promised herself silently, *soon*.

As the sun set behind the trees to the west, Morinae lay upon her blanket, aware that Sha'haan was close by, and watched the stars steadily carpet the sky, listening to the sounds of the camp gradually still. Sleep found her soon enough, and her dreams were sweet: of revenge upon her scheming step-brother.

Morinae slept fitfully. She awoke with the dawn light, and soon fell into the routine of the camp, though her resolve was undaunted. Briss and Brissett were already up and active, fetching water, stirring pots of porridge over the cook-fire. Sha'haan stretched beside her, and then stood, stamping her feet to dispel the morning chill, her chains rattling cheerfully. Morinae arose too, and cast a watchful eye around the camp. She saw the Captain, E'bok walking amongst the still sleeping guards, nudging them with an ungentle toe.

The camp was sluggish at rousing. The clearing was idyllic, the bird song sweet as they welcomed in the new day, and the surrounding trees seemed to offer protection, their dense foliage and thick boles a comforting barrier. Only the Captain seemed fully awake, and soon enough he was bellowing orders at his men, shouting at the slaves to get on their feet and make their way to the stream. Seeing the rag-tag line of dejected souls, each connected to the next by lengths of chain at their ankles, soon brought Morinae out of her reverie.

This clearing was far from an idyllic camping ground, and Morinae once more faced her new reality. She was relatively well cared for, but as the line of new slaves trudged past her, on the way to the stream, she could see the wounds upon their ankles caused by the shackles they wore, the bruises to their faces where a fist or a boot had been used to administer punishment. Morinae stood helpless as she watched the camp awake. She balled her hands into fists at her sides; she felt tears threaten to spill down her cheek as she watched the wretched procession pass by.

"Hurry along you two!" The voice of E'bok sliced across the camp, and Morinae felt herself flinch involuntarily. She cursed herself for allowing the captain to have such an effect upon her.

She must be stronger. Her feet picked up the pace as she hurried along with Sha'haan to the stream

The numb routine took over: washing at the stream, the meagre breakfast, breaking down the camp even as the sun rose above the trees. Morinae made her way to the horses, finding the chestnut gelding she had been assigned. The steed made a soft blowing sound as her chained hands gently stroked the side of its face. She climbed into the saddle with the help of Sha'haan, and then sat waiting for the guard that held her reins to clamber onto his own mount. Another day was about to begin, another day of travel farther and farther away from her homeland.

The slaves were chivvied into line, the pack horses were loaded and gathered, their pans and wares clanking and banging. The horses neighed loudly and their riders swore and jested with one another as they began their daily march. Ahead, as ever, the Slaver bounced along on his poor, overburdened steed. E'bok rode up and down the line, keeping a close eye upon the slaves, and ensuring the mounted guards were alert.

Sha'haan walked beside Morinae, her hand resting upon the stirrup. It was as the slave Captain trotted by, his face like stone, though his eyes hot as they fell upon the two high born ladies of Asgulun, that Morinae became aware of a sudden change in the atmosphere around them. At first, she thought perhaps it was just E'bok's leering eyes that had unsettled her, but no, she was used to his stares and veiled threats, and she knew that she was safe enough from him and the other slavers, as her value would be impaired should she show signs of brutality. It took her a moment more to register what the matter was, and she saw the same thoughts cross the face of the captain.

The sounds of the forest had stilled.

Morinae could hear no bird song, no rustling in the undergrowth, that constant and comforting commotion that had been present since they entered the woodland. Save the creak of saddle leather, the jangle of tack and chains, the scuffling footsteps of the slaves and the muted clopping of the horses' hooves upon the grass, there was silence.

E'bok met her gaze, and she could see he shared her concern. Seconds seemed to drag by. A gentle zephyr whispered through the trees, pulling at Morinae's golden hair with soft fingers.

The strange peace of the moment was shattered by a piercing scream from the rear of the line. Morinae flinched at the sound and turned her head just in time to see a guard topple from his horse, a long, black feathered shaft sticking from his chest.

Everything became chaos.

There were more screams as two slaves went down, arrows thudding into them. Instinctively, the rest of the slaves tried to run, but they were each shackled to the next. They tripped and fell, clawed and screamed in panic and fear as more arrows flashed from the trees.

Morinae watched in horror as men and women fell around her. Within moments, the trail was carnage. She could hear E'bok yelling at the men, saw him draw his sword, even as the trees spewed out charging, screaming figures. Bandits. Outlaws. The very dregs of humanity, savage and lustful in their greed.

The guards rallied, drawing swords, and for a second or two Morinae thought the advantage of their horses, armour, and discipline might help win through.

But the hope was brief lived. As more and more of the rogues leapt from the trees, it soon became a rout. Several of the outlaws headed towards Morinae and Sha'haan, wild haired with unkempt beards, wearing filthy rags, eyes mad with bloodlust. The leader of their group looked more beast than man, a head taller than Morinae, and built like a bull. Both Sha'haan and Morinae screamed in terror as he raced towards them. He came within ten feet, when suddenly a horse barrelled into him, crushing his ribs and sending him flying like a broken toy.

E'bok reigned in his horse and chopped down with his sword at another brigand, Morinae watched in shock and horror as the Captain laid about him, shouting orders to his men as he did so. So skilled was he with the sword from horseback, that soon enough, the outlaws were keeping a wide berth about him, making for easier targets. The slaves were helpless before the onslaught, those chained together died together, without hope.

Terror loaned strength to the arm of the Princess as she leaned down and grabbed the wrist of her friend Sha'haan, already kicking her heels into the flanks of her horse as she did so. Even hindered by the chains she wore, Sha'haan was able to scramble up behind the saddle, and they were off. Morinae curled her fingers in the horse's thick mane, and clung on, with her friend hanging on to her as best she could. The horse shared their terror, its eyes rolling wide as it ran through the tumult, the screaming and the smell of blood.

Morinae had only brief glimpses of the caravan as she bent low over the neck of the panicked animal, they were more than enough. The raiders killed indiscriminately: they were there for gold, for food, for whatever they were able to steal. A prisoner was just another mouth to feed, easier to kill. She cast frantic eyes about her. Looking for the sweet sisters, Briss and Brissett, she could see little amongst the carnage. She hoped they had made a break, finding refuge in the forest, even as she herself hoped to do. She knew it was a forlorn hope.

And then she was in the trees, keeping low over the neck of her mount, dodging the sweeping foliage. The horse thundered on, its breath loud and harsh as it strained for speed, yet leaped and swerved over and around trees and bushes, roots and rocks. Morinae was aware that her horse was following another, perhaps more than one. She knew also that there was at least one behind them too, and as the brigands were on foot, it had to be one of the slavers, but at that moment she didn't really care. At that moment the slavers were better than the brigands.

At last, they slowed down. They must have travelled miles at the breakneck pace. She could hear Sha'haan's panting breath in her ear, feel the heat upon her neck. The two riders were spent, their nerves fraught, stretched to breaking. Morinae was aware of a rider trotting past, gathering up her hanging reins as he did. She saw it was one of E'bok's chief cronies, a sneering, squint-eyed specimen by the name of Black Deeds. She didn't know how he had come about such a name, but as he cast a sidelong glance her way, and she saw the merciless set of his face, she worried that she may yet find out.

Just then, E'bok himself came trotting along the trail, his hair unkempt, blood was thick on the sleeve of his black leather tunic, more splashed over his face, but that didn't stop the wide white grin that he showed as he saw Morinae and Sha'haan. He looked past them, counting survivors, even as the gross Azif Bae came wheezing and sweating to rest his horse beside that of the girls.

"That was a close call was it not, Captain?" called the Slave Master once he had found his breath. He took a water skin from the pommel horn of his saddle and leant back on the cantle, drinking noisily. Sated, he smacked his lips with relish. "At least we kept the valuables, eh, E'bok? Not like that time on the Weeping Plains, three years back, when half the damned slaves were taken by lions eh?" He chuckled at the memory. "So many lions!"

"We were lucky to break even on that venture," E'bok replied.

The Captain motioned farther along the trail. "There's another stream just ahead, we can rest there and take stock, give any stragglers time to catch up." With that, he pulled on the reins and turned his horse into the forest. Black Deeds followed as did Azif Bae, and a couple more of the surviving guards.

True to his word, E'bok led them to a shallow stream running fast through the lush sward and trees, letting their mounts drink now they had cooled somewhat after the mad chase. After half an hour or so, only one other guard had appeared; the cook, as it happened. Morinae wished it could have been any of the other guards, if it meant more of the tasteless fare that he served up.

Morinae let her eyes wander around the men, as she and Sha'haan huddled together by the stream. There were just six of them now, and one of them was the Slaver: his power lay in his purse and coin, not in any useful trail skill.

E'bok and Azif Bae had their heads together as they made their plans for the continuing journey. The other four men were gathered together, their voices too low for Morinae to hear, but the look that Black Deeds gave the two of them was enough to send shivers through her, as if spiders were crawling over her scalp. Deeds muttered something to his fellows, and they laughed, a harsh rasping sound, with little humour to it. Deeds stood up, a smirk upon his lean face. He made his way towards the two slaves, glancing towards the Captain and the Slaver, then back to Morinae.

Hard eyes. Cruel and hungry.

Black Deeds licked his lips in an exaggerated fashion, as though anticipating a favourite delicacy. His eyes burned as they took in the Princess. Even dressed in a simple tunic stained with travel, baggy shapeless woollen trews, Morinae was more than eye-catching. Her golden hair still shone, though it was knotted after the mad ride through the forest. Her fine boned face was exquisite, beneath mud and sweat. Her green eyes shone bright with fear as they met those of the approaching Black Deeds. Seeing the fear there, Deeds' grin grew wider, his eyes growing crueller.

Deeds began to undo his belt, his intent clear. "Killing has always put me in the mood for a little spice," he said, letting his belt fall to the ground. He reached quickly for Morinae. Bizarrely, she had time to notice the fingernails on the grasping hand were dirty and broken. Then, those fingers curled around the neck of her tunic, and yanked mercilessly, not only tearing the garment almost in two but throwing Morinae to the ground with a pained shriek. The sight of her flesh excited the guard all the more, and he fell on her like a beast, his grimy fingers fumbling with her breasts, his mouth trying to close on hers, all the while trying to drag down her trews.

To Morinae, the world descended into kaleidoscopic madness: terror, and pain, overwhelmed her. She beat at him with her fists and raked him with her nails, but he seemed impervious, made of steel, not flesh. Deeds tried to force his tongue past her lips, bruising in its brutality, his breath as foul and hot as a furnace, his hands scratching and tearing at her clothes, at her flesh. She uttered a piercing scream. For an instant, Deeds was startled by the shrill sound and rocked back a little, though a grin still split his face.

Events seemed to speed up. Morinae was still numb. She screamed again as Deeds laughed at her helplessness. Sha'haan launched herself upon Deeds' back, whipping the loose chain binding her wrists about the would-be rapist's neck.

Even as Sha'haan struggled with Deeds, E'bok's raging voice bellowed threats and fury. Morinae could hear the other guards too, shouting encouragement to Deeds, their voices deeper with their passion. Surreally, over all the sounds, she could hear a high-pitched wailing, and knew the sound issued from the gross slaver Azif Bae, as he stood watching his valuable goods being molested and ruined. He peered from behind slug-like fingers as his caravan descended into madness, and he keened and wailed.

Through wide eyes she saw Deeds viciously smash his elbow back, saw the blood suddenly erupt from Sha'haan's nose and mouth, heard the sickening crack as her friend's head snapped back. She watched in paralysed horror as Sha'haan collapsed, lifeless, to the ground.

Morinae could not move. She was frozen in fear, a fear beyond anything she had ever imagined. She wanted to curl into a ball, to ease the pain in her body and the terror of watching her friend robbed of life, but she was unable to do even that.

And then E'bok was there, his boot caught Deeds in the face, sending him sprawling, spitting curses as he tried to crawl away, but E'bok followed him relentlessly kicking and stamping.

Morinae couldn't breathe, her throat was too tight, her heart beating so fast it was like the galloping of a horse within her chest. For an instant, just a moment, she dared to think herself safe, and then the cook appeared silently behind E'bok, a great knife in his white knuckled fist. Morinae tried to warn the Captain, tried to shout, but all that issued from her lips was a low, wordless moan. The cook struck fast, pulling E'bok's long hair back, exposing his throat. The knife sliced and then the cook leaped back as E'bok spasmed, his eyes wide with shock. He flailed about him, a wretched gurgling noise filling glade. E'bok went to his knees, though even as his life flowed out in a crimson tide, the Captain tried to strike back. The cook danced away from the dying man, staying just out of reach of his blade.

E'bok took time to die.

Not quick like poor Sha'haan, who now stared lifelessly through her sapphire eyes at the next world. Morinae couldn't stop looking at her friend, great wracking sobs suddenly bursting from her. She began to crawl away from the scene of sudden death and carnage.

She moaned in pain and fear as she heard voices behind her. Black Deeds' voice. "Captain E'bok." She heard the killer laughing, heard a meaty thud, and knew that the dead Captain was being kicked, again and again. Black Deeds was laughing loud now. "Not so tough now, eh, Captain?" Kick and thud. "No more hard marches and poor rations from you now, eh?" Kick and thud.

Morinae continued to crawl. She could hear the others laughing with Deeds, she could hear Azif Bae's shrill pleading as they advanced upon him. Snatches of their taunting voices reached her. There was much talk of gold, of missing wages, of how they would carve up the fat slaver like a hog. Morinae crawled and crawled, like a wounded animal, all thoughts gone from her save escaping, getting somewhere safe, somewhere to curl in a ball and shut out the world.

Rough hands suddenly grabbed her hair, pulling her head up viciously. She half expected a blade across her slim throat, an end to the terror, to be sent to the afterlife with Sha'haan and E'bok. But as she opened her eyes, she was confronted by the bruised and battered face of Black Deeds. The cook was hovering at his shoulder, shaking with excitement as he drank in the sight of the half-naked girl, cowering upon the bank of the stream.

Deeds grinned widely, and the Princess saw that a tooth was broken, where one hadn't been earlier. Good for E'bok, she thought. A spark of defiance was lit within her, as she saw the evidence of the beating Deeds had just taken. The defiance was short lived. Deeds spoke to her, his voice gloating, rasping. "We have unfinished business, you and me Princess, so don't be rushing off now." He cast a sidelong glance over his shoulder at the two men advancing on Azif Bae. "Check his saddlebags!" he called, "and the Captains', neither of those two would be far from their coin!" Still grinning, he turned back to Morinae, and his next words chilled her more than ever. "Your brother Juvaal sends his regards."

Morinae stared, wide-eyed.

"You would never have reached the slaver's block Princess. Your brother was sure that fat old Azif over there would try and double his money, put you on the market so to speak... Me and

Cookie here, and a few others of the guards, we were his insurance against you making it to the South." Now Deeds knelt over the Princess, his face only inches from hers, his sour breath hot and damp. "He wanted you dead in the desert, buried in the sand, but I reckon dead is dead, and in the forest, the foxes and the crows will pick your corpse clean soon enough. No one will ever know what became of you, or how you screamed in the last few hours of your pampered, miserable life."

"Get on with it, Deeds" hissed the cook. "I want a turn!"

"I'm savouring the moment Cookie," Deeds shot back. "I can smell her fear, royal fear. Pampered terror." He breathed in deep through his nose, as if sniffing a favourite bloom. "Can you smell the terror Cookie? It's sweet as any wine." He leaned closer and once again smelled her neck, her face, her tangled hair. "Sweet."

"Enough with the sniffing, Deeds. There's still a forest full of bloody outlaws that could be on our trail. Get to it, then rest of us can take a turn, then we can be off with a full purse and know the job's well done."

Black Deeds closed his eyes, and took a calming breath. Morinae tried to squirm from beneath him, but he was too heavy, too strong. "You take all the fun out of everything Cookie." Deeds said at last. "But you have a point about those forest folks. Right, hold the bitch still...."

Morinae began to scream.

CHAPTER 11
DESTINY

Steeleye sighted along the arrow, and controlled his breathing. He pulled back the string a fraction farther, and then waited. Ten paces away, swimming unawares in the crystal-clear waters of the stream, he spied a fat brown trout, and Steeleye meant to be cooking it soon enough. Any second now...

He had been wandering through this forest for six days, keeping close to the streams, setting snares along the game trails, foraging for roots and mushrooms and herbs as he went. Life was good, he thought. He didn't know where he was: somewhere warmer than the North, that was for sure. Here, spring was turning to summer, the grass was sprinkled with nodding Bluebells, dainty Yellow Rattles, pink Corncockle, and slim stemmed Columbine. Their heady scent filled the air. The sound of bees lazily zig-zagging from bloom to bloom, the merry chirrup of a thousand birds in the tree tops, were the only sounds of life that he had heard these six days, those and the scurrying of rabbits and hares in the undergrowth, the careful tread of an occasional soft eyed-deer.

Six days ago, he had defeated the Stormchild and was gifted

the finest blade ever made. The Morriggu had been true to her word, and had taken him from that strange, many mooned world with its green and yellow skies, and he had awoken refreshed and healed of wounds, lying beneath the spreading branches of an ancient oak. The oak was so old it may well have seen the times of Aihaab and witnessed the Gods walking the land for a final time.

He had checked the sword was present as soon as he awoke. It rested in his worn wooden scabbard, plain to look upon, yet when he let his fingers curl around the dull metal of the hilt, he could almost feel energy pulsing there. A wondrous piece of smithery it was; its beauty lay in its simplicity. Wondrous and terrible in equal measure. Yet for the job he had in hand, a terrible weapon would be necessary, he was sure.

Once fully awake, he had surveyed his surroundings, and was pleased to see the idyllic woodland. What was it the Morriggu had last said to him? He would find his guide to lead him on the path? He had looked for Wolf, but there was no sign of the lupine creature. He felt a pang of regret at that, for he had come to feel an attachment to the beast. As he had no idea where he was, nor where he was heading, he struck out on a course that he thought was downwards, and within half a day came across a stream. His bow and water skin were with him when he awoke, and he'd smiled as he bent the yew and fastened the string.

Since then, he had followed the course of the stream as it meandered East, then South, then East again, its crystal-clear water cold and refreshing, the trout plentiful and fat. Easy victims for a fine archer that knew his trade. Life had settled into an easy routine for him: walk and hunt, eat and walk, eat then sleep. He mulled over his predicament often. He thought of Freija, and her cruel death. His jaw set at such times. Had his soul not been held ransom, he would have merrily led the Northmen to battle with the Grimm and their ilk. He had thought his vengeance sated with the killing of Kuur'shock, but it was not the case.

His dreams remained troubled. Though he no longer stood upon the ramparts of the Fae Keep in his nightmares, instead he would sit upon a great horse upon a plain of golden grass. He was dressed in the trappings of war, the sword of the Stormchild in his hand, raised high, searing fire pulsing from the glowing blade. At his back was a host of mounted warriors, each bathed in a bright silver aura. Ahead of him, over the golden plain, a great shadowy horde of gibbering lunacy and hate: The Grimm, endless in number, their lust for blood driving them into a mindless frenzy. Seated upon a great winged serpent at the head of the Horde was the silver haired beauty from his nightmares. She wore her familiar scarlet plate armour, though now, it seemed to run with blood; Steeleye knew it to be the blood of the thousands slain by the Grimm Horde.

Her sapphire gaze searched him out each night, a triumphant smile upon her lips.

"Soon brother, soon shall come the days of blood! Look to the South, I shall come from the South, with a Host the likes of which this world has never seen!"

STEELEYE SIGHTED along his arrow at the fat brown trout. Even before he let fly, he knew his aim was true, and that it would be fish for breakfast.

The screams came from farther downstream. A woman's scream, raised in terror. It took Steeleye a moment to register the sound as real, after so long in the wilderness alone. The screaming came again, persistent and shrill, filled with pain and horror.

Steeleye was galvanised into action, the skewered trout forgotten. He ran along the bank of the stream, drawing another arrow as he went. His booted feet slipping and sliding upon the grass, but the pitch of the scream drew him on faster and faster.

He was aware of other voices, men's deep guttural cursing, harsh laughter, a strange, piping sound, wailing, but the anguish and terror in the scream drove him on.

It was as he rounded a bend in the stream, his reckless advance shielded from view by thick bushes, that he wondered how many men were here. More than one, that was for sure. It could be an army for all he knew, yet the screaming went on and on, and Steeleye ran full tilt into a company of Slavers.

He took in the scene in an instant. He saw a raven-haired woman sprawled upon the sward, her face a mask of blood. With just a glance he could tell the poor wretch was past help. Another body lay close by, this one a hired sword by the looks of him. He lay on his back, sightless eyes staring at the sky, a jagged maw beneath his bearded chin. The shrill piping sound came again, and he saw two rough looking men, dressed in mail and leather, pushing and shoving a fat peacock of a man, all coloured silk and necklaces and rings. They laughed in his face as they began to punch and kick. Without thinking, Steeleye let fly his arrow at the men.

But he did not wait to see his arrow hit the mark. He ran, not towards the peacock and his attackers, but instead at the two men that were engrossed in trying to strip the clothes from a screaming girl, even as she tried to crawl away, sliding down the bank into the icy water of the stream.

"Hurry up, Deeds!" shouted one, the shorter of the two. His voice had a hungry whine. Steeleye barrelled into him, his shoulder catching him in the chest, throwing him into the stream. The one called Deeds moved fast, faster than Steeleye expected, and it was only by an inch that the sword missed him. Steeleye rolled aside, coming to his feet with his own sword drawn, his face like thunder.

"Hurry up, Cookie!" snarled Deeds at his companion, who was now getting to his feet, drawing a long-bladed dagger. Steeleye saw the screaming girl was slowly crawling away. He saw her chains, the tattered clothing and the scratches upon her exposed flesh, her long golden hair was in disarray and covering much of her face. He could see beauty there, but also terror in her wide, green eyes.

The would-be rapist called Deeds launched a blistering attack, even as his companion, the one called Cookie, attacked at Steeleye's blind side, but Steeleye was prepared for such a move, and was fast enough to parry Deeds' attack and duck beneath Cookie's dagger thrust. Cookie died quickly as Steeleye spun away, the dull silver blade licking out, taking the man clean through the heart.

Twice more, Deeds attacked, and twice more Steeleye parried, keeping a wary eye upon the fourth assailant who was now running from the prone dandy, his sword above his head, a wild scream on his lips. Steeleye feinted a cut at Deeds, who, in a panic, fell back tripping over his britches as they dropped from his waist. Steeleye met the charge of the fourth man with a charge of his own; sparks flew as the blades met. *Clang, clang.* The third time the blades met, the Stormchild's blade cut clean through the other man's steel as if it were glass, and sliced deep into the man's collar, hacking into the chest. The guard died with a look of wide-eyed shock.

Steeleye swung his blade through the air several times, crimson droplets sprayed upon the grass. At last, he turned to the man called Deeds. The fellow was hastily fastening his belt, his eyes narrowed as he sought out an avenue of escape. There wasn't any. Only the yellow-haired stranger, who had already killed three of his companions, and had humiliated Deeds into the bargain. For all his faults, and the list was long indeed, Black Deeds didn't lack for courage. Seeing that there could be no escape, the stranger standing between him and the horses, Deeds gripped his sword tight, drew his dagger too, and launched himself into the attack.

* * *

FROM WHERE SHE LAY, half in the stream and half out, peering through her fingers, Morinae watched Black Deeds die. She saw her abuser quick as a cat stabbing and swinging, but his whistling steel met only air, as the yellow haired stranger ducked and weaved away from the blows. And then it was done. The stranger stepped in close, catching the dagger hand in a vice like grip, and Morinae watched transfixed as the stranger's blade burst from Deeds' spine in a fountain of gore. Slowly the blade twisted, and then withdrew, leaving Deeds to crumple onto the grass, staring sightlessly at the Princess.

For long moments nothing happened, Morinae lay still as a statue, her breathing coming in short ragged gasps. Panic still surged through her veins. What did this mean now? Who was this stranger, a rescuer? Or was he yet another tormentor? Her heart beat so fast and loud she felt it would soon burst. She felt her senses swim, and her vision darken. No! She must not faint. She found her eyes drifting to the face of the stranger, and found his clear blue eyes were locked upon her. They remained thus, and long seconds passed. Gradually, Morinae began to hope that the worst of her ordeal was over, and her hands slowly came away from her tear-streaked face.

Steeleye wiped the blade clean on Black Deeds' clothes. The fat peacock of a man was by the horses. His piping screams had subsided, and now he was complaining loudly, and to no one in particular. "Half my stock gone; how can I ransom a dead girl? Perhaps her father would pay for a body...no, best cut my losses on this accursed venture. I've still got the Princess. I've still got the jewel of the crown, and now no Captain and crew to pay off. Perhaps, all is not so bad, not so bad..."

Steeleye furrowed his brow as he listened to the nasal ramblings, and watched the gaudily dressed man wring his hands, jowls trembling as he spoke to himself. In the North, slavery was rare. Aye, men were taken on the field of battle now and again, and they would be put to work for a time, for the good of the community, or released early if their clan or family would offer ransom. But slavery was frowned upon, and Steeleye soon enough realised what he had stumbled upon here.

He glanced at the girl, who was now crawling trembling from the stream, making her way to the side of the dead girl. There she lay beside the body, her hands stroking the bloodied face, a thin keening sound issued from her lips, a sound Steeleye was all too familiar with. Her shackles jangled softly as she tried to hold the body, to cradle the head in her lap. The golden-haired girl rocked her dead friend, as she would have a babe.

Steeleye felt the anger cool in his breast, until his resolve was as cold and hard as iron. He sheathed his sword, and slowly made his way to the gaudy peacock. "Give me the keys to her chains," he said, his voice flat, his face set. The peacock stopped his jabbering as Steeleye's shadow fell over him, his eyes deep within the folds of flesh darting from side to side.

"She is my property, paid for in coin and now blood," stammered the slaver. He was trying to sound authoritative, but seeing little compassion in Steeleye's stare, his fingers fumbled at the keys clipped by a ring to his silken girdle. He handed over a small key, almost surprised at his hand's treachery, and for a moment he hesitated. Steeleye held out his own hand. "Key," he said, his tone brooking no argument, and the slaver's own resolve crumbled. He handed over the key, and then sat upon the sward, holding his head in his hands.

Steeleye made his way to the keening girl, and knelt silently beside her. Her green eyes were staring, vacant, and Steeleye knew she was in deep shock. For a moment, he was transported back to the terrible cell, where Freija had met her grisly end. Once more, he was knelt in the stinking blood and gore, cradling her sweet head in his arms. With a great effort, he pushed the image aside, fighting back tears he thought had long since dried up, and brought his attention back to the slave girl.

Carefully and slowly, he unlocked the chains from her wrists, throwing them into the stream. Her skin was bruised and livid from the chaffing. He felt helpless to do more, so he left her to mourn whilst he checked the horses and the saddlebags. He soon found what he was looking for: a clean and thick blanket, rolled tight. He took the blanket, and gently laid it over the grieving girl's shoulders, hoping its warmth would give some comfort. He sat close by, keeping a wary eye on the surrounding forest, and the slaver. Steeleye waited.

Long minutes passed when Steeleye became aware of the girl's eyes focused upon him. He met her green stare, and managed what he hoped was a reassuring smile. He could hear the slaver moving around somewhere, just beyond his eyesight. Probably gathering his valuables and preparing to sneak away. Steeleye didn't mind the slaver leaving, but before he allowed that, he would be looking through the saddlebags and provisions. As he stood up to check the slaver, the girl moved quickly, grabbing his wrist with a surprisingly strong grip. "Don't leave me with him!" she implored; fear writ large on her lovely face. Steeleye patted her hand.

"You have nothing to fear now. I only wish I had arrived sooner, to help your friend." He spoke the truth; he felt a pang of guilt as he looked at the raven-haired girl. If only he had been a little closer, had run a little faster. But he would ensure that the surviving slave was safe. He made a silent promise to himself, that he would see her to safety, no matter what. "I have just a little business with the brightly dressed popinjay over there, and then, we can see about laying your friend to rest properly." With that, Steeleye set off towards the slaver, a grim set to his jaw.

Azif Bae was indeed preparing to leave, searching through the saddlebags of each horse to find the choicest goods. Steeleye pushed him aside unceremoniously. The slaver whined. "But this is all I have left! These goods, these horses all belong to me. If you take them, you would beggar me..." His voice trailed to silence.

"Where I was raised," Steeleye said slowly, emphasising each word with care, "we do not keep slaves, nor do we sell one another for coin. I find the practice contemptible. Had you been involved in the assault upon the girl over there, be under no illusion, you would be burning in the Pit by now. As it is, I am still tempted to let the girl loose upon you with a blade; would she be lenient with you, do you think?" Steeleye cocked his head to the side as he regarded the now quaking slaver.

"You would not!" piped Azif Bae, his eyes wide and staring. "She would kill me!"

"Perhaps that is what you deserve? But anyway, I have a better use for you just now." Steeleye unfastened a shield from the saddle of a fine black stallion. The horse rolled its eyes and tried to bite at the young man, a fiery beast indeed. He handed the shield to the slaver, indicating the sharp point at its base. "Go to the dead girl, and start to dig. If you dig deep enough and quick enough, I will let you leave with a horse and provisions, not deep enough and too slow... Well, I will let your former slave decide." Azif Bae looked long and hard at the swordsman. He was a good judge of character, and so, he snatched up the shield and scurried over to the crumpled form of Sha'haan, ready to dig as deep and as fast as he could.

There were seven horses in all, each a fine and healthy specimen, and though no expert in the saddle, Steeleye could ride, and knew enough about horses to keep them healthy upon the trail. He carefully looked over each of the mounts, choosing a fine gelding for himself, and another for the girl. He had already decided that he would be taking her along with him, whether to her home or some other safe harbour, he wasn't yet sure. But he would see her safe. In the North, that was the way of things, one didn't leave a job half done. Steeleye had saved the girl's life, so to abandon her now would be unthinkable. He was musing upon such as he rummaged through the saddlebags.

Four of the bags were obviously those of common soldiers or sellswords. They contained spare clothes, iron and flints, whetstones, needles and threads and the like. He carefully selected clean clothes that could be made suitable for the girl, and turned to find her only a few tentative paces away. Her wide green eyes were in focus now, and darted about the forest. She pushed golden hair from her face, then quickly pulled together her torn tunic, as the fabric threatened to fall away from her.

Wordlessly, Steeleye handed her a plain cotton shirt from one of the bags. It had once been a rich purple colour, though time and many washings had now left it a pale lavender. But it was clean and well mended, and was large enough to fall almost to her knees. The girl accepted the shirt, and turned away to pull it over her shoulders. The colour suited her, Steeleye thought, though he was sure that style was far from her thoughts just then. He found a sash of garish yellow silk, property of the slaver he thought, and gave her that too, indicating she should use it for a belt. It wound about her slender waist three times, and as she knotted the silk, she looked at her rescuer full.

The girl was still terrified: of the forest, of her recent ordeal, and aye, even of him, and he couldn't blame her. But, as he returned her stare, he could see a resolve, an inner courage and determination that was vying mightily with the fear. "Thank you, for what you did..." she said, and though her lips trembled a little, her voice was calmer and steadier.

"My name is Morinae" she continued. "Sha'haan," she indicated the prone form a little distance off, besides which the slaver dug with vigour. "Sha'haan and I were taken from my home, over a month ago by these slavers. They sought ransom from my friend's parents; for me, they had other plans. They were taking me somewhere in the South, somewhere where princes and kings bid for high born slaves. I have heard there is an Empress there too, who collects nobles and even royals as pets." Morinae shuddered at the thought.

"Earlier today the slave train was attacked by dozens of bandits. We few here were all that survived." Her voice caught in her throat, and Steeleye could see the memory brought with it intense pain. "The slaves stood no chance. They were chained together, like so much livestock, and slaughtered by the bandits. Most of the caravan guards were killed, only those you see here escaped." Her eyes grew wide once more, and Steeleye could see fresh tears begin to well. "The guards became like animals," she said, and her voice broke in a wretched sob. "Poor Sha'haan tried to save me, to pull Black Deeds from me, but he killed her. Just like that, he killed her, then he and the cook killed Captain E'bok too! And I had hated the Captain, but at the end, he tried to stop them, but it was too late... too late for Sha'haan." Her speech subsided, and she wept for the death of her friend.

Steeleye gently patted her shoulder. He was at a loss of anything else to do. Her grief was too raw, too fresh for placating words, and he knew this from bitter experience. Grief must run its course, and it was different for everyone. All he could do was be there to keep her safe, be there to reassure her.

As her weeping quietened a little, Steeleye returned his attention to the saddlebags. Morinae's account of the raid by the bandits was troubling. If a full caravan guard was overpowered by numbers, he was sure that he wouldn't fare much better, no matter how skilled with a sword he was.

He quickly gathered the things he thought would come in useful: pans, a lantern, two thick and quite rich looking cloaks, water canteens, bags of horse feed, the list went on and on. He decided to take six horses, and seeing as how the slaver, grunting and sweating with the effort of digging a grave, was working hard, Steeleye decided to leave one horse for him. The foul tempered black stallion would do nicely.

Steeleye also found coin. An awful lot of coin. In fact, when he gathered it all together, he was sure that here was more gold and silver than was in the entire treasury of Aelrik's Keep. Blood money, he was sure, but he would take it all the same. He would put it to a better use than the slaver would, he was sure of that.

And then he found the real treasure. A map.

Hand drawn upon linen, and well worn. As Steeleye unrolled the fabric, he could see details of his surroundings: forests, rivers, mountain ranges, and even what he presumed to be large towns or cities. With a grin he took the map over to the near exhausted slaver.

"Where are we, on this map?" he asked, pushing the fabric under Azif Bae's nose. The slaver broke off from digging with the shield to glance at the map, and stabbed a muddy finger into a forest. "Around there," he wheezed. Sweat beaded his face, dripped from the tip of his nose to splash upon the linen map.

"Careful there," Steeleye said, brushing the droplets away. "And where did the bandits attack?"

Again, he pointed a pudgy, ringed finger. Steeleye looked for the directions key, and found an ornate cross drawn in the corner with the legends North, South, East and West inscribed. "So, you were attacked west of here? How far?"

"It was a hard and fast ride to escape, but I should think we rode at least seven, perhaps eight miles" replied Azif Bae. "Is this deep enough?" he was standing in a ditch knee deep. Steeleye glanced at the grave and shook his head. "More."

He returned to where Morinae was now sat beside the stream, the blanket wrapped around her shoulders, though it was far from cold. He sat down a few feet away from her, careful not to startle her. When she looked his way, he unfurled the map and pointed to where the slaver had indicated was their present location.

"This is where we are, I think. This line here is the stream, or perhaps a river farther along?" He pointed a little to the west. "Around here is where the bandits attacked, so we need to make a wide berth around that area, but if you can see your homeland, we can make a safe route." After a few moments, she looked at the map, and her brows drew together in concentration.

"There," she said, pointing with a slim finger at a spot that appeared to be on the coast. "Asgulun. It rests on the shores of the Sea of Storms. We have travelled two moons from there, but with a detour...." She wiped tears from her eyes, pushing her hair from her face. Steeleye was struck by her beauty, even in such a traumatised and dishevelled state. "Can you take me there?"

"Asgulun it is, then," Steeleye replied with a nod. "I have been wandering through this forest for long enough, it feels good to have somewhere to be aiming for. We shall get you back to Asgulun, you have my word on it."

With that Steeleye got to his feet and strode back to the slaver, who was still digging and scraping, his breath coming in ragged sobs. His fine silken garments were caked with mud and dirt, the green leather boots soiled and ruined. As the swordsman approached, Azif Bae ceased his labour and wiped the sweat from his brow, smearing more mud over his forehead. He was wheezing alarmingly, his face flushed. "I can dig no more," he whined, throwing down the shield and climbing out of the grave. Once clear of the ditch, he fell to his knees and began to cough and retch. Steeleye glanced at the grave, nodded, and then tenderly scooped up the still form of Sha'haan. He laid the young woman in the ditch, brushing her raven hair from her face with his fingers.

"May the Morriggu see you safe to the afterlife. You were taken too soon, but in the hereafter, I pray you will be blessed with joy eternal." He spoke quietly, kneeling beside the grave, and so was startled when Morinae spoke at his shoulder.

"Those were kind words, for a girl that you never knew." Her tears had dried now, though there was pain and remorse as she looked upon her friend in the dirt. "There needs to be a reckoning, when I return to Asgulun. Sha'haan should not be here, left alone like this, miles from her people."

"If it makes you feel any better, I know Sha'haan isn't here; this is not your friend laying here. The Morriggu has sent her upon the path to the next life. Already, I should imagine, she is meeting with those of her family that have gone before. The dead are never alone, Morinae, it is the living they leave behind that suffer. They must endure the loss and the loneliness." He stood and fetched a blanket from the piled provisions, then carefully laid it over the body. Next, he took up the shield, and began to cover the form with dirt. It didn't take long, and he was sure that the creatures of the forest would be quick enough to dig up the grave, but he didn't mention that to Morinae. Instead, he looked down at the small mound of earth, his face sombre. "Think of her as she was."

"We had better be gone from here," came the nasal whine of Azif Bae. "There's no telling where the bandits are, they could be following our trail even now."

Steeleye nodded in agreement, then walked to the great black stallion, avoiding its teeth as he gathered its reins. Next, he threw a slim set of saddlebags over the horse's rump and beckoned the slaver. When Azif Bae joined him beside the horse, Steeleye held out the reins. The slaver looked dumbstruck. "This is Captain E'bok's mount," he stammered, "and even he had to fight it every day! The only reason he rode the damned beast was he thought it made him look dashing."

Steeleye shook the reins under the slavers nose. "You need all the help you can get, to look dashing, believe me on this," he said with a grim smile. "In the saddlebags you will find food and water for a few days travel, enough coin for lodgings at an inn, should you come across one." He pointed West. "There are the bandits. Morinae and I shall be travelling along this stream here, and making a wide berth around them." He gestured to the rest of the forest with his free hand. "You have plenty of options, but I suggest you head East. I imagine Asgulun won't be a safe harbour for you. And should I see you again, someday, take to your heels, for I may not be as level tempered the next time."

Azif Bae took the reins with a trembling hand, and looked beseechingly at the swordsman, but there was no mercy there, only an ice-cold resolve. It took him many attempts to get into the saddle, the stallion kicking and stamping, but at last he made it, shortening the reins to try to control the muscular beast. "I beg you," he whined, "let me accompany you. Princess! Surely you would not set me loose in this wilderness? How am I to survive?" There was panic in his voice, and the horse snorted, tossing its head, and Azif Bae almost toppled from the saddle

"Princess, please! Show mercy?"

Morinae walked silently to the stirrup, and without a second's hesitation, she slapped the stallion's rump with a resounding *smack*. The horse took off at a mad gallop, the slaver hanging on for dear life.

"That is more mercy than you showed to the poor devils that you took up and sold on the block." Her voice, though quiet, was edged with steel.

CHAPTER 12

THE GUIDE

S teeleye led his new charge at a leisurely pace. They had good mounts, were well provisioned, and the stream that they followed meandered through pretty glades and woodland, filled with the chirrup of birdsong and the scent of spring blooms. Everywhere he looked there was colour. From the rich green of the swards, to the blue of the sky glimpsed through the canopy of verdant leaves, the yellow of buttercups, and the rainbow sheen of pebbles on the stream bed.

He was at peace with the world, or would have been, had it not been for the knowledge that the Morriggu was watching him, a precious, tiny, glass vial in her slender fingers.

Morinae too seemed to be more at ease, though she still cast nervous glances at the surrounding forest, and at Steeleye himself. The first day of their journey, Morinae had hardly spoken at all; she sat slumped in the saddle, her shoulders hunched beneath her newly acquired cloak, her eyes downcast and hidden in shadow. The first evening, she had eaten the soup that Steeleye prepared, and if she enjoyed the flavour, she made no mention of it. Through the night, she thrashed beneath the blankets, her voice raised in piteous cries. Steeleye could only sit by the small fire and watch, feeding dry twigs to the crackling flames, until tiredness overcame him and he dozed himself.

The second day was much the same, with glorious blue skies and glades full of poppies and bluebells, the green of the grass almost drowned by the carpet of snowdrops and daisies, oceans of daffodils bending their heads and nodding in the warm breeze. Towards the evening, the magic healing of nature was at work upon the girl, and her green eyes were searching not only the shadows, but also the splendour of the forest and the bushes and brambles alongside the game trail that they travelled.

That evening, as she sipped her broth from a wooden spoon, Steeleye saw her brows raise as she registered the flavour, and her eyes moved to where he sat across the fire from her.

"Wild onions," he said, with a smile. "I saw them beside the trail earlier, as we took a break. They have a bite to them, do they not?"

Morinae returned his smile with a nod, and sipped more of the broth. Her sleep that night was still troubled and restless, and she cried out several times, once so loud she startled the horses, but towards dawn, she quietened and her sleep deepened. As the sun rose higher, Steeleye let her sleep on. Sleep was nature's greatest healer, Hewla always told him. As he unrolled the map to plan out their next step, he kept an eye upon the girl, and was struck by her fragility. The cuts and bruises to her body would heal with time, but the damage to her psyche, those scars were harder to cure, and would be tormenting both her waking and sleeping world for a long time to come.

Steeleye found a smudge upon the map, a little distance downstream: it seemed the meandering water would be joined by several other tributaries to make a river called the Esker, and upon the banks of this river was what looked like a sizeable settlement, not a city, but larger than the smaller squares of ink he presumed to be villages. A town then, no doubt owing its life to the river and the trade that could be plied upon it, and the rich farmlands thereabouts. He had no scale or key to judge distances, but he was confident that he was on the right track. All he had to do was follow the stream and eventually it would become the Esker, which in turn would lead him to the Sea of Storms and finally Asgulun.

The third day saw Morinae coming out of her shell a little. She sat taller in the saddle, and Steeleye was struck that she was a much better rider than he was. She had no trouble guiding the gelding with her knees, and her gentle swaying in rhythm with the horse's canter showed her assurance; she barely used the reins, which lay slack in her hands. She even urged her horse on into the lead for a time, letting the beast stretch out its legs a little in a short gallop. Steeleye struggled to keep up, leading the train of spare mounts and pack animals. He saw her glance over her shoulder at him lagging behind, and he thought there was the ghost of a smile upon her face.

That night, they sat side by side before a small fire, waiting for their supper to cook. The aroma was delicious. Two fat trout, carefully skinned and boned, sizzled upon a skillet which was balanced on the flames. Alongside the fish, wild mushrooms and onions cooked, blending juices with the trout. Morinae's stomach grumbled loudly in the still night, and after a brief moment, the pair of them burst out laughing. It was short lived levity, for soon enough Morinae grew withdrawn again. After her supper, she wrapped her blanket tight around her, and was soon asleep. She mumbled often, and her legs thrashed as if she were running or fighting in her dreams.

Steeleye let the fire die down, then put a second blanket over the girl. As he was camped only a few feet from the stream, he cleaned off the skillet in the cool waters, then sat on the bank and stared at the night sky. Stars in their thousands winked upon the velvet blackness. The moon was only a quarter full, so did not eclipse the splendour of the heavens. A shooting star hurtled by, and then another. Steeleye sat transfixed as he watched the glory of the cosmos. He must take advantage of this peace whilst he could, he thought, for soon enough he would be drawing the Godsteel blade once more. He had seven Demons to hunt, and they could be scattered anywhere in the world, yet the Morriggu had seen fit to place him here, in this forest, at a time when the slave girl Morinae needed a sword. This was no coincidence. He was certain that Morinae was to be his guide to the demons, whether she knew it or not.

* * *

ON THE FOURTH DAY, as the sun was at its highest, a bank of grey clouds came scudding from the North, and soon enough rain began to fall, light at first, and warm as it ran down their faces. But the clouds darkened, and the rain became heavier, a cold wind moaned amongst the trees and sent ripples along the surface of the stream. As one, the pair led the horses into the partial cover of the forest, where Steeleye set up a canopy using waxed cloaks and the branches of an old oak tree. The horses too gathered beneath the spreading boughs, cropping at the rich grass.

"We may as well get comfortable," Steeleye said, as he spread a blanket upon the ground and then sat against the great trunk, resting his head upon the rough bark. Morinae pushed her damp hair from her eyes and sat down beside him. She shivered a little as the breeze raised goosebumps on her arms. Steeleye fetched more blankets from the packs, and draped them over the girl's slim shoulders. She smiled gratefully as he slid back to the grass, once more resting his head against the old tree.

As the rain drummed upon their makeshift shelter, Steeleye

closed his eyes and relaxed, enjoying the proximity of the oak. "The slaver called you a Princess," he said at length, "was that a pet name for you or is it your title?"

"Does it matter?" Morinae responded, a little guardedly.

"Not to me. Whether you are a milkmaid, a princess, or a harlot, it makes no difference. I would still be taking you home, have no fear of that."

Morinae cast a sidelong look at her companion. His profile was relaxed, his eyes closed. She found that she trusted him, though they had spoken hardly at all over the last few days. He had not even offered his name. She was aware that she was fully dependent upon him: his hunting skills, his foraging, even building the canvas shelter that kept them dry. Without this stranger, she would be near helpless in the wilderness. It wasn't a feeling that Morinae was used to, and it irked a little. The fog of despair that had clouded her every thought since the death of Sha'haan was lifting slightly, and Morinae found that she had a need to talk, to interact with someone, just to hear a voice not raised in anger, lust, or terror.

"I am Morinae of the House of Balkar, daughter of Rodero, King of the Asgulun," she said at length, pride in her bearing and tone despite her present circumstances. "And yes, I am Princess by birth and by right of blood." As she spoke, she watched him carefully, but he remained still, eyes closed as if dozing.

"I am Steeleye, late of the Northern lands, and, until I came across you and that precious map, I was completely at a loss as to where I was, or where I was going." His lips quirked in a brief wry smile. "And I am pleased to meet you, Princess Morinae, of the House of Balkar."

"What sort of a name is Steeleye?" she asked, relief evident in her voice that they had at last started a discourse.

"It is the name a wise woman of the Northlands gave me. It could have been much worse, or so I was told." The laughing face of Freija came unbidden, her playful mockery, and the way she would mimic his earnestness. The pain of her passing was still with him, muted perhaps, an ache rather than a searing pain, but an ache that he knew he would carry with him all of his days.

"It is a strange name, very bold." The Princess nodded at her summary. "I like it."

The rain had lessened somewhat. The patter of raindrops upon the canvas slowed, and the dark clouds raced along on their urgent path. The cool wind died too, and the pair sat beneath the cloaks and watched as wan shafts of sunlight once more lanced through the trees, leaves tipped the rain as if it were morning dew, to fall and glisten upon the rich moss and grass of the forest floor. Birds took up their song again, rejoicing at the coming of the sun and the passing of the shower. In the branches of the oak, blackbirds and sparrows sang, wood pigeons cooed somewhere close by, and Steeleye's thoughts ran to a couple of plump birds roasting on a spit.

It was as they gathered up their packs, and Steeleye was rolling up the cloaks, that their visitor arrived. Steeleye was bent to his work with his back to Morinae, but he heard her exclamation of surprise. Looking over his shoulder. He saw a large glossy crow perched upon the lowest branch of the oak, its shiny eyes regarding the Princess, head cocked to the side.

"Speaking of bold, look at this chap." She was smiling, a bright smile that lit up her entire face. The crow cawed, and then hopped to the ground. It was a big bird, its head as high as Morinae's knee, its beak black and fierce. Morinae's smile faltered a little at this odd behaviour. Crows were usually seen in the sky, or in the fields pecking at crops or carrion, not inviting themselves into the company of people.

Steeleye gave a sigh of relief as he saw the bird, particularly as it seemed to be taken with the Princess. He had been right then: Morinae was somehow to be his guide, and in helping her, he would be helping his cause. The arrival of the crow was a subtle reassurance from the Morriggu, he felt sure. He finished rolling the cloaks, and as he tied them to the pack horse saddles, he heard Morinae screech. The crow had alighted upon her slim shoulder, its beady eyes close to hers, its pinions were spread wide as it sought its balance, though its clawed feet were gentle enough, Morinae stood stock-still in shock, her green eyes wide as they looked at the strange creature.

"Steeleye!" Morinae wailed. "What is it doing?"

Steeleye walked over to the Princess. She stood as if petrified, as if the sharp gaze of the raptor had turned her to stone. "What is it doing?" she repeated, her lips hardly moving.

"I think it is saying, 'hello'." He moved closer, and raised his arm next to Morinae's shoulder. The bird obligingly hopped onto the proffered perch, shuffling its feet a little as if to get comfortable.

"Is it yours? Is it a... pet?" Morinae let out the breath she only now realized she had been holding. She watched as Steeleye ran a finger across the bird's glossy head.

"Not mine, but I did know a crow once, its name was Morrigh, it lived with the wise woman I spoke of, Hewla." He lifted his arm higher and the crow spread its wings, taking flight into the branches of the tree. It sat there. Watching. "He is a good omen I think, come to wish us luck upon our journey."

With that, Steeleye untethered all the horses, and swung into the saddle of the gelding. Morinae followed suit, keeping an apprehensive eye on the branches above her, wary of the crow. She guided her horse beside that of her companion as they moved off, the first time that she had done this, usually letting Steeleye lead, with her trailing after.

After an hour on the trail, with twice that remaining before the day's light left them, Steeleye turned in the saddle to face his companion. "So, tell me about Asgulun, is it a good place to live?"

She smiled at his clumsy attempt to draw her into conversation, but Asgulun was her life, she was born to serve the country, and was lost without it. "Asgulun is beautiful," she said wistfully, her eyes growing dreamy as they looked upon a place far from the forest. "It has miles of coastline, with fishing villages and towns dotted along both the Sea of Storms and the Narrow Sea. Inland, the land is rich and green, the soil black with health, and our farms grow crops aplenty. Our neighbours are Ashanaar over the Narrow Sea, and little Ish, a land of plenty like no other, or so it was when I was taken. I fear for our neighbour." She chewed upon her lip for a few moments, a habit that she had Steeleye had noticed.

"Asgulun was once a city state, and its capital is still known by the name Asgulun, a lovely city that perches upon the headland overlooking the Sea of Storms, and the Narrow Sea both. Its walls are high and white in the sunlight, as if hewn from the cliffs themselves. There are towers within the city, and spires that rise two hundred feet and more. The walls are thick as well as high, and the sentries can patrol them six abreast." Morinae paused, transported back to her home.

"There are banners and pennants that wave proudly upon the battlements, proclaiming the names of all the noble families and barons that support the crown. Each morning, the street traders can be heard shouting their wares, vying for customers, the smell of baking bread from all the early to rise bakeries, the rich colours and heady scents of the flower sellers...." Morinae paused, and smiled at her companion. His question may have been clumsy, but it had worked.

"My father, King Rodero, is getting along on years, but he is still beloved of the people. Not so much my half-brother, Juvaal, nor his mother the Queen, a spiteful snake of a woman. Her name is Vasha, and it is her son who is responsible for my being here in the wilderness, sold to a slaver who was supposed to bury me deep in some valley, or sink me in some isolated lake. Black Deeds himself told me this: Juvaal paid him to see the job done, and Juvaal does nothing without his mother adding steel to his spine. But they didn't count upon the greed of the slaver Azif Bae, who took their coin, and had it in mind selling me on to boot." She paused, surprised at the venom in her voice, and the fact that she had blurted out so much. "They didn't count upon you either, did they? Wandering the woods, just where you were needed. It is fate I think."

High in the trees the crow cawed a raucous cry.

On they rode, side by side, with Steeleye leading the fine spare mounts now reduced to pack animals. Morinae spoke of her homeland with a smile, but there was worry in her eyes also, particularly when she spoke of the land across the Narrow Sea. Steeleye learned of the King of Ashanarr, Betod, a fine and fair king who led his country in peace and to prosperity. A good trading partner for Asgulun, and their smaller neighbour Ish. But then, only two years ago, the Queen of Ashanarr, Betod's beloved wife Meera had died suddenly. She had developed a cough, then a fever, and within a week she was gone. Betod was destroyed.

It was only two months later word came to Asgulun that Betod was to remarry, and a party of nobles and royals from Asgulun attended the wedding feasts. So too did the great and the good from Ish, with Prince Andar looking with besotted eyes at Morinae, a match would be made there no doubt, the Princess told Steeleye as she recounted the events of the feast. The new Queen was a striking woman, tall and regal, fine boned with skin so pale as to be almost like snow, it contrasted sharply with her hair, which was as black as sin, and fell below her waist. This was She'ah, the new Queen of Ashanarr, and for the first year all had been good and peaceful. But as time went on, She'ah began to show her true colours, and her influence waxed greatly.

Steeleye listened to his companion's concerns, the talk of

trade crumbling, of tensions rising, how this new Queen was building an army of mercenaries, and seemed intent upon forcing her will upon her neighbours, particularly Ish, a jewel of a land, rich in farms and precious mineral mines to boot. In the old tongue, She'ah meant the Slithering One, or the Serpent. How apt, Steeleye, thought.

That night, they camped upon a plain, the forest curtailing behind them. The stream they followed had widened considerably, and had joined several others as they rode through the day, until now it bore more resemblance to a river than stream. It ran fast and turbulent after the earlier rains, and where streams joined there were fierce white waters leaping over rocks and stepped falls. This must be the River Esker, Steeleye mused as he sat by the fire listening to Morinae as she mumbled and whimpered in her sleep. She fared better every day, but he feared her ordeal had scarred her deeply. He sat deep in thought, until at last he dozed, and though his chin fell upon his chest, his hand never left the hilt of the hard-won blade.

THE SUN ROSE to find Steeleye already preparing breakfast, two fat trout sizzling upon the skillet. He brewed hot spiced tea, which he had found amongst the packs. Its taste was revitalising, the spices unfamiliar but tasty. Morinae awoke at his clattering, and accepted the proffered mug of tea with a tired smile. "Fish?" she asked nodding at the skillet. Steeleye grinned at her feigned enthusiasm. Their diet had been a healthy one, and trout was good to eat, but he supposed a princess would be used to a more varied menu.

"I can prepare porridge if you would prefer? Like that the late Cookie would have made you?" His grin widened at her look of distaste.

"Fish is lovely." She sipped her tea. Hugging the warm mug in both hands, she breathed in its aroma and smiled, no doubt the scent triggering some pleasant memory. Once the fish was ready, Steeleye served up, and soon they were setting to, the fresh air sharpening their appetites, the trout filling.

"Looking at the map, I think if we follow this water course, which I believe to be the Esker, we should come upon a town or settlement in three or four days. There we can perhaps find an inn, and a plate of roast beef." Steeleye popped the last morsel of trout in his mouth, and chewed with relish.

"And bread!" Morinae said. "Fresh baked bread. It seems an age since I tasted it..." Her eyes grew dreamy as she thought of a comfortable inn, a deep mattress, and a meal sat at a table rather than sitting cross-legged, balancing a rude plate on her knees. "And wine, just a cup or two, and singing, perhaps there will be singing? There was no singing in the slave train." Thoughts of the poor slaves, now dead and butchered back in the forest, sobered Morinae's gaiety.

Together they collected the breakfast pots and pans, and made their way to the river. As Steeleye scrubbed and rinsed the plates in the fast-flowing water, Morinae idly plucked several daisies that grew nearby, her nimble fingers quickly manipulating the stems into knots, making a chain, and then a crown of tiny white blooms, which she popped upon her head. "Sha'haan and I would make daisy chains in the palace gardens," she said, sadly, letting her fingers dip into the cold river. "She was the sister that I never had, and now she is dead because of me, buried in a shallow grave, where none will ever visit, nor pay respects, all because of me..." Her tone dripped melancholy, and her lips trembled. "Because of me." She repeated.

Steeleye laid their dishes aside and gently put his arm around her shoulder. "Not because of you, Princess, because of Azif Bae's greed, because of Black Deed's lust, and because of your brother's treachery." Morinae put her head against his shoulder, and he could feel her tears through the linen of his shirt. "Your brother must hold the lion's share of the blame here," he continued, "not you. And won't he be surprised when you return home, safe and sound, and with such a tale to tell?" He felt a subtle change in her at that moment. The grief was still there, along with her guilt at surviving at the cost of her loved one, yet also there was a determination, a resolve.

"Juvaal shall rue the day he conspired against the House of Balkar. My father, Rodero, may be under his thrall in his dotage, but my bastard brother Bryann, and the nobles of Asgulun, will be appalled and furious by the actions of that viper." She looked up at him, and he saw a new steel in her green eyes. "We must make what haste we can to return me home. I fear for Asgulun, with the fool Juvaal steering our father, and She'ah bristling for war in Ashanarr. These are perilous times."

Steeleye nodded his understanding, and rose to return to their camp. He liked the new set of the girl's jaw. Even her posture was changed as she walked alongside him. Gone was the slave that he had rescued a few short days ago, here was the Princess. He smiled, eager to be off himself as he swung into the saddle. Side by side they set off, though now Morinae dictated the pace, and the horses seemed glad to be stretching out their legs.

The next evening, they could see cultivated lands in the distance, and by the afternoon of the following day they passed the first isolated farmhouse, single storied and painted white, its roof well thatched, the fields about it tilled and well-tended. The game trail that they had followed became a track wide enough for carts to travel along with ease. As they left the wilderness behind, Morinae's confidence soared, and she rode with a beaming smile upon her lovely face.

CHAPTER 13
TALES OF THE EMPIRE

The town was bigger than Steeleye had expected, nestled in a wide bend of the river Esker. From where he and Morinae sat on their horses, half a mile up the track, which had now turned into a definite road, he could see plenty of houses in the town. Some were even two storied with tiled roofs, though most were timber affairs with good strong thatch to keep out the rain and the cold. Though the sun was dipping towards the west, there was still a good few hours' daylight left, more than enough time to find lodgings for the night, and hopefully a good stable for the horses.

Paying for both would be of no problem thanks to Azif Bae.

They passed plenty of farms, with families and field hands hard at work on the land. Morinae waved at each party and gave them her most radiant smile, but most of the workers looked away, concentrating on their early crops, or tilling the earth with their wooden hoes. Back breaking work by the looks of it, Steeleye thought. He had always thought of country folk as cheerful characters, especially when living in such idyllic surroundings as these, but apparently not. They had even gone so far as to approach a couple of the farmhouses, but as they drew near, doors were slammed and windows shuttered quickly. It was Morinae that suggested that perhaps these farms, so close to the wilderness and the forest, were cautious of strangers for good reason. After all, had she not seen first-hand what the denizens of the woods were capable of?

There were no cobbles upon the streets, nor paving flags, but the ground was hard packed with much use. Even now as the day drew on, there were folk aplenty out of doors. It seemed there was a market of some kind being held in the town square, a large space to which all the streets ran. Stalls had been set up, with bright coloured canopies, where locals hawked their wares, animal pelts, yarns and bolts of linen, furs and leather goods. There were stalls with vegetables, fresh from the soil, apples and pears, shone on the traders' tunics, herbs and spices, earthenware jars containing who knew what stacked waist-high on the ground.

All around the square, there were well made shop-fronts, a baker, a fish merchant, a smithy that smelled of sulphur and dry heat, stinging the nostrils. There were farm goods aplenty too, with shops selling sacks of seeds and grain, hoes and ploughs, great leather yokes for horse or oxen. Steeleye found his senses reeling with all the hustle and bustle. He was unused to seeing so many people around in one place. In the North, there had been market days sure enough, and festivals through the summer, but here there seemed less space, everyone was crowded upon one another, their voices raised in raucous calls as they sought to entice the day's last customers to buy their wares and goods.

The smells too were almost overpowering: livestock, pungent tobacco smoke, herbs, dyes and of course manure. It seemed the market had earlier been used to sell cattle and sheep. The air was thick with the stink of their leavings.

"Is that an inn?" Morinae leaned close to him in the saddle, to speak above the din. The building she gestured towards did indeed have a painted sign outside, atop a timber pole. It read quite simply "The Wheat Sheaf". The sign was made of wooden boards, and at some time in the past a picture of yellow wheat had been painted beneath the legend. The paint now faded and flaking, still served its purpose.

The Wheat Sheaf was by far the largest building to face into the square: two storied and its timber walls painted white. A sidewalk of wooden planks encircled the inn, so during the rains mud would be kept out. Posts were available for mounts and cattle, even a water trough for thirsty animals, whilst the owners took a drink inside or sat at one of the many tables arranged on the wooden walkway. Steeleye led them to a rail, and clambered from the saddle, tying his horse to a post and the pack animals next to it. Morinae dismounted with more grace, and considerably more skill, and joined her companion as he threw his saddle bags over his shoulder, heading towards the open doors.

Inside, the inn was a surprise for Steeleye. He had expected very basic standards, but instead he found a large common room which, judging by the number of lanterns dotted about, would be well lit and cosy even when the daylight failed. Now, however, the afternoon sunlight poured in through the many wide-open windows. He barely noticed the newly fitted shutters at each aperture, nor the heavy metal bolts fixed to them.

Sturdy tables and benches were set about the room. In one wall was set a large hearth, with a cheery fire blazing. About this fire were several overstuffed chairs, with small tables for drinks beside them. All was clean and brightly painted. Behind the bar, a highly polished wood affair that ran along the wall opposite the fire, stood a couple in their middle years, both dressed simply in cream tunics, with spotless aprons about their waists.

The pair behind the bar looked nervously at the newcomers. The man, the landlord Steeleye presumed, was polishing a tankard with a clean rag. The metal cup gleamed, yet he continued to polish industriously as he stared. The other behind the bar was a woman who looked in fine health, her greying hair held up in a bun, her eyes a bright blue, shifting from Steeleye to Morinae and back, fixing upon the sword at his hip. It was Morinae who spoke first, leading her companion to the bar, flashing the gawking pair with a white reassuring smile.

"What a lovely inn," she began, her poise and bearing suddenly quite regal, and not at all what Steeleye had become used to. He found himself staring at the Princess the same way the pair at the bar were. Morinae pushed a lock of golden hair from her face, and continued, her attention solely upon the innkeepers. "Have you a pair of rooms? One with a bath, if you can arrange it? I feel as if half the forest has taken root in my hair." Again, the smile, the poise. Even bedraggled as she was, wearing borrowed clothes, and, as she said, with half a forest of spattered mud and the odd leaf and twig in her hair, Morinae had a presence about her. The woman behind the bar was bobbing her head. "We have rooms set aside for the Baron, for when he would come to market and festivals. They are not in use, and there is a bath that I can have filled."

The man behind the bar, the husband Steeleye presumed, nudged the woman with his elbow. "What if the Baron shows up?"

The Landlady tutted. "We've seen neither hide nor hair of anyone from the castle for nigh a year, not the Baron, not his men, nor even his tax collectors. I would as soon have this lovely girl making use of our best room, rather than see it empty." With that, the woman turned her eyes back to the travellers, and her tone became more normal, business-like, hidden behind a smile. "It's our best room, but not often used. I can get a girl to light the hearth, if you would like? There is room for two...?" Her voice trailed off, her question hanging in the air. Morinae raised her brows in surprise, and looked from the landlady to Steeleye and then back.

"The room isn't cheap," piped up the husband, at last setting aside the tankard, avarice seeming to have overcome his nerves.

"That's not an issue." Steeleye hoisted the saddlebags onto the bar, the tell-tale rattle of coin loud in the empty common room. "There are horses outside that need stabling overnight. Their shoes need checking too. The Lady will take the finest room you have to offer, and whilst we wait, perhaps a meal..."

"Anything that doesn't swim." Morinae broke in, "and bread!" putting her hand upon Steeleye's arm to hush him, as she once more took over the conversation, it was a subtle move, but one that the pair behind the bar noticed. Here was a lady used to getting her way, surely high born, no matter her present condition. "And you mentioned a Baron? Which would that be?" She oozed confidence now. The city life was her element. "Word should be sent to him of the brigands in the forest hereabouts. Why, I am lucky to be alive, and if not for the brave action of the captain of my guard here- "

"Captain?" Steeleye asked quietly.

"Yes, a deserved promotion after your bravery," Morinae replied matter-of-factly before she continued. "We are all that is left of my retinue, and we have been traipsing through the forest for days, half-starved and hunted by brigands!" Half-truths spilled from the Princess in a torrent, and Steeleye could only watch in wonder at the transformation from the slave girl of a few days ago to this self-assured young woman.

As the Landlady hurried off, shouting directions at a group of serving girls, peering from a doorway Steeleye presumed led to the kitchens, he listened with half an ear as the landlord explained that the local landowner, the Baron Meska, lived a day's journey over the fens to the north, and that as his wife had said earlier, they had not seen any sign of him through the winter nor the spring. It was a little strange, but the townsfolk and farmers hereabouts weren't complaining. After all, the absence of revenue men was a blessing to be celebrated in his opinion.

He busied himself once more polishing an already gleaming tankard, as Morinae said she was familiar with the Baron, and described him to Steeleye conversationally as a fussy little man with too little hair upon his head and too much upon his lip. The landlord guffawed at this, and seemed to relax somewhat. Obviously, the description rang true, and was probably something the townsfolk said out of hearing of the Baron himself. The innkeep was at last letting his guard down with the strangers, and asked if they would care for a drink whilst they waited for their rooms. It all seemed a little odd to Steeleye; surely an Inn so far from any major city should be glad of passing trade, not so wary of it?

It was as the innkeep was taking the cork from what looked like an expensive bottle of wine, that Steeleye saw another customer making his way down the stairs from the bedrooms. This newcomer was a white-haired, spindly limbed fellow, dressed in plain tunic and trews, yet with a flamboyant red silk cape about his shoulders. A similar coloured beret, with a peacock feather sticking out of it on his head. His face was clean shaven, with deep laughter lines about his eyes. The long white hair fell lose and well-groomed to his shoulders. Steeleye was watching when the newcomer's eyes fell upon Morinae, as she stood by the bar, and he saw those eyes go wide with recognition.

"We are blessed indeed today," said the innkeep, as he too spied the man entering the common room. "Visitors from afar, and a singer of tall tales as well. The locals will be thrilled and no mistake, to share the room with such company." He grinned, dipping the tankard he had just polished into a barrel behind the bar, and presenting the foaming jack to the apparent singer. The white-haired man nodded appreciation at the landlord, and then he scooped off his hat and made a bow before Morinae, whispering out of earshot of the innkeep, "Is M'Lady travelling incognito? Or is it safe for the town to know it has a royal visitor?"

Steeleye let his hand fall to the hilt at his waist, he seemed relaxed, but in truth was as taut as a bowstring. Violence, as ever, was but a moment away. Morinae saw the movement, as did the singer, who swallowed nervously. "I think it best that I remain a mere noble born lady for the present." The Princess guided the fellow to the hearth as she spoke, her manner natural and friendly enough, but with the looming presence of Steeleye at her shoulder, the singer was under no illusions that he had best follow her lead. They found comfortable chairs out of earshot of the bar, and sat down together, Morinae smiling, the singer wary, and Steeleye silent yet menacing.

Once all were comfortable, and the newcomer had taken a slurp of his ale, Morinae fixed him with a piercing green stare. "How do you know me?" Her smile remained friendly enough, but her eyes were another matter. Steeleye could feel her tension.

The story teller wiped foam from his lip, and keeping his voice low and his eye on Steeleye's blade replied, "I am Artfur the Bard, Lady. I had the honour of recounting the tale of the Battle of the Morinorn, two years past at the court of Asgulun. You and your, er, half-brother, the General Bryann, were kind enough to remark how rousing you found the telling. There were many Tellers there that day, and I would understand should you not remember me." Artfur took another sip of ale, and screwed up his face a little. "How the mighty have fallen," he muttered to himself. "Two years ago, I sang in the Court of Kings and supped fine wine, now I tell bawdy songs in market taverns for a bed and a sour beer..." He looked at the pair with a morose expression. "One dalliance too many, and I swear she said she was a widow..."

"I do remember you!" Morinae exclaimed, her face lighting up at the memory. "Though, you were presented better than you are here. Hard times seem to have found us both." She beckoned the innkeep for her wine to be brought over, and a pitcher of ale for Steeleye too. Once served, and the cosy fire warming them through, as well as the drink, Artfur leaned forwards to speak in confidence, even though only a few other patrons occupied the inn, and they were all by the bar ordering food and drink after a day's work, well out of hearing.

"Though I have not been to Asgulun for many months, the telling of your disappearance has been told far and wide. Some blame the Bitch of Ashanarr, others say that you have run off with a lover..." He cast an eye at Steeleye before continuing, "but the word is that you are sorely missed, Princess, and I would humbly urge you to make haste home. Ashanarr has taken Ish in less than a week, I have heard, and eyes Asgulun next." Morinae choked on her wine, a coughing fit drawing curious stares from the bar.

"Ish has been invaded?" she asked, shocked.

"Aye, the Ish were brave enough, but it's said that, as well as a mercenary force, Ashanarr has darker allies, beast-men that feast upon flesh and live for killing. The men of Ish didn't stand a chance, and were overrun in short order. It was pure luck that so many escaped over the Sea of Storms and were welcomed by your own father."

Steeleye interrupted the telling with a question of his own. "Beast-men?" he asked, "do you mean the Grimm?" The intensity in his voice surprised Morinae, and the question itself seemed to take Artfur aback.

"In truth, no one likes to think that the Grimm have returned, and the name is not one to bandy about. But from the stories I have gathered over the last year or so, I would have to say; yes, the creatures serving Ashanarr are the same that served the darkness eons ago." He once more sipped his ale, and cast a furtive eye about. "In fact, far to the North, I have heard that The City of Kings, as was, now the City of the Dead," he paused for dramatic effect, "has been invaded by the Northerners, and hundreds if not thousands of the Grimm were slaughtered there. It is said a King has risen in the North, and all the tribes have sworn their swords, and that he leads men south in anticipation of a great war.

"That will be Aelrik Bearslayer, then." Steeleye nodded deep in thought. When he saw his drinking companions staring at him, he explained shortly "I was present at the first encounter, at the Western gate..." As Steeleye spoke, he once again felt the bite of Kleave's black steel in his side, felt the loss of his friends. And he missed Wolf as much as Freija, odd that the creature that had led him for so long, to ultimately leave him in the underworld had wormed her way into his thoughts and affections so much.

He returned his attention to the present. Artfur was speaking, wide eyed. "The story of Aelrik at the Great Gate has spread south, already. Why, I myself am considering composing a song about the brave band that ventured into the city, to root out the evil ones. Shining armour and brave knights are ever popular at Courts." Artfur leaned forwards in his chair and his scrawny hand clutched at Steeleye's arm in his passion. "An eye witness account would be wonderful," he breathed, "it could well be the making of me, a tale from the front line, so to speak." He sipped the ale once again, his leathery skinned face showing his thoughts on the brew.

"I don't recall any shining armour at the gate." Steeleye muttered softly, "I remember snow melting in my comrades' hot blood, the stink of fear, the bedlam of battle and the pain of loss. I remember seeing the Grimm, slavering jaws and tearing teeth." He paused a moment to take a sip of his own beer: it was not so bad as the story teller made out. "Not something that I would wish to endure again, but if Aelrik is bringing men south, then I should think we had all better sharpen our swords, and fletch arrows aplenty. My Lord has a knack for finding a fight."

Artfur squirmed in his chair, his excitement palpable. "Can I use the bit about snow melting in the blood? I'm sure the dainty ladies at Court would swoon at the thought."

Morinae cleared her throat, bringing all attention back to her. "Does my father still rule? Is the Sea of Storms still safe?"

"Aye Princess, your father does indeed rule, and fair as ever so I hear, though Prince Juvaal has taken up your place as advisor, and he seems a little keener than you to throw Asgulun into war. Bryann is solid, as ever, and a fleet has been manned to patrol both the Narrow Sea and the Sea of Storms, but my news is old by a week at best. Out here in the back of beyond tidings travel more slowly. For all I know, a peace could have been brokered already, though I doubt it."

Morinae mulled this over, sipping her wine, yet not tasting it, for all her anticipation of the drink. The landlady came over then, letting them know their rooms were ready, and water was being heated for a bath; a private dining room had been made available, and should the Lady and her captain wish to sit and listen to the Tale Teller and his apprentice, a seat by the fire would be kept empty for them. The woman was still babbling as she led Morinae to the stairs, to show her to her room. Three serving maids excitedly following in their wake, eager to be of service to the Lady.

Steeleye watched them depart over the rim of his tankard. In truth, he too could use a change of clothes, a rest on a down mattress, but he had other ideas just now. Artfur was beginning to stand, ready to take his leave, no doubt to prepare for his audience, but Steeleye put a strong hand upon his arm to keep him in place. More farm workers and tradesmen had entered now. The room was filling with both noise and tobacco smoke. It seemed every table had someone puffing away on a noisome clay pipe; the odour made Steeleye's eyes water.

"Sit with me a while longer, if you will, Artfur." Steeleye leaned closer to make his voice heard above the raucous din without shouting. "I have been long in the wilderness, and I am unsure of how the land lies hereabouts. For instance, why does such a fine establishment as this see fit to build new stout shutters, on the inside of the windows no less? And those bolts look like they would withstand a battering ram." He smiled as he saw the singer hunch forward, ready to reply, Artfur enjoyed his own voice, which was handy, Steeleye thought, as he was sure there was much to be learned.

"It's not just the inn, Captain, most every building locks up tight at sunset hereabouts. Why, if not for the fact that I am here," he puffed up his scrawny chest a little, "ready to entertain the rabble, I have no doubt the inn would be empty already." He waved vaguely at the windows. "See? The sun goes down, yet more are coming into the common room, whole families see. They bring their children to hear the tales of wonder and merriment, I have no doubt the innkeep will have a floor full of sleeping farmers ere the night is done." He frowned, a sudden thought occurring to him. "I should have asked for a percentage of his take, not just a meal or two and a bed. They look set to make a pretty penny this evening, yet how was I to know they would be so deprived of news and scandal?"

Artfur drained his cup, and held it aloft. It wasn't too long before a girl scooted along bearing a pitcher. She filled Artfurs' cup and made to replenish Steeleye's own, but he put a hand over it, shaking his head and smiling at the girl. She curtsied and blushed before hurrying off, weaving amongst the tables. Artfur guffawed loudly at the exhibition, though not unkindly. Here was a man used to every standard of life, from the highest to the very bottom of society. "She is taken with you!" he exclaimed, nudging Steeleye in the ribs, then rubbing his elbow as it had scraped against the plated mail of the shirt. "Were I your age, I should be spending a pleasant hour or three in yon lass's' company." He grinned widely, which faltered as he saw Steeleye staring at him.

"No?" he sipped the brew as a way to mask his embarrassment at misreading his companion.

After a few moments of awkward silence, Artfur launched once more into speech. "Aye for nearly a year, the nights have held terrors for the local folk. It began with sheep and cattle found dead in the fields, gutted and mauled. At first everyone thought a bear had wandered out of the forest, but the savagery was too much for even a bear, so I'm told. The townsfolk gathered and a delegation was sent to the Baron. After all, this is why we pay taxes is it not?" Now Artfur looked over his shoulder, a furtive gesture to ensure what he said was not overheard. "The delegation was never seen again. Four men, good and true, fathers and husbands..." He snapped his fingers loudly *click!* "Gone and never returned.

"Two more groups were sent, as several outlaying farms were attacked, the farmers butchered or taken the gods know where. Both groups failed to return. It is as if a curse had been laid upon the land. The Baron nor his men have been seen for months, yet strange looking shapes running over the Northern Fens have been seen, shambling creatures, letting out unholy bawling and gibbering. Cursed." Artfur finished, slapping his palm upon the table.

The innkeeper surprised them both, for he had moved within earshot whilst they spoke. Now he sat with them, a worried frown upon his honest face. "The singer tells the truth, sir. Why, even within the boundaries of the town of late, there have been reports of noises through the night, shadows seen flitting amongst the buildings, and look at yon shutter!" The keep pointed at a stout shutter, and Steeleye soon gouge marks in the wood, four deep scratches, as if made by a bear marking its territory. "The glass was smashed just two nights gone by, and I awoke to find we had been visited." He worried at his lip with his teeth, his hands unconsciously wringing the apron at his waist.

"The town is becoming unsafe, as well as the farms. See how

many have come to us tonight? They are here for the comfort of company, not just to hear our honoured guest here." He looked apologetically at Artfur, "though I am sure your presence has bolstered the numbers. My wife and I, aye and our girls too, we are ready to hop on a boat and make our way to the coast." He laughed nervously, surprised at himself for speaking so. Then making his excuses, he rose and went to shutter all the windows, lighting the lamps as he went.

Steeleye and Artfur looked at one another for several moments in silence. It was Artfur that finally spoke. "Was it really the Grimm, do you think, at the Western Gate?" His voice was subdued, the landlord's words hung heavy upon the both of them. Steeleye nodded, then, blowing out a breath, he beckoned Artfur closer.

"Something is happening in the world, something dark. It's not just here in the backwaters, but everywhere. As if..." He struggled for the word, "evil, is growing. I have heard from both you, and the Princess about this new Queen, this She'ah that now sits beside the King of Ashanarr- "

"Nay friend," Artfur broke in, "she sits the throne of Ashanarr alone. The old King Betod is dead, found broken upon the crags beneath his palace window. It is thought he jumped, missing his dear first wife Meera. She'ah alone is responsible for the new wars, though rumour has it that she is in turn but a puppet of the Southern Empress." Artfur rolled his eyes at the mention of the Empress, and made a swift sign with his fingers to ward off evil. "Now, there is creature of darkness, if the rumours are true." Again, he hunched forwards, relishing his rapt audience.

"None know where she came from, though many have speculated it to be the Pit, or some other gods forsaken place, but she is said to be unmatched in sorcery and brutality. The South is now hers, so I hear, from the icy Mythran Wastes, to the Fire Isles, the desert lands have bowed, as have many of the lush and ancient

Forest Lands. She paves her way with the skulls of the fallen, she builds temples of sorrow to unknown gods. Her army is legion, and is as bestial and monstrous as she is beautiful. Hair like spun silver, and eyes so blue as to be painful to look upon... what ails you?" Artfur reached out a hand of comfort, as he saw his companion suddenly blanch.

"*I shall come from the South.*"

Steeleye, waved away the hand, and paused a moment to compose himself. The description of the Empress had sent shivers down his spine, and his half-forgotten nightmare came back to him with stark clarity. The Huntress, that achingly beautiful creature that stalked him amongst the bones of the vanquished, that followed him each night through his dreams and called him Lightbringer, called him brother! She was the Empress?

Before he could fully recover and question Artfur, a lithe figure glided between the two men, and snatched up Artfur's jack, taking a gulp before the old man could react. "Dammit Helgen!" spluttered the singer, though Steeleye heard no anger in the voice, and could see only fondness in the mock stern gaze he turned upon the newcomer. Helgen was a girl of perhaps twelve summers, auburn hair left to grow long and wild, eyes that could be green or could be brown, depending upon the light. Her small face was pinched and looked half-starved though the huge grin she displayed at the two men belayed any indication of maltreatment, the girl was just naturally wiry. "Shall I warm up the audience uncle?" she asked, pulling a flute from her tunic and brandishing it eagerly. "I thought I could play a dance or two, and then juggle knives."

"You can play the tunes right enough, but you juggle *batons*," Artfur interjected firmly. Helgen rolled her eyes, and muttered something the two men couldn't quite hear, and then bounded off into the lamplit common room. Steeleye watched her snatch up a bag as she went, then jump up onto a table, laughing at the startled faces of the customers sat there. From the bag, she took three blades as long as her forearm and began to juggle, throwing them high into the air one by one. Catch and throw, catch and throw. The blades shone in the lamplight as they whirled through the air as if bewitched. Helgen winked at her uncle, then laughed merrily as the old singer shook his head with resignation. As Helgen tossed the blades, she began to dance and caper upon the table top, her skinny form in its homespun tunic and trews a comical, though engrossing, sight.

As if on cue, the landlord began to clap a beat to her steps, a wide smile upon his face. Soon enough near everyone in the room was clapping or slapping the table with their palms, stamping their feet, keeping time for the young entertainer's dance. The noise filled the room, and laughter rose to the rafters.

"My late sister's girl." Artfur raised his voice above the din. "She is a natural, can dance, juggle near anything you throw at her, play the flute and aye, is even passable with the harp, though that is a bit high-brow for such a place as this." He was smiling distractedly, his head bobbing in time to the audience's clapping. "When she came on the road with me, a few years ago, after her mother died of the wasting sickness, I thought she would be a burden." He shook his head at his own folly and levelled his sober gaze upon Steeleye. "How wrong can an old fool be?" he asked. "She has become as a daughter to me, and she will rise far above any station that I had hoped for myself; she has real talent, she does!"

Steeleye smiled despite himself. The old man clearly adored the young firebrand, and his eyes followed her every step and trick. The dread brought on by the talk of the Empress was still with him, sat like a stone in his heart, but when was dread not with him? Dread was a constant companion, one that he had learned to live with.

On the table, Helgen had just performed a somersault, her feet landing flat and square, the blades still spinning from hand to hand. Again, the innkeep reacted to his prompt, this time instead of leading the applause, which had suddenly increased in volume at the acrobatic feat, he thew a wooden rolling pin, still dusted with flour from the kitchens, towards the girl. Without hesitation Helgen caught up the pin, and it twirled amongst the knives over her head. The crowd roared its appreciation of the feat, Helgen laughed all the more, loving the attention.

As Helgen finished her act, catching the blades and tucking them into her bag, Steeleye clapped with all the rest of the towns-folk. There were a few whistles and whoops too. For a town so far from a major city, and one with such recent and ongoing tragedy, this was a rare feast of celebration indeed, an opportunity for many to put aside their cares and woes, to simply be entertained. Helgen knew her audience. She was well trained by her uncle, and he in turn had many years of experience on every stage, from royal courts to the meanest of common rooms. She held the customers rapt; they were in the palm of her hand.

Tossing the bag to the landlord, who fumbled the catch and dropped it to the floor, much to the merriment of his customers, Helgen performed two backflips to the bar. Once there, she hauled herself onto its shiny surface, pulled her flute from within the folds of her tunic, and then paused with the flute at her lips. All eyes were focused upon her, and she waited thus, until all noise in the common room died down. Once she was sure she had every-one's undivided attention, she began to play. The tune was well known, a merry dance, and everyone here knew the words to the song that accompanied the tune. Though only a slip of a girl, her command of the audience was complete. On she played, the notes twirling just as had the blades when she juggled.

She tapped her foot on the bar in an exaggerated fashion, stamping out the beat. The landlord winced as he saw his glorious bar top being used in such a manner, but he too was swept up in the joy of the moment, clapping his hands now along to her beat. Before long all were once more clapping, snippets of the songs' lyrics could be heard here and there as the audience relaxed even more and joined in.

"She taught herself this tune in a day." Artfur raised his voice with pride, and Steeleye felt himself grinning along with the old entertainer.

"She is very good," Steeleye said, finding himself once more clapping along with everyone else. When the tune finally finished, and the applause was at its highest, Helgen bowed exaggeratedly on the bar top, then motioned for quiet as she called out for requests. The response from the crowd was loud and instant, every table it seemed wanted a different favourite performed. Steeleye could make out some of the names, some he was familiar with, many more he wasn't.

"Play *Lucky Jack and the Kissing Game!*"

"Nay, *The Prince and the Milkmaid!*"

More and more titles were called, and Helgen beamed ecstatically at the attention, her eyes bright with excitement. She put her hand to her ear feigning that she was hard of hearing, and the crowd grew louder still. Steeleye was a little bemused, and he let his eyes wander about the room. It was packed with grinning, happy people. There were at least thirty tables in the big room, and each was full, plus there were men, women, and children standing in every available space: along the walls, by the bar, even on the steps leading to the second storey. As he watched the stairs, he saw Morinae begin to make her way down. She now wore a simple yellow gown, high of neck and long in length. Her hair was damp, no doubt still wet from her bath, and simply combed back from her face, falling long down her back. Her green eyes met his briefly, and she grinned with pleasure, seeing so many happy patrons. The Princess wove her way through the melee, to the chair that the landlord had kept empty for her, and fell into the cushion.

"That felt wonderful!" she said to Steeleye above the noise. "I've not bathed in an age." Her eyes found Helgen, strutting to and fro on the bar. The flute had gone back into her tunic, and from the bag she had pulled a fiddle and bow. She was sawing away at the strings, but the crowd was so loud the party by the fire could barely hear a thing.

"My niece," Artfur told Morinae with pride, "she is warming up the crowd for me, getting them ready to be entertained by a master singer." He shook his head ruefully. "It won't be long before I am doing the warm up, and she is the main event!" There was no bitterness in his tone, and only love in his eyes, laughter on his lips. At length, the old singer got to his feet, winking at the Princess and her companion. "Let me show you how it is done!" he said loudly, starting to make his way through the throng.

What happened next was both sudden and brutal. In one moment, the room was filled with happy laughter, families crowded together participating in simple, joyous entertainment, and the next the shuttered doors and windows burst inwards, shards of glass and splintered wood scything through the crowd. There was barely a moment to register what was happening, Steeleye caught the briefest glimpse of a black, apelike shape leaping through the shattered window. He heard the screams of the injured and the terrified, bodies and furniture seemed to suddenly be thrown everywhere, tables were smashed, blood sprayed, and, in the confusion, Steeleye pushed Morinae to the side and surged to his feet, just as an enormous howling figure came crashing through the window nearest the hearth. The wooden shutters exploded inwards, sending timber flying, the black iron of the lock catching Steeleye on the side of the head, felling him instantly.

He lay amongst the shattered furniture and shards of glass,

dimly aware of a great torrent of sound washing over him: the pleading and screaming of women and children, the cursing and hollering of their men, and over it all, the howling and insane gibbering of the invaders. Darkness began to crowd his vision, and he desperately tried to remain conscious, but the crack to his temple had been fierce, and even he, strong as he was, succumbed. The last thing he saw before oblivion claimed him was Morinae being dragged screaming by her hair through the chaos of the common room, by a hairy, taloned hand.

CHAPTER 14
CAPTAIN OF CROWS

Steeleye awoke to a blinding pain in his head. For several moments he was unable to move, nor see. His entire being centred about the pain radiating from his temple. It beat and throbbed like an enormous heart, with each beat a wave of nausea washed over him. Gradually he became aware of sounds outside of his head, muted, indistinct.

There was a voice, close by his ear. He tried to ignore it, to once more embrace the darkness, escape from the pain, wrap himself in the cloak of unconsciousness. But the voice would not let him be. "Captain!" said the voice, louder and more urgent. "Can you hear me? Captain?"

Steeleye cracked open an eyelid, and regretted it instantly. Lamplight pierced him, colours swirled in a chaotic vortex, and with it an overwhelming nausea. He rolled to his side and retched, feeling the sour ale burn his throat, even as it splashed amidst the ruins of the inn floor.

"Thank the Gods!" the voice piped up, heavy with relief, "I feared you were lost to us! That is a fearsome wound to your head, it looks like you were kicked by a horse. Can you understand me? Captain?"

Steeleye groaned, and tried to push the nagging voice away, but instead felt hands dragging him further into the waking world.

"Is he with us?" From beyond the fog of confusion, Steeleye heard more voices. He dimly recognized them, and with great effort managed to open both eyes. For a moment the world tilted, and again he felt bile rise in his throat. Gradually the nausea subsided, and the spinning slowed until he felt confident enough to look about him. He found himself on the floor of a large room, tables and chairs smashed and scattered all about; shadows danced and leaped, threatening to set him back to retching. But, at last, his vision steadied, and he was able to focus upon the face hovering over him.

"Artfur?" His voice was cracked, more a growl.

"Yes Captain, it is me, Artfur. Can you sit up? Do you remember where you are?" Seeing the leathery face, and hearing the familiar voice, brought memories crashing in. He remembered the townsfolk, clapping and stomping their feet, laughing and singing. Then the explosion of glass and wood as nightmare shapes burst into the room, the screaming and the pleading, the wretched howling of the injured, the tortured sounds of the dying. The chaos as the room was invaded. The creatures, all tooth and claw, killing and maiming, gibbering and laughing. Once again, he felt the crashing blow to his head, saw the bestial face, the red burning eyes filled with a lust for flesh. He saw again the lovely face of his companion, shock and fear writ clear, then pain as her still damp golden hair was violently yanked and she was gone.

"Morinae!" The name burst from him like a battle cry, and he lurched to his feet, pushing aside the singer. "Morinae!" he cried again. He reeled like a drunken man, stumbling over the remains of a chair and falling down to his knees, hard. The pain jolted him to greater awareness, and now he cast wild eyes about the room, feeling his blood run cold. The room was a shambles, even in the dim light cast by the few remaining lanterns: broken bodies, sprays of gore. He could now hear clearly the lament of the survivors. Here, a woman sobbed kneeling over a mangled corpse, a child judging by the size; there, a man wailed uncontrollably, like a beast, as he held the body of a woman to his breast, her neck hanging at an unnatural angle, her lifeless eyes staring at Steeleye, piercing him.

He looked away. Guilt and grief vied within him. Everywhere he looked it was the same: death and pain, destruction and horror. He found it hard to breath, his chest feeling as though rocks were piled upon him, crushing him down. His throat tightened, as if a strong hand throttled him, his heart beating loud and fast.

"Captain!" Artfur was shouting now, shouting in his face, his old hands clasping his shoulders, shaking him. "I need you to focus, I need you to help us." But the words seemed meaningless to Steeleye, and he tried to bury himself, to shut out the sights, the awful sounds, the smell of death and despair. On his knees, amid the devastation, Steeleye was shockingly reminded of a dungeon in the North, of the horror at finding Freija... Would it never end? Would he never be free of the guilt he felt for not being with her at the end? In anguish, Steeleye covered his head with his arms, falling to his side, curling tight into a ball, making himself as small as he could, seeking out a safe haven within himself, somewhere the terrors of the world couldn't reach him.

The sounds and the smells faded away. The pressing pain in his chest diminished, and Steeleye was falling into a blessed void. A sanctuary of darkness, peace, and solitude. He crouched in the primordial night. He hid within the shadowy confines of his mind.

But he was not alone in the darkness. He became aware that the shadows swirled like ebony fog, and from this tortured maelstrom stepped the Morriggu. Her brows were arched, the eyes grey as a stormy sea, softened as they looked upon his cowering shape. Her gown and raven wing cape were mere blurs in the dark, yet her face, her beautiful, terrible face, shone pale and distinct. There was understanding in her expression, there was pity and mercy and a forgiveness that was boundless, for she had lived countless eons, and had seen all the despair and fear that the world could offer.

Her pale hands rested upon his face, and she raised his head to meet her gaze.

"Your path, is not here," she said, her voice at once silk and thunder. "Here lies only death and defeat. This is not who you are." She paused, letting her words sink in, her eyes boring into his. "You are the Lightbringer, you are chosen to be the Bane of Shadows." Now, she took her hands from his face and pointed a crimson tipped finger directly at him.

"You are my sword, and you must be stronger than this." The Morriggu seemed to grow in the darkness, to loom over his kneeling shape. "There is too much to do, to linger here: you cannot give in to despair." Steeleye realised he was sobbing. He felt fear, and a twisting self-loathing.

"I have failed again," he blurted. "First, I lost Freija to the Grimm, now I have failed Morinae, and she trusted me with her life!" He pounded his fists in to the unseen floor, his voice becoming louder, wracked and anguished. "I failed yet again, and again another has paid the price! I am lost, Morriggu. I am not the sword that you hoped for, I am not worthy of your faith, not worthy of the trust that Morinae placed in me." Tears ran down his cheeks, and his sobs were loud and raw in the still black void.

"Morinae still lives, Steeleye, Grimmsbane." The voice of the Morriggu was suddenly as a whip, cracking harsh in Steeleye's ears. "She, and many others that you shared company with this night are still alive, though they are in dread peril. But I am yet to reap their souls, for they are still clinging to life. Would you abandon Morinae now?" The question cut him as deeply as Kleave's blade had. "Will you kneel here, whilst she is tortured, her body wracked with terror? Would you leave her, and all the others, to the mercy of Janovis?"

The name of the demon, one of the Seven Sisters, wound its way around the void like a slithering beast.

"Ah, I see a there is still a spark of my champion within you." The Morriggu continued in a softer tone, seeing that Steeleye had raised his head at the demon's name.

"Janovis is responsible for the destruction of the inn?"

"And much more besides. She sits in the seat of the old Baron, in the Northern Fens, Like a poison, her evil seeps into this land. She is a curse upon the world, a deceiver, a vile succubus preying upon mankind. Through the ages, thousands have fallen victim to her gross appetites, but here you are, Lightbringer, bearer of the Godsteel blade, one of the few weapons capable of killing a demon of such power. You are sworn to vanquish Janovis, and her kin...so close now. Only one more day, and you can strike your first blow against the Darkness. You have the strength Steeleye, you are far more than you know." The voice of the Morriggu trailed into silence. He was alone again in the shadows, though now it seemed the darkness was not so total, his misery not quite so absolute.

* * *

"Captain?" Again, the familiar voice of the old story teller drew him back to the horror of the Inn. This time Steeleye looked at the old bard, and nodded. The pounding in his head continued, and his vision swam, but these were conditions he could cope with. He could persevere.

"What happened when I was knocked out, Artfur?" The old

bard reached out and helped him to move to a chair that was still serviceable. Once Steeleye was sat, and more alert and in his right mind, Artfur launched into his tale.

"Creatures," he began, "creatures that I have sung many a song about, but up until this night didn't truly believe in... They burst in through every window, took the door straight off the hinges with brute force. They were so fast, so many of them too, maybe twenty, thirty even, and they began to smash anything and everything, and anyone..." Artfur paused in his tale, and gestured towards the bar. There, laid side by side, were a dozen or so bodies of the slain; men, women and children. They were covered poorly with hasty shrouds, made of coats, curtains, whatever had been at hand, but the covers could not mask the horrendous wounds inflicted by savage teeth and rending claws. Steeleye could feel the bile rising once more as he caught sight of one particular shape, tiny in size. It could only be that of a small child, an infant.

Artfur followed his gaze and placed a hand upon his arm. "Do not berate yourself Captain. I saw you felled, and you are lucky not to be laid beneath a shroud over there yourself. Why I thought you surely dead there was so much blood. No one could have done aught after such a blow."

"Why did they leave?" Steeleye's wits were gradually sharpening. "They had the place at their mercy, why did they leave so many alive?"

"They took what they came for, I reckon. Took at least twenty with them, women and children." It was the landlord who spoke. He was limping as he joined them. He held a mug of water in his hands, which he offered to Steeleye. "The rest of the town was hit too: houses, shops, everywhere. They butchered many, stole some, and left others." The innkeep was shaking, tears streaming down his face as he wandered off to help others.

"Jonn is a good man," Artfur said, using the landlord's given name as he watched him stop to right an upended table. "His wife

Leanna is laid out there before the bar; his youngest daughter, Bella, is amongst those taken."

"Morinae?"

"Aye Captain, the Princess, and my poor Helgen, all taken by the beasts."

Steeleye looked closely at the old man, the eyes red rimmed, the leathery face slack from grief, his shoulders stooped and bowed as if he carried a load too heavy to bear. Steeleye knew that burden well. The guilt would be with him forever. He sipped the water, cold and fresh drawn from a well. Then as his thirst registered, he quickly emptied the cup. "They are yet alive." He spoke quietly, almost to himself. Uttering the words the Morriggu had said to him aloud, was a spur. Even though he was still groggy and reeled drunkenly as he got to his feet, he felt his strength returning.

"What did you say?"

"It's not too late. For some, at any rate, they are yet alive."

"How can you know this? You were senseless through the attack, the savagery was brutal, the poor folk are surely dead. We need to bury these poor souls and grieve best we can, then we need to cross the river before they return. All of us. This whole province is cursed."

"Trust me, Artfur, those that were taken are not dead yet. Those creatures were the Grimm, but they were serving another, an evil that resides in the fens. We need to be going there, not across the river. We need to be gathering every able-bodied man and women, armed with whatever they can bring, and we need to go and get our people back." He was steadier on his feet now, and his voice stronger. "We need to be moving soon Artfur; are you coming with me?" The storyteller was dumbstruck for a moment, and could only stare.

"How do you know this?" he repeated his question. Steeleye was aware that several others were looking their way too, and a quiet had descended upon the inn. Many pairs of eyes, desperate eyes, were watching them, waiting for the same answer. Hopeful, yet fearful too. Steeleye struggled to find the words that would bring about the townsfolks' help. He knew how bizarre they would think it if he told them of his visitation, that he was allied with the Mistress of Crows, but he had to find a way. He doubted he could rescue Morinae and the rest, and slay one of the Seven, all alone. He wished Rolf were here, and Aelrik too, with men like those at his side, he could storm the gates of the Pit itself.

Without realizing it, Steeleye had begun a silent prayer, a prayer to the Keeper of his soul, his tormentor and his saviour. The Morriggu answered, in her usual vague though impressive way.

A sudden breeze blew through the common room. It came like a whisper, and the stilled townsfolk strained to hear the voices that were entwined within the zephyr. Soft whispers, like children at play, but just out of sight. Artfur looked about him wildly. The breeze intensified, the lanterns swinging to and fro on their hooks, casting long, wild shadows along the walls. But there was one wall that remained dark, one corner where the shadows were stygian and dense. And within the darkness, something moved, the mere suggestion of a tall slim womanly shape. All eyes were transfixed upon the apparition, though everyone there would have agreed they felt no threat, only a feeling of awe and wonder. The shoulders of this shape lifted, their shadow enveloping the wall, and from within the depths, there came a new sound, faint at first, as if far off, but gradually becoming louder.

Artfur and all the rest of those gathered there, could hear the beating of many wings, and the raucous caw of crows. Within moments, the room was full of ebony shapes, their wings beating loud as they circled the room, hundreds of huge crows, their voices loud and strident. Everyone in the room stood transfixed, and gaped: they had never seen so many. Round and around they flew, until Steeleye raised his arm, and at that signal, the largest of the crows flew to perch upon his forearm. The rest of the black tide flew through the shattered door, filling the predawn sky with their cacophony.

Once calm had returned to the room, Artfur let out an explosive breath. He looked at his companion with wide eyes, his mouth moving yet no words forthcoming. For his part, Steeleye stroked the ebon head of the crow, then swept up his arm so the bird took flight. With a great *caw,* the creature followed its brethren through the door.

Steeleye looked about him at the staring townsfolk, took in their awe at the supernatural. Many cast glances between the now bare wall and Steeleye himself. Several had fallen to their knees, mumbling prayers to their gods. Artfur was the first to speak, though his voice held a tremor. "What have we just witnessed, Captain? Who could bring such a spectacle into our midst?"

"Are you a sorcerer?" This came from Jonn, who looked fearfully now at the warrior.

"I am no sorcerer, Jonn, have no fear of that. You have just been visited by none other than the Morriggu, the Lady of the Long Sleep herself. The crows are her eyes and ears in the mortal realm. They are even now crossing the fens, in pursuit of the Grimm." He let his eyes rove over the gathering, could see the fear and the pain of loss. "The Morriggu bids me go after her crows, to win back the Lady Morinae, and your loved ones." Now Steeleye stood up straighter and he drew the Godsteel blade, and plunged its point into the stone flags of the common room floor. It quivered there, driven deep into the stone, lamplight played upon its dull length.

"I carry a sword that can defeat the Grimm, and their mistress, and the Morriggu has told me where to find them. They abide in the fortress of your Baron, in the fens to the north.

But I will need a guide, I will need companions that will stand with me. I cannot do this alone." He let his words hang in the air for a while, watching. "What say you Artfur? Will you accompany me?" The singer surprised Steeleye, and perhaps himself too, as he nodded without hesitation. His eyes like many others there were fixed upon the blade, a blade that could cleave stone.

"I will, though I will need a weapon. I cannot bear the thought of Helgen at the mercy of those creatures."

"What of you Jonn?" Steeleye asked, "will you come and bring back your daughter?"

"Damn right, I will." The amiable man that Steeleye had met just so few hours past was gone. Now here stood a man that had lost more than he had ever imagined possible, but if there was a chance of bringing back his child, he would do whatever it took. He looked at the shrouded shape of his wife by the bar. "She would never forgive me, if I did not at least try."

Other patrons of the tavern were now coming forward, many with tear-stained cheeks and eyes red from weeping, but there was a set to their jaw, and many a strong work-hardened hand came to pat Steeleye upon the shoulder. Heads nodded, and red eyes became hard with resolve.

It was Artfur that now raised his voice, rich and commanding as if he were reciting some saga. "Spread word through the town of what we have just seen!" he cried out. "The Dark lady herself has sent us her Captain of the Crows, to lead us against the creatures that haunt the fens. Bring your bows, your spears, swords if you have them, axes, clubs, knives whatever you can wield and kill with." Artfur was breathless in his fervour, but his passion lit a fire in the hearts of the gathered folk.

Soon enough, word had spread throughout the town: the Goddess of the Long Sleep was with them, she had sent to them her Captain of Crows, and he would lead them to reclaim their people, or at the very least take revenge upon the horrors that stalked their lands.

They brought with them many weapons. Some bore swords or long bladed knives, others axes made for chopping wood, though their sharp edge would cleave a limb just as well. In place of halberds, they brought pitch forks, brutal looking affairs that Steeleye would not wish to get on the wrong end of. Whether makeshift or made for war, the gathering men and women positively bristled with sharp edges. But the weapons that brought the grimmest of smiles to Steeleye's face were the longbows, the great yew bows that could feather a target at one hundred paces, and it seemed that every second member of this gathering carried such a bow.

As he looked about, the throng was gathering now outside the tavern, their number too great to fit indoors. Steeleye was pleasantly surprised to see the odd helmet here and there, an old and rusted breastplate, even a shirt of mail or two. The townsfolk and the surrounding farmers were well enough equipped, and he was sure they could see off a band of brigands and rabble easily enough, but a group of the Grimm would pose a hardier foe. Yet he also knew there was little option here: the choices were clear, do nothing and become victims of increasing raids by the monstrosities, flee and be sure the Grimm would follow, or fight, and fight hard.

With luck, their attack would be as much as a surprise to the Grimm, as their attack upon the inn had been.

* * *

"WE ARE READY CAPTAIN."

Artfur broke his reverie. Dawn was fully broken. The sky to the East shone red as a courtesan's lips, violet clouds gathering in a brooding mass, boding ill for the day ahead. "Will you be saying a few words, Captain?" asked the singer hopefully, his nerves making his voice high-pitched. Jonn stood at his shoulder, nodding encouragement.

Steeleye was not used to this, and wasn't particularly keen on speaking before a crowd, but he was aware that he had prompted this rag-tag army to be made, and he knew that he would be responsible for what befell them in the coming hours. He looked over the gathered ranks, people of all sizes, men and women both, stood watching him with eager and hopeful eyes. Gods, there must be two hundred souls here, he thought. He looked more closely, and felt his throat tighten. He saw a huge fellow, probably the towns smith, all muscle and beard. He carried a hammer in a meaty fist and looked like he could use it. Next to the smith, though not so massive in stature, stood a man armed with both a bow and a huge cleaver. Steeleye had no idea what its original purpose was, but felt certain it would serve as well as any axe. But for every two or three such armed, there was a man or woman carrying a kitchen knife, or a wooden staff, and some with no weapons at all, just their courage and desperation.

Hardly a great host, Steeleye thought, hardly the same calibre as those he had stormed the Western Gate at the City of the Dead with, but they must suffice. In every face, he saw mirrored his own grim resolve. They, like him, had loved ones, or at least those they were responsible for, beyond the fens. They were aware they would face an inhuman enemy, but they knew too that they were out of real options. Even as Steeleye began to speak, he wondered how many here, would run screaming if they knew the real enemy they would face today, a Demon of the Old Host, Janovis of the Seven, evil incarnate, with an insatiable thirst for human souls.

But he would not tell them of the Demon. He needed their numbers. With a little fortune on their side, they could engage the Grimm, giving him time to confront the real enemy. He needed them as a distraction. The thought hit him hard. Was he willing to sacrifice the townsfolk to give him a chance at killing Janovis?

"Captain?" Artfur again prompted him. The townsfolk were watching, waiting, shuffling their feet, anxious, ready to be off before their courage failed. As Steeleye began to speak, he felt a presence with him, comforting, encouraging. He felt the Morriggu close by, and his doubts were quashed, his confidence surged.

"Your Baron is dead." The words he spoke prompted a muttering in the crowd. He saw the surprise, the shock, and slowly the registering fear. "You have heard that the Morriggu has sent me to lead you, to save your people. This is true in part, the Morriggu has indeed sent me here, though I had no notion of why until last night. I followed a Princess here, and she, like your kin and neighbours was taken last night. Taken by the same creatures that killed your Baron, and have been growing in their boldness, spreading their terror across your land." He paused, watching the fear course through the crowdlike a tide.

"These creatures, these Grimm, they follow another." He felt the invisible nudge of the Soul Collector, as if she were guiding his words. "There is a great evil, sitting even now, in the keep that belonged to your Baron, and this evil commands dark creatures such as we all saw last night. The Morriggu is held by her oath not to enter the fray, but she has sent me to fight in her stead." He saw the hope kindled at the mention of the goddess, the hope dulled the fear a little. "The Morriggu knows that each of you, too, will stand before the shadow, that you good people will not bow down to the darkness that threatens you, but will instead lead me over the fens, to take back your people. To take back your land." Steeleye felt a sudden compulsion to raise his arm, and a great black crow alighted upon it, its fierce eyes raked the gathering, and it let out a great cry that sounded very much like "Morriggu!"

The crowd were awestruck. They stared with superstitious wonder at the warrior before them, at the huge black crow.

Steeleye raised his voice loud, "Stand together, shoulder to shoulder, with your kin, your friends and your neighbours. Lead me to the Baron's keep across the fens, and we shall bring the fury of the Morriggu to the evil hiding there!" There was a resounding cheer from the gathering. They were swept along by the spectacle of the crow, by the Captain of the Crows standing tall in his shining hauberk, who would fight beside them to save their loved ones. Almost as one they turned and headed North. There was excited chatter amongst them, backslapping and camaraderie like they had not felt before.

Steeleye was swept along with them, the crow taking flight, circling overhead.

As Steeleye marched, Artfur fell into step beside him. "Pretty words, Captain. But methinks it will be a little harder than you let on to bring our people home safe." Steeleye continued to walk, but he met Artfurs piecing gaze with one of his own. "I need you all to draw out the Grimm, get them from the keep, where the longbows can do their work. So long as they are kept at a distance, these good folks can win through. The Grimm are terrible to fight in close quarters, they would go through you all like a scythe, but with the longbow, you should be safe enough."

"Well, that is comforting." Artfur muttered bitterly, looking at the dagger that he carried. Steeleye grinned at his companion and whispered "I will be looking for a few volunteers to enter the keep with me." He winked at the storyteller.

"Ha, that sounds so much safer than standing behind an archer." Artfur's words dripped sarcasm. Then a moment later, he rubbed at his face and made a groaning sound. "Very well, I will find the strongest to enter the keep with you and me. That there blacksmith looks like he can handle himself, and there are a few others that used to be soldiers so I hear. They might not stab themselves by accident if the going gets a little hairy."

"You don't have to come in the keep, Artfur. You have my word

I shall seek out your niece, and if at all possible, I shall bring her out."

The old storyteller nodded his thanks, and smiled a tired smile. "For fifty years I have sung of all kinds of heroics, of battles and great deeds, yet I have never once seen any real danger. I sing of the labours of others, of events a thousand years gone by, songs passed down through the ages." He was quiet for a little while, deep in thought, and Steeleye waited. When the old man spoke next, his voice was so low Steeleye almost missed it. "Perhaps we are in a new age? Perhaps new stories are being written now, and maybe we are all to be a part of them." Louder, the Storyteller asked, "What great evil sits in the keep? What is it that the Morriggu has sent you to confront?"

For a moment, Steeleye considered lying about what the Morriggu had revealed to him, but as he looked around him at the marching throng, saw their determined faces as they gave one another encouragement, helped one another with smiles and banter, he realised they were all in this together, he had no right to conceal the true nature of the enemy, should they ask.

"It is Janovis, one of the Seven Sisters. I've been tasked by the Morriggu to slay them all." He grinned at the shocked expression on Artfur's face.

"And how many of the Seven have you faced so far?" Artfur asked at length, when the enormity of the task ahead had fully sunk in.

"This is the first!" Steeleye slapped the old man on the shoulder, and laughed loudly at his dour expression.

CHAPTER 15
MARCH INTO DARKNESS

I t took less time than Steeleye had anticipated to reach the
fens. A vast expanse of clumped, purple-flowered heathers
that crunched underfoot. A well-used road wound its way
through the shrubbery. Great ferns grew amidst the heather, their
nodding leaves pit pattering with raindrops. The sky was leaden,
the clouds low and dark. The rain fell so fine it was almost a mist,
yet soaked through the thickest of woollens. Steeleye had had the
forethought to collect a cloak, and now pulled up the hood,
scowling at the weather. This low cloud would give them cover as
they approached the Baron's keep, yet he was also aware it would
be bad for moral. Nothing made marching over a dreary landscape
worse than rain, except perhaps biting hail, though the weather
was too warm and cloying for such. He was grateful for such small
mercies.

His reverie was interrupted by the deep bass voice of the
smith. Sten was his name, and though none of his family had
been taken, close friends and good neighbours had. Sten was an
intelligent man, and he knew that the only road to peace was to
confront evil such as this head on. If he ignored it, then perhaps

next time he and his loved ones would not be so lucky. "We should leave the road and walk cross country, Captain, as the crow flies as it were." He grinned apologetically. Steeleye fixed him with a look. He had to tilt his chin upwards, Sten was so tall. "The road winds, finding the most level way for the use of wagons and such, but we are all afoot, so should travel a more direct route."

"Will it save us time?" Steeleye was dubious. He didn't want to become lost in the fens should the mist become thicker. "And is it safe?"

"It will enable us to arrive at the old skinflints keep by mid to late afternoon, rather than late evening or even worse, after night-fall. And aye, the way is safe enough if you know where to put your feet, and many here know the way well. Most of the women-folk hereabouts used to tread the fens every day collecting herbs and suchlike, before the ghouls began to roam that is."

Steeleye nodded and gave his thanks and agreement to the suggestion, and soon enough several townsfolk hurried into the lead, leaving the roadway and heading directly North over the heather and fern. They had shawls and coats pulled over their heads against the rain. Their feet squelched and splashed, yet they led on without hesitation, and if it meant reaching their destination in daylight, rather than night time, Steeleye was only too pleased to follow.

On the road, he had begun to regret leaving his horse stabled at the inn, but now walking amongst the hummocks and tufts, after stumbling several times, he was glad he was not astride a mount as he felt sure he would have led his horse on to an acci-dent by now. He watched where the leaders were putting their feet, and did his best to emulate their tread. Behind him, in a line of twos and threes, the motley gathering marched on.

The towns-folk proved to be made of stern stuff and stout of heart. Hour after hour they tramped through the rain at a steady pace. No stops or breaks were asked for, nor suggested by Steel-eye. On and on they went, heads down watching their footing. The sky darkened even more and the rain intensified, making the fenland slippery with mud, but still they ploughed on regardless.

Steeleye found himself falling in step with Sten once more. Artfur was keeping up too, and walked at his other shoulder. "Have you been to the keep often?"

"Aye, the old man was too tight-fisted to keep a smith, so I would journey there a few times each month to shoe horses, fix blades and such, but a couple of years ago he cut even that back, and would only send for me when absolutely necessary.

"The numbers of his war band dwindled too. That's why so many of us in the town use the longbow. That was the Baron's idea. We all had to train with the bow, so we were like a reserve militia, unpaid foot soldiers, or at least that is what he had in mind, but it never worked the way he intended. The brigands grew in number. Many I suspect were members of his war-band that he had let go, but whatever the Baron became more and more isolated. A shame, he was a good and fair man once upon a time."

Steeleye listened carefully. All the information he could get would be useful he was sure, as yet he had not arrived upon a plan of just what to do when he reached the Baron's holdings, and the responsibility of the many souls that accompanied him weighed heavy. He needed to know the access points to the Keep, its strengths, its weaknesses, its position relative to where they would be making their advance from.

Sten was eager to help, so Steeleye asked the questions. Sten answered, and in more detail than Steeleye had hoped. The Smith was naturally curious and had taken the time to get to know his surroundings whilst working for the Baron.

Steeleye soon learned the keep was a simple affair, a squat looking tower only three stories in height, though it had two levels below ground too. It had a courtyard, surrounded by a wall some ten feet high and perhaps two or three hundred paces in circumference, not a huge affair, and easily defended by a small body of soldiers, which suited the Baron's pocket. The courtyard housed the stables, the laundry rooms and such, with many outbuildings scattered through it. In the tower itself, the ground floor was taken up by kitchens and a hall where the men would eat with the Baron; the first floor was the soldiers' quarters, and the top floor was the manse of the Baron himself. Sten had never been onto that floor, he said, but the men had told him that the Baron lived with sparse luxury, and his quarters were hardly distinguishable from those of his hired men.

Steeleye urged the Smith to tell him more of the wall, and in particular the gate and how it was best approached, and he frowned as Sten described it. "It's nothing fancy," he said, spitting rain water. "Yet it is strong oak, and would withstand more than we can throw at it. As to its size? Well, a cart drawn by a couple of horses can pass through easy enough."

"And the approach to the gate is unobstructed I should imagine?"

"Oh aye." Sten nodded in his hood, "but I wasn't thinking of taking us to the front door...

Steeleye peered into the shadows of his companion's hood, and could see a toothy grin. "When I was there last, the Baron wanted me to reinforce a grill that covered the entrance to a passageway a hundred strides outside the walls." Sten walked on in silence for a moment or two, and it was Artfur that lost patience first.

"Well?" piped up the storyteller "What about this grill? And where does the passage lead?"

Sten stooped as he walked, to ensure his companions could hear him. "The passage leads to the lowest cellar floor. There are a few cells there, a reminder that once upon an age the keep held real authority in the area, but the grill was rusted through, and would have given way at the hinges with a few good kicks."

"But if you reinforced the grill, what good does that do us now?" Artfur snapped, his temper shortened by the weather, and the fear that twisted in his bowels. Steeleye found himself mirroring the Smith's smile, for he had an inkling as to what Sten was driving at.

"Who said I reinforced the grill?" Sten asked innocently, then winked at Artfur, and in a hushed tone continued "Baron Meska has a habit of slow payment, so I made excuses that I needed more tools and would return when I had the time. He was far from happy, but I am the only smith for miles around, so I generally get my way in such matters." Now he looked directly at Steeleye and went on, "so, we don't need to go in the front way at all."

This was unexpected, and Steeleye felt a surge of hope. His mind ran through a series of possible tactics. He was faced with an undeniably superior force in close contact, and his own forces, though brave, with many ready to give their all, were terrified, ill-trained and ill prepared. He knew that he must cause a diversion that allowed a small group of rescuers to enter the Keep, yet didn't bring the majority of his force into too much peril. Though they might have the advantage of numbers, he felt sure that if they engaged the Grimm hand to hand, there would be a rout, and few survivors.

The longbows were the answer of course. All they needed to do was lure the Grimm from the walls, out into the open, and then bring them down with withering fire from a safe distance. But how to draw the creatures out? He knew they were primitive and impulsive, their rage and bloodlust, though fearsome in battle could perhaps be used against them. If they were challenged perhaps?

"We need a way to get the attention of the creatures, a way to bring them out of their holdings, into the open so archers can bring them down. I have faced them in battle, they are wild and frenzied, lacking discipline. We need to entice them, to lure them onto the fenlands." He was speaking aloud though in truth it was for his own benefit, playing with ideas.

"The Horn of Stromphael!" Artfur suddenly spluttered, both the Smith and Steeleye turned their eyes to the excited old man. "The Horn that rallied the armies on the Plains of Morinorn millennia ago... surely a blast from such a horn, a challenge from a weaker force, would bring the monsters out into the open?" Now the old man looked horrified at the prospect of the slavering horde bearing down upon the townsfolk. Colour drained from him, and his scrawny hand went to his throat. "Gods it would be carnage," he mumbled.

"No Artfur, at least not in the way that you think. Look about you, see how many longbows we have! If these folks are half as good as Sten says, then the Grimm may not get within fifty paces of our ranks." Steeleye patted the old man on the shoulder. "But we don't have the Horn of Stromphael. If I remember my legends, the Horn shattered when the Dark One cried in anguish at the death of his beloved Arianna." He grinned at Artfur. Suddenly he felt energised, he had the seeds of a plan, a way to keep the townsfolk from too much danger, and that was a priority. There would be risks, but in warfare there were always risks.

"Not the real Horn." Artfur shrugged off Steeleye's hand and rummaged through the satchel he carried over his shoulder. Presently he brought out a curling ram's horn, tipped with brass and engraved with runes. "This," he said proudly, holding the Horn aloft, "this is a replica of the legendary horn that I had made years ago, when I would sing the songs of legends, in Kings' halls and not common rooms. I would blow the horn as I began my telling of Stromphael's last charge against the armies of Aihaab, and its tone is clear and loud. I was famous once upon a time for such theatrics..." Artfur trailed to silence as he looked fondly at the relic from his own glory days. It gleamed wetly as a forlorn shaft of pale sunlight fell from the darkening clouds.

"It will do nicely, I'm sure." Steeleye motioned for the old bard to put away the horn, and take more care with his footing. They were being led through deep mud just now, it came over the ankles of Steeleye's stout boots. He cursed as he slipped and almost went to his knees, his outflung hand saving him from total embarrassment, not to mention a thorough soaking. He pulled his hood tighter and stretched out his legs. He noticed the others seemed much more adept at walking the fens than he was, and cursed inwardly at their knack over the difficult terrain.

It was about an hour after seeing the horn that the Keep came into view, sitting dark and foreboding on the vague horizon. Its walls were a blur through the rain, hardly more than a smudge in the distance. As his eyes fell upon the squat tower, lightning forked out of the tumultuous sky, its harsh brightness cutting a jagged tear through the clouds. Deep bass thunder followed close at its heels, and as it boomed out many of the party struggling over the heather flinched in their cloaks, the thunder rolling over the fens like an ominous tide.

Steeleye beckoned for Sten to fetch the innkeeper, Jonn, to walk with him, and when he was at last joined by the landlord, Steeleye told him of his plan, such as it was, with the time he had and the information to hand. They would walk to within two hundred paces of the walls, and then Jonn, or whoever was able, would blow the horn to get the attention of the Grimm. Under no circumstances were they to go nearer, or engage hand to hand with the creatures, for that would bring nothing but swift defeat, and a no doubt horrible death. They were to goad the Grimm into the open, then feather the bastards. If they should start to get close, then the rescuers should fall back, drawing the Grimm with them, but he stressed that the townsfolk keep a good distance.

Whilst the main body of the townsfolk were engaged thus,

Steeleye and a small number of the better armed and experienced amongst them, would enter the Keep through a tunnel that Sten knew of; this would lead them to the lower levels of the Keep, where they hoped to find their missing loved ones. If they were not in the lower chambers, they would work their way upwards, floor by floor, until they found them, and brought them out safely.

Jonn met his eyes with a level stare, and Steeleye looked away first. It was a desperate plan, he knew; it was fraught with dangers, and many a chance for disaster, but it was all they had time for. He was certain that they had to act quickly, or their daughters, their sons, friends and loved ones would be butchered or put to even worse ends.

As if he could read Steeleye's thoughts, Jonn smiled ruefully and nodded. "We shall draw them out right enough, and we have bows aplenty to cut them down. But I'm thinking not all the buggers will fall into the trap. There will be plenty still within the walls, enough to give you and those you take with you, more than a little hardship."

Steeleye slapped the hilt of the sword at his side with a calloused hand. "Nothing comes easy, Jonn," he said, and, as if to give weight to his statement lightning flared again, searing the clouds. Thunder cracked.

The townsfolk, hooded and cloaked, soaked to the skin but grimly determined, walked over the heather like a slow relentless wave advancing ever closer to the Keep.

CHAPTER 16

JANOVIS

As they neared the keep, the motley army made its way back to the road. They had saved time, just as Sten had predicted, and the walls of the Keep were clearly visible even in the wan afternoon light. Now they trooped along the hard surface with grim purpose. Steeleye and Jonn had taken the lead, along with Sten, Artfur, and several others, all bristling with spears and blades.

Lined along the roadside there were wooden poles ten feet long driven into the heather. Impaled upon each of these grisly totems was a corpse. The first was the Baron Meska. The stake had been driven into his back, then hoisted upright. His arms and legs were splayed out. The skin had been flayed from his body. It was only by the shield bearing his personal sigil, nailed to the post, that the dead man could be identified. Staring up at the grotesque shape, Steeleye could see carrion had been busy: flies swarmed about the body in a black, frenzied cloud.

He felt bile rise in his throat. One of the men with him moaned in horror, and made a sign with his fingers to ward off evil. Too late for that, Steeleye thought, evil had come to the fens, and brought with it a new type of terror.

Atop the next post, a corpse was skewered vertically; the sharpened tip of the stake protruded from his silently screaming mouth. Once again, the man had been flayed of all skin. Flies were thick upon him, mercifully obscuring much of the horror. Steeleye could hear several of his followers retching, and could hardly blame them. There was a scrap of parchment tacked to the post, with brutal glyphs scrawled upon it. Time and the fens damp weather, had left the meaning of the writing illegible, but Steeleye assumed it was some way to identify the victim, as with the shield for the Baron.

His eyes searched the roadsides, and he found himself counting the totems. Twelve, fourteen, sixteen, on and on went the stakes, and atop each there was the remains of some poor wretch, tortured and flayed, half-eaten and left to rot. This was the grimmest of warnings to all the gathered townsfolk. Their own loved ones would likely soon adorn one of these monstrous spikes. Though only simple folk, steely resolve ran through the gathering. Rather than send them screaming for their homes and hearths, to cower beneath blankets and start at every creak and shadow, they gripped their makeshift weapons tighter, and turned furious eyes towards the keep's gate.

Steeleye too, looked at the gate, picking it out clearly by the brightness of a lightning bolt that tore through the sky. He saw, too, the twisted shapes upon the poles, clearly. Too clearly. He made a guess that they stood roughly two hundred paces from the wall, and gripped Jonn's arm tight, pulling his attention away from the dead.

"Here is your line, Jonn. Gather up your archers, have them stand in ranks, bows ready." He bade Artfur hand the horn to the landlord. As Jonn took the rams horn, Steeleye saw that his hand was shaking violently. Jonn saw it too and laughed nervously.

"Will you look at that?" he nodded at his hand, "I won't be able to nock an arrow with hands like that."

Steeleye gripped Jonn's shoulder reassuringly, his fingers tight enough to distract the landlord. "Think of your daughter, Jonn. Think of all those that you know, being held in there. This is where we put a stop to the creatures, this is where you and your neighbours take back the fens." Steeleye was aware that the men Sten had chosen to accompany them into the Keep were gathered close. They were doing their best not to look at the totems, to keep their anger hot, their fear controlled.

There was no need for speeches: each of those gathered knew the price of failure. Word had been passed around what was expected of them, and the signal they were waiting for. Almost two hundred strong, they waited in the downpour; their eyes fixed upon the gate. There was nothing more to do. Steeleye had made all the plans he was able, and was well aware they were woefully inadequate. He nodded to Jonn, "give us a couple of minutes to get closer, then blow that damned horn."

"Won't they see you coming?"

Steeleye shook his head, peering at the wall top through the rain. "I see no sentries, no lookouts. The Grimm are not like us, Jonn, they are more animal than man." He paused, adding silently to himself that they had new playthings to keep them occupied. "We shall be in and out, hopefully, before they even know we have been there." He grinned then, hiding the apprehension that sat in his stomach like a lead weight. "And your daughter will be with us Jonn."

Not giving the landlord time to reply, Steeleye motioned for Sten to lead them to the passage in the fens. With a nod, the blacksmith set off swiftly, angling to the East in a long loop that would take them beyond the walls, and to the damaged grill. Steeleye and the rest of the small force were quick to follow, their feet splashing through the moor. Lightning came now in constant flares, making their way easier through the gloom. The rain fell harder, and the party made swift progress and remained unseen.

Sten pulled up beyond the wall, and began a frantic search for the grill. "It is here somewhere," he rasped, blinking away rain water. "Look for a small mound," he called to his fellows. "The entrance we seek is in a small hillock." The rest of the men were quick to join the search, and only a minute or two had passed, before Artfur stumbled upon the raised ground.

"Here!" cried out the old singer, "it's here!"

The rest of the men were swift to gather round and take a look at their way into the Keep. A rusted steel grill, some four feet in diameter, was set into the small hillside. Lightning flashed and the men clustered about the grate could see a path beyond, dipping into the gloom.

"Hurry up, Sten. Clear the grill away." Artfur moved aside to let the blacksmith get to the grate. Sten didn't hesitate, he gripped the bars and began to exert terrible pressure, but the grill remained stubbornly in place.

"It should open easily," panted the smith. "It was near dropping open the last time I was here." Once again, he gripped the bars and pulled, twisted, and pushed, yet the grate was closed fast.

Peering over Sten's shoulder, Steeleye saw the gleam of new steel. Links of new chain were looped through the grill and were set fast to a ring in the tunnel beyond. Steeleye pushed the blacksmith aside and drew his sword. The men fell back from the wild-eyed warrior, and the blade flashed through the air, shearing the chain links and a bar of the grill itself, as if they were made of kindling, not steel. Without hesitation he pulled the barrier free, the loud clanging noise made them all flinch; had the noise been heard? The thunder that had seemed to be rolling continuously had fallen silent, the men waited with bated breath.

And then, into the void of silence, there came a long loud blast from a horn in the distance. The note came again, strident and savage. Steeleye grinned fiercely, he could picture Jonn with the ram's horn pressed to his lips blowing for all his worth. "It could be the legendary Stromphael himself, out there on the fens." Steeleye called to a wide eyed Artfur. "Come on, we will have to trust that the beasts will answer the call of the horn." With that he moved quickly into the passageway, Sten at his shoulder.

* * *

JONN WATCHED the small party running over the fen, aware that the rest of their band, almost two hundred souls, were gathered behind him. They were six or seven deep on the road. Many carrying the fearsome longbow, even now they were taking dry strings from pouches, bracing the lengths of yew through their legs, then bending the top down with grunting effort. Their strings, already attached to the bows' bottom arm, were stretched taught as they were looped over the top. Yard long arrows were loosened in quivers. Once set, the archers turned their eyes to the portal in the wall, two hundred paces distant.

Behind those doors were creatures beyond their ken. So too, were their wives and daughters, sons and friends. Feet shifted. The instinct to flee into the oncoming night wormed through them. Lightning flashed, thunder growled and then a stillness fell upon the fenland.

Standing at the head of the group, Jonn lifted the ram's horn to his lips, and blew.

There was a strangled piping sound that barely reached his companions. Jonn took the horn from his lips and looked back at his fellows abashed. "My mouth is too dry," he croaked. Again, he put the horn to his lips, taking several deep breaths, he once again blew.

The blast from the horn was surprisingly loud. A clear, strong note that blared over the fenlands, on and on went the note. When at last Jonn was out of breath he took the horn from his lips, and watched the wall carefully.

Nothing moved.

Once more the innkeeper blew the horn.

And then again.

The archers and the waiting townsfolk were emboldened by the sounding of the horn, as if it were indeed the legendary horn that had gathered the armies of humankind upon the plains of Morinorn, millennia ago.

From beyond the wall, there came bedlam. Screams of rage and howls of fury rose up to answer the challenge of the horn. The great oaken gate was suddenly thrown open, and a tide of monstrous creatures burst out, like pus from a corrupted wound.

Jonn felt his bladder give up the game, but was too terrified to do anything about it. He blew the horn again, a desperate sound now. All about him archers put arrows to string and drew their bows taut, shoulders straining at the poundage they pulled.

The Grimm came on with relentless purpose. Now they could be seen clearly, shambling creatures, more ape than man, long arms full of twisting sinew, grasping hands with razor claws. Slavering maws full of tusk like-teeth, gnashed and bit as if they could already taste the flesh on offer before them.

Jonn could hold his nerve no longer, the roar of the onrushing horde threatened to break what little resolve he had left.

"Now!" he screamed.

Almost as one, near forty bows let loose their steel-tipped death. The front ranks of archers aimed almost straight at their targets. The missiles punched into the horde with devastating effect. The creatures were thrown back like rag dolls, howls of pain melding with the screams of bloodlust. The archers further back had aimed higher, letting their shafts fall out of the sky like a vicious rain. More and more of the creatures tumbled, arrows feathering them.

Jonn counted to five in his head, then screamed, "Again!"

As they prepared for the second volley, the archers spread out, with several stepping from the road into the heather, making the front ranks longer. The sound of bowstrings twanging was loud, but the arrows were as quiet as a scythe as they hammered into the bodies of the Grimm.

The monsters still came on, leaping over their fallen comrades. Jonn could see terrible weapons in their fists, saw toothed blades, axes so big they could hack a horse in two. "Fire!" His voice rang loud, though cracking. Once again, the withering storm of missiles descended and dozens of the Grimm melted away, trodden into the road by those coming on behind. They were less than a hundred paces from the townsfolk now, screaming with rage.

The townsfolk roared in defiance, bows twanging, and yet more of the Grimm fell. Jonn thought there could be no more than twenty of the creatures left now; the road was carpeted with their dead and dying. Another volley arced into the sky. The targets were fewer now, so the impact less deadly, and the Grimm seemed to come on all the faster. Jonn opened his mouth to order a retreat, but suddenly there were townsfolk rushing past him, running at the oncoming horde their faces contorted with fear and rage.

Dimly Jonn saw that the leader of the attackers was familiar to him, a quiet widow of middle years; Mara was her name, a seamstress and as gentle a soul as one could wish to meet. He also remembered laying a coat over the still form of Mara's only child back in the inn, after the Grimm had left. Mara was screaming, her eyes wild, her bare feet seeming to fly over the hard-packed earth of the road. In her raised hand she brandished a kitchen knife. Others rushed by, men and women wearing rictus grins; he saw their pitch-forks and mallets, knives and wood axes.

Lightning blazed once more and Jonn was surprised to find himself running at the madness himself. The rusted sword he waved above his head had hung on the wall of the inn for twenty-five years, and before that he doubted it had ever been drawn in conflict. There was a loud screaming in his ears, and he had gone a dozen steps before he realised it was coming from his own lips. A challenge. A rage. A primordial cry.

* * *

THE TUNNEL WENT DOWN STEADILY, the way quickly lost in the gloom. It was Sten that stumbled upon the torches set in brackets along the walls, and again it was the smith that lit the first torch, with flint and steel. A handy man to have about, Steeleye thought.

As the two led the way, with the smith bending slightly to avoid scraping his head upon the mortared ceiling, he whispered to Steeleye, "What kind of blade is that? It cut through steel, and the grate itself. I've never seen anything like it."

Steeleye still held the naked steel in his fist, the torchlight playing upon its length like liquid fire. "It's a special blade, right enough," He told the smith, "Though the price for carrying it is too high, for me and those around me, I fear."

The tunnel went on and on, gradually levelling out and widening somewhat. A couple of the other men, also carrying torches pushed past Steeleye and the smith, hurrying on into the gloom. He didn't try to stop them. He knew they were sick with worry for loved ones, and there was no time for caution. A few minutes more, and Steeleye and the rest of the rescuers left the passage, and entered a wide corridor of neatly dressed stone.

Barred cells ran along one wall. The stink of death and decay was overpowering. He saw his fellows vainly pulling and shaking at the bars of a cell. It was locked fast. Within, he could dimly make out a large group of figures huddled atop one another, doing their best to hide behind each other in their terror. Steeleye pushed the men from the bars, and swung the sword with all his might, sparks showered into the gloom as again and again Steeleye struck the bars in a wild frenzy. At last, the black iron of the bars relented, and Sten and the others set to bending and clearing the shattered bars.

Steeleye quickly scanned the cell, but he couldn't see Morinae, the terrified faces were all a jumble. He turned away from the bars and began to walk deeper into the cellar. Artfur and Sten caught him before he got three steps.

"Where are you going? Most of our people are here." Sten's big hand gripped Steeleye's arm painfully. "It looks like your diversion worked. We can return back through the tunnel and be gone; we have done it." There was a desperate look in the eyes of the smith.

Steeleye shook off his hand. "Look for my companion, the princess. Find all the prisoners that you can. But my work isn't here."

"This is madness, Captain," chimed in Artfur, his face wet with sweat, his eyes darting around the corridor. "Listen to Sten. We have done what we came here to do, we must return to the fens, to help Jonn and the others." Artfur was so nervous he was practically hopping from foot to foot.

"Find your niece, Artfur, then get away, all of you get away safe. I'm going up into the keep; I have no choice in the matter. Look for Morinae, Artfur. You know where I am going." Without another word, Steeleye set off along the corridor at a jog. His mind was moving fast now. He knew what he must do, what his priorities must be.

Janovis.

The demon. As the Morriggu had called her, the succubus.

The first of the seven.

It seemed he had been on the road to this encounter a lifetime, as if each event so far in his twenty odd years had been preparing him for this. The corridor curved, and led to an arch way, Steeleye went on without hesitation, finding a case of wide stairs that he took two at a time. The stairs led to yet another corridor, this one lit by flaming brands in sconces along the wall. There were more cells, though a swift glance through the bars told Steeleye the occupants were long past any help he could offer. The stink of a charnel house hung like a thick veil along the corridor. Steeleye wished the torches had not been lit, to save him from seeing the horrors within the cells.

He prayed to all the gods that Morinae was not among the wet, glistening heaps of flesh that he glimpsed. He reached the end of this corridor too, without seeing any other living soul. It seemed his hasty plan had worked, the Grimm were outside, hopefully every one of them dead with a dozen arrows skewering them.

More stairs. He raced upwards, his heart beating fast, more from anticipation and fear than from running. At the head of these stairs was a door, thick and well made of oak. It gave to a shove, swinging open on squealing hinges, and Steeleye found himself in the Keeps main hall.

Thirty paces across, the hall was circular, with an open stone staircase twisting around the circumference, leading on upwards. But it was not the stairway that held his attention. Rather, it was the dozen or so men, flayed and bloody that hung crucified around the walls. Like so much artwork, to entertain a sick and twisted mind.

So drawn was he to the remains of the hanging men that at first, he didn't see the three shapes lurking in the shadows. He hardly had time to acknowledge the ruin of the room; the great long table that was now no more than a charred heap, the once exquisite chairs, made of lacquered wood and vibrant velvet, now smashed for kindling, the great stains upon the cracked flagstones of the floor that drew clouds of flies. All this his eyes barely registered before he heard the quick rushing footsteps, the grunting breath, the scrape of steel from its sheath.

Steeleye spun to face the attack, the Godsteel blade cutting through the air with a savage hiss. The rushing Grimm found its outstretched hand chopped off at the wrist, the same swing lopping off the top of the creature's head, a gout of ichor and brains spraying over the floor. His return swing blocked a halberd that was thrust to skewer his bowels. Steeleye danced to the side, letting the snarling Grimm rush by, his outstretched foot tripping the creature so it sprawled head-first into the stone floor.

Steeleye had little time to set his feet before the third Grimm struck. Towering over seven feet tall, the monster wielded a great war-hammer, its heavy head full of spikes. Steeleye felt the wind of the hammer's passing as he leaned away from the blow, then the Godsteel blade leapt forward, almost of its own violation, taking the huge Grimm in the throat. As it fell to its knees, its lifeblood jetting from the wound, Steeleye turned his back to confront the halberd carrying foe once more. He didn't give it time to stand. Instead, he swung the sword as the monster was on its hands and knees. Its head rolled to the wall, landing at the feet of a crucified man.

He hoped the shade of the man had seen justice done.

Steeleye looked around the room with a little more care now, but he was alone, save for the dead. The door that led to the courtyard was wide open. He hurriedly went to peer outside. The courtyard was a wreck. Sten had told him there were stables and wash houses, outbuildings of all kinds, but all that remained were blackened shells and piles of rubble. Burnt timbers sprouted from heaps of rock, like the bones of a cadaver. He could see the gate in the wall too, and the roadway beyond. He saw the road littered with the dead, and further on a mass of figures, a melee of confusion and slaughter.

Steeleye looked away. He had told Jonn not to engage, to keep a distance, to keep safe. But he knew well enough the chaos of battle. Plans were just that; a plan. They were all well and good until the first arrow flew. With a curse, he turned and ran to the stairs, bounding up two and three at a time. He must block from his mind the townsfolk; he must not dwell on thoughts of sweet Morinae. There was real evil here, evil that would grow and grow, infect the land and bring nothing but horror to the world. He ran faster, the blade in his fist naked and stained with gore.

On the next floor, that which had been the dormitory for the war-band, once again Steeleye found only destruction; the beds were now mere kindling, the chairs and tables smashed and ruined. He only paused to ensure there were no Grimm lurking, and seeing nothing, thankfully not even crucified men, he made for the stairway, a twin to the one that he had used from the ground floor to the first.

Gathering his breath and his wits, he pounded up the steps, his boots ringing loud on the stones. At the top of the stairs there was a landing, and a door.

Ajar.

Now Steeleye became cautious, his grip tightening upon the hilt. He strode silently, his steps bringing him to the door. Steeleye took hold of the handle, an iron ring. He pulled and door swung wide, there was the faintest of squeals from its hinges; Steeleye caught his breath at the sound, and waited sword raised.

Nothing came hurtling through the door. No slavering beast, or ravening monster. Steeleye pushed open the door fully and stared into the dead Baron's private quarters. It took his eyes a moment or two to adjust to the gloom. When at last he could see, he wished fervently that he could not.

Bones littered the floor, discarded like rubbish. Here a skull;

there, a spine snapped and bent. He saw several rib cages, strips of meat still visible on the bone, though they had been well gnawed before being discarded. The once fine flagstones were now stained black with dried blood, and there were huge splashes of it over the walls too, as if a bucket of it had been hurled at the stonework. Steeleye felt bile rise in his throat as his eyes came to rest upon what else decorated the walls.

Human skins, some near complete, were nailed to the walls as a lord might hang a tapestry, or a hunter a fine pelt.

"Oh gods." His voice was but a whisper, but in the quiet room it carried, and there came a soft response.

"Steeleye?" A chill ran along his spine, and dread gnawed at him, for even in a whisper, he recognised the sweet voice.

She came slowly out of the shadows, naked and shivering with fear, her skin torn and bitten, ravaged and bleeding. "Steeleye?" she asked again, staggering, as if her injuries were too great to even stay on her feet. Her golden hair was matted and thick with blood from a gash to her scalp, it ran down her cheeks like crimson tears.

"Morinae!" All else was forgotten. He moved swiftly to catch her in his arms as she stumbled. She flung her arms around his neck. He could feel the warmth of her nakedness as she collapsed against him, her breath hot and sweet so close to his cheek. Steeleye felt a fog descending upon his mind. He was confused, dizzy, as if he had drunk too much wine; the room felt to be spinning madly. As if from a distance, he heard a clanging, clattering sound. His sword had slipped from numb fingers, yet he couldn't find the will to take it back up. Darkness threatened to engulf him, and he tried to pull away from the girl, but her arms tightened. Like steel cables they twined about his neck, pulling his head down towards hers.

Steeleye pulled with all his might. He pulled until the tendons in his neck stood out and sweat poured down his face, his entire body shaking with the effort, but to no avail. He seemed as weak as a kitten in her arms. He tried to speak, but only a low groan escaped his lips. He stared into those vivid green eyes, struggling like a mouse in the jaws of a cat; it was useless.

The green eyes swam, they grew and enlarged. The lovely green was gone now, replaced by a black so total it could have been the carapace of a beetle. The face too was changed. No longer was he staring at the fine beauty of Morinae, the pride of the Asgulun. Instead, a face from nightmare was before him, scaled and sharp, its mouth red and raw and filled with razor teeth. Steeleye silently screamed as his head was pulled ever closer, and the terrible mouth fixed upon his.

* * *

Morinae awoke with a scream on her lips as rough hands shook her. She tried to scramble away, to hide, to press herself against the cell wall and become invisible. In her mind she prayed for someone else to be taken, to please not let it be her. Slowly she became aware that her name was being called. Human voices, friendly voices, issued from mouths without too many teeth.

"Princess Morinae! Thank the gods you are safe. Come princess, we are getting you all out of here. Hurry!" The urgency in the voice dragged her to her senses. She opened her eyes to see the bright flames of a brand waving about in the gloom of the cells. Lit by the torch, she could make out the features of the old bard, the one she and Steeleye had met in the tavern. Her mind groped for his name but she could hardly remember.

What she did remember were brutal fingers dragging her by the hair, seeing her rescuer and friend laid on the tavern floor with his brains dashed out. She had fought vainly kicking and gouging at her abductor, screaming and writhing until the crea-ture had delivered a cruel back handed blow to her jaw, stunning her. Then she was hauled over a stinking shoulder, and the beast began to run, in a tireless loping gait that she was sure would tire out a horse. She was aware that she was not the only abductee. Many shapes loped along the road, each carrying or dragging a burden.

They reached a battered, towering keep in the middle of nowhere, and she and the others were quickly dragged into a cell far below the ground.

Then the horror had begun.

The townsfolk were not the first prisoners. The cells held a few of the Baron's men at arms, several travellers that had been snatched from the road, even farmers that had been taken from their fields. One by one, the prisoners were dragged kicking and screaming from their cells, hauled along the corridor and taken upstairs.

The screams would haunt Morinae for as long as she lived. Again, and again the brutish creatures would come shambling along the corridor, with their great saw-tooth blades, and each time they returned they were covered in more and more blood and gore. The screams of those taken away from the cells seemed to become louder and more hysterical. Morinae couldn't imagine what could make a person scream so.

One by one the cells were emptied, until at last only their own cell remained. All those from the inn had been bundled together and now they cowered in the shadows, each trying to hide behind another. When the creatures came back, the first of the townsfolk they grabbed was the young juggler, Helgen. She screamed piteously as the hairy paw gripped her ankle like a vice. Without thinking Morinae launched herself at the creature, her weight driving the beast onto its back, her fingernails drawing blood from the apelike cheeks. In shock, the beast released Helgen, but caught the princess a mighty buffet at the side of the head. She fairly flew across the cell, crashing into the rough stone wall. She saw Helgen crawling back into the press of townsfolk through swimming vision, saw the beasts grab another girl by the hair and drag her out in to the corridor.

Darkness engulfed the princess... until the rough hands shook her awake.

Artfur! That was his name, Artfur the Bard, as she remembered him from court. The young juggler Helgen was clinging to the old man's arm, her look of shock and terror mingling with a dawning hope. "Hurry, Princess." Artfur was now pulling on her shoulder, trying to drag her towards the doorway of the cell. Morinae realised she was the last prisoner, the rest were scurrying along the corridor, men with torches hurrying them along. Standing in the doorway was a giant of a man, tall and broad, but there was the look of fear about him for all his size.

"Artfur, we need to go. Now!" the giant hissed

"Give me a moment, Sten, the girl is barely conscious."

Morinae shook her head, trying to clear the fog that clouded her thoughts. Her golden hair, now matted and coarse, fell over her eyes. She squinted into the corridor, remembering the scrawny girl Helgen, and the gnarled hand trying to drag her through the door of the cell. "Are you alright?" she asked the girl. She knew she ought to be moving, but her brain and her body didn't seem to be communicating properly.

"I'm fine, thanks to you." Helgen seemed to be blushing under the streaks of dirt and sweat that covered her face. Artfur rolled his eyes at his niece, making shooing motions trying to get her to move along, but Helgen wasn't moving without the princess. "She saved me uncle, they were dragging me out, taking me to the screaming room, but she leapt upon the creatures' back...." Her voice trailed off as she remembered her paralysing fear.

Morinae was regaining focus, her mind sharpening, her vision clearing, though the pain in her head throbbed liked the devil. She walked a step or two. At each step, it seemed she would pass out again, or vomit. The cell swam and she reached out instinctively. The huge fellow, Sten, caught her, steadied her.

"We must make haste, Artfur," said the big man. "We have everyone, there is no point in lingering."

Morinae was nodding her agreement. She wanted to leave this ghastly place, to return to Asgulun, to lock herself in her room and never leave it. She let Sten help her along the corridor into the gloom, eager to be away. Little Helgen was holding her free hand, gripping it tight as if her life depended upon the contact. Ahead, Morinae could see lights bobbing in the darkness, lit brands carried by the townsfolk. Hope flooded through her, she was going to be free, she was going to get away, to walk beneath the sky!

It was Artfur's voice that stopped her dead in her tracks.

"I'm not leaving without the Captain," he said. Morinae looked back to see the old man still by the door to her erstwhile cell. He was shaking visibly in his terror, yet his voice was resolute.

"My captain?" she asked, confused. "Steeleye is here? But I saw him killed in the inn..."

"Not killed, Princess, though it was only his thick skull that saved him. He led us here, then bade me find you, whilst he went to seek out the commander of the Grimm." Artfur pointed away from the bobbing lights, away from safety, along the corridor where the prisoners had been dragged, towards the screaming place.

Morinae found herself pulling free of Sten's helping hand, freeing herself too from Helgen's grip, as she made her way back to Artfur. "Is he alone?"

Artfur nodded, his lined face grim. "He says there is more afoot here than we know, there is another here in the Keep, one worse than even the Grimm."

"Worse than those vile creatures?" Morinae had returned to

stand with the bard; she could see terrible conflict in the old man's eyes.

"Princess, there is so much more going on here than I have time to tell, save to say the Morriggu herself came to the inn, and bade us come to this terrible place. The Captain is about her bidding now, I fear."

"The Morriggu?" Morinae remembered the strange crow in the forest, how it had flown to her rescuer, and how he had shown no real surprise at its unnatural behaviour. Slowly her eyes looked to the ceiling, as if she could see through timber and stone. "Who is he hunting, Artfur?"

"A demon, Princess. He told me it was Janovis, one of the Seven Sisters from the time of Aihaab. He means to kill it."

Morinae struggled to take everything in. The blow to her head was surely dulling her wits. Demons? The Morriggu? Could it all be true? But then she remembered the taloned hand grasping her hair, the screams of her fellow prisoners as they were dragged along the corridor to their grisly fate.

"Princess, please hurry." Helgen's small voice broke through her reverie. The girl still stood beside the big man, and was now near hopping from foot to foot in her desire to be gone. Sten the smith looked no less eager.

Yet, Morinae lingered.

Steeleye had saved her life. He had kept her safe, fed her, and guided her. He had brought her out of the wilderness and had promised to see her home safe. Morinae could feel her posture straighten, her chin lift as she met the old man's eye. "Sten, take the girl to the others." The authority in her voice was natural, her old self waking up. She had a duty to her friend, her captain. And Morinae knew all about duty. "Artfur, lead the way, if you are coming. I will not desert Steeleye in a place like this."

Artfur smiled gratefully as Morinae took charge. He bade Helgen follow the smith, locking eyes with the fellow even as he did. There was no need for words, and Sten picked up the now sobbing Helgen, and hurried after the rest of the rescuers.

Morinae watched them go, then followed Artfur in the opposite direction, almost stepping on his heels. "Hurry up," she hissed in a whisper. "Before I change my mind!"

The pair found the stairs and hurried up them with all haste. Morinae had to lift the hem of her now torn and soiled yellow dress. Strange to think so short a time ago she had beamed at her reflection in her room's mirror at the lovely dress, a gift from the landlady. She was dragged back into reality by the stink of death that greeted them from within the cells on the next floor. She doubled over, feeling bile sting her throat. Thankfully her vision was blurred with tears, and she could hardly see what was left of the prisoners. But she heard Artfur gasp in horror, could hear him muttering prayers as he rushed by the cells.

Morinae hoped that the terror of the cells would be the worst of it, but as they came to the next floor, the hall, she was aghast at the barbarity inflicted upon the crucified men. She stared in horrified fascination at the poor flayed souls, unable to look away, yet filled with revulsion at what she saw.

Artfur grabbed her wrist and pulled her to the stairs, and Morinae was grateful to be dragged from the spectacle. She noted the three Grimm, sprawled and bloody, and a fierce grin broke through her terror. Steeleye was alive yet, it seemed. She lengthened her stride, racing up the stairs, ignoring the pounding in her head. Artfur kept pace with her, though his breath came in great, rasping gulps.

At the next floor, the pair barely paused, they were drawn on, their feet fairly flying up the stairs, up and up, round and round. They reached the well carved door to the Baron's quarters, and burst through. Together, they came to a skidding halt.

Morinae bit the back of her hand to curb the scream that

threatened to tear past her lips, her green eyes wide at the horror that confronted them in the dimly lit chamber.

There, in the centre of the room, was Steeleye. He was gripped tight by what seemed to be writhing serpents that held him two feet from the floor. Morinae struggled to comprehend just what she was seeing. She could see the terrible face of the creature, its lips locked upon those of her Captain. Great leathery wings grew from the demon's back, as well as a dozen or more tentacle-like appendages, scaled and clawed, that gripped the suspended man tightly. She could feel her blood turning to ice just at the sight of the horror, yet instinctively she ran forwards, shrugging off Artfur as he tried to stop her.

Morinae made a desperate dash towards the mesmerising creature, snatching up what may have been a thigh bone as she ran. The creature, Janovis, was so intent upon its dangling captive that it wasn't aware of this new danger. Not until Morinae ran in and swung the thigh bone with all her desperate strength at the head of the demon.

CHAPTER 17
FIRST OF THE SEVEN

Steeleye felt the world fade away. His heart, drumming fast in his ears, his only anchor to his body. He floated in a void, empty of feeling and sound, a great black nothingness, cold and inhospitable. Time had no meaning in this terrible realm. He was unsure if he could see, or if he was blind, for the expanse was blacker than night. There were no stars as focal points, only an eternal emptiness.

He felt a sudden pull. He was moving through the void; cold wind bit at him, freezing the blood in his veins. The loud beating of his heart slowed, the *dub-dub* faltering, then stopping altogether.

Steeleye ceased to breath, hurtling through the dark. Yet still he lived, encased in ice. Terror clawed through him as he sped on. Ahead, there appeared a pinprick of light. It grew in brightness and size as he neared, blinding white, a tear in the darkness, and then he was *inside* the light. He felt a pressure bearing down upon him, being squeezed by a giant fist.

Feeling returned in a rush of pain as his every cell was crushed and torn beneath the immense pressure. He had no breath to scream, and still he was moving, faster and faster. He felt the skin on his face dragged back, as if it would tear from his skull. His eyes bulged as they were assaulted by the blinding light. And then he was beyond. Wherever he had been, he was there no longer.

Steeleye was suspended in a new cosmos. There were giant blue suns, ringed planets speeding on their travels. He could see a strange amorphous mass of pink and blue, yellow and green; like a cloud floating in the depths of space. The strangeness threatened to overcome his fear, until he saw that he was not alone here.

He became aware there were unseen eyes hungrily watching. Sounds, too, penetrated the dark, like a mournful piping lament. He floated, helpless.

He saw at last the singer of the song, and his sanity teetered.

Enormous. Its size was beyond his reasoning, a huge sphere of glistening flesh, its colour a sickly grey, reflecting the blaze of giant suns. From its bloated surface there sprouted a thousand waving tentacles, the tip of each bearing a slavering maw. Great eyes, the size of moons, fixed upon his helpless form, and Steeleye felt the dread of an ancient evil, undreamed of by humankind.

A voice came to him then, a sibilant whisper that slithered through his consciousness.

"Lightbringer!" The voice was excited, a woman's voice. "Can you see the wonders of my realm? Or is your sanity blasted already?"

Steeleye knew who the voice belonged to, just as he knew somehow that he was still in the topmost floor of the Keep on the fens. All this that he saw about him, was deception, a vision of the demon's realm that she showed him, to torture him with its horror. He screamed in terror and frustration.

The voice laughed at his helplessness.

"See my God, pitiful man. See the nameless one that awaits in the darkness, just beyond sight. This is my God, and He is a devourer of worlds."

Steeleye's existence flickered, and once more he was in the keep, the terrible mouth fixed on his, his limbs crushed by what felt like bands of corded steel. He stared into the cold black eyes, and they seemed to mock him, to taunt him. "I shall eat your soul, man, for that is all you are to me, just one more soul to consume. Your name strikes fear in the shadows, but not to me, Steeleye. Lightbringer. Grimmsbane. To me, you are just.... food."

A searing pain shot through Steeleye's head, as if an axe had bitten into his skull. Again, the pain shot through his head, even more intense, until he felt his eyes must melt and his brain explode. His body convulsed, shuddering in the demonic grip as Janovis tore apart his psyche, searching for the tiny light, the morsel he called his soul.

On and on went the pain, like a corkscrew twisting through his brain.

Deep within Steeleye, there came a curious sigh, and then a strange scratching sensation. "What is this?" came the hissing sibilance of Janovis. "No soul to feed on? But I have found a wall, Steeleye Lightbringer. A wall within your memories. Like a dam in a river, it holds your truth from you, I think. Would you like to know what I know, oh tiny man? Would you like to know the truth about your world, and the Empress? My mistress will soon rule all the lands, and set free my God from his cosmic prison."

There was more scratching in his head, then it felt as though his brain were in a vice, squeezed and squeezed, like an orange to produce sweet juice. His secrets oozing out. "There is a door within the wall," came the voice of the demon, "and within the door a lock, but I don't have a key." There came more scratching, louder, more insistent. "I don't need a key, I am Janovis of the Seven, I shall break the wall as easily as I could break your skull." Steeleye flinched as there came a hammering noise, a noise that only existed inside his head. A crashing sound, as loud as an avalanche, harsh as thunder, on and on it went. He wanted to scream, to cover his ears, to fall to his knees and cover his head, anything to stop the terrible hammering in his skull.

The first memory came so fast and vivid that it sent his body into rigid shock. There was a flash of yellow in his mind's eye, and he was running along a stone-dressed corridor, he was racing his sister Maeve, his twin, and they were six years old. He was laughing, exuberant as he ran. Maeve suddenly pushed him, and running at full speed as he was, he overbalanced easily, crashing into the sone wall, grazing his shoulder, then spinning to the flagstones, where he banged his knee so hard it broke the skin. Maeve ran on, her silver laughter trailing after her. "I win!" she shouted, her bright blue eyes shining with childish excitement. "I win!"

The six-year-old Steeleye staggered to his feet, fighting back tears, his lip trembled. "You cheated, Maeve." His voice was high, almost whiney. "You would never have beaten me if you ran the race fair."

"Don't pout, little Aluin, winning is all that matters." Maeve's voice was all sweetness and honey, a talent she had, even at so young an age. "Father says, 'In all things, do what needs to be done to be victorious!' does he not?"

The quote was of course correct, their father lived by the simple principle that in life, anything was acceptable if it meant that you could vanquish a foe. As Maeve had just defeated her twin brother, Aluin.

Steeleye blinked in shock. For a moment, the pain and hammering within his skull was forgotten. He'd had another name, once upon a time.

The sneering voice of Janovis was louder now. "My mistress always wins, Lightbringer. She will bring the entire world under her dark cloak, and when she does, the shadow folk shall feast upon the marrow of humankind and their screams will drown out even the thunder in the sky."

Another flash and Steeleye spasmed, the pain of this next memory twisted his innards. He felt fresh tears in his eyes that had nothing to do with the torture he now endured in the grip of the demon. He was seven, and he and Maeve were about their daily weapons practice under the keen eye of their father, Bardok, the warlord of Clove. They fought with weighted wooden swords, both were fast, both were strong for their age, yet Aluin was more skilled. The boy put in hours of extra practice every day: his forms were exquisite, his speed unmatched even by members of Bardok's war-band.

Maeve's fighting style was wild and out of control. Had young Aluin not been so fast, his sister would have knocked him senseless. He ducked and swayed, parried swing after wild swing, resisting the opportunity to put an end to the mock duel for fear of hurting his sister. She came on now harder than ever, her lovely face twisted with rage. Aluin countered her thrust easily, tapping the side of his wooden blade against her unprotected chest. "A hit!" he shouted instinctively, turning a beaming face to his father.

Maeve let out a scream of blind fury and swung her blade edge on, to catch her twin on the side of the head. As the boy collapsed, sprawling headlong in the dust of the practice yard, he heard his fathers' booming laugh, his voice filled with joy and admiration for his daughter's actions. "Well done, Maeve! That was a canny blow and no mistake, keep fighting until you can fight no more. And Aluin, what kind of a tap was that? For all the fancy footwork and swordsmanship, if you are not willing to strike a real blow, you may as well stay in the library with old Nestus, or with your mother at her potions!"

The laughter of the gathered swordsmen smarted as much as the blow to his head.

The laughter of the demon mingled with those of the men in his memory. "Oh, how my mistress bested you, bested you at every turn!"

The demon inside his head was still cackling with uncontrolled glee when suddenly, she stiffened, her mouth tearing away from Steeleye's own as she emitted a shriek of pain, the muscular tentacles that held him spasming, sending him sprawling into the bone strewn floor.

Steeleye hit the paving stones hard, his head banging down, sending a shower of stars before his eyes. He fought to remain conscious, to get distance between himself and the creature that he had come to slay. The demon was screeching with fury, the long appendages lashing about her, great wings spreading from her back and beating at the air. Janovis hovered four feet from the ground, and cast her beetle black eyes about. They fell upon her tormentor the same time as Steeleye's own.

Morinae.

He saw the Princess's dirty yellow dress, her wild hair, her lovely face contorted with fear. In her trembling hand she held what looked like a man's thigh bone. The Princess must have struck the demon with the thigh bone; there was no way such a blow could have damaged the scaled and misshapen head of Janovis, but it had hurt enough to distract her, for her to momentarily release him.

His eyes now fell upon his sword, within easy reach from where he lay. His bruised and bloody lips stretched into a grim smile.

Even as he reached for the hilt of the sword, Janovis was snarling at the now cowering Morinae. The tentacles thrashed and writhed. They shot at the girl, whipping about her waist, lifting her screaming in terror and agony into the air.

"A thigh-bone?" shrieked the demon. "I am Janovis! I was old when your pathetic world was first born. I have been shot with arrows, stabbed with poison blades, even impaled upon a lance, and you thought to kill me with a scrap?" The screeching voice rose into a maniacal laugh; the muscular appendage that held Morinae throbbed and squeezed. The Princess was shaken like a rag doll. Slowly, the succubus drew Morinae towards its hideous mouth, a gross purple tongue, long and bloated, licking the bloodied lips,

"I am hungry for souls, and seeing that your Lightbringer seems to have had his hidden from me, yours will do."

Morinae was screaming hysterically as she was lifted to the waiting maw.

Steeleye curled his fingers about the hilt of the Stormchild's sword. He felt a new strength surge through him, like fire in his veins. His eyes became as suns, shining a pure white light as hot as twin stars. Yet, he remained unburned.

He struck, fast and hard, the keen edge of his blade hacking through the limb that was crushing the Princess. Black stinking ichor spurted from the thrashing stump. Morinae hit the floor dazed, almost unconscious, and Steeleye moved to stand over her. He raised the sword high in a two-handed grip, and roared a primal, wordless challenge to the now howling demon.

Janovis came at him, all writhing limbs and gaping maw, foul curses spat from her lips like venom, the cruel eyes blazing with fury. Steeleye met her snarl for snarl. He felt strength coursing through his limbs, as if he shared his body with another, stronger, faster entity. Janovis tried to overpower him with sheer brawn, the lashing limbs wrapping themselves around him like serpents, her great wings beating about his head, yet Steeleye fended her off, the sword screaming in great arcs about him, painting the air with the demon's gore.

The two of them refused to give an inch, trading blow for blow, until at last Steeleye saw an opportunity and leaped forwards, the Godsteel plunging deep between Janovis' breasts.

Even as the demon realised the steel had pierced her heart, her eyes growing wide with shock, then pain, Steeleye wrenched out the blade, and with a great cry of rage, swung the dripping sword again. The demons head fairly leapt from her neck, a gout of ichor fountaining as the creature spasmed and then finally collapsed.

It was over so fast, yet Steeleye was far from unscathed. His fine mail habergeon was in tatters, his arms cut and scratched, as if he had battled for a day, not minutes. Blood ran freely from cuts to his brow and cheek, but he stood tall as if unhurt. His shining eyes fell upon the dazed Princess, and she shrank from him, cowed by his savage appearance. Slowly, the fire in his eyes dimmed, and as it did, the rigours of the battle took their toll. Steeleye staggered as the pain of his wounds erupted across his body. He grimaced and winced; everywhere seemed to hurt at once.

He carefully prodded a tentacle with the toe of his boot. It remained inert. As he turned to Morinae, he saw Artfur sidling towards them, his eyes huge as he saw, up close the enormity of the demon. He helped Morinae to her feet and the pair of them looked cautiously at Steeleye, as if expecting him to scream and begin slashing about him with the gore-stained blade.

He smiled ruefully through the blood that streaked his face.

"Well, at least you know now why I was named Steeleye. The witch that raised me thought my eyes looked like the sun reflected from burnished steel, when I suffered from an episode." He grinned; his teeth white against the crimson mask. "She is very poetic in her own way, is Hewla the witch."

Artfur was the first to find his voice, though it was little more than a whisper. "To be honest, Steeleye, I was unsure who to be more afraid of, you or the creature at your feet."

"I am truly sorry for that, Artfur. When the Shining comes, it almost takes over me, as if I am no longer me, I am sharing with another entity, though I feel nothing evil in the Shining."

271

Morinae at last was able to look at her Captain again, Steeleye saw her fear of him abate, or at least she hid it well. "That was bravely done Princess," he said at last, breaking their awkward silence. "Attacking a demon, with a thigh bone no less! I'm sure Artfur will sing a song about that. My thanks, Morinae. You undoubtably saved my life, the succubus had bested me."

"I didn't have time to think," she said, her voice tremulous. Steeleye watched as the realization they had survived dawned upon the princess. Colour came to her cheeks, and the glaze of shock lessened in her eyes. A hesitant smile tugged at the corners of her lovely lips. Steeleye carefully wiped the blade on a leathery wing, the stink of the ichor made his nose wrinkle.

He had killed the first of the seven, and he was still alive.

There was a sudden flash behind his eyes, and he saw a lovely elfin face, hair like spun silver. He knew at once that his memory was showing him his mother, all at once he could *remember* her. The gentle laugh, her wise words, so in contrast to his father, he cherished the memory, felt warmed by it like a child with a favourite blanket.

A strange rattling drew his and his companions' attention, to the dim corner of the chamber. The grisly head of Janovis was there, propped against the wall, where it had come to rest after it had l been lopped it from its neck. Steeleye felt his flesh crawl as the dead mouth cracked open, the swollen tongue licking again at the rictus lips. The black eyes blinked and swivelled to look at the three humans, loathing emanating from the gaze like a physical force.

"I see you, Lightbringer." The voice was like stones grating together. "And my sisters see you. Your dark mistress cannot shield you forever, and my sisters will be waiting." The voice trailed to silence, and all relief and joy the trio may have felt at surviving the encounter evaporated, like a mist before the rising sun.

CHAPTER 18

MEMORIES

S teeleye, Morinae, and a very shaken looking Artfur, left the demon's chamber, making their way to the entrance of the Keep on slow and weary feet. In his left hand, Steeleye gripped the lank hair of the now dead and silent head of Janovis, the creature that had terrorised the land, had killed countless travellers and feasted upon their souls even as her minions had feasted upon their bones. Janovis' face was set in death, the black eyes lifeless, staring wide into whatever hell awaited her. The jaw of the demon hung loose and slack, revealing row upon row of vicious teeth.

Steeleye felt revulsion carrying the grisly trophy, yet he had no notion of what to expect out upon the fens. Perhaps the Grimm were still waiting, gathered upon the road, cracking open the bones of the townsfolk. If that was the case, he hoped seeing the head of their leader would take the fight out of them.

As it happened, there was no need to have worried.

The weary trio came cautiously down the final stairway. Artfur carried a torch lit from a brazier on the floor above. Full night had fallen without, and, as they stepped into the hall, there came a great commotion from the doorway. Lights bobbed and massed voices murmured and mumbled with apprehension, and then there came a booming voice, Sten the blacksmith's: "There!" The voice echoed around the empty hall. "They are still alive!" There followed a dozen voices, each shouting questions, each mingled with the next until no single voice could be discerned, nor understood.

Steeleye saw Jonn at the forefront of the mass. In one hand he held a fiery torch aloft, his other gripped that of his now rescued daughter, tightly as if he would never let it go. Sten stood beside him, tall and imposing, yet a look of soft relief on his face upon finding the trio alive and relatively well. The townsfolk surged forwards, and then came to a staggering halt as they saw what hung, lank and dead, from Steeleye's fist.

"By Heros' beard, is that the thing that led the creatures?" Jonn had found his voice first, his eyes wide as they took in the horror of Janovis.

Steeleye lifted the head a little, the eyes glinting in the torch-light as if they were alive, Steeleye suppressed a shudder. he hoped the demon had passed on for good, and held no more surprises. "Aye," he said at length. "This was Janovis, one of the demons from the old times. She had taken up residence here a while ago if the bones and the trophies we have seen, are anything to go by." The townsfolk had fallen silent, they were gaping with awe and revulsion upon the twisted features of the demon.

"By the looks of you all, you were able to best the creatures out on the fens?" Steeleye broke the silence, directing his question at the tavern innkeep, who seemed to have stepped into the role of leader quite naturally.

"The bows were the key. We were able to kill most of them at a distance. Things did get ugly towards the end, though, and we finished the job hand to hand." Jonn pushed out his chest with pride, and Steeleye saw the look of adoration in his daughter's eyes. "We lost good people in the last few minutes," he continued, a little less cock sure, "though we outnumbered the monsters twenty perhaps thirty to one, they were hard to kill, and had no fear in them." Jonn let his voice trail off, and Steeleye guessed he would relive that melee in his nightmares for all of his remaining days.

"Yet most of you survived." This was from Morinae, even filthy and ragged she managed to look regal. It was the tilt of her chin, her forthright stare as she surveyed the townsfolk. "You have taken back your fens, and ousted the creatures that brought terror to your lands," Her white smile broke through the grime on her face, radiant. "You have saved many souls this night, and I for one, shall be eternally grateful."

Steeleye watched the crowd, they ate up Morinae's words, and he found himself wondering idly if perhaps the royalty were unknowing wielders of magic, so rapt had the crowd become at the girl's words. He looked at Artfur, and found the poet staring fixedly at the trophy in his hand. "Are you going to keep it?" he asked, licking his lips nervously.

"This?" Steeleye gave the head a little shake, spattering gore upon the flagstones. "Nay, this is for burning, and perhaps grinding to dust."

Just then there was a commotion amongst the crowd, and Helgen wormed her way through to the front. Seeing the three alive she gave a squeal of delight and ran forwards, heedless of the demon's head in Steeleye's fist. Artfur crouched down to receive his running niece, a relieved grin splitting his lined face, but Helgen ran straight to Morinae, and threw her arms about the waist of the shocked, yet beaming Princess. "I knew you would come back!" Helgen's voice was muffled, as her face was pressed tight into the folds of Morinae's tattered yellow dress. "I knew they couldn't kill you!" The child now looked up at the Princess, the same Princess that had saved her in the cells from being dragged to the screaming room, and she sobbed in her happiness and relief.

Artfur, straightened up, rolling his eyes with mock hurt, though there was nothing pretend in the love that he had for the girl, that was clear as day in his old tear-filled eyes.

* * *

Steeleye and Morinae remained in the town for five more days.

In that time the town mourned, celebrated life and survival, and sent burial groups over the fens, back to the Keep. The old Baron and his men were cut down from their grisly perches. The bloody skins were torn from the walls and laid to rest. The remains of the demon and her followers were stacked high, and set alight, the stench of their burning hung in the air for days.

At the inn, windows were repaired, furniture restored, and life began to return to a new normality, one with private grief, yet also, a guilty thankfulness for survival. Jonn and his daughters were busier than ever, filling the gaps in their daily routine left by the death of their matriarch, but work was better than idleness, for when there was no work to do, then the grief had to be faced square on. And that grief was still raw, like an open wound. It was best left unscratched for a while, given time to heal.

Sten the blacksmith was also busier than ever. As well as his usual work, making and mending hoes and plough blades, fashioning shoes for horses and the countless other tasks that fell to a smith, now he made spear blades, and arrow heads by the score. The town had survived by the skin of its teeth, with pitchforks and carving knives, clubs and staves, but Sten had an inkling the world was changing, and if ever their community was threatened again, he intended they be better prepared.

Artfur spent his days strumming upon a lyre, humming to

himself, or scribbling on parchment as he composed his newest, and most personal poem. How many singers of songs, he wondered could lay claim to actually being at the great events they sang of? He still shook at every creak of a floorboard, and shivered when a cloud passed over the sun. He had seen things that should not exist in the world of mankind. His perceptions had been forever changed in that grim Keep. He had looked upon true evil, dark, and stinking of corruption, had seen real heroics in the actions of the Princess and her Captain, and they were not at all as he had sung of before. He had seen the fear and the pain, the terror, and yet still the pair had stood up to the demon.

Artfur had also come to realise he was a spectator, not a participant, in this game of heroes. Whilst Morinae had lunged at the creature that had entwined about her Captain, Artfur had stood frozen in the shadows, the sight of the demon filling the old poet with such bowel loosening terror that he would never be able to convey the feeling in song. Instead, he would tell the tale of Steeleye and the Princess and keep it focussed on them, though already it had changed somewhat; instead of a torn and bloody habergeon, the Steeleye of his story wore shining steel plate, and had ridden to the keep on a white charger. The great sword, however, remained the same.

Morinae, too, was different in his tale. Gone was the dishevelled girl, shaking with fear and stinking of sweat and filth. Instead, the Princess was a proud and fierce individual, seeking out danger with relish and a carefree smile upon her lovely face.

Artfur knew his audiences well. They would not cheer and toss coins his way to hear of the blood and the horror that had made its home in this quiet backwater, nor of the death and its ungodly stink that even now cloyed about his nostrils, and made him gag when he remembered it too vividly. No, he reasoned, give the audience the hero they expected: smiting evil and protecting the weak and the innocent; give them hope that there were such paragons in their world.

Of Steeleye's savage countenance, with his eyes blazing with unnatural fire, Artfur would remain silent in his song. He had felt as afraid of the Captain as he had been of the demon during that confrontation. Better his audience heard of a more traditional heroism, he thought.

The world was changing, he feared, and not for the better.

FOR MORINAE, the five days were more pleasant than many she had experienced for a long time. She had a new shadow, a skinny talented shadow that could juggle and tell jokes, could play the flute in a way that melted the hardest heart, and looked upon the Princess with adoration and devotion. The apprentice entertainer, Helgen, had found in Morinae a surrogate mother, sister and exemplar all rolled into one. It was a role that Morinae was pleased to fulfil, as it distracted her from the terrifying, and all too real circumstances that she found herself in.

Morinae, much like Artfur, had been almost as fearful of Steeleye's flaming eyes and the sheer violence he displayed fighting the demon, as she had been of the demon itself. She still felt safer with her captain than with anyone else, save perhaps Bryann her half-brother, yet now she was fully aware that there was far more to her companion and saviour than she had at first thought. She had been a witness to an ancient evil, and had seen it thwarted and destroyed in a manner she would never have dreamed possible. She had seen the Grimm, beasts out of myth and legend, and found them to be of flesh and blood, as real as she was herself.

In the space of a day and a night, Morinae's understanding of the world had been turned upon its head. Her world, and that of every man, woman, and child, was changing, and she believed that her companion, Steeleye, was in some way a catalyst for this change.

FOR FIVE DAYS Steeleye rested his weary bones, letting the cuts and bruises delivered by Janovis heal. More than this, he delved into the memories of his life before the Northmen had found him. Somehow the demon's vile kiss had broken down the barriers in his mind, the wall holding memories at bay was sundered, and a kaleidoscopic barrage of images and snippets of half remembered events assailed him.

Slowly, Steeleye was working through years of the unknown, like a reader turning the pages of a treasured book. Though unlike a book, the memories came to him in no particular order: events flashed before his minds' eye, jumbled and nonsensical, leaving him reeling and confused.

Steeleye stood upon the banks of his memory, casting out his net, unsure just what he would reel in. There was much to cherish, like his sweet mother, Ardanya, a rare beauty of sapphire eyes and silver hair, a laughing mouth and keen wit. Most memories of his mother would bring a tear to Steeleye's eyes, and a lump to his throat. It seemed he had not had the happiest of childhoods, yet almost every image of joy he could recall involved the lovely Ardanya.

His father, Bartok, was a brutish thug of a man, though even he behaved with a semblance of decency around Ardanya. But when his mother wasn't present, then Bartok had shown his true colours to his son, and should he not perform in his martial training as well as the warlord expected, he would not spare the rod upon his son's back, often beating him till he bled. Maeve, Steeleye's twin, was the favourite of their father, and she would use that knowledge without hesitation to escape punishment or chores, often with a sly smile and a secretive wink at her sibling.

The memories flooded and whirled. There were still many gaps, but he gathered that his parents were formidable folk: his father a tactician and warrior of unsurpassed skill, his mother a sorceress, as much at home in the great libraries, studying dusty tomes as she was casting spells to aid her husband's endeavours and to help the good people of Clove.

They ruled their small, though rich, province, South-West of Morinorn, with a firm yet just hand. As to Steeleye, or Aluin as he was then, and his wild twin Maeve, they were schooled with fierce vigour. Texts and histories were drummed into them by their tutor Nestor, and their mother too, when she had the time, and any waking moment they were not immersed in books, and scrolls, they were at the archery butts or the practice yard swinging weighted wooden blades.

Or so it seemed in Steeleye's fractured memory.

One memory in particular tore at Steeleye and wounded him deeply. He sat in little boat, alone and afraid. His mother and father were standing waist deep in a rolling surf, pushing the little craft beyond the breakers. Bartok looked over his shoulder often. He looked afraid, an expression that young Aluin had never seen before on his stern father's face. This in itself was enough to scare the child, but there was more, for he knew what Bartok feared.

Ardanya clung to the craft as a wave lifted them all, she was muttering a spell, her eyes out of focus as she recited words that made no sense to the boy. On and on she mumbled, as her long fingers wove intricate patterns in the air, and Steeleye was sure he could see faint auras of light where the fingers danced.

"She is coming." Bartok hissed, his face now turning stern and hard. He laid a callused hand gently upon Ardanya's shoulder. "See the boy safe, I shall do what I can." Bartok the warlord had never looked so humble, nor so frail as he did at that moment, as his eyes locked with those of his son. "I wish I had been a better father to you, Aluin. Perhaps it is best you will have no memory of me." With that, he turned away from the boat and began to wade towards the shore.

Ardanya shuddered, and tears fell from her sapphire eyes. "Look at me," she told the boy, distracting him from his father's receding figure. "You will be safe, there are good people awaiting you, far in the north. There, you will thrive, there you will be free to live and grow." Ardanya was swimming now, still pushing the little boat, the waves were clutching at the craft too, pulling it away from the shore, away from his mother. Ardanya was once again locked in concentration, her smiling lips forming soundless words. Steeleye watched in his memory as his mother released the little boat, and her striking eyes, now welling with tears sought out those of her son.

"You will not remember us, Aluin, but I hope we have prepared you to live a good life, to be a good man." Ardanya raised a slim arm from the water, her thumb and middle finger created an O shape. "I love you, Aluin!" she said softly. The little boat was getting further away. "Maeve loves you too, but she will not know it..." Ardanya snapped her fingers.

Steeleye awoke as his little craft ran upon the shingle beach, his breath frosted in plumes, and he shivered uncontrollably from the intense cold. There was a mist cloying the beach, and shapes were emerging, like phantoms. Several huge men dressed in furs and steel, and with them, an old woman, white hair pulled back and braided tight, Steeleye felt relief and a comfort he could not understand when he saw her. Hewla the seer hurried to the boat, to care for the lost boy.

* * *

"Captain?" Morinae's voice brought him back from his wanderings.

He was sat outside the inn, at a bench upon the wide deck. About him, the town bustled with its daily activity. Normality was returning, albeit a little different to what it had been before. For Steeleye, there would never be normality, he thought, no pleasant daily chores about town, no fields to plough or sheep or cattle to take to market, no family to sit before the hearth with, or children to watch grow. For him there was a different path, one he expected would bring much bloodshed, and loneliness, even if he did have companions to share his journey from time to time. He knew well enough that ultimately what he needed to do, to reclaim his soul, he would need to do alone.

Thoughts of his twin, Maeve, came unbidden. He thought of her as she had been, full of playful spite and childish malice, and as she seemed to be now: Empress of the South, steeped in darkness, leading a horde of Grimm and demons that adored her. Steeleye shuddered. Maeve was a problem for another day, he hoped, though he knew now that the huntress from his dreams was waiting along the road of his future, waiting with an ice-cold smile and a heart as black as a raven's wing.

He did his best to shrug off the melancholy as he turned to Morinae. She was neatly dressed in woollen trews and a fine homespun tunic of emerald green, no doubt a gift from a starry-eyed townswoman, who would be filled with joy that a royal wore her garments. Morinae's hair fell in lush golden waves, and Steeleye was struck that he had never seen the girl look so clean, nor well presented. At her side was her little shadow, Helgen, similarly dressed, though still looking like a waif and stray for all her new clothes and brushed hair. Artfur stood behind the pair, a woollen cloak over his shoulders, and a slouched hat upon his head.

"The horses are all saddled and ready to go." Morinae was

eager to be on the road, keen to return home to Asgulun and resolve its treacheries. She grinned at her Captain her green eyes bright. "Jonn says there is a good chance we can be at the coast in under ten days, and from there we can get passage to Asgulun."

Steeleye nodded and got to his feet with a sigh. Five days. He had not been idle in his time, he had spoken to many a merchant in the town, and with their help had plotted a course upon his map. They were headed for a fishing port called simply Fishtown, and if Jonn was correct, ten days would see them all there, bar any unexpected delays. As he walked to his horse, Steeleye messed the hair of Helgen and the girl squealed with indignation, Artfur laughed at her vanity as she sought to rearrange her mousy locks.

His time for reflection was at an end. It was time to be once more upon the business of the Morriggu. As if to confirm his thoughts there came a raucous cawing from overhead. Steeleye squinted into the morning sky, and sure enough he could see the silhouette of a crow, wheeling above them.

Steeleye quickly took stock. He now sported a fine habergeon of fine mesh; its sleeves just shy of his elbows. This had been brought from the keep by Sten. His professional opinion was that it was too fine a garment to be used in a funeral pyre. Steeleye had agreed heartily. He also wore leather archer's wrist guards, a gift from a townswoman whose husband had been a great hunter, before going to petition the Baron over a month ago, never to be seen again. Steeleye had accepted the gift solemnly, for he had an inkling of her husband's fate.

The Stormchild's blade hung from his belt, along with a long bladed poignard, another gift from the town's busy smith. "Very well then, if all our farewells have been said, I suppose the time has come to press on." He found his horse fully packed, with a rolled cloak behind the saddle, and a waterskin looped over the horn. Their supply mounts were now two short, as Artfur and

Helgen would be using them for riding. It had been agreed that the pair would join them on the journey to Asgulun.

As Steeleye settled in the saddle, Jonn the innkeep and Sten the smith came to watch them off. It seemed half the town paused in its routine as the travellers made ready to leave.

"Keep a watch on the fens, the two of you," Steeleye cautioned the pair. "And keep the archery training going too." He grinned at the men, who were nodding that they would do as he bid, though they had gone through this a dozen times already.

"You take care, out there in the world," Jonn said grimly. The four of them heeled their horses into a steady walk. Ten days ahead of them lay Fishtown. Plenty of time, Steeleye thought, to sift through his new memories, to find out how he became as he was.

Morinae brought her horse to ride alongside him. "I saw the crow."

Steeleye nodded. "Aye, I think there will be many more crows in the days ahead."

Morinae shuddered at his tone.

PART THREE

CHAPTER 19
PHANTOMS

T was on the very first night of their journey, as the group lay around a small fire, wrapped in their blankets, with three of them deep in their dreams, that Steeleye met with his sister. Artfur played his lyre softly as they ate a meal of bread and strong, tangy cheese. Morinae and Helgen sat quietly talking, the young girl's eyes wide with wonder, as the Princess told her of life within a palace. The bread was fresh and tasted wonderful to Steeleye, reminding him of Hewla and the fare she seemed to produce at a moment's notice.

The night was pleasantly warm. He had lit a fire more for comfort than necessity, and, of course, to boil water for tea. As Steeleye sipped his brew, hot and spiced, he watched the night sky. The moon was almost full, lending a luminescence to the few clouds that scudded by. The stars were silent and blinking, vast in their array. Unimaginable in their number. He became aware that the lyre had fallen silent. Artfur had put the instrument away and pulled his blanket tight up to his chin, his slight frame curled in a ball as sleep came upon him.

Morinae and Helgen soon followed the old singer's example. Steeleye listened as their breathing deepened and became rhythmic. Morinae made a soft snoring sound and Steeleye smiled at its daintiness. The Princess was full of surprises he was finding. She was beautiful to look at, there could be no doubt that she had been blessed by the gods in that respect, but also there was a quality within her greater than her beauty: she elicited trust from those around her; she had the capacity for compassion and an iron resolve. Both traits were needed, though not always present, in those who were to become leaders.

Tiredness was creeping upon Steeleye too, but he pushed it away, sipping his tea to keep his mind clear, watching the stars to keep his focus, and all the while listening to the sounds of the night. He waited.

The Morriggu stepped from the darkness like a phantom. Soundless, like a dream. Her sable attire blended with the shadows of the night. Long raven hair moving gently as in a breeze, though the night beside the campfire was still. So, reasoned Steeleye, this was but a projection of the goddess, an image that she had sent forth into this world. He was surprised that he'd had such a notion, at the calmness with which he accepted the image of the goddess.

It seemed the Morriggu shared his thoughts, for a smile quirked the corners of her lovely mouth, amusement shining in her eyes. "So, you have become bold, I see." Her voice was soft as velvet, and sent shivers along his spine. "And you are now a Captain, no less? A Captain of Crows, I hear." Her smile broadened, showing sharp white teeth. "Janovis the Demon is now suffering at the hands of my brother." The Morriggu seemed to shiver slightly, as if the scale of the demon's suffering was extreme even to a goddess. "I come with congratulations, and with news, Captain of the Crows. Janovis' sister, Ixtchel, awaits you beyond the Sea of Storms, and her mistress..."

"My sister," Steeleye broke in softly. "My twin. Maeve, is the Mistress of the Seven."

"Of course. The kiss of the succubus has broken down the walls within your mind. Can you remember everything? Can you see what set you and Maeve upon this path?"

"Not everything is clear to me yet. Most of my memories come in brief flashes, like drops of morning dew falling from a leaf. Memories drip into my mind at their own pace." Steeleye was watching the goddess as keenly as she did him. "Can you not tell me what happened? Why did my parents see fit to cast me adrift, and why did my mother set a spell in my mind to block out all knowledge?"

The Morriggu nibbled her perfect lips with her sharp white teeth, and stared intently at her Captain. "I could put you on the path, perhaps... a nudge in the right direction may not constitute a breaking of the Great Oath."

"You refer to the oath all gods took after the Dark One smote the earth."

"Indeed." The Morriggu was all focus now, her eyes lambent as they rested upon Steeleye. "Already, some of my brothers and sisters insist that I go too far in my meddling, that I bend the rules of the oath so much I am close to breaking them entirely. Your own coercion to the cause of Arianna is but one instance. I have nudged you here and there, even saved you from death a time or two, and such things are frowned upon these days." The perfect brow furrowed a little, her raven winged cloak stirred and lifted in a breeze Steeleye couldn't feel. "But time is short." The Morriggu continued in her breathy voice, "And the Enemy is not constrained by oaths nor rules."

Steeleye listened, yet didn't fully understand what the goddess was saying. It was as if she spoke to herself and he was just a coincidental listener. Who was the Enemy? Surely, he had enough of those just now? He already had a further six demons to contend with for the sake of his soul, plus his twin sister would need to be confronted, sooner or later, and he seemed to have attracted the ire and hatred of the Grimm too. Not to mention mortal enemies that he seemed fated to attract, such as Black Deeds and his cronies. Any one of them could have slipped a blade between his ribs and sent him to the afterlife for good. No, Steeleye thought, he had enough enemies already.

Whilst Steeleye sat at the fire, and the Morriggu stood in whatever realm she spoke from, deliberating on her oath, a third figure appeared out of the darkness, bringing a feeling of dread and unfathomable evil with her.

Maeve.

Her keen beauty rivalled that of the goddess, though there was no compassion or kindness about her. Maeve's beauty was fierce, like a hawk. She seemed as a great storm barely held in check. Her silver hair whipped about her like a banner. Her crimson cloak likewise snapped and flew. She was dressed for war, her armour shining red as blood, sculpted to her feminine form. She stepped closer to the fire, some ancient deity of war and carnage. Her eyes, once as blue as their mother's, were now empty black pools.

Steeleye was on his feet in an instant, the Stormchild's blade hissing from its sheath. But the Morriggu held up a staying hand to her champion, and looked at the newcomer with hard contempt. "Be still, Lightbringer. Like me, your sister is elsewhere. This is merely a phantom, unable to harm you."

Slowly, Steeleye lowered his blade, though he did not sheath it. His knuckles were white he gripped the hilt so hard. He heard a low growling, menacing in its primal intensity, and there at the feet of the Morriggu there came a black, bristling shape. Wolf, one eye the yellow of a spring bloom, the other as blue as a summer sky, the great beast, her hackles standing almost straight on her back, stood before her mistress, lips peeled back from cruel teeth, her growl seeming to rise from the very bowls of the earth.

Steeleye found himself grinning at the lupine form, and even here, faced as he was with a goddess, and the Empress of Dread, he felt his spirits buoyed somehow by the wolf's mere presence. The wolf growled on; a trail of saliva looped and dangled from her jaws.

At last, Maeve spoke, her voice as Steeleye remembered from his dreams, calling over the valley of bones beneath the pink dawn, and in the shadow of the great keep, though now all the spite and malice he had known her to be capable of was magnified a hundred-fold.

"Put the bitch on a leash, Crow." She looked coolly at the goddess, not in the least cowed or intimidated by the power that emanated from the sable figure. "Or I will be wearing its pelt as a cape."

Wolf bunched her muscles, as if preparing to pounce, but the Morriggu laid a slim white hand upon her head, calming the beast. "Another time, little Wolf," she spoke softly. "Return to watch my sister..." Wolf cast a glance at Steeleye, and for a moment as their eyes met and locked, Steeleye felt a strange thrill surge through him. He had missed his shadow, his truest of friends. Silently, Wolf turned and was gone into the darkness, as if she had never been. Steeleye's three companions slept on unaware of the drama that unfolded by their fire.

Once Wolf was gone, Maeve turned to Steeleye and gave him the widest of smiles. Though her face was one of beauty, the smile combined with the pitch-black orbs of her eyes was unsettling, and Steeleye shuddered in spite of himself.

"Brother..." Maeve breathed, licking her lips slowly, as if tasting the word, the black eyes half closed in ecstasy. "Soon, we shall meet in the flesh, not in dreams, nor magical theatrics such as this, but as we were, in the witch's womb." She tilted her head in the direction of the silent Morriggu, the smile becoming fixed and glacial. "No more hiding your champion now, is there, Crow? Janovis has seen to that, picking apart the wall that mother dearest built to hide her precious Aluin from me." The eyes flicked to Steeleye, wicked mirth even in their glossy emptiness. "And you, Aluin, Steel-Eye, Light-Bringer, Grimms-Bane..." she pronounced each name and title with careful contempt, "you collect names like that wolf bitch collects fleas."

"Enough, Maeve." Steeleye surprised himself. His voice was calm, filled with authority. He faced the apparition squarely. Within him, he could feel the Shining begin to stir, to awaken, an alien power that surged through his veins, filling him with confidence.

"I see you." Maeve pointed a cruel nailed finger at her brother, though he wasn't sure that she spoke to him. "There you are, hiding still, but your hiding places are fast dwindling." The Empress of the south stood taller, growing even more impressive. "You have grown to resemble our mother, Steeleye. Shall I call you Steeleye? Has little Aluin gone for good?" She didn't wait for a response but instead continued, her words like the sharpest of blades. "I think father would have been even more ashamed of you than usual, had he lived to see you running from me. Perhaps it was a mercy, my killing him upon the shore, whilst our mother waded into the sea, building her wall of spells within you, hiding you from me. From yourself." Maeve smiled slowly, slyly, as she recalled the events on the sea shore when their mother had saved her son. "She died screaming. Did you know?"

Steeleye felt the words twisting in his guts, like a red-hot blade.

"She screamed and screamed and screamed." Maeve stared at her tortured twin, and shivered visibly with pleasure. "I made the torment last as long as I was able, but back then, my skills were not honed, not as now." She looked to the Morriggu, dark and silent. "What do you say, little Crow, shall I nudge him along? Shall I save you your precious oath?"

The Morriggu nodded, almost imperceptibly "As you will Maeve, you seem to like theatrics much more than I."

Maeve laughed then, loud, and Steeleye flinched at the harshness of it. "Theatrics? I am not the one hiding behind crows and wolves, playing games of prophesy. No, Crow, the theatrics have all been from you, but tonight we shall start afresh, it is past time that Steeleye saw the whole picture."

"Speak on then Maeve," Steeleye reeled at the knowledge that his parents were dead, he was still finding memories of them, still getting to know them, and now they were gone. His sweet mother Ardanya, his saviour, gone. "Enough of this dancing, if you can help me regain all my memories, then lets at it." There was a flicker of light within his eyes, like sparks when flint strikes steel.

"The book, Steeleye, remember the book!" Maeve's voice was raised in excitement, so loud Steeleye wondered that his sleeping companions did not stir. But that simple word, book, had burst open a doorway within his mind, and Steeleye was catapulted into his past, to a time before crows and wolves, before Northmen and seers, before the name Steeleye Lightbringer.

ALUIN WAS awoken by the crash of thunder. Lightning forked outside his window, lighting his bedchamber brighter than any oil lamp. He rubbed the sleep from his eyes, and groggily made his way to the stone sill to stare into the raging storm. The sky seemed to boil, jagged lightning tearing through the clouds, bursting with fury. Behind him, he heard the door to his chamber open, and in the way of twins, he knew that Maeve had been awoken too and had come seeking her brother.

"What do you want Maeve?" he asked, a sulk in his tone. He had gone to bed that night with his arse sore from the birch, and that had been down to Maeve and her tricks, leaving her twin to take the punishment for her own wrong-doing. Aluin would never tattle tale upon his sister. Though he would have loved to dearly, it just wasn't in his nature.

"Mother has left open her study door!" Exclaimed the girl, her face lit with excitement, her silver hair still in disarray from sleep. "Hurry, Aluin, we can sneak a look at all her witchery things!" Maeve was literally hopping from foot to foot in her excitement.

"No! If we were to be caught, imagine the beating I would get from father." Aluin didn't think Maeve would suffer, not even if they were caught in their mother's most private sanctum. Maeve seemed blessed with a knack for passing on blame, usually straight to Aluin.

"Just one look, Aluin, to see what has been keeping her so occupied of late"

It was true: Ardanya had been spending much more of her time locked away in her study. When Aluin had enquired what she was doing, a shadow passed over her lovely face, and she and Bartok had exchanged an almost fearful glance. Maeve had seen the look too, and her fearless curiosity was piqued.

Even as they'd begun their argument, Aluin knew it was a lost cause. He would follow where his sister led, if for no other reason than to keep her from causing too much damage.

And so, the young Aluin pulled on his breeks and soft boots, and followed his twin from his chamber, along the corridors and passageways of their parents' sturdy castle, up flights of stairs, dodging patrolling men-at-arms, until at last they came to their mother's study, high in the east wing.

"How do you know the door is open?" Aluin whispered, abashed that he had only just now, standing outside the castle's most secure portal, thought to ask.

"I came by earlier," Maeve replied.

"What were you doing up here?" Aluin could feel his stomach churning. He really didn't want to be here, not only afraid of a beating should they be caught, but feeling disloyal to his mother; it did not sit well with him.

"I was just mucking about!" Maeve's exasperation was clear, she wanted to be on the other side of the door, not out here in the draughty corridor, arguing with Aluin.

"Mucking about? What do you—"

"Hush!" Maeve hissed, louder than either of them had been speaking. "Just shut up and follow me." With that, the girl reached for the iron handle, and pushed open the door. Without hesitation she stepped into the sanctum, pulling her resisting twin in her wake. The twins stared about them in wonder, for this was the first time either had ventured into their mothers most private domain, and it was hardly what they expected. Firstly, there were no dusty scrolls, nor cauldrons. No jars, filled with questionable fluids or strange creatures. In- fact there was nothing in the room to suggest it was the workplace of magic at all. A huge window dominated one wall, and through the glass the children could see the storm outside, they could even glimpse the raging sea when lightning came cracking across the sky.

In the centre of the room there was a simple desk, with one high backed chair tucked neatly beneath it, and that was all, no other furniture, no bookcases nor vases, no tapestries upon the walls nor carpets on the floor. The room was completely empty save the desk and the chair.

And what sat on the desk.

A book.

"There is nothing here." Aluin gushed, obviously relieved.

Maeve scowled at him, her eyes like a cat's. "Nothing here? Nothing here?" She made to slap his ear, but he jerked his head away. "What do you call that, sat in the middle of the desk?" Maeve seemed to be vibrating with pleasure. "Can't you feel it, Aluin?" She stepped close to the desk, her fingers dancing as they often did when she intended mischief. "It is calling to me Aluin! The book is singing in my head."

Aluin looked at the book doubtfully. "It's just a book," he said, shrugging his shoulders.

"*Just a book?*" Maeve looked at her brother as if he were a simpleton. "This is not just any book, you dullard, it is *the* book. Aihaab's book!"

Aluin knew his history well enough, and he blanched at the mention of that terrible name. "All the more reason to be away from here then, Maeve, there's nothing good can come from meddling with that. Come away." The boy made his way to the door, his hand making it as far as the handle, when he heard the squeal of pleasure from his sister. Glancing back over his shoulder, he saw Maeve reach out and, with shaking fingers, flip open the book. "No!" cried Aluin, deserting his post at the door and instinctively running to his twin.

By the time he reached Maeve's side, she was staring wide eyed at the open page before her. "Can you hear it, Aluin?" she was whispering, engrossed in the text. "It knows me, Aluin. It sees me for who I am, who I really am."

"Look away Maeve! There is no sound coming from the damned book." Aluin was now becoming short tempered. What if his mother should come by? This was a stupid idea, another stupid idea of Maeve's, and one that was sure to result in Aluin not being able to sit down for days. "Come away now Maeve, *please!*"

"In a minute Aluin in a minute, I'm listening to the book."

Maeve let her fingers hover over the sable text. It was written in a language long forgotten, great looping characters and shapes that looked entirely alien to the twins, yet somehow strangely familiar. Aluin peered over his sister's shoulder and gave a gasp. The words on the page were moving! They lengthened and thinned, they merged and slowly began to rotate, like ink in a pot stirred by a quill, round and round and round.

"Maeve! What are you doing? Stop it!"

Maeve turned surprised eyes to her brother, her hand almost touching the swirling letters on the page, the girl had no notion of how her fingers had come to be so close. She exhaled sharply, and began to withdraw her hand. At that moment, thunder boomed directly overhead of the tower, and lighting flared so bright as to make both the twins flinch and duck.

Maeve's fingers brushed against the parchment.

She let out a piercing scream, her young body suddenly rigid, so taut it seemed she might snap. Aluin recovered quickly from his fright of the thunderclap, and reached to help his sister. Even as he did, to his horror, he saw the swirling words spreading over Maeve's skin. Within moments, it looked like she had dipped her fingers in an inkwell. Seconds later, her hand was jet black, and tendrils of the swirling words inched up her wrist.

Maeve screamed on. So high was the scream that it hurt Aluin's ears, so loud he feared it would shatter the very glass in the windows. He grabbed at his sister's arm, feeling the limb as tense as an iron bar. He yanked at her arm to pull her away from the book. But he might as well have tried to uproot a mighty oak. All the while he called her name in a panicked desperation, and all the while Maeve screamed and screamed.

To young Aluin, it seemed he was there for an age, fear and rage waging a war within him. He was terrified of the book, yet his love for his sister wouldn't let him leave her, no matter her malice and stupidity, so he redoubled his efforts, pulling with all his might on his sister's unheeding arm. When the door to the room burst open, and his mother and father came dashing over the threshold, Aluin near burst into tears with relief, no matter the beating he knew was coming his way.

"God's have mercy what have you done Maeve?" Aluin could just hear his mother's voice over the shrieking of his sister, could hear the shock, the fear in her tone. Bartok was silent, but he looked terrified, standing there besides his wife, watching as his daughter screamed. Aluin, for one absurd moment, thought that for all this time Maeve had yet to take a breath, but surely that wasn't possible? The boy now changed his tactics. Instead of pulling at her arm, he reached over her chest and tried to bodily pull her away, to prise her from the book. All to no avail. Maeve was as a statue, immoveable. He looked into her face, pleading with her to move her hand. Her mouth was stretched impossibly wide, the tendons on her neck standing out like wires, her eyes staring, unfocused.

"Nononononononono!" Maeve's scream suddenly changed, her eyes widened even more and she began to shake and tremble. The black tendrils spread further and further, now past he wrist, past her elbow, spreading faster. "Pleasepleaseplease!" she was gasping for breath now, sweat standing out on her face.

Aluin could bear no more. His parents were still frozen with terror, so he did the only thing that he could think to do. He snatched the book from the table, slamming the pages shut. There came a furious roaring sound from the book, and Aluin was hurled away from the desk like a rag doll. He set to against the legs of his father, who seemed at last snap out of his shock, reaching down to cover his son with a protective arm.

Aluin scrambled to his feet, staring aghast at the book, which now rested harmless upon the flagstones. Maeve lay curled in a ball beneath the desk, great wracking sobs making her whole-body shudder. As one, Aluin, Bartok, and Ardanya rushed forwards, the latter two at Maeve's side, but Aluin went to push the book farther away with a booted toe.

Even as his toe came upon the binding of the book, the scenario in the study worsened.

Ardanya put a comforting arm around her daughter, cooing soft words of comfort, Bartok too was hovering over his beloved daughter, the very apple of his eye, when the twin suddenly shuddered and fell silent. For long moments, she remained still, and then her body began to spasm as if in great sobbing grief, but the sounds she issued were not of grief, not by a long shot.

Maeve was laughing.

As she uncurled from the floor, she turned her twisted, maniacal face towards Aluin, pushing her father away as if he were the child. Ardanya tried to hold on to her daughter, but Maeve lazily struck her with an open hand. Ardanya was sent sprawling next to her husband. Now, only Aluin remained standing, his toe still nudging the book.

"Maeve, all will be well." Aluin heard his own voice, but didn't agree with the sentiments; how could all be well? Maeve was no longer Maeve. Her look of mischief had now gone, replaced by malice. Maeve moved towards her brother, the nails on her fingers suddenly long and sharp as knives, dancing *clickety click*.

Aluin was rooted to the spot. For the life of him, he could not move a muscle as his sister advanced. She was laughing louder now, and Aluin knew his sister was lost to him. He knew also that she meant to kill him, to kill them all. The book at his foot vibrated, began to thrum with power and energy, and there came to Aluin's ears wondrous voices, singing out in rapturous glory.

Aluin flipped open the book with his toe.

There came a blinding light, as if the sun had been hiding within the pages of the book and was now released. It shot from the parchment and engulfed Aluin. The glorious singing became louder still, yet over this, he could hear his sister screaming with rage, howling like a banshee. She pushed past her parents as if they were no more than stalks of wheat and fled the room.

* * *

"THE BOOK!" Steeleye exclaimed. "Maeve, you awoke the book!"

Maeve raised a brow towards the Morriggu, smiling slyly. "You knew, of course?" she asked the goddess, "when you enlisted my poor dullard brother, you knew that he bore a part of the book?"

"I knew he carried the Light," replied the Morriggu softly, "just as I knew that the darkness held within the book had passed to you, his sister." There was a sadness in the look the Morriggu gave to Maeve then. "The darkness sought out a weak will, a vessel it could control and corrupt, though not too much corruption was needed in your case, unless I miss my guess?"

Steeleye stood stock still, the Stormchild's blade forgotten in his fist. He remembered clearly now how his mother had hugged her son, how his father had grieved for his daughter, keening softly as he fell to his knees.

The book had poured its shadowy bile into the mind and body of young Maeve, and then, had infused him, Steeleye, with an opposing power, the Shining as he had come to know it.

He looked across the fire to his twin. She glared at the Morriggu without fear. In fact, there was triumph in her face, and slowly, the blackness of her eyes began to swirl, like paint in water, then fade, leaving the fierce sapphire orbs that Steeleye knew and had once loved.

"I am so sorry, Maeve." His voice was choked as he spoke, his vision blurred with tears, and he could feel them coursing down his cheeks. "I should have stopped you opening the book. I should have been stronger and pulled you away."

Maeve gave her twin with a confused look, then her face broke into a wide smile, and she laughed at her brother's misery. "You are still a dullard, aren't you?" she spat. "Still trying to save me? It's past time you realised I don't want to be saved, Steeleye." She said his name with disdain, her lip curling as if she tasted something bitter. "The book searched for me for a thousand years. It knows me. It understands me, more than you or mother ever did, more even than father, and he knew me better than most. No, brother, there was no way you could have stopped me opening the book, I was waiting for it my whole life!" A look of pure pleasure lit up Maeve's face. "You cannot imagine the power the book has given me, the things it has shown me, the realms that have been opened to me. I am becoming more than human, Steeleye, this empire that I am building is just the start. I have the Horde at my command, I have demon lords clamouring to do my bidding, begging to be let join my host. I am... more!

"In the South, I am worshipped as a god! Whole nations crawl on their bellies before me. They flinch at my name; they pull out their hair in despair when they see my banners before their gates. The book has given me all this, brother. From the moment I was born the book was waiting for me, to bring me to it."

"Only a part of the book." The Morriggu spoke calmly, softly, the very opposite of Maeve's passion. "The book holds far more than mere power, more than the darkness that you embraced so eagerly: it holds the balance of things, hence the giving of the Light to your twin, once you had taken the Darkness. Even as you carry the corruption of the book, Steeleye carries the Light that will balance it out. The cosmos must have a balance, light and dark, day and night. One cannot exist without the other."

"Wrong, Crow," Maeve spat, and Steeleye was taken aback by her venom, particularly as it was directed at a goddess. "There shall be only the way of the darkness. Its way is the natural way of things: decay follows all splendour, every fruit rots no matter how sweet on the branch, corruption is the natural order of mankind.

You need only look to the courts of the great kings to see that. Why already the nations near here send me platitudes, they would betray their people to the Horde, to save their own skins."

"And yet your plans in the City of the Dead were met with failure; *good* men rose to meet your armies. In fact, isn't it true that the farther your empire spreads, the more resistance it finds?" The Morriggu now let steel enter her voice, and her eyes lost any compassion they had shown. Sitting there between his mad twin and the collector of souls, Steeleye for the first time felt real fear of the immortal, her face was as Death. From within the shadows of her robes, the Morriggu drew out her silver scythe, and held it before her, so Maeve could see it clearly.

"Even you, Maeve, shall meet with me at your end; this is the way of things, for I have seen the birth and the death of worlds in numbers that you cannot fathom. When your time comes, *this* Crow shall whisper your fate in your ear, even as I pluck what is left of your black, corrupted soul from your body."

Steeleye saw Maeve's bravado falter.

"So you believe, Crow." She regained her composure with difficulty. Her crimson cape suddenly lifted, as if caught in high winds. Her silver hair too was pulled and whipped about her. "I have done what I came for, I have twisted the knife in the dullard's guts. I have shown him that he faces more than he could ever hope to defeat." Maeve turned to stare with utter contempt at her brother. "Our mother was the greatest witch of her age, and she tried all she could to destroy the book, but she failed utterly. She should have embraced the book, as I have." As she spoke, Maeve was suddenly holding the great book in her silver taloned hands. The ominous presence of the tome seemed to bear down upon Steeleye, and even the fire he stood by seemed to shrink and falter.

"The Sisters are waiting for you, brother, they champ at the leash to get to you, and yet your *goddess* would send you to them, and gladly." Maeve began to turn from the little gathering, but looked back over her shoulder at her twin. "I have despised you, for all time, brother. I should imagine I hated you, even in the womb. You are everything that I loathe in the world, and that was before I joined with the entity of the book. You are... weak.

"If by some miracle the sisters do not find you and rend you, know that I am waiting, even as the Crow thinks she will be waiting for me."

With that, Maeve stepped back, and returned to whatever storm-tossed location her body truly resided.

The night seemed to breathe again.

Steeleye and the Morriggu locked their gaze. "She will kill me, I think," he said softly. "I have never seen so much hate... She was always wild and full of mischief, I can remember that much, but I think her very look could kill me had she been here in body."

"Maeve was ever a dark soul. Whether she came by the book or no, she would have grown to be a tyrant. The book has merely amplified that which was already there, as it has with you." The Collector of Souls looked upon the sleeping companions. Morinae shuffled a little, making contented sounds.

"I have sent them pleasant dreams, dreams to rest their spirits, after the trauma of Janovis and her Grimm." The hardness had left the Morriggu now: there was compassion in the look she gave the trio. "Strong companions, these," she mused. "The Princess has more steel in her bones than you know, Steeleye, and I think it a good thing she is on the side of the Light, for there is plenty of darkness within her too, which I think her brother will undoubtably find out." The Morriggu smiled at the thought of the prince of Asgulun getting his comeuppance.

"You know of his treachery then?"

"I know much, Steeleye, but the oath we gods took is strong, and not one I would break, I must keep some things to myself, though perhaps I can let you know this: Ixtchel awaits you on the shores of the Asgulun. The demon sister has taken the form of the Queen of Ashanarr, and is even now leading the Grimm to Morinae's homeland. Look to my crows, they will guide you, and Morinae, she will be a firm ally I think, and the old windbag too." She smiled, and Steeleye was surprised to think she looked upon him with fondness.

"Make haste to Fishtown, charter or steal a boat: Morinae is needed in Asgulun, and your place for now is at her side, as she fights for the Light." With that, the goddess stepped back into the shadows of the night and was gone. There was no farewell, or ceremony, she just blended with the night, and vanished as if she had never been.

Ixtchel. Another of the Sisters, no doubt enraged by the death of Janovis. He felt the thrill of fear along his spine, a sensation he was becoming all too familiar with. But along with the fear, there came relief. Ixtchel was a stepping stone to reclaiming that which the Morriggu held, stoppered and trapped in her glass vial. But Ixtchel was for another day, along with all the other Sisters. For now, he had to deal with the pain that Maeve had just visited upon him.

Steeleye scowled into the fire. He wished the succubus had never broken the seals of his memory. His past was not a happy one: his father had been a good man, yet a bully where his son was concerned, ever wanting more than the young Aluin was able to achieve. His mother had loved him dearly, and he returned that love tenfold. Most of the memories that brought a smile to his lips involved his mother. The pain he felt at her death was a physical sensation, a torture.

And Maeve. His memories of his twin were difficult to unravel. His love for her was boundless, more so than even his mother. For Maeve, he had taken beatings, suffered ridicule, become her partner in petty crime about their parents' keep. Yet now he knew that she didn't feel the same. Any love she might have shown him had been a ruse. Even though she had been the cause of much of Steeleye's past issues, Steeleye felt only an immense sadness at what Maeve had told him as she left. It left him with a strange empty feeling, a void as real as the one left by his missing soul.

He sat down and watched the fire till it died. He was still awake as the sun poked its head over the hills to the east.

CHAPTER 20
FISHTOWN

They came upon Fishtown just as the sun reached its zenith in a cloudless sky. The town was built around a wide natural harbour, with steep cliffs guarding two sides of the horseshoe bay from the worst the Sea of Storms could throw at them. The bay itself was near a mile across, and from their vantage point on the headland above the town, the company could see hundreds of brightly painted fishing vessels bobbing about on the waves.

Though they were still a good mile from the town proper, they could smell the sea in the briny air, and the catch that gave the town its name. Steeleye turned in his saddle to look at his companions, though they had travelled far, they looked much refreshed after their perils with Janovis and her horde. Morinae in particular had flourished on the journey—she was after all, heading home to her father and brother—her golden hair seemed to glow in the sunlight, and a smile was never far from her lips. Of her intentions towards her step-brother, the scheming prince that had been responsible for her abduction, she said little, but

Steeleye had come to know her well enough to understand the matter was far from closed.

Artfur had practiced his lute, singing songs of heroes or long-lost kingdoms. Though getting on in years, his voice remained strong and clear, and his company eased the rigours of travel. Helgen was still smitten with the Princess, and spent any spare moments hanging on her every word, but still she practiced the flute each day, and its tone was so sweet it might charm even the birds from the air.

Steeleye had spent the rest of the journey, since the visitation from Maeve and the Morriggu, deep in thought. His memories came to him more easily now, and he thought often of his home, Clove, a small barony along the coast from Morinorn, which his father had ruled as if he had in fact been a king rather than a warlord, subject only to the whims of the Queen of Morinorn. It had been his father's duty to maintain the peace in the area, and secure the coast for the crown, and, until his death, he had been capable of both.

Steeleye often wondered whether perhaps when all this was over, if he still lived, there would be a place for him in Clove? For a long time, he had thought himself homeless, vagrant, yet in recent days he remembered that this was not always the case. He had a home, even if there were no kin left there. He had roots, a place to return to.

"The place stinks." Artfur put into words what everyone was thinking, the muttered comment breaking Steeleye from his reverie.

"Agreed," Morinae said, wrinkling her nose. "We should get down there and charter a vessel, then begone. The smell is likely to put me off sea food for life, and I live on the coast!" As good as her word, Morinae heeled her horse forwards, leading the small band down the track towards the bay below.

It was mid-afternoon by the time they arrived on the main

street of Fishtown, the smell of the sea drowned out by the over-powering stench of fish, both fresh and rotten, and smoke billowing from the seemingly endless smoking sheds. The town was all hustle and bustle. Even here, a few streets back from the quay-side, children pushed hand carts teeming with crabs, oysters and gutted fish, ready to be sold to the taverns and house-holds. They declared the freshness, the value, the splendid taste: the descriptions they shouted could hardly be further away from the grimy, and blood-stained carts that they pushed to and fro.

"I think perhaps I will be looking for beef stew for supper," Steeleye remarked as they passed a particularly filthy lad pushing his noisome cart. Artfur chortled merrily. As a well-travelled man, he had seen it all before, the bigger and busier the town, the worse such sights and smells became. And Fishtown was quite a size. As they passed by the quay, they saw it was lined with perhaps fifty or so two storey buildings, warehouses, whore houses, ale houses and smokehouses. In the streets further from the docks, there were more dwellings, and stores of other trades too: stables and smithies, rope-makers and sail makers, coopers and jewellers, all the trades a town could need, mixed amongst several good-sized taverns and inns.

"Have you been here before, Artfur?" Morinae asked. She guided her horse around a cart piled high with furniture. It was a good thing the streets were wide and well cobbled, else the cart would have blocked the way like a cork in a bottle,

"I have, Princess, though it was not so hectic as this." Artfur too had noted the wagon stuffed with a family's belongings. He looked about him at the all the activity. "And may I suggest that we steer clear of the taverns called *The Saucy Nymph* and *The Fisherman's Rest*? If memory serves, I may not be too welcome in those establishments."

Young Helgen made a disgusted, tutting sound as she rode next to her uncle, to which he waggled his white eyebrows and gave an exaggerated wink.

"Cards, was it? Or dice?" asked the girl with a frown

"A little of both, and perhaps more besides," Artfur replied with a grin.

Steeleye grinned along with the old man. "We shall need a decent inn for the night, and once we are settled, I shall make my way to the docks to find us passage to Asgulun. It will needs be a sturdy ship, I reckon a day's sailing at least, hugging the coast of the Narrow Sea, and then a day or more to cross the Sea of Storms." He looked about him at the activity on the street. "The town has the smell of war in its nose, I think. It looks like half the populace is getting ready to pull up sticks and move on. The situation with Ashanarr must have worsened." He chewed the inside of his cheek, thinking hard, this would make their passage to Asgulun more precarious.

"What do you think Artfur? Will we be able to get passage? We will be heading into a possible war zone, not away from it, like so many seem to be?"

"There are always those willing to take a risk, if the price is right." The old bard smiled to himself, he obviously had an idea or two. "Once we get the ladies' settled, you and I should take a walk along Smugglers Warf, I'm sure there are rogues aplenty there willing to take a risk."

"Very well then, but I'm not too keen on using smugglers for passage. What is to stop them making extra demands once we are at sea?"

"You are!" Artfur grinned. "You and that pig sticker that hangs from your belt. You are handy with a blade, and such rogues as I've a mind to speak with will respect that. Or fear it, either will work as well for us."

The four of them reined in their mounts outside a large and well-tended hostelry at the start of the evening rush, Steeleye dismounted and stretched his back, hearing a few disturbing popping cracks from his spine. He grimaced, while Morinae laughed at him good naturedly.

"I would have thought you were used to the saddle by now," she chided.

"I don't think I ever will," he mumbled, motioning them all to stay put whilst he looked the tavern over. The building was large and made of stone and timber, two storied and painted a bright white that hurt his eyes as he looked at it. A sign proclaiming The Jolly Moon, swung gently on a chain above the door. The breeze that moved the sign hinted at the sea, less overpowering than the stink of the rest of the town.

The door to *The Jolly Moon* was open wide, and Steeleye made his way inside. He found himself in a very large common room, with plenty of tables and benches dotted about, lanterns hung from black painted rafters, giving off a welcoming yellow light. At a glance, Steeleye guessed there were perhaps thirty patrons gathered in the room, most already tankard in hand, many sitting with platters of bread and cheese, or a fish stew on their tables. For all the people present, it wasn't long before a man Steeleye presumed to be the landlord, appeared at his elbow. The man was of middling height and thinning red hair, his face flushed.

"Good evening to you, sir," he said. "Welcome to The Jolly Moon, Fishtown's finest inn. Good clean beds, home cooked food, and the very best ale and peach brandy in all of the province of Barr. Will you be wanting a table? A meal and a room perhaps?" Steeleye nodded absently at the man. He was busy looking around the patrons, searching for anyone or anything suspicious. At last, satisfied all was well, he asked the landlord if he could arrange for six horses to be stabled, provide two rooms, and a table for four.

The landlord was all smiles and nods as he rushed to get a couple of lads to go outside and take care of the horses. Steeleye waved the rest of his companions in, and they soon found a table. The landlord himself served them, taking an order for food and wine, and a pitcher of water to dilute the wine for Helgen, much to her disgust.

The four of them ate in a leisurely fashion. The fish stew, for all Morinae's misgivings, proved to be excellent, and the wine was welcome after days on the road. Artfur guzzled, and young Helgen had stern words for him. The four of them relaxed for the first time in days, feeling that the end of at least one part of their journey was at hand. Morinae spoke of her homeland, and though she worried at the prospect of war with Ashanarr, she was confident in her brother's military skill to defend Asgulun. In fact, as Steeleye listened to her speak of Bryann he had to smile, she was so obviously proud of him.

Their talk soon turned to Juvaal, Morinae's other brother. Helgen wanted to know just what would happen when Morinae sailed back home, not only alive and well, but knowing that Juvaal had been responsible for all her recent woes, and was indirectly responsible for Sha'haan's death. "Nothing will happen." Morinae told them. "At least, not at first. Juvaal will welcome me back, as if he had done naught but fret over me all the months that I have been gone, and I shall play along, and bide my time. My first duty is to Asgulun. I must find out how my father fares, how the land lies with Ashanarr. Once that has been settled, whether it be war or peace, then Juvaal will be dealt with."

"A fall from the battlements perhaps?" Artfur had drunk a little too much, but Morinae didn't reproach him. Instead, she sipped her wine and said quietly, "Something like that: life at court can be full of perils."

A shadow fell over the group, and Steeleye turned to find a wizened old sailor looking at them in a confused way, as if he knew them, but didn't know from where. "Can I help you?" Steeleye asked the man, carefully. He was well aware that Barr's borders were open with those of Ashanarr, and that there was the risk of Morinae being recognised.

The old sailor looked Steeleye in the eye. "I've been having dreams, sir. Of you, I think." The sailor looked bewildered, lost. "I was told in my dreams to seek you out, if your name is Steeleye?"

"It is." Steeleye was intrigued.

"I am to tell you to be at the harbour at dawn, sir. The lady in my dreams told me to tell you this: be at the harbour at dawn."

Steeleye felt a chill, though the room was warm. The lady? Surely not Maeve, she would have come to him as she had at the campfire, or into his own dreams to taunt him. Could it be Ixtchel? The demon that posed as the queen of the neighbouring country and was even now doing her level best to spread the empire of her mistress north.

He waited patiently for the old man to continue, feeling no threat from the fellow. He saw his companions had likewise ceased their own chatter, and were now waiting for the sailor to speak on. Moments dragged by, then Helgen, plagued with the impatience of youth, blurted "Who is the lady in your dreams?"

The sailor started at Helgen's voice, as if awakening from a trance "Hewla, little miss," the sailor said softly. "She said her name was Hewla, and the one called Steeleye would know to do as she said, or suffer the consequences."

Steeleye barked out a laugh, his face breaking into a genuine smile, perhaps the first in days. Hewla! Sending messages through dreams was a new trick, but he didn't doubt that the witch was capable of it.

The sailor suddenly gave a yelp, as the landlord grabbed the scruff of his tattered coat and pulled him away from the table. "How many times must I tell you, Rob? Keep away from paying guests, they don't need to be hearing your drunken prattle."

The balding innkeep cast an apologetic glance at Steeleye and his party as he marched Rob over to the bar. "I'm right sorry for my brother," he said over his shoulder, tapping his temple with a finger. "He's not quite all there I'm afraid. One too many knocks on the head while at sea. But he means no harm." And with that, Rob and his brother went behind the bar and beyond into what Steeleye thought may be the kitchen.

Steeleye watched the brothers go, then looked back to find his companions all staring at him expectantly. He was still grinning. "What?" he asked of them all. "Have you never seen a man passing on a message?"

"Delivered to him in his dreams?" Artfur choked.

Steeleye chuckled. "We should find our rooms. Artfur and I will share, as will you two ladies. We have an early start, and I for one don't intend keeping Hewla waiting!"

DAWN FOUND the three of them wrapped in their cloaks against the early mist and chill, standing at the stone harbour wall. The sea fret was damp and cold, plastering their hair to their heads, reducing visibility to only a few yards. "So, the lady that bade us come here, she is a good witch you say?" Artfur had asked the same question couched in different words a dozen times, since the sailor Rob had delivered Hewla's message the previous evening.

"She can be menacing, right enough," Steeleye responded, his tone hushed yet carrying strangely in the mist. "But there is no evil in her. She is a powerful healer, and has knowledge well beyond the norm. I for one, was relieved to get her message. She is a worthy ally."

Artfur made an unconvinced noise in his throat, and stamped his feet on the damp stones, trying to dispel the cold.

"Who goes there?" A man's voice drifted through the fret, and the companions turned as one to see a yellow ball of illumination approaching them. The yellow light soon revealed itself to be a lantern, held high by a man dressed in a heavy coat, a felt cap pulled tight on his pate. "What are you about at this time of a morning?" the newcomer asked, suspicion writ on every line of his face. Steeleye noted that several more men, vague shapes in the mist, were standing close behind the speaker.

"Who is asking?" Morinae stepped up beside Steeleye. She wore a rich purple cloak, the hood of which was pulled up, hiding her face in its shadows. Her tone and the obvious quality of her clothes caused the newcomer to look closer. Spilling the yellow light of his lantern over the waiting group.

"I am Berry, the night harbour-master, miss. You cannot be too careful in times such as these." He motioned at the vague shapes behind him. "These lads are the Harbour Watch, here to keep the peace, so to speak." The harbour-master looked over the four of them, noting the sword at Steeleye's hip and the gleam of his mail shirt beneath his dark cloak. "We aren't looking for any trouble, miss, just doing our jobs, is all." He licked his lips nervously, his eyes moving from Morinae's shadowy cowl to Steeleye's sword, then back. He seemed to have decided the richly dressed woman was in charge, so he addressed his comments to her.

"These are strange times, Lady, and I'm tasked with keeping the docks safe from smugglers and the like. May I ask again your business here at this hour?"

"We are meeting a friend, is all." As she spoke, Morinae let her hood fall to her shoulders. Her hair shone like burnished gold in the lantern light. "We mean no harm, nor pose any threat, Master Berry."

"A friend? In weather such as this? Please tell me they are not hoping to come ashore from the sea, at least not until the fret has lifted. When the sun breaks full the fret will slowly melt away." Berry looked genuinely concerned, and Steeleye could understand why. As he peered into the harbour, he could see shadowy indistinct hulks, vague and looming in the fog, dozens of vessels, large and small, anchored overnight in the security of the harbour.

Steeleye was about to ask the watchman how long he thought it would be before visibility would improve enough to allow the docking of a ship, if that was indeed what Hewla's message had meant, when out of the fret there came a distorted call. All Steeleye's companions and the harbour-master and the men of the watch gathered together at the harbour wall, eyes narrowed as they tried to see where the call had issued from.

"Halloo," came the disembodied voice again, drifting, muffled, through the fog.

"What madness is this?" Master Berry was incredulous that someone would be trying to manoeuvre through the anchorage with such poor visibility.

Another voice came from the grey, grumbling and forlorn. "If I had lost both my eyes and not just the one, then by Heros' breath, I swear I could still do a better job at the helm than you are right now."

The two parties on the harbour wall exchanged bemused glances. Now they could hear the sounds of oars dipping into the sea, slow and rhythmic.

"Steady now lads, steady. Watch your oar there, lad! Keep it slow and steady!" A new voice drifted from the fret, and while the watchmen peered mouths agape, Steeleye felt a slow smile spreading over his mist-damp face. He had thought the first voice was familiar; he was even more sure that he recognised the second, but what were the owners of the voices doing here, a month's journey from where he had last seen them?

"That is Rothgar and Rolf." Steeleye breathed the names in a whisper. "I know those voices, I'm sure of it." Just then, a blurred yellow light became visible in the mist, gently bobbing like a will-o-the whisp. Soon, a large shadow began to emerge from the misty gloom.

"Backwater!" a voice called, louder and clearer, the sound of the oars changed at once, the sound of straining timber floating to

315

the harbour wall. Slowly, the outline of a high, sleek vessel emerged from the mist. Standing at the prow, one hand gripping the carved mane of the horse figurehead, the other holding aloft a lantern, was none other than the grizzled northern veteran Rolf, his white beard and hair as wild as ever Steeleye remembered.

The prow of the ship visibly slowed as it came nearer, masterfully handled by the helm and the oarsmen. The ship came to a stop with a soft thud against the great stone wall of Fishtown harbour, it remained indistinct in the fret, but its shape was recognisable. A Northern war galley, built for speed and for battle, the figure-head a charging horse, fierce and wild, just like the Northmen that crewed the ship.

Berry, the harbour-master, stood open mouthed. "This is most unusual!" he muttered, staring up at the bearded figure brandishing the lantern. "You can't just come in here as you please and tie up! There are ledgers to fill in and tithes to pay!" Berry was getting over his surprise at seeing the near silent vessel, his responsibilities as a harbour-master taking over. He motioned for the watch to come forwards, ill paid men in sodden boots and cloaks, poorly armed with halberds and bronze studded clubs, men more at home breaking up a tavern brawl than confronting a ship load of warriors from the north.

"Be at ease, lad," Rolf called to the master, his voice kind enough for all his wild appearance. "We are to be gone in a moment, just picking up a few passengers, and then we will be back into the Narrow Sea before the ink has dried on your ledger. As for the tithe?" Rolf tossed down a small leather pouch, which Berry caught deftly. Steeleye heard the sound of coins rattling together. "That should cover the cost of a mulled wine or two for you and the boys there."

Berry peered into the bag, then turned to the watch. "I reckon *The Saucy Nymph* along Smugglers Wharf should be serving breakfast right about now boys, so seeing as there is nothing amiss here, we should be moving along." The watchmen were only too pleased to depart, soon fading into the fret along the quay. Berry was about to follow, when he turned back to the companions. "I see you there, Artfur Fleetfingers. A good thing that you are leaving Fishtown. Marked cards can mean a week in the stocks around here. We have enough cheats and swindlers of our own without the likes of you." With that, Berry rushed into the mist, keen to be gone from the strange ship and its passengers.

"Well then Strawtop, are you getting aboard, or what?" Rolf called down from the prow. "Hewla is expecting you and the Princess at Asgulun, and we all know the crone doesn't like to be kept waiting."

CHAPTER 21

ASGULUN

Morinae, Helgen, and Artfur, followed Steeleye as he bounded up the wooden plank that was pushed ashore for them. The huge white-haired man came forwards to meet Steeleye, wrapping his arms about him in a fierce embrace. "It is good to see you, boy," he roared joyously, near lifting Steeleye off his feet in his enthusiasm. Steeleye returned the embrace, clapping the giant upon the back as he did so.

"I can scarcely believe it is you," he wheezed. Rolf released his bear hug. "What brings you here? In a war boat, and in a fog thick enough to carve?"

Rolf did not answer. The old man gestured for the party to come on deck. Even as the plank was pulled back aboard, oars once more began to slice into the water; Rolf watched with satisfaction as the harbour wall seemed to dissolve into the mist. At length, he put an arm around Steeleye's shoulder, steering him along the deck to a raised cabin at the stern. "Come, into the cabin, we can catch up over spiced tea."

Steeleye looked to either side of him as he was led to the rear of the galley, northmen sat in pairs, strong hands gripping oars, leaning forwards then heaving back, legs braced on boards before them. These men were warrior elite, dressed in hauberks of mail, swords at their hips, hard sinew in their arms and iron in their eye. They grinned fiercely at Rolf and their new passengers as they made their way aft, as if they knew that wherever the yellow haired warrior went, then the clash of arms was close behind. These men lived for the thrill of combat.

Morinae found herself hurrying to keep close to Steeleye, though the men around her had offered no harm, they looked savage, and she had heard tales of the Northern clans in their sleek galleys. They were feared throughout the world when they ventured from their frozen wastes. She was grateful for their assistance. It seemed they were intent upon taking them to Asgulun, but what were they doing so far from their mountains and fjords? Why were they spiriting them from Fishtown like spectres in the fret?

The answers to her musings came soon enough, as Rolf opened the cabin door and bade them enter.

"Welcome, to the captain's cabin." Rolf grinned easily. He motioned that they should be seated. The cabin was only several paces square, with a shuttered window behind a bolted down desk, opposite the doorway. To each side benches were affixed to the walls, rude cushions strewn on them. As the group sat about the benches, Rolf twisted a screw on the side of the single oil lamp that hung from the cabin roof by slim chains. Yellow light filled the cabin, giving the illusion of warmth and cheer.

"Tea will be along soon enough; nice and hot. These damned fogs can chill a man to the bone." He sat at the captain's chair; it creaked alarmingly under his weight. "To business then," he said, eyes wrinkling in smiles. "Hewla waits for you in Asgulun, along with Aelrik and a thousand men, and a dozen galleys, the same as this one."

"There is a fleet in Asgulun?" Steeleye was bewildered. "And Aelrik too? How?"

"Why?" chimed in Morinae. Her concern at so many armed men from the north in her beloved Asgulun was writ clear on her face.

"Be at ease, Princess." Rolf soothed. "We have come to lend our steel to yours against this Empress of the South."

"But it is Ashanarr, not the Empire, that threatens our borders." Morinae was indignant at Rolf's easy assumption that Asgulun should need the warriors of the North, and more than a little worried he mentioned the Empire.

"Ashanarr is but a catspaw of the Empress in this game," Rolf responded, "and it is more than just threats to borders, I'm afraid. There is war upon the Sea of Storms, and aye, along the shores of Asgulun as well. The Ashanarr have made landings, burning and looting. Threats are long gone, Princess, and your wizard, Al'hainn, he sent word to Hewla the seer that Asgulun would soon bear the brunt of the Empress' wrath, and so we came to stand shoulder to shoulder with the good folk of Asgulun."

Morinae sat shocked. Her mouth worked soundlessly for a moment or two, and then she blurted, "Al'hainn? Al'hainn the wizard? He is a drunken sot! A hermit that lives in a cave! He is no more a wizard than Artfur here." Morinae seethed, and Steeleye, who sat next to her, could feel her shaking with fury.

"Drunken sot or no, when he called to our own, to Hewla the witch, she bade us come to the South at once." As Rolf spoke, the door to the cabin opened, and a tousle-haired lad brought in their tea upon a tray. The ship must have cleared the harbour, for it began to buck and roll gently with the waves of the Narrow Sea. Once the boy had gone, the group gathered their tea, sipping the hot spiced liquid with trepidation, Morinae made a surprised sound as she recognised the taste.

"Made with the berries of the ashan tree, from the East." Rolf commented, noting the princess' surprise. "We trade in the spring fairs with all nations, Princess, and the North has a taste for the exotic."

Morinae blushed a little, and stammered how nice the brew was. She was caught off guard by the civility offered by so wild a looking man. Steeleye grinned at her discomfort, sipping the tea with relish. "Hewla makes it better," he remarked.

"Hewla takes the best of the leaves, that is why." Rolf winked at Steeleye, obviously still very pleased to see his old comrade. "Much has happened since you and that beast of a wolf of yours wandered from the Stone Gods. I'm not complaining the beast isn't here mind," he lowered his voice a little, and spoke into his cup, "handy in a scrap, but the thing gave me the willies."

"You had a wolf?" Helgen interrupted excitedly, her eyes wide as she stared at Steeleye. Rolf answered in his stead. "The wolf didn't belong to him, more the other way around I think," Rolf chuckled softly. "A huge beast it was, with jaws so wide they could snap a man's head off." Helgen's eyes grew rounder still as she pictured the wolf. "At the gates to Ash Ul M'on, the wolf saved many a man, including Straw Top there."

Steeleye smiled, but a shadow passed over his face as he remembered the gate, the carnage and the loss. That was where he had first come to realize there was a greater evil than he had ever imagined stalking the world. He thought again of Freija, with her flaming hair and ready wit. The denizens of Ash Ul M'on had taken a great deal from him. "Wolf and I parted ways at the Bridge of Glass," he said, not mentioning that he went down into the abyss, nor that he had seen the silent beast a time or two since, shadowing her true mistress, the Morriggu.

"You say much has changed?" Steeleye steered the conversation back on track. He well remembered Rolf's tendency to ramble.

"Aye! Changes aplenty in the North. Aelrik called all the clans together after the death of his boy Rannulf, and that monstrosity that you killed in the circle of stones. The North is big, and hard to manage, but Aelrik brought us all together under one banner, and we returned to the Dead City, with ten thousand men and maidens. We lit every shadow with fire, killed every skulking creature there, and then under the command of Aelrik, we began to bring the city down. It will take years to complete, but Aelrik commanded that not two stones should be left atop one another. He plans to destroy the very memory of the place."

Rolf sipped his tea, and looked at each there, ensuring he had their attention. "The city is an evil place. For centuries, the Grimm thrived in its shadows; their evil has permeated the very stones of its walls, so Hewla tells us, and she would not brook any argument on that. Runners were sent South, East and West once the spring thaw arrived, and word was sent to those that would listen; dark days are upon the world once more. The Grimm are returned to the world. Many scoffed, but there has been enough strangeness of late for some to listen, and now, like in the old days, nation speaks to nation, hands of friendship are held out, and alliances are built. Hence, we are now gathering at Asgulun, ready to stem the advance of this... Empire." Rolf spat out the word in conclusion.

"You have been to Asgulun then?" Morinae had listened with awe, as she heard the tale of Ash Ul M'on. To her and most of the folk not of the North, the city was a myth, a tall tale, told to keep children entertained and frightened of a winter's eve. But she had seen with her own eyes the Grimm, and worse, she had seen the demon Janovis too; Morinae was a believer now in the macabre, ancient tales.

"Is the king, my father, well? When I last saw him, he was not at his best." Morinae could well have said that the kindly old man that she knew as her father, was vanishing a little more every day, confused and forgetful as age took its toll, more malleable to those who had his ear. But Morinae was more tactful than that. Her life had been shaped by politics, by veiled truths and half answers, the game of court, and she knew it well.

"King Rodero still sits the throne, Princess, but to an old man like me, he seems to be taking a bit too much advice from that son of his, Juvaal, and I know he is your brother and all, but he doesn't strike me as a leader-"

"Half-brother," Morinae corrected. "Juvaal is my half-brother. The queen, Josksa, she is my step-mother, and you are right, he is not fit to lead." Her tone was clipped, her eyes hard, and not for the first time Steeleye was aware of the inner metal of the Princess; there was a capacity for great love and charity within her, the way she had taken young Helgen in was evidence enough of that, but there was also a harsh, resolute side to her, a side that would not easily forgive a wrong.

"As you say, Princess, half-brother it is. Well. Al'hainn has been scouring the land for you, rolling bones and the likes, I've no doubt. He said he had seen you and Straw Top there making your way back to Asgulun, and he was mightily pleased at that I can tell you. So, he and Hewla got their heads together, and sent me and this here ship to bring the pair of you back a little quicker." He smiled at Morinae then, a wicked knowing smile. "Your *step-brother* knows nothing about this. Al'hainn was very keen that he be kept in the dark. He probably wants your return to be a nice surprise for the prince." Rolf smiled innocently as he spoke.

"You know," Morinae said flatly, "that Juvaal had me abducted? He probably thinks that I am dead, at the bottom of a lake somewhere."

"Aye, your wizard thought as much, though proof is lacking. He is a canny soul is your wizard. Likes a grand entrance too."

"I still cannot think of Al'hainn as anything but a drunken hermit in filthy rags and with a beard to put even yours to shame. If he is as wise as you say, no wonder then my father pandered to him." Morinae turned grim. "Juvaal must not know that we are aware of his complicity in my abduction. There is too much at stake here, we need to be united against our enemies, not divided. There will be time for a reckoning with Juvaal, once Ashanarr has been hurled back over the Sea of Storms, with its tail between its legs."

* * *

FOR TWO DAYS the swift ship hugged the coastline as it made its way up the Narrow Sea. On the third day, they entered the Sea of Storms under a cloudless sky, the ocean like a mirror. The northmen plied their oars with vigour as they made their way North and East, and for a day and a night the ship carved its swift passage. Twice on that first day they spied ships in the distance, great lumbering things, loaded with men from Ashanarr, bound for the fair shores of Asgulun, but the hulks could not match the speed of Northerners' craft, and each time, the ships were left behind, lost beyond the horizon. They made good time, for all of the lack of a wind; the oarsmen were tireless, the sea was in their blood and they thrived upon the salty air.

On the dawn of the second day, as the sun's heat dissipated a light, clinging mist, the ship began to roll gently as the waves began to swell. Within an hour, a wind was up and the single square sail was unfurled. The red and white striped canvas cracked and boomed as the wind grew and filled it out, the ship leaping forwards, like a sprinter at the start of a race. Rolf was at the prow, his strong hands gripping the carved mane of the wild figurehead. Waves grew and rolled. The ship plummeted into deep troughs, then sped back onto the crest, white foam running from its sides. Again, and again the ship rocked and pitched. The oars were shipped, and the oarsmen clung to their seats as waves crashed over them. The wind howled with fury, and the North-erners howled with glee.

Within the captain's cabin, the four passengers clung to anything they could to stop being pitched off their feet. Artfur had his hands wrapped around a wooden bucket. Every so often he would curse the sea and all those that sailed upon it, whilst Helgen tried her best to balance on her feet, laughing at the new experience. Steeleye watched his companions with a smile, even proud Morinae, clinging to the bench she sat upon, looked a little worse for wear, though she suffered in stoic silence.

At length, Steeleye made his way to the deck. As he opened the door of the cabin, a thick spray of brine broke over the gunwales, making him stagger. The noise of the crashing sea, the creaking of the ship's timbers and the howl of the wind were far louder outside, and much more intense. A strong hand caught his arm to steady him, and Steeleye found himself grinning into the face of Rothgar, whose one eye was bright with excitement. "Never more alive than at brink of death, eh lad?" the old man shouted above the crack of the sail. When Steeleye was steady on his feet, the old warrior rushed off, nimbly ducking beneath flying spray as he made his way to the stern.

It was the front of the ship Steeleye was aiming at. He noticed a series of ropes that had been set up along the deck, safety lines, and gratefully caught hold of one just as the deck seemed to disappear beneath his feet. Moments later it bucked back up, and if not for his grip upon the ropes, he would have been washed along the deck by a huge wave that broke over the gunwale.

He remained on his knees, arms wrapped around the line, shaking his hair out of his eyes. Three feet from him, he could see the rowers, their heads tucked beneath the cover of the gunwale. They were watching him with wide white grins, their hair and beards soaked and wild in the wind. Determined not to look too much of a fool in front of the North-men, many of whom he recognised from his life in the lands of Aelrik, he lunged to his feet, and made his unsteady way to the prow, where he could see Rolf, still gripping the figure head, glaring at the wild ocean in front of him, so steady he could almost be a part of the carving itself.

As Steeleye caught hold of the rail near the prow, Rolf looked down and laughed joyously. The ship plunged through a cresting wave with a crash. "This is living!" the old man shouted to be heard above nature's tumult. Steeleye would have preferred his feet upon solid ground, but he nodded and smiled gamely. The sky was darkening with the oncoming of night. For all the gales and rough sea, the sky remained relatively free of cloud. "By the dawn we should be in sight of Asgulun," Rolf shouted, guessing the reason for Steeleye venturing into the wild weather.

"Is this normal?" Steeleye jutted his chin at the great swelling sea.

"It's not called the Sea of Storms for nothing," Rolf came back with a fierce grin. "Our captain tells me we are making good time, and he thanks the gods that the weather has been kind to us."

The captain was a dour north-man, called simply Bo. Steeleye had seen him a time or two, rushing hither and yon, a serious faced fellow, but evidently an expert seaman, and more than capable of taking on the battering waves. His ship ran smooth, with every hand knowing just what they were about. For all the pitching and rolling, the vessel always burst free of the sea's chilly grip, surging out of the troughs like a cork from a wine bottle.

Steeleye stayed on deck most of the night. He found a perch amongst the rowers, where he was protected from much of the spray, and like those he sat amongst, he snatched sleep when he could. Every now and then, when the ship seemed to slide down the side of mountainous waves, only to be thrust back into the air with breath taking speed, he would hear old Rolf laughing above the noise of the storm.

The rowers he sat with grinned at the old man

"They are all mad!" Steeleye told himself, but he found himself grinning along with them, unsure if it was the relief of surviving each wave, or the sheer lunacy of being out upon this treacherous sea in the first place.

With the first golden rays of the sun, the sea calmed. A light zephyr, warm to the skin, did its best to dry the sailors, many of whom stood to greet the dawn, relishing the warmth on the breeze.

"Land!" came a shout from the mast-head.

Steeleye craned his neck, not to see the welcome smudge of Asgulun upon the horizon, but rather the shape of the man high in the crow's nest that had remained there throughout the storm. Madness, he thought, though he grinned, the dried salt upon his face splitting and cracking.

Within an hour, Asgulun was clearer, as was the fleet of defensive ships, both sleek Northern vessels and Asgulun war ships, with great crossbows and catapults visible upon their decks. More than a hundred moved back and forth at a leisurely pace through the now calmed sea. Farther out, black specks could be seen, moving parallel to the coast, but more than a mile from shore. This was the fleet from Ashanarr. Their number crowded the sea, like a flock of starlings blackening an evening sky.

Morinae joined Steeleye at the rail, and she cast a pensive eye at the horizon with its many ships. "There are so many of them." Her voice was little more than a whisper, but old Rothgar One Eye heard and moved closer.

"They cannot gain landing nearby, Princess," he said, meaning to reassure her. "The harbour is the only safe place for miles, and between the Asgulun fleet, and the longships, it's too heavily defended, hence the patrols you can see hereabouts."

Morinae found herself staring with a morbid fascination at his empty eye socket. "Then where will they try to land, do you think?" She tried but failed to look away from the grisly wound.

"I hear tell there is ample beaching some twenty miles along the coastline, once these white cliffs of yours give out." Rolf spoke of the great white chalk cliffs, a natural rampart against any sea invasion, save one cove that had been made into a wondrous harbour. The cliffs rose up from the sea and ran for miles either side of the cliff top city of Asgulun.

"The cliffs give way to many beaches." Morinae was thinking aloud now. "But there are many towns, and even the city of Mash'aar, which is a not equipped to withstand a large attack."

"Aye, that's the name I heard bandied about: Mash'aar." Broke in Rothgar, "but not to worry, your step-brother, Bryann, is a canny leader, and already the city is being evacuated, the fighting men making their way to Asgulun to bolster the troops there; the civilians are being led inland to safety." Morinae nodded, appreciating Rothgar's assurance, though she still looked worried.

Steeleye looked from the fleet, to Asgulun, and caught his breath as the great harbour came into view. A natural horseshoe bay, that had been built upon over the centuries, so that a towering wall swept around the harbour. At the end of each of the horseshoe's arms, there stood an enormous statue, at least two hundred feet in height. Steeleye was agog. He had never seen such incredible sculptures. Each figure was that of a woman, her head and shoulders covered by a shawl, reaching into the sky with one hand, and in that hand holding a huge lantern, which even now in the dawn light could easily be seen. He could well imagine that at night time, the lanterns could be seen for miles out at sea, beacons to bring seafarers safely to the harbour.

"They are called the mothers." Morinae noticed her companion's awe. "They have stood there for centuries, representing the hundreds, nay thousands of women that have stood upon the harbour, staring out to sea, waiting in vain for the return of their loved ones." She rested her hand upon the rail as she spoke. "The Sea of Storms is full of wondrous fish, but it is not named lightly, it has claimed many of our ships, and many of our brave fisherfolk have set sail on a sea as smooth as glass, never to be seen again."

Now, the Princess looked at the great ships that were moving alongside the Northern vessel, a look of pride in her face. "The Sea of Storms is harsh indeed, but its very reputation keeps our seaward borders safe." After a moment, she looked back to the horizon, at the tiny specks that seemed to fill the sea. "At least, until now."

STEELEYE CRANED his neck as their ship sailed by the great statues and into the harbour proper. As he passed between the mournful mothers, he could not help but be touched with sadness at what they represented. The harbour itself housed over a hundred ships he guessed, of every size and shape, with crews visibly swarming about on their decks like ants. Everything about the place was huge in scale. Not only the statues, but the great stone blocks that made up the harbour wall seemed to be over ten feet square; their size and obvious weight was staggering.

The harbour town was all abustle, with taverns and shops, merchants and tradesmen's' units, all packed together alongside the quay. Ships seemed to be loading and offloading as in any port, as if unaware that just beyond the great stone horseshoe, a fleet bearing an army of enemy soldiers made its way slowly to their shores. As their vessel slowly coasted to a docking station, with sailors casting thick lines ashore, to be wound about great iron posts, Steeleye watched the cobbled street that ran the length of the harbour. Even so early, the street thrived. Sailors, vendors, whores and merchants went about their business, the poor and ragged rubbing shoulders with the well-to-do.

Beyond the harbour, the ground rose sharply with a well-travelled roadway that wound to and fro up the hillside, until it reached the great walls of the city proper. Morinae followed his gaze to the splendid walls, and the many towers that could be seen beyond.

"From the sea, Asgulun is nigh impregnable," she told him. "The harbour is not only guarded by ships, but great crossbows and catapults can be lined upon the harbour walls at a moment's notice, with a goodly range. Should any great number of ships manage by some miracle to bypass our own ships, and weather the ballistae, then there is a grim reception that awaits." Ensuring that she had his full attention, Morinae continued quietly. "The great statues are more than just kindly lights for seafarers, or tributes to those that have been lost at sea. Their true purpose is more military. From the lanterns they hold, a stream of oil can be let run into the harbour. Once set alight, no ship nor crew within the area can survive."

Steeleye shuddered at the thought of the sea set ablaze, at the panic that would ensue, the death and destruction that would follow. A strong hand upon his shoulder broke his reverie, and he found Rolf standing close by. "Time to disembark. We'll go up to the city and find Hewla and Aelrik. And for you Princess, time to go and spin a yarn to the city council and your father too. There will be time aplenty to confront your half-brother about his actions."

Though he spoke of caution, Rolf grinned at the prospect of the invasion, and at the thought of Morinae's revenge upon Juvaal.

"For now, we have a bigger problem: we have a thousand ships bearing down upon us."

CHAPTER 22

THE GATHERING

"So, this is the sword that killed Janovis?" The speaker was a tall, spindly character, with a stoop so pronounced it gave him the appearance of a vulture, his hobbling gait and tattered robes furthering the look, though his odour was more reminiscent of a back-alley midden.

Steeleye wrinkled his nose, and moved the hilt of his sword out of the reach of the grimy, long nailed fingers.

"Legend has it that no blade made by man can kill any of the Seven, only the Morriggu with her silver scythe can bring the demons to an end, and as she and the rest of the Gods are strangely quiet these days..."

The tall man was Al'hainn, a sorcerer, or a hermit, some said a drunken half-wit, but as he stood at the shoulder of Hewla, and she often asked his opinion, Steeleye would defer a negative judgment for the moment. Though, he had to admit that Morinae was usually a good judge of character, and the Princess still gave the man disbelieving looks.

* * *

ROLF HAD LED THEM ASHORE, through the mad bustle of the harbour, with its miasma of the sea, and the press of refugees. The journey to the keep, or palace as Steeleye had come to think of it, for he had never seen a more beautiful looking castle with all its towers and marble halls, had taken half a day. Travelling through the harbour itself, and then the thriving Lowtown, was hard work: so many people rushing here and there. Stalls and market vendors were everywhere, as were soup kitchens set up by the palace. City watchmen were greatly in evidence too, their scarlet cloaks and tall plumed helmets dotted liberally through the throng. The noise was a constant wave, pressing upon Steeleye's ears, a vast assault of cries and shouts, hammering smiths and snatches of song and music, the snort of horses and the rattle of wagon wheels upon cobbled streets.

Steeleye did his best to blot out all the sights, sounds, and smells, to walk with his companions, shouldering through the press, but by the time they reached a huge guarded gateway, its towering doors shut and barred, he felt dizzy and awash with the sensations of the chaotic abundance of human life.

Once Rolf spoke to the guards, the great doors were pulled open. Steeleye and his companions were led through, and he looked slack jawed at the steep winding roadway leading up the cliffs to the summit, where the great structure of the palace sat, dominating the skyline. The group were given horses, for which Steeleye was grateful, even as fit and tireless as he was, the way to the palace looked a hard walk. Even mounted, he was sure it would have its challenges.

It was at this point, that Morinae spurred her horse into the lead, flashing a white smile at her companions. "Home!" she sang out. "I had begun to think I would never see it again." And with that she was off up the roadway, leaving her friends to follow the best they could.

That had been half a day ago, and since their arrival at the palace Steeleye and his friends had been met by a constant barrage of well-wishers and back slappers. It seemed the entire palace had turned out to gawk at the returned Princess and her companions. Steeleye was uncomfortable with the attention, and as they made their way through crowded hallways and marble pillared courtyards, he kept mostly tight lipped, grateful that Artfur was the garrulous type, and needed little encouragement to take centre stage. Steeleye couldn't help rolling his eyes as he heard the bard chatting to some puffed up noble, hearing their exploits exaggerated, more outlandish with each subsequent telling.

Steeleye was happy enough when the doors to the audience room closed behind them, and the crowds were shut away, at least for a while. Morinae had told them there would no doubt be a feast, much to Steeleye's dismay, and to Artfur's glee. Within the audience room, the travellers found themselves facing perhaps a dozen men and women, and he was glad to see familiar faces amongst the gathering.

Aelrik, King of the North, strode forwards to greet them, his huge size and warlike demeanour daunting Morinae and little Helgen, who seemed to have become affixed to the Princess' skirts. The child stared wide eyed as the great King lifted Steeleye off his feet as if he were a child too, slapping him on the back as he did so.

"It is good to see you again, Young Buck," he said through the tangle of his beard, his eyes full of joy.

There were new faces too, Steeleye was introduced to Prince Bryann, and took to the man instantly. The commander of the forces of Asgulun held out his hand, and his grip was firm and strong as he thanked the gods that Steeleye had brought back his half-sister. She was, he said, needed now more than ever, to help their father.

Morinae's other half-brother, was a different matter. Juvaal stepped forwards to greet the party, and though he hid it well, Steeleye could see the venom in the smile he lavished upon the Princess, could hear the lie in his voice as he congratulated her upon her fortitude and return to the palace, where, he said, she belonged. Steeleye tensed, wanting to split the oily Prince's skull, but the words of Morinae and even wild Rolf calmed him.

Politics.

Juvaal's loyal men were needed for the defence of the Asgulun, so for now, it had to seem as though the Prince's treachery was unknown; they would allow him continue with his schemes.

But only for now.

Juvaal stood tall, slim, with a dancer's grace, dressed all in silks, not in the trappings of war like most others gathered here. His hair was long and dark, curled and oiled so it shone like a raven's wing. Steeleye knew he would have disliked the Prince, even if he had not known he had sold his own sister to slavers.

When Hewla grabbed his arm and steered him away to speak with her and the stooped hermit, Steeleye was eager to oblige. Bryann and Aelrik followed along, and of course, wherever Aelrik went, Rolf wasn't far behind, whether invited or not.

* * *

STEELEYE LOOKED AT THE TALL, stooped figure carefully: there was something about the hermit that made him cautious, like the jellyfish that would wash up on the beach at Clove when he had been known only as Aluin; they were innocent enough to look at, but could deliver a nasty sting, and in some cases, if help were no sought out quickly enough, even death.

"The blade was made by Narissa," Steeleye offered, his fingers curled around the hilt protectively. Even as he spoke, he got the feeling that Al'hainn knew very well from whence the sword came, but there were others here too that needed to know that he brought with him a useful weapon in their fight against the Grimm, and the Witch Queen of Ashanarr.

"You travelled the roads between realms then? You actually trod the ways that Hewla and I can only look along?" Al'hainn looked impressed, bright eyes taking stock of the young swordsman anew.

Hewla, for her part, looked concerned. Aelrik, Bryann, and an eavesdropping Rolf all looked confused.

"I was shown the way between realms. I walked along an endless corridor with doors beyond counting." He saw the surprise clear now on the faces of the hermit and the witch, but he continued on with his tale. "A door led to the world of the Storm-child. I went to his temple and took this sword from him. It cut Janovis' head clean from her shoulders, and I am sure it will do the same to all her sisters. Ixtchel first, if I can get near enough,"

"What was it like, the other realm?" Al'hainn was eager to hear more, but Hewla shushed him, and gripped Steeleye's arm in a claw-like grip.

"We have seen much of your adventures, Steeleye. We knew that you had somehow come into possession of a god slaying weapon. A weapon capable of killing even the Seven, that is why we have been waiting for you so keenly, we knew that the Queen of Ashanarr was Ixtchel the Cursed, and without the means to see her dead, then no other battle plan we concocted had the slightest chance of success." She drew her breath in, steadied herself, leaning upon his arm. "The Grimm are too many to be defeated by conventional means. Al'hainn and I believe there is a way, but not if the beasts are controlled by a higher intelligence. We need them wild and unfettered, not held in check by their mistress."

Now the witch grinned at Bryann, and the King of the North. "It will fall to these two to stand their ground against the creatures. They will meet them upon the great steppe to the West, half way from their beaching point to the city. There, the grass is long and dry, and there is a slope that runs down to steep cliffs. The Grimm must be held there, and held at all cost. You, Steeleye, you will seek out this creature Ixtchel, and destroy her. She will likely be at the rear of the ranks, where she can see the battle, and where her will upon the Grimm will be strongest." Hewla paused, to let the import of her words sink in. "Until you strike the demon dead, we will be as chaff before their scythe. You must find her, and kill her, then the Grimm will revert to their bestial state, uncontrolled and wild. Only then will our plan have a chance of working,"

Aelrik burst out laughing at the look upon the young swordsman's face. "If the task is too much, young Steeleye, then lend me your sword, and I will kill this bitch."

He returned the King's grin with one of his own.

"And I suppose I would have to then meet the Grimm in your stead? No, I fancy my chances against the demon more than I do yours against the Horde."

Rolf howled with laughter at this, throwing back his white maned head, holding his spreading stomach as if it hurt. "But what a fight you are passing up on, lad!" he wheezed. "And as you were kind enough to bring along a bard, well, we can take him along too and all be immortalised in song. It may be a fool's stand, but think of the glory!"

"Think of all the glory you like, Rolf Whitebeard," snapped Hewla sharply, ever the planner and the cool head. "But you won't be taking a slice of it. You are to lead one hundred picked warriors to escort Steeleye, and to hold his hand if needs be until he gets the chance to slay Ixtchel and break her power over the Grimm. Otherwise Aelrik's glorious stand may well be the shortest in history, and Asgulun will be overrun."

Instead of looking hurt, Rolf grinned even wider, slapping Steeleye upon the arm. "If your good fortune holds true, the demon will be in the thick of it, surrounded by only the biggest and fiercest of the Grimm, and there will be glory for one and all!"

Hewla rolled her eyes. The old warrior was incorrigible, but she knew he would do all he could to see Steeleye safely through to the leader of the Grimm. There was no one else she would trust with the task.

"Couldn't you just, I don't know, *send* him to the Queen somehow?" This from came Prince Bryann, who had snagged a goblet of wine from somewhere, and took a gulp. "Or better yet, send *her* somewhere else?" He was looking at Al'hainn and Hewla expectantly.

"That isn't how our magic works." Hewla was scowling now, as if she could see the shortcomings of her and Al'hainn's efforts. "We can manipulate the spirits of the air, and those of fire too, at least a little, and can see along the paths of the many tomorrows, but to send a man, or a woman physically from one place to another, those arts are long lost to the world. Since the gods departed our realm, magic has withered, and those of us that now practice the arts are much less powerful than those in times gone by."

"What you are lacking in spells, grandmother, you more than make up for with your wise council." Aelrik was quick to defend his seer, and with his intimidating size, there were none who were going to argue with him.

As they spoke, Prince Juvaal came to stand with them. He too carried a goblet of wine, and by the look in his eye, it wasn't the first. He stood next to the King of the North, his slender frame dwarfed by comparison, the top of his head not reaching the giants collarbone. Yet for all this, the Prince managed to look down his nose at the gathering.

"Please continue." He waved a hand airily at the witch and the hermit. "Did I hear that the great and mighty Al'hainn is not up to the tasks that lie ahead?" His speech slurred, but his barbs were sharp enough.

"Hewla and I will do our part, your Highness, you can rest assured on that." For a moment, the old hermit seemed to grow in stature, his eyes intense, even the stoop lessened. "And you, Prince Juvaal? Will you be riding out to meet the Grimm at the side of your noble brother?" Steeleye could feel the tension between the two, and could see that Al'hainn's words had hit their mark.

Juvaal took a swig of wine, spilling some down his chin, then grinned, his eyes sliding by his half-brother, taking in the gathering around them, resting at last upon his father, the King. The old and frail Rodero watched the gathering without interest, instead beaming his pleasure at the return of his daughter.

"I think not, hermit. I am next in line to the throne, after my dear sister Morinae of course. It is more fitting that I remain behind the walls, along with my father and sister. The family line must be assured to save chaos in Asgulun. Can you imagine, if there were no hands upon the tiller?" Now Juvaal let his gaze rest upon Bryann, and his lip curled a little as he spoke. "Besides, I would not wish to deny the bastard his little bit of glory, it is why royalty have a few spares for, is it not?"

Steeleye and the Northerners all looked to Bryann, expecting the general to drive his fist into the smug, sneering face of his half-brother, or at least counter the remark with some anger, but he did neither. There was a little colour in his cheeks, and the muscles in his jaw bunched as he fought back his anger. When he had been Aluin, Steeleye had experienced this chain of command first-hand, and knew what it took to hold back such rage. He could understand Bryann's reaction. The Northerners were used to a looser structure in their courts, where the highest were expected to give those of a lowlier station respect. Though not so civilised as Asgulun, Steeleye knew the North to be a more noble place.

Juvaal tossed the remaining wine down his throat, and stalked off, chuckling at his own wit, and the fact that, because of who and where he was, had kept all his teeth.

"That man is an arse," Rolf muttered, with his usual diplomacy and tact, which meant that anyone within ten yards could hear him.

"A very dangerous arse," enjoined the hermit, though his voice was low so only their small gathering could hear him. "He had the balls to have Morinae taken from the very palace gardens, and I'm not sure that he would care if he knew that we are aware of this. He is popular with many of the soldiers. He knows how to speak to the common man, even if he despises them." Making sure that the prince was indeed out of earshot, the tattered hermit continued. "We shall deal with him anon, but for now, there is an army of Grimm landing upon our shores, and come first light, Bryann and the bulk of the troops must be off to meet them."

"The bulk of the troops?" Steeleye chipped in. If the army they faced was as huge as they assumed, then he would want all the men the Asgulun could muster.

"War is a fickle thing." It was Bryann explained, having calmed himself after his brother's insults. "Asgulun must be protected, and though we hope to gather all of our enemies upon the grasslands, we must remember that they have a huge fleet, and Asgulun has a harbour, so men must be left to man the Mothers, and to guard the Asgulun itself. I am sure Juvaal can manage to oversee that, with the help of Morinae." He cast a sharp eye about his comrades, as if taking stock.

"We had best be off: I have spent too much time away from the army as it is, and there is still much to do."

With that, the Bastard Prince set off for the door, Aelrik and Rolf at his shoulder. Steeleye hesitated only a moment, then, nodding to Hewla and the hermit, he too set off. There was no fanfare or farewells for the Prince and the Northerners as they left; the court was too busy feting their returned Princess, and watching their doddering King.

Especially Juvaal, who even now watched his sister's every move through hooded eyes.

CHAPTER 23

NORTHERN SWORDS

Steeleye sat easily in the saddle. The time he had spent bringing Morinae home, had at least taught him to be a little better on horseback. Beside him, Rolf sat upon a huge gelding, its glossy hide as black as night, tossing its head and chomping upon the bit. Impatient with waiting, just like the old swordsman himself.

"I'm boiling already," Rolf complained, though half-heartedly. His mail shirt was lined with soft leather over a quilted jupon, made twenty years ago by his late wife; it had been repaired and patched so many times, that little of the original garment remained, but he was always proud to point out that it had been made for him by his love. Clipped to the shoulder of his mail was a thick fur cloak that made him resemble a bear more than ever. Sweat beaded his forehead, sticking his wild white hair to the pate.

"Lose the cloak then." Mari, the shield maiden, sat with the two men, watching the sun rise out of the sea. She was dressed in a finely scaled vest of mail, leaving her arms free of weight, though from elbow to wrist they sported thick leather guards, rings of iron sewn upon the hide capable of turning a blade, and protecting the soft inner flesh of the forearm from the cruel sting of the bowstring. Mari, like most of the maids who followed Aelrik to the Asgulun, had cut her hair brutally short, protection against the heat as well as lice; the bane of all armies.

"The cloak is expected of a great warrior of the North," Rolf grumbled through his beard, "You maidens wouldn't understand, it is a man thing."

"I understand you are already too hot, and the sun is hardly up. Hewla and her hermit will be working the weather magic today, it will be warm enough to fry a fish on a stone, and you are sat wearing a bear." Mari's tone was short and clipped. Though there was laughter in her eyes.

"Mari has a point, Rolf." Steeleye had been given a new hauberk of silvered scale, falling halfway to his knees, the sleeves reaching his elbows. On his saddle horn rested a steel helm, with finely wrought cheek guards and a proud crest of scarlet. He wore no cloak. At his side he carried the Stormchild's blade. On his arm an iron rimmed wooden shield was strapped. Hanging from the saddle horn with the helm was a canteen of water. Killing was thirsty work.

Rolf sniffed, wiping his brow with his forearm, then unclipped the cloak and let it fall to the brittle grass. He tried not to show his relief at losing the great weight. There were a few chuckles from the men and women behind them, and he cast a baleful eye over his shoulder. Lined up in neat ranks were men and maidens from the North, one hundred of them. For the most part the men were veterans, getting a little long in the tooth, but still strong in the arm.

When Aelrik had asked for volunteers to ride with Steeleye to strike at She'ah the Queen of Ashanarr, and leader of the Horde, nigh every man that had been at Ash' Ul Mon raised his hand and called out his name, as did many others that had seen the young outlander best the creature wearing the skin of their King's son in the Stone Circle.

The maidens had elected to accompany the outlander as they reasoned wherever he went, the fighting would be thickest.

Steeleye was glad of every sword, for the ground began to vibrate, and he knew it was due to the stomping feet of the Horde, even now cresting the rise to the west. The sheer mass of bodies was enough to send a mind reeling, a great broiling, glinting, roaring, sea of anger, surging towards the waiting lines of the Asgulun and their allies.

"God's help us," Steeleye heard Mari whisper at his shoulder. At his other side he could hear Rolf's teeth grinding.

"How the hell are we supposed to stop *that?*" Rolf hissed, though even as he spoke, he was pulling on his helmet and tightening the chin strap. With the threat of battle looming, Rolf no longer looked so old: the stoop of his years suddenly gone, his huge shoulders squared, straining the links of mail. There was a look of fierce joy in his eyes, for all his doubt that so huge an enemy could be thwarted.

Steeleye felt a shiver as fear ran its icy fingers along his spine, but managed to keep his voice firm and steady, loud enough to be heard by those gathered behind him.

"We don't have to stop them all," he said, slapping Rolf on the shoulder. "We just have to find their leader, and cut off her head! After that, the Horde will be leaderless, easier to out-fox, and Hewla and the hermit have a surprise or two that should help." He grinned whitely, though inside, panic clawed at his throat. *So many!*

Taking a last look at the gathered army of the Asgulun, rank upon rank of steel and flesh and bone, waiting a little below him and to the left, Steeleye sawed the reins of his mare, turning it around to face his one hundred. Already the heat of the day was oppressive, and the sun was barely a hand's width above the horizon. Steeleye was comforted by the thought that the enemy would have to contend with the glare of the sun, and not he and the rest of the allies.

Bryann had prepared as well as he could. If all went according to the plan that had been laid out for them last night, there was a chance that they might all live through the day, but in battle, a plan was not worth the parchment it was scrawled upon once steel was drawn, and the blood pulsed faster in the veins.

As if the Fates were eager to prove his last thought true, as Steeleye stood in the stirrups, ready to urge his band down the slope to join at the rear of the ranks of infantry, he spied a lone horseman racing towards them through the sun-bleached grass, the purple cloak of a messenger billowing like wings he rode so fast.

"Hold!" he was shouting, waving his arm to get their attention. As the messenger reined in hard, the horse almost sitting in the grass, its forelegs kicking the air, eyes rolling as it caught the fear of its rider. "I have a message from the hermit and the witch," he was gasping for breath, his face pale with dread. "We have been fooled, Hewla says. The Queen She'ah is not with the Horde on the plains, she says the Queen is instead sailing for the harbour, coming to take the Asgulun from the seaward side."

"Then who controls the Horde?" Steeleye said, bewildered. The Grimm were advancing in orderly lines, some power keeping the beasts on a leash, something that the creatures feared more than they loved battle and the taste of flesh. Steeleye shuddered at the thought, and found himself answering his own question. "It must be yet another of the demon princes, like Khuur'shock, coming from the City of the Dead." Wild-eyed Steeleye grabbed the messenger by the arm. On the plain below them, bugles blared, and drums pounded, signalling that the armies of the Asgulun should make ready.

"What does Hewla say we should do?" Even as he spoke, he

was turning his horse for Asgulun.

"Ride hard, she says. Enter the castle from the landward side, bolster the defences as best you can." Now the messenger looked a little confused as he repeated the next instructions. "She says you must take Ixtchel's head, though I have no idea what she meant by that, but the witch was adamant. 'Tell Steeleye', she said, 'he must take Ixtchel's head if we are to stand any chance at all'." With his message delivered, the man wheeled his horse, ready to return to the command tent, which could just be made out in the distance, where Hewla and Al'hainn were busy communing with the spirits of the sky and the plains, and evidently scrying the future with their bones and runes.

"Wait!" Steeleye caught the reins of the messenger. "Before you return to Hewla, you must hurry to Aelrik on the plain below, tell him to look for a banner. Tell him he must find the one that commands the Horde on the plain, and he must kill him, else the Grimm will remain orderly and no matter what Hewla and Al'hainn have in mind, it will be futile. Tell him I think it is one kin to that which killed his son; he will know what you mean and what to do."

With that, Steeleye released the messenger, letting him spur off towards the plain and the mass of humanity slowly readying shields and stringing bows. "Good luck!" the messenger called back even as his steed was picking up speed. "May the gods smile on us all!"

Steeleye watched the rider for a moment more, then raised his voice over the cacophony of drums and horns coming from the plains. "We are bound for Asgulun, the Queen has deceived us and intends to strike at the harbour. With me!" As he shouted this last, he was digging his heels into the mare's flanks, feeling the great muscles of the horse bunch beneath him. Then he was off, clinging on for grim death as he and his one hundred pounded at full speed back towards the city.

CHAPTER 24

THE GRIMM HORDE

Prince Bryann, commander of the armies of Asgulun, and her allies, stood upon the very edge of the grasslands. A huge swathe of rolling pasture run wild with tall poppies, buttercups, and foxglove. The vast palette of colour was striking, as the wild blooms opened to greet the sun, already bloated and hot, rising from its slumber in the East. Bryann took a deep breath, savouring the freshness of the air, before the oppressive heat of the summer day took hold.

The chinstrap of his helmet chaffed at his throat. He longed to take the damned thing off, so ornate with its crimson horse-hair crest and engraved cheek guards. He swore it weighed more than his head, making the muscles of his neck ache, adding to the tension he already suffered in his shoulders. He blew out a breath noisily, his gauntleted hand patting the hilt of the sword he wore at his hip.

He brooded over the day ahead.

He had been wracking his brains for a fool-proof battle plan for six days, ever since his beloved sister Morinae was miraculously brought home. Six days since the great fleet from Ashanarr had been sighted cruising past their harbour, making for landfall in the West, a little more than ten miles from where the Prince now stood, fretting over his decision to commit such a large portion of his forces upon this one gambit, this one all or nothing, throw of the dice.

There had been clashes already of course. His men had been bloodied, but had fought bravely when they came upon their enemy advancing upon Asgulun's lovely city. The men of Ish, carrying their proud leaping deer banners, had twice fallen upon the flanks of the advancing army, harrying and retreating, playing cat and mouse. Bryann was under no illusions as to which was the mouse.

Today the full might of both human and Grimm would collide. Bryann commanded near forty thousand troops, mostly infantry, like those that stood in such motley ranks behind him, and though they carried spears and shields aplenty, a closer look would show that they were not seasoned troops. Many had been conscripted from the land, from the fishing fleet, from anywhere that Bryann's recruiters could find them. Their training had been sparse, their armour and equipment sparser still, yet Bryann had been honest enough with them all. It was fight or die. There was no third option, there would be no terms, no surrenders, that was not what the Queen of Ashanarr was here for.

At his side, the great warrior King, Aelrik, shifted. The huge bear of a man rolled his shoulders, stretched his neck from side to side with a loud cracking sound. "Ahh, that's better." The King's voice was deep and steady, and Bryann hoped he looked half at ease as the Bearslayer did. But then, Aelrik had fought this enemy before, and won, and because of that, Bryann was eternally thankful that the Northerners had sailed South to lend their might. Not only had they brought steel and muscle, but the witch

Hewla gave sound council, and she and that drunken hermit Al'hainn would be pivotal to any victory today, should things all go to plan.

"Shouldn't you be making your way to your heavy horse, young Prince?"

Aelrik was right of course. In such matters, he was always right. Bryann would lead the mounted charge, when the time was right. Over the ridge, there were two thousand of the finest cavalrymen in the world, The nobility of Asgulun had not shirked when asked to supply men; all the lords and barons had been quick to answer the call of their Prince. And hidden there, beyond the rolling grassland, waited a great wave of steel and horse-flesh. They would ride under at least fifty banners, but each banner had deference to Bryann and his office.

The responsibility weighed heavy upon him, but he knew that the lords would not have come together for any other, and so he would persevere, whatever the outcome.

"I had hoped to get a first look at this enemy of ours," he said at last, straining his eyes to the green horizon. He licked his lips. Damn, but he was thirsty. He knew that every man standing behind him felt the same, so he remained stoic.

"They aren't pretty, I can assure you." Aelrik's face split in a broad grin behind his beard. "But we will hear them first, I should think. They are great ones for making a noise are the Grimm."

"And will we be making a noise?" Bryann wondered softly.

Aelrik laid a hefty hand upon the Prince's shoulder, and leaned down to catch Bryann's eye with a steady gaze. "You have done all that can be done, and you have done it well. It is in the hands of the Fates now. Your plans are well thought out, and to use Hewla and Al'hainn as you intend was inspired, as is this location." Aelrik looked out at the grasslands, the dry blades bent under a breeze. Like waves, the grass and wild flowers undulated, as if racing down the sloping ground to their right, where a mile or so away, the land ended suddenly at a two-hundred-foot cliff, against which the Sea of Storms crashed relentlessly. Even on as fine and warm a day as this.

"Do you feel the breeze, Aelrik?" Bryann could barely mask his excitement

"I do, it would seem that the winds can be coaxed after all."

Even as he spoke, Aelrik felt a slight tremor underfoot. And again. He and the Prince shared a glance, and Bryann whispered, "I asked Hewla for a wind, not an earthquake."

"Oh, that little ruckus is no earthquake lad..." Aelrik squinted at the horizon again, and now came to their ears a steady droning noise. Aelrik beckoned his captains to him, and they responded at once, crowding around their leaders, eager for orders. "Get your-selves to your groups, lads. Keep everything calm-like. We here are about to get a glimpse of the Grimm, and I don't want anyone taking off back to the city, or there won't be a city come this time tomorrow." With that, the captains were off, their horses dashing through the dry grasses as they returned to their posts and their war bands.

Even as the riders departed, Bryann saw movement out in the grassland. Moments went by, and soon a dark line was visible, a stain upon the grass that was coming closer and closer, the droning getting louder and louder. Bryann again felt the thumping in the ground.

Rhythmic and insistent.

It was, he realised, the stamping feet of the Horde. The droning noise was now more defined, guttural roars of rage coming from the throats of the advancing army.

"God's help us." Bryann couldn't help his prayer. The Horde was vast, the numbers seemingly endless. Their feet stomped, their spear butts hammered into the dry earth like thunder, their bestial voices rose in a deafening challenge, and Bryann felt his knees wobble.

"Steady lad." Aelrik was grinning at the advancing host. "Remember, if Steeleye and his band of rascals can cut the head off this serpent, there will be chaos in their ranks. Just now they march together, held together by the will of the Witch Queen, the demon Ixtchel. All we need to do is hold them here, until Ixtchel is dead."

"But what if they cannot kill her? What if the Horde remain organised?" Bryann was glad that none of the men were close enough to see the fear in their commander.

"Then, I would say we are buggered." Aelrik grinned broadly once more, and slapped the Prince upon the back. "Go on, get back to the horses. I will hold them here. You just wait until you deem the time is right, and heed Hewla, she will know what is happening long before you or I."

Bryann took a deep steadying breath, the sound of the enemy growing louder and louder. "Asgulun owes you a debt, Aelrik," he said. He set off to find his horse, and make his way to the head of the mounted contingent. He knew that he should be here, with the first of the Asgulun to face the enemy, but he was also aware that without his presence beyond the ridge, the lords would soon enough be squabbling as to who should have the honour of first blood, or some other such nonsense, even in the face of oblivion.

Wait until they catch sight of the horde, Bryann thought, *there is more than enough blood to go around.*

As Bryann crested the rise, he looked back at the gathered ranks of his infantry. He had to admit, from a distance they looked bloody fierce. He could see Aelrik, twenty paces ahead of the lines, a huge figure, like a god of war.

As Bryann watched, the Northern King raised his sword high into the air, and roared a challenge at the advancing host. A moment later, Bryann felt a surge of pride for his countrymen, as they too raised their voices in defiance at the Horde. Gritting his teeth, the Prince put his heels to the horse's flanks, and sped to the gathering of horsemen and nobles. In the distance, he could just make out the enormous tent, in which Hewla and Al'hainn were busy summoning the winds.

CHAPTER 25
WALL OF STEEL

Aelrik spat a curse as he listened to the messenger. The lad was looking out over the steppe, watching the great tsunami of fury moving towards them, slow and steady, like flowing lava. Irresistible. Unstoppable.

"So, Steeleye has gone after Ixtchel?" He had to roar above the clamour of drums and pounding feet. Someone had brought a set of pipes and were blowing hard at some tune or other, though Aelrik couldn't discern what it was.

"Aye, Your Highness, and he says you are to kill whatever is keeping those monsters in check." As he spoke, the messenger motioned towards the Grimm. "He says there will be a banner, and beneath it a general, is what I think he meant."

"He and I have seen their generals before, lad, they are not a pretty sight." Aelrik remembered all too well the gigantic Kleave. That creature had almost done for him. Had it not been for Steeleye and his wolf, and old Rolf too, who had only just regained full use of his sword arm, Aelrik would doubtless be lying dead outside Ash Ul M'on.

"The way I see it, little has changed. We must bring the

Grimm to the plains and hold them. Bryann will harry them, and we shall do all we can to find their battle leader and kill him. After that, we must pray that our magic wielders in that tent yonder..." Aelrik nodded towards the distant pavilion, a safe distance from the grasslands, "Have the power to bind the forces they are seeking. For now, all we can do is stand and fight."

"There are other messengers still at the pavilion, could I fight alongside you, King Aelrik?"

Aelrik looked the lad over: his burnished armour gleaming, cruel on the eyes in the morning sun, his purple cloak pleated and neat, spread out over the horse's rump. The lad's face was free of whiskers, his eyes clear and eager to prove himself.

There came a sudden clamour from amongst the Northerners and the Asgulun, and a one-eyed old warrior came up alongside them. He reeked of brandy and stale sweat, the hauberk he wore was missing several scales, and had obviously seen better days. His grey hair was thinning and blew wild in the raising wind. He grinned gap toothed at his King. But it was not the tattered look of the man, nor the gruesome empty eye socket that caused the messenger to blanch. It was the evil looking sarissa, a huge spear some twenty feet in length, topped with a spear-head as long as the span of a man's arm, elbow to finger tips. The sarissa was a terrible weapon against cavalry when used correctly, and it was clear from the sudden forest of long shafts making their way to the front of the line that Aelrik planned to use them to halt the charge of the oncoming Grimm.

Old Rothgar set his single eye upon the messenger. "What's this then?" He shouted to make himself heard over the din; there was a slur in his voice. "More meat for the Grimm's stew, is it?" He stumbled as the sarissa got entangled in his legs. "Bloody hell! I'm going to war carrying half a tree!" He laughed loudly, and a woman covered in mail from neck to knee, with her hair cut off in a savage fashion, stepped up to help him with the ungainly pike.

The messenger was at a loss for words. He had been so keen to stand beside this great warrior king, yet now as he looked about him, he could see the true rag-tag nature of this army: farmers and stable hands mingled with Asgulun watchmen and wild Northerners. The latter all seemed to be passing around wine-skins or flasks of brandy, save for the shield maidens, who were all sober, though they laughed and jested along with the men, as if they had not a care in the world.

"Are you drunk?" the messenger asked the one-eyed man incredulously.

"Not quite." Rothgar was still grinning as he raised a flask to his lips. "But I hope to be, before those creatures get here." He belched loudly "I cannot understand anyone who would stand and fight something like that when they are sober!" He was laughing as the woman helping him with the sarissa slapped him around the head. Her grin was all the more terrifying for the fact that she was obviously sober.

Aelrik took the messengers reins in one huge hand, and beckoned the rider to lean closer, to hear his words clearly. "Return to your prince, lad. He and his cavalry are just over yon rise, and he could use every able horseman he can get. Don't you fret, there will be killing aplenty to go around. Seek me out after the fight, and we will swap stories." The King let go the reins and patted the horse's rump, setting it dancing.

The messenger swallowed heavily. Hauling on his reins, he nodded to the King, and began to ride away. Behind him, he could hear the one-eyed man wagering with a fellow Northerner that he would get more Grimm stuck upon his sarissa than any other there. There was a roar of laughter as the veteran tripped over the pole yet again.

The messenger rode for half a mile, cresting the hill that hid the prince and the heavy horse, before he looked back. Though numbered in the thousands, the army looked thin and pitiful before the great sea of Grimm that even now began to move faster, their shambling, savage shapes eating up the ground.

Aelrik's forces looked in better formation from this distance, and there were several rows of the giant pikes now clearly visible, perhaps a thousand, all pointing at the onrushing mass, a glinting wall of steel.

Several rows back, the messenger could see line upon line of archers. They bent their long bows, aiming high. The bright morning sky was almost hidden behind the sudden angry swarm of yard long shafts lifting higher and higher, before plunging down into the advancing horde. A great wave of the rushing creatures fell, hundreds were killed instantly by the deadly accuracy of the archers. Hundreds more were felled with wounds, only to be trampled by their comrades.

A second and third volley of arrows darkened the sky, and the Grimm now fell by the thousands, but still they kept their ranks, howling in rage and fear as the air about them was filled with whistling doom. The messenger watched in awe as rank upon rank of the creatures fell, melting into the ground. Yet the surge continued on, unabated. If anything, the charge accelerated as the arrows fell faster. From his vantage point upon the hill, the messenger could feel the ground tremble with the rushing, stomping feet of the Grimm.

He watched horrified as the great wave of snarling fury crashed upon the wall of shield and sarissa. He saw the line waver and ripple as the great weight of the horde pressed upon them, but it did not yield. Even from the hill, the messenger could hear the clang of axe and sword upon shield, hear the screams of the dying and the terrified roars of defiance as men and women stood, and fought, and died.

Though the army of the Asgulun numbered in the thousands, it seemed the horde outnumbered them ten to one, a never ending, undulating mass of tooth and claw, steel and hate, obliterating the grasslands. Their numbers were so great they began to outflank even the long lines of the Asgulun.

The messenger watched helpless as a thousand or more of the Grimm circled the right flank of the Asgulun. He knew it would only be minutes before the creatures fell upon his countrymen, upon the unprotected and out of formation stragglers, yet there was nothing he could do to prevent it. He found himself chewing upon his knuckles. He had wanted so much to be down there, with the legendary King of the North, perhaps even creating his own legend. But now, watching the devastation below, to his anguish and shame, he felt only relief that the King had sent him away, for surely, nothing could stand before that unending mass of fury.

There came the loud blast of a horn behind him, and as he turned, he was overjoyed to see the heavy horse of the Asgulun, the pride of the army. Banners from fifty noble houses snapped and flew above the knights, and at the head was the general of all the armed forces himself. The Bastard Prince, beloved of all the Asgulun.

Bryann adjusted the shield upon his left arm, hefted the spear in his right into the air, and dug his heels into the horse's armoured flanks. The huge horse danced, and then set off at a gallop down the rolling hill, hundreds upon hundreds of horsemen letting their voices ring loud, their armour bright and dazzling. For a moment, the messenger hesitated, seeing the impossible odds that his countrymen charged, but only for a moment. Soon his purple cloak flew out behind him and his sword cut the air in a fierce salute as he thundered down the slope, joining the river of steel as it smashed into the oncoming Grimm seeking to outflank the infantry.

* * *

IN HER SCARLET PAVILION, a goodly distance from the battle lines, Hewla sweated over a strange series of glyphs and shapes gouged into the earth at her feet. Her thin lips mouthed impossible words, and her ancient fingers drew shapes in the air that seemed to be tracings of fire. She had been thus for several hours, starting long before dawn, and the toll it was taking upon her was evident. Her straight back was bent, those hard eyes now filled with tears and pain, yet still she sought to open a way to the realms of the spirits of air and fire, to bind and to harness their power. Such a feat as this had not been attempted since the Great Gods had withdrawn from the world, making such practical magic nigh impossible.

Al'hainn stood across from her. His eyes had rolled back into his head, his body shaking with the strain his spellcasting put upon him. If not for the old staff that he leaned upon, he would have collapsed to his knees long ago. As it was, he was near the very limits of his endurance. The spirits they sought had left the world of humankind, and they were hard to find amongst the twisting paths between realms. For the longest time the pair had harboured doubts they would ever find the aid they needed.

And then, almost as if they had been waiting for the summons, the spirits came to their call, and not a moment too soon, for both the ancients were trembling with fatigue, dizzy from their efforts.

The interior of the pavilion became suddenly hushed. The braziers snuffed out, as if a giant had laid its hand upon the flames, and then the very fabric of the tent began to billow and stretch, to snap and blow as if it were a sail upon a mast.

"The spirits are here!" Hewla exclaimed. She staggered a little, but managed to keep her balance, her thin grey robes suddenly tugged about her, her hair caught in a gust of wind smelling of spring flowers.

Al'hainn stood as straight as he could, grasping the staff with both hands, his wild hair and beard flying about him like the seeds of a dandelion. "Spirits of the grasslands, hear our plea!" His voice was deep and powerful, at odds with his weary frame. "The people of the Asgulun, your ancient allies, call upon you to help us against the Enemy. The Grimm have returned to this realm, and we stand alone, as the gods are holding true to their pact. But you, sweet spirits of the air and the fire in the hearth, you have always been the allies of our kind. Come now, we beseech thee, send us a wind from the hills, to race to the sea. Spirits of fire, harken to our call, and give our meagre flames the power to ravage our enemies, the enemies of all the realms, of all the gods and spirits, the fore-runners of the Dark that threatens to engulf us all!" As he spoke, Al'hainn's voice grew louder and louder, until he was almost shouting. As he finished, he punctuated his plea by striking the earth with is staff. The braziers burst back into life, and the door flaps to the pavilion, though tied secure, burst open.

The guards standing outside were bowled over by the shrieking wind that tore from the tent, and anything that wasn't secured was suddenly lifted into the air. Saddlebags, canteens, blankets and cloaks, all suddenly danced in a spiralling vortex, as the spirits of the air were let loose upon the grasslands.

Hewla burst from the tent moments later, her eyes wild with joy at their accomplishment. She grabbed the sleeve of a messen-ger, who was trying to get back to his feet. "It is time!" Hewla shouted. "Ride, all of you ride... tell Aelrik he must strike the Grimm's commander now, or all will be lost. Sound the horns and beat the drums! Bryann must be told to harry the Grimm, and keep them on the grasslands at all costs. Go! *Go now!*"

CHAPTER 26

OLD ALLIES

A elrik found himself holding the shaft of a sarissa, stabbing at the wild faces rushing at him. The sound of battle buffeted him like a physical blow. Snarls and curses rose as both sides pushed and shoved, muscles straining, spittle flying from stretched, grimacing mouths. Sprays of blood, bright crimson, spewed over the heads of the armies, obscuring the blue of the sky. The sun, a merciless golden disc, beating down upon the steppe.

The King of the North towered over the Asgulun and Northmen alike, and wielded the sarissa as if it were a spear of normal proportions. Even in such close quarters, the twenty-foot-long pike was a terrible weapon. The razored tip tore out throats, shattered shields, and skewered screaming Grimm. As he yanked the blade free from a corpse, another beast bounded to take its place. Old Rothgar caught its wildly swung axe upon his shield, allowing Aelrik the time to free his pike, and strike once again. All along the line, the sarissa held the Grimm at bay, even though some of the shafts had to be held by three men. They stabbed and pierced in a frenzy that matched that of their bestial enemy.

For over an hour the armies strained, chest to chest, the shield wall of the Asgulun battered and wavering, yet somehow continuing to hold. Wherever a man fell, and fall they did for all the bloody success of the long spears and the arrows that still filled the sky, another of their comrades would leap into the gap, shield up, head down, blade stabbing and curses screaming from frothing lips. The Grimm were relentless in their attack. Though those at the front were near certain to die, still they came. As they fell, their grisly comrades stomped over them, some striking down their own brethren in eagerness to reach the shield wall.

Time crawled, as if through syrup. The sun seemed stuck at its zenith, and Aelrik was feeling his age. His throat became parched from shouting and screaming commands. His arms felt like lead. His fingers ached, from gripping the haft of the long spear so tightly. But he knew there was nowhere else he would rather be. If this should be his last day, his last hour, then he would greet the Morriggu with a grin, for it was only when life was a hairs breadth from being snatched from him, that Aelrik felt truly alive.

He struck again and again. A huge thrown axe burst from the melee, skimmed over Rothgar's shield, its wicked edge hammering into Aelrik's helm, making his head ring like a bell. With a roar he thrust the sarissa into the axe wielding Grimm, lifting it clear off its feet in his fury.

It was as he shook the corpse from the spear tip that he spied the banner. It fluttered and billowed in the rising wind, only twenty yards away: a tattered black cloth, adorned with crudely painted skulls. Yet, for all its crudity, Aelrik was certain this was the banner of the Grimm's general. Before his view was obstructed by more charging Grimm, he caught a glimpse of a giant creature, all muscle and rage, snarling threats and curses at the Grimm, lashing them on with its fury.

Aelrik stepped back, pulling Rothgar with him. Three maidens filled the gap he left, two with a spear the third carrying a huge shield, which she not only hid behind, but smashed into the face of a screaming Grimm, smearing the metal with gore.

"The banner of the Grimm is just there! Gather twenty men and form up a wedge! I want a crack at that big son of a..." Aelrik had to break off his shouted orders, as a monstrous form suddenly broke through the ranks of the maidens, impaling one on a cruel saw-toothed blade. He turned dark eyes upon the King. Discarding the dead maiden, like an undesired trophy, he lunged at his new prey.

Aelrik met the charge full on, his spear smashing under the chin of the beast, almost taking its head off. One of the Maidens obligingly yanked the body from the end of the spear by its long, greasy hair. She grinned savagely at her king, as he stepped into the breach beside her, his roar lost amidst the cacophony of screams, striking steel, and pounding feet.

The killing and the chaos continued. Arrows filled the sky, falling like rain into the ranks of the Grimm. Both sides now stood upon the bodies of the fallen, in some places three or four corpses deep. They shoved and pushed, shield to shield, slipping in the gore at their feet, heaving and straining with every sinew in their bodies, with hardly room to swing an axe or stab a sword.

The sun beat down upon the grasslands, and the spirits of the air rode a breeze over the steppe, causing the brittle blades to bend and sway, to undulate like gentle waves, a green tide that rolled and swelled towards the cliff tops and the Sea of Storms.

THREE BATTLE BARGES of Ashanarr hid behind the veil of mist, just beyond the harbour of Asgulun. Upon the foremost, lounging upon a pile of crimson cushions and exquisite silks from the far-off Eastern provinces, was the demon, Ixtchel, though her form was couched in that of the supple beauty of the late Queen

She'ah. This apparition stared with a sultry contempt at the Grimm that laboured at the oars of the barge, her hair as glossy as oil, slicked past her buttocks, her slender frame as white as alabaster, as if never kissed by the sun. Upon her slim arms there was a king's ransom in jewelled bangles, their emeralds and sapphires glinting in the wan, mist shrouded sunlight. Low upon her hips, she wore a chain of golden links, from which hung a filmy square of some gauze-like material, as red as a setting sun.

Ixtchel presented the image of the perfect barbarian queen, and the Grimm cowered and grovelled at their oars, heedless of the backbreaking labour, or the blisters on their palms, that tore and bled, making the oars slick. They whimpered like dogs upon their benches, in terror and awe of their mistress, who sat with such haughty calm at the aft of the barge.

Behind the queen's black, kohl-rimmed eyes, Ixtchel stared out at the bent backs of her crew. Beyond the mist, a simple gift from her mistress, she knew Asgulun waited. A ripe fruit to be plucked, to be skinned, squeezed dry and devoured. Her plan had been a simple one: she had sent the vast bulk of her forces to advance upon the city from the West, thus drawing the mighty armies of the Asgulun out onto the plains, along with the wretched Northern King that had seen fit to join with them. As the forces clashed and died in their thousands, Ixtchel and her three barges waited safe within the mist.

Now she led her three hundred Grimm into the harbour. She led them with promises of the blood of babes, the fair flesh of the women of the Asgulun, and the threat of her whip and her wrath if they should shirk from her commands.

As her barge nosed into the harbour, shedding the mist like an old coat, she watched the sudden chaos and panic upon the wharf-side. She delighted in the fear of the Asgulun people as they ran to and fro, seeking escape from the sudden appearance of her mighty battle barge. She could see the long, winding roadway that led to the upper city; even at this distance she could discern that it was packed with ant like figures, flooding upwards towards the brittle safety of the city and its walls.

Ixtchels barge passed between the huge welcoming statues of the Mothers.

Her crew bent their backs, and the vessel fairly flew over the still harbour waters towards the quayside. Behind her, the two following barges approached the great statues, holding aloft their lanterns. She could hear the barge captains shouting in their guttural tongue, shouts that quickly turned to screams of fear and dread as, from the stone lanterns jets of black oil spewed, splashing into the water and upon the decks of the barges and upon the bodies of the Grimm.

Flames chased the oil from the lamps. Running along the black stream like lightning through stormy clouds. The flames swept along the sea, engulfing the two barges and their scream-ing, terror filled crews. Ixtchel watched as her Grimm, flames already eating at their flesh, sought refuge in the waves, yet the waves were now a sudden hell of churning flames and billowing smoke.

For days, the Grimm had toiled at the oars of the barges, had suffered the whip of the bosun, the sheer paralysing fear that they felt of their demon mistress. They had endured agonies to reach the promised feast of flesh, waiting behind the walls of Asgulun. Yet within minutes, the hardships of the Grimm had ended in an excruciating inferno of burning oil and choking smoke. It seemed that even the waters of the harbour were afire.

Watching the devastation and the maelstrom of fire, as it devoured her Grimm as surely as they would have devoured the children of the Asgulun, Ixtchel laughed with joy to see such carnage. Her beautiful borrowed face now contorted with glee.

"More blood and flesh for us!" she shrieked to her remaining crew. They flinched and hunched over their oars, as if expecting to feel the biting sting of the lash. The barge thumped into the quay, and the Grimm turned their crimson eyes to their mistress.

Ixtchel stood with a languorous grace, stretching her arms above her head. Without haste, she broke the chains at her waist, the gauze slipping away to puddle at her feet like a small pool of blood. Naked, Ixtchel savoured the fear and the hunger that emanated from the Grimm as they looked upon her with lust and terror.

What a beauty the queen had been, Ixtchel thought, as she ran her fingers over the smooth flesh. Without a doubt one of the fairest women to ever have trodden upon this realm. She was almost a rival for the Reader of the Book, Maeve, that silver-haired enchantress who could match the cruelty of any demon a hundred-fold. The very thought of Maeve, the Bringer of the Darkness, made the queen's naked form shiver in ecstasy.

The thought of Maeve made the demon queen's eyes roll into her skull. The image of the silver haired sorceress was lodged in Ixtchels brain, Maeve the bringer of death, the singer of the dark spells that would open the doorways to all realms, ushering in the Old Ones, those dark, brooding entities that dwelt in the spaces between realms, banished by the Creator of all things before time began.

But they waited still. With eyes the size of burial mounds, and their many limbs the length of rivers, they waited in the cold, lifeless, blackness, between the realms of life. The key to end their waiting, resided in the Book.

The pretender Aihabb had tried to master the Book eons ago. The Book that was written by the First Being, containing both the Light and the Darkness of all eternity within its script. Aihabb, though an evil man, could not contain the dark knowledge of the Book, and the light was denied him. Just one line alone had been enough to drive the man beyond insane.

But the Book had found Maeve, and she not only read the

words, she had welcomed the Darkness, absorbed the Darkness into her being. Maeve had become the Darkness, drawing all the evil and corrupt of the realms to her, binding them to her irresistible will. Ixtchel and her sisters had been no different: the creature within the beauty remembered all too clearly when she had received the call of her mistress. The blinding, terrifying wave of sheer malice that had lanced into her brain, sent her senses reeling, leaving her with nothing but the desire to serve, to glorify the apparition that had come to her in dreams, to bring the world of humankind to its knees before the Reader of the Book.

As Ixtchel strolled along the decking, with the fierce Grimm falling to their knees, grovelling and writhing upon their bellies, seeking to lick her naked feet, she imagined the joy her mistress would feel when she pulled the proud Asgulun into the sea. She wondered at her reward; would she sit at the side of the Empress? Would she be granted the honour to serve the Reader of the Book for all eternity? Again, she shivered with pleasure at the thought of those azure eyes falling upon her.

But first, she must crush the Asgulun, and crush them she would. She would suck the very flesh from their bones, she would gnaw upon their marrow before the day was done.

Behind her, the inferno continued unabated, with flames reaching twenty feet or more, black smoke billowing and pluming, hiding the open sea better than even the mist that Maeve had sent. The screams of the Grimm continued too, and with the screams came the smell of burning flesh.

The Grimm manning the surviving barge rushed to tie the craft to the quayside, then hurried to kneel before the barge, making living steps of their bodies, to ease Ixtchels descent. Without haste, the demon in the form of the lovely queen stepped from back-to-back of the abased Grimm. Those that felt her dainty feet press down upon their flesh cooed as if in rapture. At last, her feet found the cobbles, and Ixtchel breathed deep of the air, relishing the moments before she would release the slavering Grimm to savage the town, and then the palace itself.

Drawing herself to her full height, Ixtchel drew a crimson fingernail above her perfect left breast, the nail bit through skin and flesh, blood welled in the deep cut as she dragged the nail down, over her ribs, blood now running in torrents over her belly, streaming down her milk white thighs. The finger continued to dig and cut, past her navel, to her groin. The cut blossomed like a flower in the summer sun, opening wide. Ixtchel raised her finger to her eyes, to look curiously at the gore-smeared nail. She licked at the blood hungrily; her tongue was thick and forked.

Ixtchel dug her nail into her right breast, dragging it down to the juncture of her thighs. With a sigh of pleasure, she dug her hands into the cuts, and began to tear away at the flesh, *rip and tear, rip and tear*. Great gobbets of flesh spattered to the cobbles, thick red gore raining upon the stones as Ixtchel stripped off the flesh of the Queen, inch by gory inch, revealing her true hideous nature. Like an artist, presenting a masterpiece to an adoring crowd, Ixtchel unveiled herself before the watching, spellbound Grimm.

The demon stretched, her spine cracking and lengthening. She shook off the dainty hands as if they were gloves to be discarded, revealing long and narrow fingers ending in razored talons that flexed and bent with too many joints, the fingers making strange and repellent shapes. The talons tore at the sweet face of the Queen, blood spraying over the watching Grimm, sending them into a frenzy. They howled and screamed, beating their breasts with huge fists, stamping the cobbles with their splayed feet, watching entranced as their mistress cast off her disguise.

At last, the long silken hair of the Queen of Ashanarr was hurled to the cobbles, the bloodied scalp and strips of a pale face staring up out of the grisly wreckage. Ixtchel rolled her shoulders, feeling her neck stretch and crack, free of the confines of the puny vessel that had hidden her for so long. Her skin resembled the scales of a serpent, grey beneath the remaining shreds of crimson gore. Her face as much like a great toad as a human, though jagged tusk-like teeth protruded from the lower jaw, her upper teeth were sharp and glinted as if made of steel. Again, she stretched, now reaching her full seven feet of height, her arms long and full of coarse muscle. Down her naked back, there arose a row of sharp spines that stood like dagger blades, running to her buttocks, and from there followed the length of a muscular writhing tail that whipped and flailed at the air, fully ten feet in length.

About her, the Grimm writhed and moaned, their savage, brutal fingers reaching to touch her, to caress her with their worship. At the forefront of the swarming shapes, a huge beast, hungrier than his brethren perhaps, or maddened beyond any reason by the sight and smell of human blood, reached out and scooped up a strip of queenly flesh, quickly shoving it into his maw, the great jaws working furiously as they sought to chew on the morsel.

Ixtchel turned baleful eyes upon the feasting Grimm, eyes that held no pity, that had seen an eternity of savage torture and had revelled in it. She watched as her creature gulped down the bloody flesh. It remained blissfully unaware of her scrutiny, even as its fellows backed away, leaving it alone, gorging on the discarded flesh of its mistress.

Like a great serpent, Ixtchel's tail silently snaked towards the beast, who even now was gathering more gobbets of flesh and pushing them into its mouth, now swallowing without chewing, as if in a race of gluttony. It forced more and more bloody meat into its face, and its crimson eyes glazed with pleasure. Soft mewling sounds issued from around the grisly feast as the Grimm was transported to a realm of pure rapture by the taste and texture of human flesh.

When Ixtchel struck, it was with a speed beyond the ken of the Grimm. There was no time to plead, nor to even move to defend itself. The great tail coiled about the creature in an instant, pinning its great arms to its sides, squeezing and crushing so that half-chewed pieces of the Queen of Ashanarr spewed over the cobbles. Ixtchel slowly dragged the Grimm to her, its eyes no longer glazed, instead burning with terror, his soft moans of ecstasy replaced by breathless pants of panic.

Ixtchel laid a great, many-knuckled hand upon the creature's head. Her fingers walked along his face, finding his wide staring eyes, the great talons thrusting deep into the sockets, the fingers tightening like a vice, squeezing and crushing the skull. The Grimm struggled and spasmed, its teeth snapped and snarled, yet Ixtchel was indomitable.

Squeeze and crush.

The head shattered in her gore-streaked fist, and Ixtchel raised her hand and licked the blood and brains of the Grimm from her fingers, as if it were the most precious delicacy.

She now turned her pitiless gaze upon the remainder of her trembling crew. She gave them what may have been a smile.

"Go now, and take the city upon yonder cliff." Her voice was deep and wet, as though it came from a swamp, gurgling in her throat.

"The Empress will smile upon us all once the palace has fallen, and I will smile upon the Grimm who brings me the head of the Asgulun King." The split tongue licked at the gore that hung from her lips, and the Grimm trembled with desire.

"Go!" she snapped. "Fetch!"

The Grimm leapt to do her bidding, racing through the swiftly abandoned harbour town, battering down the gates that led to the city atop the cliff, and surging up the steep roadway, their howls and screams enough to turn the blood of any warrior to ice.

CHAPTER 27
THE BURNING

The wedge of shields and spears cut into the ranks of the Grimm. Aelrik stood near the front, hovering behind an enormous Asgulun. The fellow stood but a hand's breadth short of the King's own impressive height, yet was even broader in the shoulder and chest. Rothgar had called him The Bull, and Aelrik could see why. Bull held a great rectangular shield in his left hand, taller than an average man, but he hefted it easily enough, pushing forwards step by bloody step. To either side of him were Rothgar and a spear maiden. They poked javelins through the small gaps between Bull's shield and the shield bearers to either side of him.

The formation was an inverted V shape, with twenty men per arm, its centre packed with Northerners and shield maidens, the former cursing and screaming as they sought to stab and hack at the Grimm over the shields, the latter singing raucously, their javelins darting into the press of the Grimm with deadly effect.

Soon, the wedge was forced to step over the bodies of fallen Grimm, their boots wet with gore. The heat was overpowering, the press of straining bodies claustrophobic. Aelrik struck at a figure in front of Bull, his spear tearing out the Grimm's throat, yet the beast didn't fall. Enraged, Aelrik drew his sword and with a mighty overhead swing, split its head from crown to chin, but still the Grimm stood, wedged against Bull's shield and its monstrous comrades to every side, dead, yet unable to fall.

The big Asgulun gave a mighty heave, his spear sweeping high before him. Despite their compact ranks, the Grimm fell back, if only for a moment. A moment was all that Aelrik needed. Once again, he spied the tattered banner, the huge Grimm standing beneath it shouting his orders, his voice so deep and guttural it made the King's toes vibrate. In one swift motion, Aelrik jerked the sarissa to his shoulder, gripping the twenty-foot-long shaft as if it were a mere javelin. With a roar, the King drew back his arm, then, every sinew in his mighty frame straining fit to snap, he hurled the sarissa.

The huge spear flew true, hammering into the chest of the Grimm general, a full thirty feet away. The force of the cast lifted the huge creature off its feet and flung him back into the press of his troops like a rag doll.

A huge cheer went up from the Asgulun.

The Grimm general drowned out their voices with a murderous, raging challenge as he staggered to his feet. Fifteen feet of the sarissa protruded out from his chest, the rest dripping with gore and bone from his back.

Aelrik swore under his breath, pushing Bull and Rothgar aside so he could get a run at the wounded general. The Grimm parted before the enraged King, uncertain what had happened. Their fierce, unstoppable leader was sorely wounded, his absolute authority upon the Horde diminished, and with it their cohesion.

Aelrik took advantage of their confusion, his sword slicing off an arm here, a head there, black blood fountaining over the melee. The King's feet slipped and slid in the gore as he closed with the general.

The monstrous creature gripped the sarissa in its taloned left fist, his right hacking his sword into the slick, bloodied wooden shaft imbedded in his chest, heedless of the damage each stroke did to his own body.

This creature was sure of its death, yet still its red eyes fixed upon the King running towards it, saw the sword raised high in both hands. The general showed tusks in a grim smile, it coughed, and black blood spewed down its chin, over its chest. With a final chop, the shaft of the sarissa broke, and the general cast the free length away, raising his sword just in time to catch that of Aelrik, as the King swung for its head.

Sparks flew as again and again the titans struck; each blow more ferocious that the last. Like a smith beating at an anvil, Aelrik gave no pause. The battlefield rang with the clang, clang of their steel. All about them, Grimm and men fought, the sound of the dying loud, the cry of the desperate louder still.

Aelrik could see the monster was tiring. In its crimson eyes he could see that it knew its fate was upon it, yet still the general met his steel with its own, ichor pumping from the grisly wound in its chest with every move. Aelrik heard the horn blaring from his own ranks, ordering their retreat. The plan was going ahead, whether the Grimm were still organised or not; he should have slain the general faster, driven the Horde to panic sooner.

The horn sounded again, persistent, strident. Men began to fall back, orderly, tight-packed, their captains keeping them under control, leaving Aelrik and the mortally wounded Grimm general trading weaker and weaker blows.

The general heard the horn too, and thinking the men were running away, fresh vigour coursed through its wracked and tortured body. It raged at the King, this upstart human who had delivered its doom. Striking with panther-like speed, the general struck out with a vicious sweeping blow. Aelrik managed to meet the steel with his own, but so strong was the general, that Aelrik's sword was wrenched from his numbed fingers. The King scrabbled back, his heel caught in the harness of a dead Asgulun, and he fell. The general's backswing whistled over Aelrik's head, shaving hair it passed so close.

The King sprawled amongst the bodies of friends and foe alike, the wind knocked out of him by the impact. He stared up at the huge general, who swayed, life ebbing from the great wound in its chest. Their eyes met, and Aelrik knew that the Grimm had enough vitality left to send him to the afterlife before it. He grinned even as the general raised its great blade. Aelrik could smell smoke, could feel the strengthening wind on his sweating face, as it blew over the grasslands towards the sea. He would likely not live to see it, but Hewla's plan was underway; even now Bryann would be charging into the Grimm's flank, sowing panic and disruption amongst their ranks.

"Have at it then." He spat at the huge figure standing over him, relishing its triumph.

"All men will die, and the Empress will bring home the Old Gods."

Aelrik could barely understand the words, so deep was the voice, so guttural, as if the throat was choked with blood.

"Bastard!" Aelrik shouted, refusing to be cowed even in the final moments of life, refusing to go meekly to the Morriggu.

The general began to laugh, to cough, the sword raising higher, the edge of the steel glinting in the sunlight.

And then the generals head sprung from its neck. A torrent of black, stinking blood splashed over the sprawled King, and he could only stare at the enormous corpse, blocking out the blue of the sky. With a sudden twitch, the general's knees buckled, and the huge shape crashed to the ground. More meat upon the battlefield.

"Bloody hell, they have set the grasslands afire already!"

Old Rothgar tottered a little, regaining his balance, a huge axe in one fist, a wineskin in the other. He took a quick swig, red trick-ling down his chin, his one good eye rolling with pleasure. "We had better join the retreat, or I won't be alive to boast of saving your arse once we get back to the North." He threw aside the skin, and reached down to help his King. "I reckon that there creature is bigger than the bear you killed, all those years ago. Should be a song in this somewhere."

Aelrik gratefully accepted the one-eyed man's hand and stag-gered to his feet. All about him was chaos. The Grimm Horde was in a panic. The defeat of their champion had unsettled them. It was as if there had been a psychic link between the general and the rest of the Horde, and now he was gone that link had been severed. The Grimm were vulnerable. Around the King stood the remains of the fighting wedge: Bull, and a dozen others, maids and warriors all bloodied and panting.

Aelrik showed his teeth, snatched up his sword and nodded at Rothgar. "Lead the retreat then, and let us hope we can outrun Hewla's fury!"

* * *

Hewla the witch left her pavilion, her grey robes billowing in the wind. If she listened hard enough, she fancied that she could hear the soft, gay laughter of sprites upon the air. Beside her, Al'hainn stamped along, now leaning heavily upon his staff. The sprites pulled at his beard and hair, making it wilder and more unkempt than ever.

"I can hardly believe that our magic was so strong, Hewla." The hermit was short of breath, the exertions of summoning the winds had drained him, yet he looked elated for all his exhaustion.

"Nor I," Hewla answered, her voice faraway, as was her mind at that moment. She and the old hermit were strong in magic, yet no one had been powerful enough to summon winds upon the scale that they had just done for centuries; or, at least, no *human sorcerers*. All she could reason was that the gods had lent them the power. *It must be that*, she thought. Ever since the gods had turned away from the world, magic had dwindled, or at least the kind they had used today.

Witches and wizards were manifold throughout the world, yet their skills were most often in healing, divination, the ability to see beyond the veil that covered the eyes of mortals. But evocation, the ability to conjure up a wind that could sweep miles upon miles of grassy steppe, that was quite beyond the ken of today's sorcerers. Until today. Hewla could feel magic in the air, could almost taste it. Is this what it had been like to be a witch or a warlock when the gods were free with their gifts? When magic was strong in the realm of humankind?

Or was it the meddling of Maeve, the Empress that sent out the Horde, and demons too, to do her bidding? Had her reading of the Book somehow invited magic back into the realm?

Hewla looked at the huge swarm of figures below her on the grasslands. At her signal, the retreat had been sounded, and the Asgulun and their allies had begun to back away towards the city. Aelrik must have been successful in overcoming their leader, for she had witnessed the moment when the beasts had suddenly slipped their leash, when their order and discipline had evaporated. The horde must have feared the leader, and he in turn, must have been able to communicate to the entire ranks by some terrible magic, as if they were of one mind, utterly controlled by their general.

But now, the Grimm had been reduced to savagery once more, driven by hunger and hate, but also by fear and panic. The sudden withdrawal of the Asgulun had confused them. They milled about in their thousands, and the wind blew the grass flat at their feet.

Next, Bryann and his cavalry had struck, their horses flowing over the savannah like a great wave. Hewla watched impassively as the horses charged through the Grimm. Even at this distance, she and Al'hainn could hear the screams, could see that the Horde was already turning towards the distant sea.

Again, and again the horsemen struck.

A line of archers broke from the retreating ranks of the infantry to dip arrows into the fire pots that had been secreted in the earth, and marked by tall, waving flags. The archers drew back their bows and released their flaming arrows into the massing Grimm. All the while, the Asgulun and their allies continued with their hasty retreat. The arrows flashed through the sky, leaving oily streaks across the unbroken blue, before landing. The bone-dry grasses erupted in flame.

Hewla could see the Grimm were being slaughtered like sheep, by the fire and the horsemen, the survivors herded towards the distant sea.

"Now is the time, Hewla," Al'hainn whispered, and watched with rapt awe, as the witch raised a clenched fist to her face. She opened the fist, and there, dancing in the palm of her hand, was a crimson flame, a sprite of fire that the mages had coaxed to return to the realm of mortals, had bound to their bidding with spells that would have been beyond them just a few short years ago.

Hewla blew at the flame, gently, and the sprite leapt from her palm, to dance with her sisters, the sprites of the air. The fire sprite flew and danced, flew and danced, glad to once more be free and returned to this realm. It was carried by the wind until it reached the burning grasses, where it spread itself amongst the flames.

The grassland fairly exploded. A wall of boiling flames ten feet high blossomed and bloomed, its roaring cry drowning out even the screams of those Grimm too slow to keep ahead of the maelstrom. Thick black smoke billowed from the inferno, almost covering the sky, but Hewla could see, though the sight made her sick to her stomach, and she forced her flint hard eyes to watch her handiwork no matter the pain of the stinging tears.

On and on the Grimm were pushed, the supernatural wind and the mage-wrought flames relentless in their work. The Grimm were running now, all thoughts of fighting gone from their heads. Fear and terror gnawed at them as the wall of agonising fire advanced upon them. So intense was the heat, that even before the fire reached them, some burst into flames as they ran. Their rusted armour melting, as did their flesh. The stench of burning Grimm was overpowering. They ran and ran, casting their spears and swords aside, clawing at one another trying to outdistance the horror that came upon them with crackling glee.

Those leading the stampede, farthest away from the flames, were the first to see the doom that awaited them. They did their best to stop their headlong run, digging their heels into the grass, only for the thousands behind them, being harried by the wall of flames, to collide into them. Hewla made herself watch as row upon row, hundred upon hundred, of the creatures were pushed by their own terrorised momentum over the edge of the cliffs.

She knew the sharp jagged rocks, two hundred feet below the lip of the cliffs, would offer the most brutal of ends, yet still she watched, and the fire that she had conjured swept the plains. Behind the flames, the land was blackened, peopled only by the grotesque dead, burned and melted, burst and cooked, their jaws agape in silent screams. Those that didn't reach the cliff, to die upon the jagged teeth of rocks, or pulped by the waves that pounded upon them, were incinerated as they ran.

None were spared.

The Asgulun cheered and whooped at their victory. Surely the gods themselves had returned to lend a hand in their hour of need. Upon the hill, Hewla held out her hand, and the fire sprite landed, dancing quite harmlessly upon her wrinkled palm. Looking at the devastation that she had wrought through this tiny, harmless-looking ally, Hewla felt a sickening dread at what she had done.

Even though the Grimm were unrelenting killers, eaters of babes and worse besides, she would forever have the lives of thousands upon her conscience; she was sure that the horrors she had just witnessed would be waiting for her to relive whenever she closed her eyes.

She was still standing looking at her empty palm when Aelrik made his tired way up the hill, and laid a heavy, bloodstained hand upon her shoulder. "It was a terrible thing that you did Hewla, but history will thank you for it. The men that stand there upon the plain, alive, and able to return to their wives and children, they thank you for it."

Hewla nodded absently, turning to make her way back to the pavilion, the screams of the dying thousands ringing in her ears.

CHAPTER 28

GRIMM

Steeleye led his one hundred veterans clattering through the gate in the city's landward wall. A guard, a captain by the look of the braid on his shoulder and the fine plume of snow white horse hair cresting his mirror bright helmet, rushed forwards, grabbing the reins of Steeleye's horse in a leather gauntleted fist.

"Thank the gods!" he yelled, his eyes wild, his face pale with fear. "How many of you are there? Are there more following?" The guard peered back along the line of mounted warriors, out of the gate. In the distance palls of inky black smoke billowed into the afternoon sky.

Behind the guard, Steeleye could see plumes of smoke too, rising from the harbour. His horse danced, keen to be off once more, even after the mad dash over the plains. Rolf heeled his horse forwards, nudging the guard with his boot. "How long until the Grimm reach the city gates, lad?" His gruff voice, and fierce appearance seemed to calm the guard somewhat.

"Perhaps an hour, sir, maybe less. They are as fast as horses coming up the Winding Way from the harbour, there must be a hundred or more of them! I've seen them through the looking glass upon the battlements, they are terrible looking things, and their howls..."

Steeleye laughed, though not unkindly. He well remembered his first sight of the Grimm. "A hundred? That doesn't sound too bad. Your countrymen yonder..." He jerked a thumb to indicate the plains beyond the gate behind him. "They have had to face a hundred *thousand,* of the creatures. Gather all the men you can, and bolster the defences at the walls overlooking the harbour: we must stop them gaining entry to the city, it would be carnage if they were to get amongst the families packed in there."

"But what about guarding the landward gate? There is a battle raging out on the plains, surely we should be there too in case the Grimm overrun our forces?"

Rolf heeled his horse past the captain, calling over his shoulder "If the Grimm get past the forces on the plain, the city is lost anyway. A few guardsmen won't stop those numbers, but you may make the difference against a hundred or so coming up from the harbour. Do as Steeleye says, and make for the walls."

"Is that where you are going? To man the walls?" The captain was young; very likely his family had bought him a commission in the guards, liking the uniform, no doubt. It was painfully obvious to these bedraggled veterans clustering about the gate that he had little or no experience in the art of soldiering.

"We are away to see where we can do the most good, captain." Steeleye pulled his reins free of the man's grip, and grinned down at him. "Whether that is to meet the Grimm on the Winding Way, or bolster the defence at the gate, we will leave it to you to ensure that any that get past us don't get into the city. Clear enough?"

The captain nodded, clearly unsure, but at last he fumbled a salute of kinds and stepped out of the path of the warriors. As they thundered by, he heard a savage looking woman, all scalemail and braided red hair calling to him "Are all the Asgulun as pretty as you?"

There was a wild laughter burst from the throats of several of the shield maidens as they urged their mounts faster over the cobbles through the narrow streets towards the seaward gate.

* * *

MORINAE STARED in shock down into the harbour. From her window, high above the cliffs, secure in the palace, she had seen the three great battle barges emerge from the sea fret. She had called young Helgen to her, and they had watched together, as the enormous Mother statues vomited flames and death, setting alight the very waves. So fierce was the fire, that Morinae fancied she could feel the heat of the inferno even here, nearly a mile or more away.

The Princess saw that there was one surviving barge, and bade Helgen fetch her a spyglass, which she quickly returned with. Morinae peered through the glass, a wonderful affair of brass tubing and mirrors, and saw the remaining barge reach the harbour walls. She could just make out the slavering Grimm, lining the gunwales; she could almost feel their anticipation, their insane hunger and hate.

She saw the naked Queen of Ashanarr, and though she did not know the woman well, she was mortified by the Queen's brazen appearance. Strangely, she felt more affronted by the woman's nakedness than she was by the Grimm setting foot upon her beloved Asgulun. She watched the lithe yet voluptuous queen begin to caress her body, and though the image in the spyglass was still small, so far away was the barge, Morinae could see well enough what followed next.

Her green eyes went wide with horror, as she saw the figure begin to shred her skin, to peel off her flesh, and let it fall in bloody ruin upon the cobbles. If the sight of the mutilation sent fear through her bones, the emergence of the demon from the discarded skin sent her mind reeling and into a panic. Morinae fell away from the window, abandoning the spyglass.

"God's help us all!" she breathed when at last she found her voice. "A demon has come to Asgulun, and our forces are all upon the plains!"

Young Helgen had snatched up the spyglass, and after a moment, made a disgusted retching sound. "It just squashed the head off a monster!" she reported to the Princess. "Just like that, squashed it like an orange. Now they are leaving the barge... they are running through the streets, making for the gate to the Winding Way. I can see watchmen there, guardsmen, perhaps a dozen of them. Oh!" Helgen put down the glass with shaking hands, her face drained of blood, pale as a ghost. She stared at the Princess. "The watchmen were torn apart, bits and pieces thrown and scattered about."

The Princess put a comforting arm around the child, and drew her close in a fierce hug. "The Winding Way is long, Helgen. The watch will have seen the barge dock. These walls are thick and high. The gate has never been breached, and my brother Juvaal has men aplenty in the palace. Enough, I am sure, to defend the gate." Silently, Morinae prayed that what she said was true. Her scheming brother was far from reliable, and those that rallied to his cause were of a similar ilk.

"Thank the gods all the people from the harbour town were brought into the city," Helgen said. "Imagine if there had been *families* down there!"

Morinae could well imagine, and she felt bile burn in her throat. Fear gnawed at her, every instinct was to run away, to flee, to go to the stables and find the fastest horse that she could, ride out of the gate and never look back.

Helgen shivered violently in her arms, and the Princess made reassuring cooing sounds. "It will be alright, Helgen. Why, we have seen the smoke from the plains, have we not? And we know that means Prince Bryann, my brother, and his allies, have set alight the plains. That is all part of the plan, is it not? I'm sure that even now there are a thousand men making haste back to the city"

"Do you really think so?" Helgen raised her tear-filled hazel eyes to meet those of the Princess.

As if on cue, there came a knock upon the chamber door, and a guard stepped in, snapping to attention when he saw Morinae and the child. "Princess, the Grimm are upon the Winding Way. We must get you somewhere safe."

"Where could be safer than here, high in the palace?" Helgen wanted to know.

Morinae was more concerned with the sigil of a serpent like dragon stitched upon the breast of the guard's tabard. "Are you one of my brother's men?" she asked, tightening her grip upon Helgen.

"Aye, Princess, and Prince Juvaal himself, bade that I come and bring you to safety."

Morinae was suddenly very aware that there was only one exit from the chamber, and that it was now blocked by one of her brother's men, and he looked broad and fierce in his chain mail and tall, conical helmet.

"Where exactly does my brother deem safe?"

"Why, with him, and your father, the King, of course."

Morinae felt a chill run along her spine. The guardsman smiled, showing white teeth, but somehow, the smile didn't reach his eyes, reminding Morinae of a reptile. Aware that for the moment she had no recourse but to follow the man, she bade him lead on.

As the three of them exited the chamber, the guardsman first, followed by the Princess, young Helgen pressed something into

Morinae's palm. Cold and hard, Morinae gripped the hilt of one of the throwing daggers Helgen used in her act.

"Clever girl," Morinae mouthed silently, smiling and closing one eye in a reassuring wink.

* * *

STEELEYE REINED in at the head of the Winding Way, remembering the exhausting journey up its length just a few short days ago. It had taken him nigh half a day to make the journey, yet now, as he stared down the white paved road, he could see the Grimm swarming along the Way, heedless of the steep fall either side of the road, heedless too of the distance they ran or the incline.

From this vantage point, he could see the harbour. He was higher even than the Mothers, holding out their still smoking lanterns, a guide to fishermen, and doom to invaders. The two battle barges that had been caught in the fiery spray had all but sunk, their charred and bloated crew floating upon the burning waters, like so much flotsam.

"We seem destined to meet these buggers at the gates to great cities." Rolf had drawn alongside him, doffing his helm to better view the devastation in the water, and see the writhing tide of figures coming towards them.

"It seems an age since we stood on the plains outside Ash Ul M'on," Steeleye replied, thinking on all of his adventures since that grim day, the friends he had lost, the trials that he had endured.

"But back then, we were trying to keep them *in* a city," Rolf said. "This time it falls to us to keep them out!" Steeleye grinned at the old man's words.

"And we have numbers and the high ground this time too..."

For all his bravado, Steeleye was well aware that now, unlike then, there was a creature leading the Grimm far stronger than the monstrous Kleave. This time, there was a demon from legends cracking her whip over their savage backs.

He looked down the Winding Way. Judging by the speed the Grimm were charging, Steeleye knew they would be upon them in much less than an hour. In fact, the closer the creatures came, the faster they seemed to swarm.

"Do we take the fight to them, Rolf? Or should we man the walls and kill them as they come?"

"I'm for getting behind a wall. This roadway is fifty yards wide, that's a lot of space to hold against a charge, even on horseback. As it is, the gate is huge." The white-haired old warrior chewed his beard, and looked at the walls behind them. They were tall, true enough, but made of rough and weathered stone. Steeleye and Rolf both knew the Grimm could scale them easily enough. "Even behind the wall, we will have our work cut out for us I think."

Steeleye nodded his agreement. Rolf had the spirit of a wild and reckless fighter, so if even he thought that caution in this instance was prudent, who was he to argue? "To the walls!" Steeleye roared at the top of his voice, wheeling his horse as he did. It danced on its hind legs kicking the air with its forelegs. Steeleye clung on, desperate not to fall from the saddle.

Rolf was laughing loudly, his own horse fully under his control. "Aye, lad," he called over his shoulder as he rode back into the gateway, "I'm not sure you are ready for a cavalry charge just yet."

Steeleye finally brought the horse under control, and fairly jumped from the saddle, leading the horse by the reins back behind the walls. Mounted shieldmaidens rode by hooting good naturedly at his novice horsemanship. "You need to control it with your legs," called one, young and fierce, her red hair gathered in a braid that fell down her back. Her legs were bare and tanned, gripping the horse soundly. "Let him know who is in charge!" She grinned, making the horse dance this way and that, using only her hips and her long legs. In her hands she held her shield and javelin like a veteran, for all her lack of years.

"Once Kallis gets her legs wrapped around you, that is it, you will do whatever she wants!" an older Maiden shouted loudly, winking at Steeleye, then laughing all the louder to see him blush. Kallis was renowned throughout the North for her beauty, and her fierce appetites.

"Leave the lad alone, he has enough on his mind without Kallis distracting him!" Rolf said. He had dismounted, and was wheezing his way up the steps to the wooden walkway that wound around the inside of the walls. At the summit, he leaned on the balustrade and looked about the courtyard. The one hundred Northmen and maidens were packed behind the gate, several of them working together to swing the great portals closed, then sliding the huge planks into their brackets, locking the gate fast. There were not as many of the Asgulun guardsmen as Rolf had thought.

He caught the elbow of a lad staring over the wall at the Winding Way, at the Horde coming swiftly towards them. "Is this it?" the old man asked. "There are only two dozen of you here."

"There were more of us, until they saw those things coming at them. Most have families, children and the like." The lad paused to adjust his oversized bowl of a helmet; it continuously slipped over his eyes. "I can't see the point in running to be honest, and I reckon we have a better chance of killing them from up here than we have fighting them in our homes." The helm slipped again, and the young lad cursed, wrenching it off his head.

"Put a rag in the bowl, lad, it will pack it better. Should soften the blow too should an axe land on your head." Rolf grinned as the lad snatched up his pike and ran for the stairs, holding his helmet on with his hand.

"Is he running away, or going to pack his helmet?" Steeleye

asked, as he mounted the platform, behind Rolf. The maidens and the veterans made their way up the stair, spreading out along the battlements above the paving of the Winding Way.

"I'm not sure, perhaps we should have sent Kallis up here first, she has a way of rallying men about her." The old man was chuckling softly as he looked down the paved way to the harbour. His mood sobered soon enough, when he looked at the ruin of the barges in the harbour. "Thank the gods that not all three barges made it through, eh? And that the harbour town was mostly evacuated. Can you imagine the carnage had there been people down there when the barge docked?"

"Arrows!" came a call, loud and strident from further along the walkway. For a moment Steeleye thought one of the men had taken it upon himself to order a volley. He was about to shout that the distance was too great when a yard long black shaft struck the wall a mere foot from where he stood. Chips of stone flew, so hard was the impact. "Damn it, but their archers can shoot a long way," he said, lifting his shield above the ramparts and glaring at the Grimm. They were closer than he would have thought possible in so short a time. Perhaps an arrow or two of their own would slow them down.

Moments later, twenty shafts lifted from the walls, then plunged amongst the Grimm, only two fell, to be quickly trampled beneath steel-shod feet. The other arrows either missed or were deflected by bucklers.

"Get ready!" Rolf shouted; his eyes grew wide as the creatures sprinted towards the wall. A hundred yards, then fifty. The white-haired warrior chopped the air with his hand and more bowstrings twanged. Seven of the creatures fell, but now they were milling at the gate, shields lifted above their heads, like a turtle's shell. "Shoot them!" Rolf bellowed, and volley after volley showered down upon the shields.

Now there came the rhythmic boom, boom as the Grimm ran

against the wooden gate, using their very bodies as a ram. "Ha, they can do that all day!" came a voice from along the wall. "That gate is reinforced with bronze, the latch is layered with iron. The bloody wall will break before that gate!"

Steeleye grinned, slapping Rolf upon the back. "Perhaps Aelrik will be back before the bastards get in then, eh?" But Rolf wasn't listening. He was looking along the roadway.

"What in the nine hells is *that*?" he gasped. Steeleye caught sight of what had brought the exclamation from the old war horse. Running towards the gathered Grimm was a huge, spindle limbed apparition. It ran upright like a man, but its feet ended in talons that struck sparks from the paving, the long arms ending in scythe like claws that seemed to tear the very air. It was female, Steeleye thought, gaping at the thing's naked form, clothed only in blood and gore.

But it was the face that made Steeleye swear: all tusks and teeth, with a great tongue, thick as a man's wrist, cloven like the hoof of a ram. The eyes were huge, slanted and brimming with malice. They burned with a palpable hate even as they fell upon Steeleye. Great spikes rose from the creature's spine, running down its elongated body, and along the long whip of a tail that lashed and flailed about.

"Ixtchel!" Steeleye hissed, his hand snatching the hilt of the Godsteel blade, pulling it with a rasping snarl from its scabbard. Rolf staggered away from his young friend, putting an arm before his face, as Steeleye's eyes suddenly burst with a blinding white light.

"It's the Shining!" cried the old warrior, even as the demon below charged through the Grimm, and for all the talk of its invulnerability, smashed the gate to kindling. Like a river breaking its banks, the Grimm flowed through the shattered entryway, a black tide, full of crimson eyes and snarling teeth. The Northerners in the courtyard met them with shield and spear, their countrymen upon the wall quick to draw arrows and shoot into the writhing mass of muscle and bone. Others drew blades and began to hastily run down the stairs to bolster the ranks of their comrades, Rolf amongst them.

Steeleye was tempted to throw himself into the fray, but he held himself in check. He was here for the demon, he was here in service for the Morriggu, and to retrieve his soul. He scanned the melee, searching for the terrible creature that led the Grimm. Beneath the wall was chaos, the Grimm were outnumbered, but their ferocity evened the odds and then some. Steeleye watched as some of the creatures broke free of the fight, howling and yapping like dogs, running towards the palace.

The palace would have to fend for itself just now,

Steeleye pushed by an Asgulun guard and began to head down the steps into the courtyard where he knew he would find Ixtchel. A young Asgulun lad was hurrying up the steps, hoping to find safety on the wall. He held his helmet on his head with one hand, the other gripping a pike so hard his knuckles showed white. He skidded to a halt as he saw Steeleye advancing towards him, eyes shining like suns, great broadsword naked in his fist. With a wail, the lad quickly spun about, running back into the furious clashing and clanging below, the wail turned into something of a battle cry, as he found his courage, plunging into the fighting.

It didn't take long for Steeleye to find Ixtchel. Her scaled and misshapen head stood a foot above even the Grimm. Her wide, glaring eyes roved the combatants. There was a terrible lust in those eyes, a lust for horror and pain, for blood and misery.

"Where are you, Lightbringer?" Her voice was loud as cymbals, as raw as hate. "Come and face Ixtchel, let's see how you fare against *this* Sister!"

Their eyes met, just as he reached the courtyard. Ixtchel hissed a challenge, the Grimm scattering out of her way as she began to run at the wall. One of the creatures was not quite fast enough, and the whipping tail lanced through its chest, lifting it writhing and screaming, then tossing it away like a gnawed bone.

Steeleye stared at the horror running towards him, feeling the energy brought on by the Shining coursing through him, his entire body vibrating with the surging power. Unbidden, a roar tore from his throat, and the Shining charged to meet the demon. Steeleye barely felt in control. He felt he was riding upon a storm, his sword lightning, his voice thunder.

MORINAE COULD HEAR the screams from without the palace, and she knew the flimsy defence mounted upon the walls had been breached. She paled at the thought of the Grimm loose within the city, rending and tearing. Even though only the one battle barge had made it to the docks, she had seen first-hand the savagery they were capable of, and the creature that led them was worse, far, far worse.

Their escort walked confidently along the palace corridor. They passed no one. As if every living soul cowered behind their doors, or had evacuated the palace altogether, making a break for the walls away from the harbour. Morinae wished she had done the same, she was feeling more and more vulnerable as the three of them walked the corridors, their feet echoing hollowly upon the flags.

"Where are all the guards?" she asked at length. The quiet was becoming oppressive, fraying at her nerves. "Watchmen, the palace servants?"

"The guards will be at the wall, Princess, and all the servants will be in their quarters I should think, or running home to their loved ones. But don't you worry, your brother has asked that I take care of you, personally." Again, that lizard grin, the eyes flat.

As they passed the head of a great stair way, there came the sound of a wailing shriek. Higher and higher rose the scream until it gurgled away into silence. Morinae peered down the wide stairs. They were on the fourth floor; the scream had come from perhaps two floors below. "God's help us, they are in the palace. Hurry and take us to the King!" Even in her fear, Morinae found her royal voice. she turned to face the guardsman, and found him shaking his head.

"There will be no orders given to me, save by your brother, *Princess*." He fairly spat out the last word. "Why couldn't you just stay lost? Why did you have to come back at all?" As he spoke, the guard let his hand fall to the well-worn hilt of the sword at his hip. "With you gone, Juvaal could wait out the old fool on the throne, knowing that in time he would ascend to his birth right. But no, you had to come back, to bring these creatures with you too; why couldn't you just stay gone?"

He drew the sword slowly. Its silver steel caught a bar of sunlight falling through a nearby leaded window. Morinae could tell he was relishing the drama of the moment, the fear in the lovely green eyes before him, her trembling full lips. "With these creatures running around the palace, many a deed will go unremarked," he whispered. "When they are ousted, a new day will dawn for the Asgulun, a new King, new advisors. Come now, Princess... there is a balcony along here, with a view of the harbour." The guard's free hand quickly caught a handful of Morinae's hair, dragging her towards him. "Can you fly, Princess?" he asked, his voice a hissing snarl.

Something small and bright flashed past Morinae's face, and the guard reeled away, his hand still entangled in her hair, pulling her with him. Something hot and wet splashed over her cheek, red and sticky. The guard was suddenly howling in pain, freeing his hand to grab at the small dagger stuck in his right eye. Horrified, Morinae staggered away, seeing young Helgen snatching a second throwing knife from her tunic, her young face set and grim. The girl drew back her arm for the throw, but Morinae was faster. On impulse, without thought or plan, she thrust her own borrowed blade into the neck of the guard, above the mail of his shirt.

The guard let out a gurgling, choking sound as he staggered back, but Morinae was away, she grabbed Helgen's wrist and was running, running as fast as she could away from the treacherous guard and his wet, choking sounds. Away, too, from the stairs, up which she could picture in her mind, the shambling shapes of the Grimm rushing with fangs and claws. Panic took hold, and she and the young juggler fairly flew along the corridor.

CHAPTER 29
TOOTH AND CLAW

Steeleye ran at the demon, Godsteel blade raised high, the sun shining along its length almost as bright as the Shining in his eyes. Ixtchel barged through friend and foe alike, her talons tearing armour and flesh, arrows and spears bouncing off her impervious scales. The din and the chaos dimmed from Steeleye's mind; his concentration fixed upon the demonic adversary making its relentless way through the throng towards him.

He saw the snaking tail raise, like that of a scorpion, then flick with a blinding speed. Great spines fully a foot in length flew from the tail. Like fingers of bone the spines mowed down men and Grimm alike, piercing mail as though it was parchment. Steeleye caught one of the spines upon the flat of his sword, more by luck than design, sending it harmlessly to the cobbles. An Asgulun guardsman close by was not so fortunate, a spine driving through his conical helmet, flinging him back, nailing his head to the wooden scaffolding that held up the perimeter walkway. He twitched and spasmed, his heels drumming against the wood for a second or two, then falling still.

Steeleye could barely give the guard a glance: one more death amongst a kaleidoscope of churning strife.

The demon and the Lightbearer met with snarls and curses. Steeleye found himself weaving away from snapping teeth and tusks, rending talons and lashing tail. Twice he struck at the demon's head, twice she knocked aside his blade with talons as long as daggers. The serpent tail lashed, sending him reeling, staggering back. He tripped over the bloody remains of a shield maiden, his head striking the cobbles, sending stars spinning before his eyes. Spines from the demon's tail drove into the cobbles beside him. For a moment, blackness engulfed him, snuffing out the Shining, casting away the energy it brought with it, and Steeleye was left befuddled, barely clinging on to consciousness.

A huge, sinewed hand plucked him from the cobbles, the talons piercing the collar of his habergeon. He was lifted bodily, held close to the face of the demon, the cloven tongue flicking over a cut on his chin, tasting his blood as if it were a fine wine.

"Not so simple to kill as my little sister Janovis, am I Light-bringer?" The demon spoke in a sibilant hiss, reminding Steeleye of serpents, and crawling, slithering things. Gradually, the darkness receded, and his vision cleared somewhat. When he saw the fangs and bloated tongue, the malevolent unblinking eyes just inches from his face, he wished for darkness once more.

Just for a moment. He hung limp in Ixtchel's grasp. Beaten.

"It is a shame, you will not see Empress Maeve conquer all the nations of this realm, see the kings cowed and on their knees before her; you will not live to see her usher in the return of the Old Ones." As she spoke, the demon gently traced a talon over his face, from his brow to his chin. "I collect trophies," she hissed, "I have the skins of kings and queens, the swords and the bones of champions spanning a thousand years, but I think your eyes, yes, your eyes shall have a place of honour in my collection." The froglike mouth spread in a vile, tooth filled smile.

Steeleye struggled weakly to pull his face away from the talons, yet he was held firm by the monstrous fist. Again, the tongue slimed his face, and the creature shuddered with pleasure. He shook his head, clearing away the fog that threatened to send him back into oblivion. The rank smell of Ixtchels breath assailed his nostrils, like smelling salts, sending him into a fit of coughing and wheezing.

The demon laughed.

In his fist, the Godsteel blade began to vibrate. Was it his imagination? Or was the god forged steel trying to bring him to his senses? He growled, an inhuman sound. He cursed as he sought to bring the sword to a position of some use. He roared as the sword point at last came to rest upon the scales of the demon.

Steeleye pushed the sword into the creatures bloated belly.

Ixtchel let out a piercing scream.

The clawed hand let go Steeleye's head, and instead gripped the blade, vainly seeking to stem the slow, agonising penetration. Blood, black as sin, oozed down the steel, not only from the stomach wound, but from the cuts to Ixtchel's hands too. So tight did the demon grip the razor like steel, that one of her fingers was near cut from her hand.

Too slow, Steeleye saw the tail whipping over the demon's shoulder, it struck the already groggy warrior a blow to the side of the head, throwing him back, gasping. His fist still gripped the sword, stained with gore to the hilt. Again, the tail lashed out, Steeleye knew he would be unable to avoid the terrible projectiles at such close range. Instinctively, he planted his feet, and swung the sword in a blind arc. Its keen edge ripped through the tail, sending five feet of writhing muscle and bone spinning into the air.

Ixtchel screamed again, a shrill piercing sound. In a frenzy, the demon lashed out, her razor like claws missing Steeleye's eyes by a hair's breadth, but slashing the skin of his face from brow to cheek. Blood splashed, and ran freely.

Gasping for breath, wincing and grimacing in pain, the pair staggered apart.

About them, the tumult of the fight continued. Dimly, Steeleye was aware that more Asgulun guardsmen had arrived. The clash of iron and steel upon shield and helm, the thud of blades on flesh, rang loud in his ears as he warily circled the demon. He wiped a forearm over his eyes to clear the blood. Ixtchel circled Steeleye in her turn, no longer the thrashing, maelstrom of death. Instead, she held her stomach with an injured hand, as she sought to keep her entrails from spilling about her feet. Her posture was stooped, black gore still dripping from her severed tail, and fairly gushed from the wound in her stomach whenever she released pressure upon the cut.

As Steeleye reached the very end of his endurance, he felt the Shining once more shift within him. He felt strength course through his sword arm, clear his swimming vision, and straighten his staggering gait.

Ixtchel saw the fire in the warrior's eyes; it flared past the mask of blood that ran down his face, and the demon knew dread. She and her sisters had seen the death of suns, the exploding birth of galaxies, seen worlds born and end in cataclysmic fury, but never had she felt icy fingers constrict about her black heart, as they did now.

Fear coursed through her veins as she saw the Light revealed, and understood that here, in the courtyard of Asgulun, she was confronted by a force from the very beginning of time. The very opposite force to that which had vomited her and her ilk into the endless realms. With the fear came hate, with the desperation came loathing and fury. With an almost human scream of rage, the demon attacked, all thrashing limbs and a lashing stumped tail, her mouth wide and snarling as she sought to bite and chew her tormentor.

For all the energy that the shining brought, Steeleye still fell back before the berserk attack.

Sparks flew as talons and steel met. The demon offered no defence, only a suicidal attack, as if she knew her fate was sealed, her doom delivered by the Lightbringer, but determined that he should be dragged to the afterlife with her.

Steeleye's retreating heel slipped through a puddle of gore, he stumbled, crashing to the ground, the demon's claws raking the empty air an inch above his head.

Steeleye stared up at the grinning creature, and knew the Morriggu would soon be taking him to her bosom, leading him to his place in the Hall of Heroes, one more figure in the vast army of failed questers.

Even as Ixtchel raised a sinewy arm high, the talons on her hand glinting cruelly, Steeleye knew he wouldn't be fast enough to deflect or parry the attack. He braced himself for the pain and the agony, that would come from being skewered by the demon.

A sudden blur, and Rolf barrelled into the creature. He knew his sword would have no effect, but his rush and his body weight pushed the demon back a step. Raging, Ixtchel took a swipe at the old warrior, but he rolled clear of her reach, a grin splitting his face. Again, the demon staggered backwards, this time with a pike thrust into her side. Though not penetrating the scales, the impact was enough to push the creature back another step. Steeleye felt his own face split in a grin as he saw the pike-wielder was none other than the lad from the ramparts, his ill-fitting helm even now sliding about on his head.

Another impact sent the demon staggering and snarling further from Steeleye, allowing him to scramble to his feet. He saw Kallis, the shield maiden ducking beneath a swinging claw, hammering her shield into the demon's ribs for a second time.

Leaping nimbly back, though this time, not quite fast enough. A talon caught her head, sending her spinning away, spraying blood.

But by now, Steeleye was back on his feet. He swiped at the blood that ran into his eye, clearing his vision, then ran in at the demon once more. Though sorely wounded, the creature was far from done, and the pair of them set about delivering and receiving blows, Steeleye using the blade to deflect talons and tusks, then chopping into flesh on return swings. The demon screamed in fury. It howled in pain so loud as to hurt the ears of those close by, and on they fought, trading cuts and wounds, the demon and her bright-eyed nemesis, until at last Ixtchel fell to her knees, raising a gore streaked, talon beseechingly.

Steeleye stood before the kneeling creature, chest heaving from the effort of sucking in breath, his face a bloody mask as the shining dimmed in his eyes. "You were no harder than your sister Janovis after all." He panted gritting his teeth as a wave of pain washed over him, swaying slightly as the Shining left him, aware that this creature had come as close to killing him as anything ever had, yet determined not show weakness.

He glared at the cowering figure before him. Ixtchels slanted eyes were locked with his, black empty voids that promised nothing but death and oblivion for all. Blood ran from the cuts to his face and brow, for a moment blinding him. As he wiped at his eyes, Ixtchel struck. With the very last vestiges of her strength, the demon surged to its feet, jaws gaping. Steeleye fell back, instinctively his left hand pushing out to fend off the rushing snout.

The slavering jaws snapped shut, steel like teeth crunched through flesh and bone, and Steeleye reeled back with a cry, as Ixtchel bit off two of his fingers.

The Godsteel blade hissed through the air as Steeleye struggled to keep his feet, its tip slicing deep into the demon's chest as it sought to press its advantage. Ichor fountained over the already slippery cobbles, and Ixtchel fell to her knees with a terrible wail.

Steeleye steadied himself, and looked at his mutilated hand, the ring finger and the little finger were no more than bloody jagged stumps. He felt bile churning in his throat, a wave of dizziness threatened to engulf him, but he forced it away. His now blue eyes as hard as flint locked upon the demon grovelling at his feet.

"Hear me well, demon," he growled. "Your army here has been destroyed utterly. Before I send you to the halls of the Dark Lord, to be a plaything for all eternity, know that I will find and kill every last one of your ilk in the human realm." He paused to drag in a sobbing breath, doing all he could to ignore the pain of his savaged hand, then as a flicker of light danced in his eyes, he continued, with a voice as heavy as stone. "And when all your kind are dead and burning in the pit, then I shall find my sister, Maeve, your Empress, and I shall deliver my vengeance upon her.

The demon mewled before him, and Steeleye struck with a blinding speed, the edge of the Stormchild's blade slicing through flesh and bone, splitting the froglike head from brow to chin.

He felt nauseous. Yet again he had pushed himself beyond what he was capable of, the Shining lending him strength and speed whilst its light enveloped him, yet with every visitation, it seemed to take him longer to recover fully. He now leaned upon his befouled blade, its tip digging into the cobbles. He was aware that much of the fighting was over. There were more Asgulun in the courtyard now. They must have joined in the fray once Steeleye and Ixtchel began to fight. He was deeply grateful for that; he didn't have any more fight in him just then.

He stared, vacantly, at the bloody corpse lying before him. His breathing became more regular, the beat of his heart less thunderous in his ears. He had no idea if the battle plan out on the steppe had succeeded or failed, yet for the moment, he didn't have the energy to care. The smell of death hung, cloying, about the courtyard. About him. Was he to stink of death and terror forever?

He watched as the young Asgulun lad dropped his pike clattering to the cobbles, hooking a hand beneath Kallis' arm, helping the young warrior maid to her feet. Blood oozed from a jagged cut along her jaw, her nose seemed swollen, slightly bent at the bridge. She let the lad help her to her feet, seeing Steeleye watching them. She touched her fingers to her nose and cheek, wincing with the pain. She was still a moment or two, looking at her bloodied fingers, and then a wide smile broke out on her once flawless face. "Imagine the men that will hound me now!" she grinned at Steeleye, "I was always too pretty, I would scare away the best of men." She kissed the cheek of the lad helping her, leaving a smear of her blood upon his face, laughing as he blushed.

Steeleye watched the pair make their way towards the palace. More maidens fell into step with them. He heard them telling Kallis, that now, she looked like a true Shield Maiden. She laughed, draping her arm around the young Asguluns shoulder, she bumped her hip against him, making him stumble a little, the helmet slipping to a jaunty angle, as they entered then palace.

A strong arm circled Steeleye's shoulders, holding him steady, and Rolf's familiar gruff tones reassured him. "We have won this skirmish lad, at least here in the courtyard. It was a brutal affair, and if not for the Asgulun guard pitching in, I'm not sure we would be here to tell the tale."

Steeleye nodded numbly.

Rolf toed at the demon, lying broken and dead at their feet. He eyed the creature warily, as if he half expected her to leap to her feet. Steeleye was harbouring a similar fear. He pushed it to the back of his mind with difficulty.

"Are the Grimm all dead?" he asked at length, gratefully accepting a skin of water from a shield maiden, he grimaced as his hand came into contact with the leathern skin. Rolf winced in sympathy as he saw the missing fingers. Steeleye tipped the skin to his lips, gulping greedily at the water, Rolf shook his head, shrugging "There were perhaps a dozen or so that broke ranks early on in the fray, and made for the palace, we have guardsmen and clansmen alike hunting them down. There is nothing else for us to do just now, save gather our strength and slake our thirst." With that, the old man took the water skin and poured a long stream of the cool liquid over his head.

"And you need to let Hewla take a look at that hand, and the cut to your face, I fear like Kallis, you will not be so pretty once the blood is washed away." Rolf blew water from his beard noisily, relishing the cool liquid on his face. "I cannot get used to the heat," he complained good naturedly, laughing and waving at a clansman being helped to the shade of the wall by a couple of guardsmen. "Hedgar!" Rolf called a greeting to the man.

"I thought he had died early on," Rolf confided in Steeleye quietly, a huge grin splitting his beard. The pair of them sought out the shade of the wall, sliding their backs down the stone until they were sat upon the cobbles.

"Well, that's two down." Steeleye drank thirstily once more. "Only five more to go."

"The demons? You are still set upon hunting them down? After this one nigh carved you up and ate half your hand?" Rolf looked at his young companion incredulously.

"Perhaps the first two were the nastiest, perhaps the other five will be easier?"

Rolf sobered and looked at his young friend sadly. "I think it is there in the name, lad: demons. None will be easy, and that is if your luck holds and you find them one at a time. What if they band together, waiting for you? They know who you are now, and what you can do."

"They may know who I am, Rolf, but I don't think they know

what I am capable of. I don't think that I have scratched the surface of what it means to carry the Shining." He found a rag, probably part of a guardsman's cloak, and wrapped it carefully around his hand, Rolf helped, tying a knot to keep the rag in place. "Well, if you are rested, old man, shall we have a wander to the palace? We can help mop up if nothing else."

Rolf returned the younger man's grin, and the pair struggled to their feet, making their limping, aching way, towards the palace, leaving the carnage of the courtyard behind.

CHAPTER 30
A LITTLE MURDER

Morinae could hear the howls of the Grimm resounding along the stones of the palace corridors, could feel her bones turning to water at the ferocity of the sounds. Her hand tightened upon Helgen's, as they sped along the hallways, seeking an elusive sanctuary from the creatures that roamed from room to room, floor to floor. The weight of the slim dagger at her belt that Helgen had given her, and which she had used so well against Juvaal's man, was scant comfort. She knew the blade, though well made, would be useless against the creatures that hounded them.

The child was beyond terror. She had, like the Princess, heard these savage cries before. Had seen the aftermath. The memory of half-eaten bodies strewn mutilated in Janovis's cells were all too vivid for Helgen, and try as she might she could not erase the sight of the victims' faces, mouths wide in silent screams even in death. She shrank against Morinae as the Princess dragged her along richly carpeted corridors, up lavish stairways, upwards always upwards, the sound of the monstrous interlopers getting closer and closer.

Morinae had spent her life in this castle, she knew every room, every nook and every well-dressed stone in the corridors, yet as she ran helter skelter, footsteps muffled by the rich crimson carpets, she felt like a stranger, lost and panic stricken. She came to a tapestry, running past it, and then skidded to a halt, almost pulling Helgen off her feet. Behind the tapestry there was a secret door, she was sure. A door that led to a flight of stairs, that in turn wound its way up to a small room in a high tower with views of the harbour. As a child she remembered her father sitting her upon his knee, looking out the window at the great stone Mothers that were both guides and guardians of the people of Asgulun. He had told her then, that the palace and the keep were invulnerable, the safest place in the world, sat upon their white cliffs.

That was before the Grimm. Before Ashanarr had been taken by the demon Ixtchel, before the armies and navies of that proud neighbour were forced to fight alongside the Horde or see their families butchered. Before Morinae's world had been violently and irreparably torn asunder. She pulled the tapestry aside, revealing a slim wooden door set in its stone archway.

Morinae could not help feeling that her half-brother Juvaal was to blame for all of this. Could not dispel the image of Black Deeds' leering face as he stood over poor, dead Sha'haan, the feeling of raw helplessness as she had tried to crawl away from the slavers. Once again, she could feel the brambles of the river-bank tearing at her shift, feel their grimy, broken nailed hands scratching and bruising her flesh, smell their foul breath as they sought to cover her mouth with lusting, bruising kisses...

"Morinae!" Helgen's panicky voice penetrated Morinae's trauma, making her start like a rabbit. She was standing at the door, her hand frozen upon the iron handle. "Morinae!" again Helgen called her name, her desperate tone finally bringing the Princess to her senses, back to the here and now. And her dire circumstances.

Morinae turned the handle, and put her shoulder to the door, letting the tapestry fall behind them even as howls of rage came from a little way along the corridor, round a corner, and she hoped with all her heart, out of sight. Beyond the door was a narrow, stone stairway lit by windows along the outer wall. Their feet slapped upon the stone steps as they hurried upwards, ever upwards.

Behind them, muffled by the door and the tapestry, the fleeing girls could hear the clank of armour, and the shouts of men. The palace guard had arrived, and Morinae allowed herself to hope that their ordeal might, for a little while at least, be over. That hope lasted scant moments as bestial roars and the shrieks of both men and Grimm assaulted their ears, along with the harsh clang of steel on steel. Morinae could well picture in her mind's eye, the brave watchmen of Asgulun battling in vain against the terrible creatures.

As the screams became shriller, Morinae hastened up the stairs, pulling a wide-eyed Helgen in her wake.

At the head of the stairs, there was a landing, a door, the one that Morinae remembered so fondly from her youth, from a time when the only Grimm were from made up stories told to her by her father at bedtime. Without hesitation, Morinae barged through the door, dragging the terrified Helgen over the threshold, then spinning and slamming the door shut, turning the key that was in the lock even as she did so, resting her face against the cool wood, fighting down the scream that threatened to burst from her lips.

It was the strange mewling sound, issued by Helgen, that caused Morinae to stiffen. She could hear the soft, ragged breathing of the girl. Feeling dread weighing down upon her like leaden doom, Morinae slowly turned to face the chamber, in which she and her father had made so many fond memories.

The room was as she remembered it. Small, almost cosy, a

large arched window giving way to a balcony with matchless views of the harbour and the Sea of Storms. The room was furnished with overstuffed chairs and a writing desk where tutors had worked tirelessly with the wilful Princess, who had been more concerned with hearing the call of the gulls beyond the window, or the ribbons that she would wear in her hair that evening, than studying her histories. Everything was just as she remembered.

Except the crumpled body of her father, lying in the centre of the floor, blood from a great wound in his stomach still glistening wet and red upon the white marble of the floor tiles.

Morinae bit down on her hand to stifle a scream, but she could do little or nothing to stop poor Helgen, who moaned louder and louder until it became a keening wail. The shrill sound galvanised Morinae into action, and she quickly scooped the girl up, her hand clamping over her mouth. "Hush!" she hissed, her instincts for self-preservation warring with the need to kneel beside the body of her King, her father, to cradle his poor head to her breast, to mourn and to keen herself. "The Grimm will hear!" she whispered into Helgen's ear.

Morinae stared into the wide, dead eyes of her father, as she pulled the child over to a chair.

"Sit here."

She unclamped her hand from the girl's mouth, slowly in case there was still a scream waiting to be let out. But Helgen remained quiet, her lips trembling, tears rolling down her cheeks, her nose streaming, eyes fixed upon the body in the centre of the room.

Morinae was tormented. She wanted to run, to hide, yet she wanted to stay with her father too. The thought of fleeing, leaving his crumpled body here for the Grimm, was almost more than she could bear. But she must think of Helgen, poor little Helgen, who had been so happy with her uncle, juggling and playing the flute as they toured the countryside, whom she had dragged away to

Asgulun, to be hunted through a castle by creatures of nightmare, all so she could have a companion, so she would feel less lonely, after the death of Sha'haan.

Guilt vied with the horror and the grief at finding her father.

Morinae cradled Helgen's quaking form, not noticing the window to the balcony edge open, as quiet as a mouse's breath. Still wielding the bloodied knife that he had used to kill his father, Juvaal stepped silently from the balcony into the chamber.

The Prince of Asgulun was dressed all in black, his hair oiled and curled even at such a time as this, when monsters roamed the corridors of the palace. His eyes were chips of stone as they found a spot in the centre of his sweet sister's back. He moved with a catlike grace over the floor towards the girls cowering in the chair. He raised the knife high above his head. What were two more corpses, when weighed against the throne of Asgulun? And anyway, Morinae should be resting in an unmarked grave in the Weeping Wastes, not here whispering in their fathers' ear, not here ruining all of his plans, spoiling his schemes.

He would be king, and be damned if the cost was a little blood on his hands. Those foul creatures running riot in the halls could be dealt with, all in good time, once the heroic Bastard Bryann returned. All Juvaal had to do was stay alive, and kill any other family members that he should come across in the meantime. A simple strategy, and one not without its pleasures. Oh, how he hated the bitch...

* * *

Morinae saw Helgen's already wide eyes pop even wider as they focused on something over her shoulder. She reacted out of pure instinct, pulling the child close and rolling away, out of the chair in one swift movement, hitting the floor with her shoulder and rolling to her knees. Only then did she see Juvaal, stepping back from the chair, brandishing a wicked, curved knife. Pain lanced through her shoulder, and instinctively she clamped a hand over the pain. She could feel a rip in her tunic, the sticky blood oozing from a narrow cut. Helgen lay several feet away, motionless on the tiles. Blood marking her temple where her head had struck the floor, knocking her senseless.

"Juvaal!" Morinae scurried away from him, half blind with tears and pain. "What have you done?" she almost shrieked. "You *killed* father?" Even though he stood there before her with the knife in his hand, she could hardly bring herself to believe he could be so calculating, so cruel as to kill their own sweet father. Games of politics were second nature to him. Having her removed from the palace, yes, *that* she was willing to believe. It was the work of a bureaucrat, sly and underhand, and it fitted perfectly with Juvaal's character. But to carry out the act of murder himself? She never dreamed that he had enough iron in him.

Morinae found herself crowded up to the door, Juvaal grinned at her terror. He wove the dagger in little circles between them, relishing her fear, tasting it with a darting tongue as if it were palpable. "So far as all Asgulun will be concerned, father dear will have died at the hands of those creatures, that even now I can hear rushing down the corridor below us. And lucky happenstance, you too will be counted amongst their victims, once our troops rally and drive them back into the sea. I'm sure the Grimm won't mind chewing the pair of you up a little. I will just have to cut you up some, to get their juices flowing when they finally figure out there are stairs behind that curtain."

"But what about you?" Morinae said, turning her head aside as the tip of the blade nicked her chin. There was nowhere else to run. She could feel blood running down her slender throat. "You will be trapped up here too!" She spat out the words, finding courage through her fear. She suddenly saw Sha'haan lying broken and dead at her feet, like a discarded toy, and felt rage burning through her veins. "They will *chew* you up just as well, brother dear."

Juvaal began to laugh at her show of bravado. Again, the knife licked. Morinae flinched back, her tunic torn above her breast, a thin line of blood traced over her pale flesh.

"Don't you fret, sister. I will be gone and safe before the brutes know what is going on. But enough play, if only you knew how long I have wanted you dead, sister. Always there at fathers' side, advising him when it should have been *me*. You say I was the schemer. But you were always scheming to keep me from my birthright." As he spoke Juvaal edged forward, Morinae watched the cruel blade draw back, there was no way to escape the razored edge.

She blurted out, "The whole court knows about Black Deeds!"

Juvaal froze, his arm raised. His grin, so triumphant a moment ago, had turned into a sickly rictus. Morinae saw an opportunity, saw her brother's hesitation. "Bryann was all for killing you outright. The only reason you are still alive is your men may have borne you some loyalty, and they were needed against the Horde." She gathered all her courage, spat in Juvaal's face, she sneered with contempt, "Black Deeds is dead, Azif Bae fled with his tail between his legs, but not before they told me that it was your coin that paid for their services. That you let them in to the palace, betrayed your own family." Morinae took a step away from the door, and her voice dropped to almost a whisper. "You are a dead man, Juvaal, no matter what happens here in this room, you are already dead."

He smiled.

"Well, if that is the way of it, I may as well follow through."

She struck fast, snatching Helgen's dagger from her belt, and slashing it with feline speed at Juvaal's throat. The slim blade fairly whistled through the air, but Juvaal was faster. The blade missed by a hair's breadth, and then Morinae was knocked clear off her feet as Juvaal struck her a back handed blow, sending her crashing into the floor, her borrowed dagger flying from her hand.

She hardly had time to lift her head before Juvaal's boot crashed into her ribs, lifting her bodily from the floor. Her vision swam. She could see the darkness of unconsciousness floating at her peripheral vision. She retched, acid bile burning her throat. She desperately clung to awareness, she mustn't give in. There had to be a way to stay alive, to escape, to get Helgen away to safety. The thought of the girl, alone and at the mercy of her brother, or the Grimm, monsters all, sent shivers through her.

Morinae, crawled on her belly over the white marble tiles, aware that the blood she trailed mixed with her father's, smearing the tiles. She sobbed uncontrollably, spittle and blood falling from her battered lips and nose, hanging like ribbons from her.

"Here lies the Princess of Asgulun." Juvaal stood over his sister, a huge grin spreading over his face, pure delight in his eyes as he watched her try to crawl from him. "What would the people think, if they could see you now? The most beautiful woman in Asgulun, crawling like a hog, trailing blood and snot. You disgust me, woman." He prodded her with the toe of his boot, causing her to gasp in pain.

"If Black Deeds had done his job, then none of this would have been necessary." He sneered "And why should I care if the court knows that I had you kidnapped? With you and father gone, I am King!"

Morinae managed to roll onto her back, fighting back a wave of nausea. "For a crown? You would be a murderer twice over just for a crown?" She rested on her elbows, beaten, humiliated and frustrated at her helplessness. Juvaal sneered again, and leaned over her, to whisper in her ear, "For the crown of Asgulun, I would murder a hundred, a thousand, but in the end all I had to do was murder one old man, and a sister I hate."

"Brother... We have never been friends," Morinae choked. "I know that, but to murder me? Let me go, I will disappear, you will never see me again, you have my word." Juvaal was so close she could see the droplets of sweat on his forehead.

"I must confess, dear sister, when I saw you and the brat come blundering in here, my first instinct was to kill you and be done with it." Juvaal leaned closer, pressing the tip of his blade so hard against her throat it drew a bead of blood.

He cocked his head, listening for the Grimm. "But now I'm thinking, why should I have all the pleasure? Surely, those creatures wandering around the corridors deserve a little fun?"

"Do you want me to beg, Juvaal? Is that it?"

"Beg? No sister, I don't want you to beg, I want you to scream. I want you to scream so loud those Grimm in the corridor below can hear you." He pressed the knife harder, until blood welled and ran freely. He smiled at his handiwork, then paused when he saw the expression on Morinae's face. Though one eye was near closed, and her nose looked as though it had been broken, her bloodied lips were spread in a smile. No, she wasn't smiling at him, she was smiling at something behind him. Too late he remembered the girl, the waif that Morinae insisted on dragging around everywhere with her.

He turned in a blur of speed, but Helgen was faster. Her jugglers blade plunged into Juvaal's back. His own knife sliced empty air, as Helgen skipped aside. He may as well have been trying to cut a shadow, so fast was the girl. Like a dancer she moved just out of the reach of the blade. With his free hand, Juvaal tried desperately to reach the hilt of the knife lodged in his back. The wound wasn't fatal, but the pain was incredible. Unable to reach the handle, he struck out again at the girl, but Helgen danced clear of the whistling steel.

Morinae's attack was swift and brutal. She had seen Helgen gather up her dropped knife, had baited her brother enough to keep his attention on her whilst Helgen had got closer. Now she staggered to her feet and half ran, half toppled into her brothers back, grasping the dagger hilt with all her strength, and twisting the blade free.

Juvaal howled.

Morinae snarled.

"Get to the balcony, Helgen." Morinae said, surprised at how calm she sounded. "There must be a way down!"

"But what about you?" Helgen was wringing her hands, caught between the need to flee and the need to stay with her only friend.

"I will be right behind you!"

Juvaal was crawling now, his blade dropped and forgotten, when Morinae had wrenched free the dagger, she had done much more damage that the initial wound. He was gasping through gritted teeth as Morinae closed on him.

"I can wait for you." Helgen beseeched the Princess

"No Helgen! It is better that you don't see what happens next." Morinae's voice had taken on a hard edge, her face grim as she reached her brother, and unlocked the tower-room door.

When she looked at Helgen and nodded at the balcony, the girl hardly recognised her friend, but she did as she was bid, scurrying out the window. Her voice floated back into the chamber, "It's here, a rope is here!"

Morinae nodded. Helgen was gone, over the balustrade and dropping hand over hand to safety. That left just her and her brother. The Prince was crying openly from pain and fear, his soft handsome face contorted in panic. "What are you going to do to me?" his voice cracked in sudden terror.

"I'm planning a little bit of murder," Morinae responded. "Not the whole thing, mind you, just a little..." Without warning, she slashed the blade behind his left knee, and Juvaal screamed. She slashed the blade through the tendons behind the right knee, hearing them twang. "That was for Sha'haan," Morinae whispered in her brother's ear. In a flash she was up and running for the balcony, grabbing the rope and flinging herself over the balustrade, even as the door to the chamber burst open, and Juvaal began to scream louder and shriller.

* * *

MORINAE FOUND Helgen waiting upon a balcony just two floors down, and the pair embraced tightly, so tight Helgen feared her ribs would snap, but she didn't care, she was just happy to be reunited with the Princess. Her terror had reached new heights whilst she had been alone, even though it was only a few minutes. To Helgen, the Princess had become her friend and protector, a fierce companion in whose company the girl felt safer than any other time.

Morinae at last released the girl, holding her at arm's length to check she was unhurt. At last satisfied the girl was free of injury, she led the way into another chamber. It was deserted, so she moved silently to the door, pulling Helgen along behind her. She cracked open the portal, and with her good eye peered into the corridor, at once giving a sigh of relief, for walking towards them were half a dozen of the wild shield maidens of the Northern army; they fairly bristled with spears and swords. Morinae almost leapt from the doorway, she was so glad to see the warrior women.

Only some primal instinct stayed her headlong rush. The set of the women's spears, their fierce grins as they stared farther along the corridor, both was ominous. A moment later, two terrible shapes came hurtling past Morinae, long arms bulging with sinew, fingernails as hard as horns tearing the carpet as they ran on all fours at the Maidens, snarling and howling. The Grimm died but two paces from the women, javelins and arrows deep in their chests.

Morinae was frozen to the spot. She had almost run directly into the path of the creatures. She trembled, feeling her knees weaken, though not with fear, but relief, as one of the shield maidens saw her and strode towards her. Morinae could only stare at the long legs, naked of armour, the red hair braided and falling to her waist, her lovely face grinning with good humour, though a recent bloody gash across her jaw distorted the smile somewhat.

"I think that was the last of them, girl," she said pleasantly to Morinae. "It's safe to come on out now." She winced as she saw the injuries that Morinae bore, helping her along the corridor. "Hey lad!" she called, and from behind the maidens there stepped a young Asgulun soldier, his oversized helmet tilted precariously on his head, the bowl obviously stuffed with rags. "Run ahead back to the courtyard and fetch a healer; this girl has been through the wars by the looks of things."

"I'm on my way, Kallis," piped the lad, sprinting along the corridor, back the way they had come. Morinae leaned upon warrior's strong arm, pulling Helgen to her other side even as she did.

She could hardly believe they had survived. Battered and bruised perhaps, but alive nonetheless. For a moment, she felt tears welling in her eyes, tears of relief and joy at their survival, but the thought of her father lying dead on the marble floor, just two floors above her, brought tears of grief instead.

"It's over, girl," Kallis whispered to Morinae, almost as she would a child. "The Grimm are dead, as is that creature that led them. There is no longer need to fear, lass. You are safe now."

Helgen mumbled from the crook of Morinae's arm, though her voice was indistinct. Kallis peered around Morinae, and looked down at the scrawny juggler "What was that child, I cannot hear you?"

"I said, she is the Queen, not a girl or a lass," Helgen mumbled a little louder and clearer.

Kallis burst out laughing, still supporting the Queen as they moved along the corridor. "It's all the same to me, child, royalty or serf, we shall see you all to safety."

Queen.

Morinae's steps faltered. Her brother and father were dead.

She was Queen.

CHAPTER 31

FOLLOW THE CROWS

Steeleye felt at the stitches in his face, absently running his fingers from above brow to cheek, along the cut that Ixtchel had dealt him. It would be a reminder of his time in Asgulun, Kallis had told him, as she had stitched together the flaps of skin. So too would the missing fingers of his left hand, still swathed in bandages and hurting like the devil whenever he accidentally knocked it, or forgot himself and patted someone's back, or went to pick up a knife at table. But two missing fingers was a small price to pay, he reasoned, when he thought of how close Ixtchel had come to killing him.

What was a scar, or a missing finger or two in this terrible game?

He remembered again the easy camaraderie with the Northerners, as he and Rolf had entered the palace after the courtyard battle. Kallis and her crew were escorting Morinae from the halls into the yard, and had come across Steeleye and Rolf, both worse for wear, plodding towards the palace. The shield maiden had allayed their fears of any more Grimm in the halls, and then set to work diligently upon Steeleye's facial wound.

"I can put your face back together," she murmured, her eyes focussed on his cheek and the needle and thread, "but there is nothing I can do for half a hand. Freija would be proud of you today."

The sudden mention of Freija, lost to him and the Maidens so many months ago, made Steeleye smile, for all the pain in his hand. "She would have been proud of us all, I think." He responded. "

Whilst she was stitching, Steeleye saw up close the ragged cut to the maiden's jaw. She preened when he mentioned it, flashing him a radiant smile. "Yes, at last I am no longer perfect, now I *look* like I am wedded to the spear and shield." She hummed happily as she stitched, proud of her battle scar, blissfully unaware that it would only add to her allure.

That had been four days ago. Four long days of pain and joy for Asgulun. Their king had been found, along with his son Juvaal, mauled and chewed in an upper chamber, victims of those marauding Grimm that had made entry into the palace. The guards that found them said Juvaal's face was contorted in fear and agony in death. His passing must have been agonising indeed. The joy was that their beloved Princess, so recently returned to them, was to be crowned Queen, and all knew of her kindness and wisdom.

For four days, the high and the mighty met in chambers, and talked of what to do now. Ashanarr was bereft of a ruler, though rumour was that a cousin of the late king had survived Ixtchel's purge of nobles. Morinae had sent a party made up of Asgulun, Northerners and the Ish, to visit Ashanarr, and set up an interim government of sorts, to ensure food and succour reached those that needed it most. Once the royal line was proven, then a new leader could be proclaimed. Failing that, Morinae had come up with a novel idea: why not let the people decide who should rule them? Let the people choose a leader from amongst themselves. The idea was met with much tutting and shaking of heads, but Morinae had been convinced it was a sound idea.

The elation of survival and victory was as strong as the agony of pain and loss to the Asgulun. And for the first two days since the Grimm had been driven onto the crushing rocks, the streets rang with both celebrations and dirges, as folks found their families alive and well, were reunited with loved ones, or waited in vain for sons to return from the scorched plains.

In the harbour town, life returned to normal quickly, the evacuees eager to return to their homes and lives, their ships and shops and smokehouses. But forever-more they would keep a wary eye upon the Sea of Storms, the charred hulks of Ixtchel's battle barges still protruding from the water a constant reminder that beyond the walls of Asgulun, the world harboured a voracious evil.

From the balcony of his borrowed room, Steeleye looked out at the Sea of Storms, its surface calm now, broken only by lazy whitecaps. Gulls wheeled and dived above the brightly sailed boats that came and went in the harbour, the fishermen of Asgulun quick to return to the sea, eager to renew their trade. The raucous call of the gulls was a constant background noise here in Asgulun, as in most ports around the world where man harvested the bounty of the sea.

He thought about all he had endured, about all Morinae had endured, and all that lay before them in this rapidly changing world.

It took Steeleye a moment or two to realize he was no longer hearing the gulls. Nor the hawking cries of tradesmen from the harbour town below. In fact, he couldn't hear anything at all, save his own quiet breathing. He peered into the harbour, and was shocked to see that the boats were unmoving. Their sails still bowed under the breeze, but there was no movement at all, as if he looked at a painted canvas rather than a vibrant, bustling town.

Casting his eyes about the sky, he came across a gull, its wings spread as it glided atop the thermals, but it, too, was frozen, as was the breeze. He could make out figures below, each was still, paused, whether walking or running, labouring or lounging. Everything except Steeleye was stopped.

When the Morriggu spoke, he flinched from surprise, turning to see the sable clad goddess only a few strides away. "Don't be afraid, Grimmsbane. I am come to congratulate you upon your victory. The immortals are pleased indeed with your adventures."

Steeleye was perplexed. He glanced from the frozen world below back to Morriggu. "How?" he stammered. He knew the gods were powerful, but to stop reality like this?

"I have plucked you from time, champion. We are between heartbeats, you and I. The world goes on as ever, but for now, we have stepped from it. Here, between moments, we can talk unheard and unseen, and I can pass amongst the living without breaking my vows." The Morriggu smiled now, that terrible, most beautiful smile, and laid a gentle hand upon his arm. "I am pleased to see you alive, Grimmsbane, and all the closer to bringing my sister back to me." As ever, her whispery voice sent a thrill through him. He could feel the hairs on his arms and the nape of his neck stand on end. He saw her fix her eyes upon the sword made by her sister Narissa, scabbarded and lying upon the borrowed bed. There was still anxiety there, he thought, but relief too, to see it safe.

"Your time here amongst the Asgulun is drawing to a close, I fear. Whilst you rest and recuperate, Maeve is on the move. She has made fast her Empire in the South, ruled for her by satraps and puppets. Her machinations are devious indeed, bringing nations to heel with words and whispers, with poison in the winecups, and daggers in the dark. She has had little need of the

Grimm in her conquests far South." Now the Collector of Souls stared full at Steeleye, and he felt himself weighed.

"There will come a time when the gods must reconsider their vows." She spoke as soft as ever, but there a new gravity to her voice, each word as heavy as the world. "Maeve is seeking to bring back to the realms the Old Ones, those endless beings that were cast beyond realities by the Great Maker, long before the stars you see in the sky were born. They are eternal in their spans and their darkness, and should they find a way to return to the realms, it would mean purgatory for all living things. Perhaps not even we gods will be a match for them." She rested an alabaster hand upon Steeleye's shoulder, as light as a feather.

"Maeve has learned the dread Book, nay, she has become the Book, and in it there are terrible secrets, terrible knowledge. The creatures beyond hunger for that knowledge, they crave it, and their influence upon the realms can be felt already. The chaos, the arrival of Maeve, and you, yes even you have been conjured up by the Fates, to balance out the darkness, brought by Maeve and the Book.

"Time is running short, I fear. There are five demons left, here upon your world. Some are at work in the desert lands to the East, in the old cities that have thrived and fallen into the sands a hundred times. There, they gather secrets and allies. Some walk amongst men without disguise and are worshipped as gods." She spat the words, her eyes narrowed, and Steeleye felt all the comfort of the room evaporate, felt the Morriggu's wrath barely contained. With a visible effort, the goddess brought her anger under control, it seemed to Steeleye that the sun was once more allowed to shine.

"You shall journey there. And you shall kill the remaining Sisters. Aihaab's curse must be broken." Her tone brooked no argument now, a general giving orders to her soldier, a queen to her subject. "Kill the demons, so we may revive Arianne, so we can gather our strength for the arrival of the Old Ones."

Steeleye was becoming used to such visitations, to magics and the supernatural, but even so, he surprised himself by asking the Morriggu if his soul were still safe. *How dare I*, he thought, *a mere mortal, doubt the word of the Morriggu?* Did he doubt it, or was he just so overwhelmed by all that he had seen and been through that he needed a little reassurance that his own reward was safe and sound?

The Collector stared at her champion for the longest time, and Steeleye could feel sweat start upon his brow.

With a smile that could melt a heart or shatter it, the Morriggu plucked from her cloak of crow feathers a small glass vial, stoppered with a silver cap. The contents glowed, strong and vibrant. "I keep it with me always, Grimmsbane. It rests next to mine own heart, so I may feel its presence and know that you are safe. Fear not for your soul, Captain, it is well tended. Always."

As ever when speaking to the Morriggu, her answers seemed to be layered. He could see threats couched in promises, worrisome promises veiled behind the mundane words. All he could do was nod and smile weakly. He had no choice in the matter, he knew that. Not only for his soul and for the return of Arianne, but because he knew that somewhere in his future, his sister Maeve awaited him in the real world, not just his nightmares.

He nodded, satisfied that for now his soul was safe, and the Morriggu's smile lost a little of its brittle edge. "Gather your strength, Grimmsbane, the crows will pay you a visit soon, and they will set your foot upon the path." With that, the Morriggu took a step back. Behind her, great shadows formed, blotting out the room, enveloping her like a shroud, she began to fade into the darkness, like the memory of a dream upon waking. From the shadows, her voice drifted to his ears, soft as a caress now, a whisper upon a breeze. "You have done well, Steeleye Grimmsbane. I shall send you a gift, what you need most in the world, whether or not you know it."

The shadows faded and were gone. Sound and the movement of the world began once more with a suddenness that made Steeleye gasp aloud. He looked from the balcony again, seeing the raucous gulls and the bobbing boats, hearing the soft gentle sounds of life in the palace all about him.

Resigned, he looked at his mutilated left hand, and wondered what other sacrifices he would need to make, before his soul was returned to him. Setting his jaw, he took up his sword, belting it at his waist, and left his rooms in search of Hewla and his Northern friends. It seemed the time for farewells was at hand.

HEWLA STARED at her young charge, and gave a resigned nod. She seemed older than before, yet somehow stronger too. Her flint like eyes had seen more of this world, and perhaps others, than should be seen.

They sat about a table within a bright, airy chamber. Huge glass doors opened on a balcony, letting in a gentle salt-tinged breeze that offset the oppressive heat of the Asgulun summer. Sat with Hewla and Steeleye was Aelrik, and as ever, with Rolf at his side, Bryann the Bastard Prince, and Morinae. The new Queen was resplendent in a gown of white silk and lace, a sash of the lightest blue about her slim waist, her hair hung in loose curls like spun gold. Her face no longer an unblemished beauty, sporting a swollen eye, though this would heal in time, and a slight kink in the bridge of her nose. To Steeleye, the injury only enhanced her loveliness, lending her character. He saw in her a new aspect of strength and determination.

Rounding out the gathering was old Artfur, sitting hunched over a parchment tablet, a pot of ink at his elbow, the scratching of the quill loud to all their ears. "He has not stopped scribbling for two days," complained the final member of the group, young Helgen, now dressed as Morinae only in miniature. She tutted and rolled her hazel eyes at her uncle, but he scratched away, oblivious of the rebuke.

"He is composing a great song," Morinae explained. "*The Defeat of the Grimm*. He stood upon a rise over the grasslands apparently, and watched the whole battle unfold, even taking notes as it happened!" She sounded incredulous, but smiled nonetheless.

The Queen of Asgulun rested her green eyes upon Steeleye, and for all the bruising and swelling, the look was tender. "Hewla tells me that you are moving on? You cannot stay, even for my official coronation a few weeks hence?"

Steeleye shrugged, uncomfortable at the attention, even amongst his closest friends. "I have been..." He paused, tasting his next words, choosing them carefully, "...encouraged, to continue with my pursuit of the Seven." His eyes met those of his companions. "I shall miss you all, and hopefully, we shall meet again along the way."

Hewla made a disgruntled sound, and all eyes swivelled to the crone. "We shall all be needed, come the final battle, mark me well." Her voice was strong, vibrant as a young woman's, and not someone of her years.

"You have seen a glimpse of the future then, Hewla?" Aelrik wondered.

"I have, Lord, and clearer than I would like. This Empress, this Maeve, she has stretched the shell of the realms thin, I fear. The gods are stirring too. All this makes magic easier. It rides in the air like pollen, easily grasped if you have the touch." The flint eyes pierced them all. "There is an ancient evil awaiting to return to our world, and Maeve holds the key to their return. We must deny her the door."

There came a harsh caw from the balcony, and all heads swivelled to see a large crow perched upon the balustrade. Its black eyes were bright and filled with knowing.

"It is time then, Straw Top!" Rolf reached over and patted Steeleye's arm, surprisingly gentle. "I shall miss you in the shield wall."

Bryann nodded his agreement, as did Aelrik. Was there a tear in the great King's eye? Steeleye couldn't help but smile. The Bearslayer wiped at his eye with the back of his hand, gruff as ever, and muttered about the sea air being a torment to his senses.

Morinae rolled her eyes at the display. "Men!" she said. "All wind and bluster, but soft as a cushion beneath their fierce talk." She grinned at the King, he had become a true friend since her return from captivity,

"Aye, Your Majesty." Hewla spoke softly. "It is us women that have the hardest of hearts, is it not?"

Morinae looked at the witch, keeping her face smiling and serene, but inside, she felt a coldness running through her veins. Did the witch know of her maiming of her brother, how she had left him to be torn and rent by the Grimm? Hewla patted her hand in a reassuring fashion, meeting her green gaze with flint. "I think you have the steel within to rule well, girl. Sometimes, to rule, you must do things that others cannot, that others would shirk from." She patted the hand again, smiling for all the world like an old woman swapping recipes with a neighbour. "Just don't make a habit of it, you and the little firecracker sitting with you."

On the balcony, the crows raised a loud cawing, as if in agreement with the witch.

* * *

STEELEYE HAD RISEN EARLY, the sun only just reaching the lip of the palest blue sky. He had saddled his horse, loading provisions upon the back of a second gelding gifted him by Morinae, to use as a pack horse upon his journey.

He led his horse from the stable, where it had shared the roof with twenty other mounts, each with a lineage any nobleman would have been proud to carry. Once in the courtyard, now clear of bodies, though some of the cobbles still bore dark, ugly stains, he tethered the horse near the gate, and walked back to the stable to collect his pack horse, and toss a copper to the stable lad that had helped him with the tack.

A crow was sitting upon a winch arm, jutting from the apex of the stable roof. It was a large bird, and as with all the Morriggu's creatures, its gaze seemed to hold more intelligence than it ought. Its beady eyes followed Steeleye as he approached the stable. He wondered idly if the crow was one of the thousand that would no doubt be feasting out on the grassy steppe. This, in turn, reminded him of the aftermath of the battle with the Grimm, and in particular, the demon Ixtchel.

The demon sister had been dragged, lifeless and broken, out of the city and onto the steppe. There she had been covered with kindling and branches to make a bonfire taller than a man. The pyre was lit, and the creature's body was consumed utterly by the flames, save for the bones. These were carefully raked from the ashes and pounded with hammers until they were dust. The dust was collected and put into a sack, the sack was then taken by boat, out into the Sea of Storms, where it was emptied into the churning waves.

The demon was gone forever, though she would still stalk through Steeleye's nightmares, of that, he had no doubt. He shuddered a little, he had enough evil things, stalking him in his sleep.

With an effort, he shook off such thoughts, and entered the stable. There was no sign of the lad, but he was not alone in the dimly lit building. Standing by his pack horse, with her back to him, was a young woman, her nakedness seeming to glow in the yellow lamplight. She was tall and lithe, yet quite broad of the shoulder, her long raven hair spilling straight and glossy to her narrow waist, almost touching her buttocks.

Steeleye stood stunned. The copper coin for the stable lad lay forgotten in his hand. As he watched, the girl efficiently unloaded the horse, then easily hefted a riding saddle onto its back, buckling the cinch beneath its belly. The horse stood, patient, cropping hay from a bag hanging from the stable wall.

"Are you going to pack up a third horse? Or just stand there looking at my arse?" The voice made Steeleye jump, he had been so engrossed with the figure. He stammered, unable to find his voice, and the girl turned to face him. Steeleye felt his cheeks colour at the girl's nakedness. Her head was tilted slightly, her hair falling over her face. Nimble fingers brushed the hair aside, and Steeleye caught his breath. Her lips were full and red, her cheekbones high, and beneath serious brows, were eyes slightly slanted and long lashed. The eyes held Steeleye rapt: one as yellow as a buttercup in spring, the other as blue as a summer's sky.

"Wolf?" he croaked.

Wolf grinned, her teeth white and sharp looking, the strange eyes playful as they saw his surprise and discomfort. She stepped closer to the lamp, its adoring light caressing her curves, her long and shapely legs. "You like?" Her brows were raised.

Steeleye found himself nodding, unable to tear his eyes from her.

Wolf bent to the saddle bags, rummaging through Steeleye's clothes until she found a cream-coloured tunic, long of sleeve and hem. She shrugged into the garment, though her smile remained at the dumb look on his face.

"My mistress bade me return to your realm, to be your guide, once more." She tapped a long, sharp looking fingernail upon her teeth, in a similar way to the Morriggu when in thought. The slanted odd coloured eyes focused intently now upon Steeleye. "You have changed a great deal since our last meeting." She stepped towards him, graceful as a cat, and ran her fingers along the side of his face, gently stroking the puckered flesh of his scar. "Being a champion for the Morriggu always comes with a price, Steeleye." Wolf paused, as if realising this was the first time that she had ever uttered his name, tasting it upon her lips. "A scar, a finger or two is a small price to pay, when balanced against the good you have done." Wolf smiled, almost sadly, "sacrifices must be made..."

With a little shake of her head, Wolf came from her reverie and locked eyes with his.

"Your sister is on the move, and time is running short, will you have me as your guide, Steeleye Demonsbane?"

Steeleye's brain was finally catching up, and he grinned at Wolf. Suddenly, the future didn't seem so bleak after all. "I will, and gladly," he replied. "But, let's not be leading me onto any slippery bridges, eh?"

Wolf's laugh was full and boisterous, her odd eyes sparking in the lamplight.

"No promises," she replied.

About the Author

Nicholas Appleyard is an author, Christian, Biker, Seeker and Yorkshire man; lover of all things ancient and slightly crooked. It goes without saying that Sword and Sorcery fiction is his passion... along with baking cakes and proper music.

Proud husband to Donna, whose patience is boundless as she picks up and sorts out after a tunnel-visioned workaholic, and keeps everyone bobbing along. And father to Ella Narissie, the most wonderful gift Donna and he could ever have received.

Grimmsbane is his first book, but hopefully not his last.

Printed in Great Britain
by Amazon